Praise for Rea Frey
NOT HER DAUGHTER

"A cleverly constructed novel that will have you questioning everything you believe about right or wrong. Frey skillfully tangles you up in these two women's lives and never lets up on the tension all the way until the dramatic conclusion. A remarkable portrayal of motherhood, in all its beautiful glory and heart-wrenching despair."

—*New York Times* bestselling author Chevy Stevens

"In *Not Her Daughter,* Frey pulls off a difficult task: balancing a nail-biting plot with a thought-provoking question—is a crime committed with the best intentions still a crime? A chilling, powerful tale of love and sacrifice, of truth and perception, *Not Her Daughter* will make you miss your bedtime, guaranteed. A stunning debut."

—Kimberly Belle, internationally bestselling author of *The Marriage Lie*

"A deft and beautifully written examination of taboo maternal fantasies: Can a kidnapping ever be justified? Can motherhood be undone? Engrossing and suspenseful, Frey writes her characters with depth and compassion, challenging readers to question their own code of ethics."

—Zoje Stage, internationally bestselling author of *Baby Teeth*

D0187559

"I couldn't put Rea Frey's *Not Her Daughter* down, and once finished, couldn't let it go. So much more than an engrossingly suspenseful novel, it's a thoughtful exploration on the extremes to which motherhood and love and loss can drive us. An amazing debut."

—Christina Kovac, bestselling author of *The Cutaway*

"In her provocative debut thriller, Rea Frey takes us on an emotional ride where the line between right and wrong begins to fade, and all that remains are the tears of a child. This story pulls you in from the very first page, and unlike most in its genre, you won't know how you want it to end until it does."

—Wendy Walker, bestselling author of *Emma in the Night*

"Women who do not embrace motherhood or 'bad mothers' are a taboo subject—in both real life and fiction—but Frey tackles it with aplomb in her taut debut, *Not Her Daughter*. The story begs the question: who is more mother—the one who gives birth or the one who rescues? The plot twists here are brave, the themes are both poignant and unsettling, and the resolution is deeply resonant. A page-turner with heart!"

—*New York Times* bestselling author Kate Moretti

"Harrowing and heartfelt, *Not Her Daughter* is a gripping novel about the amazing power of mother love."

—Rebecca Drake, author of *Just Between Us*

"A compelling mix of high-wire tension and superb writing. *Not Her Daughter* will linger in the memory long after the final page has been turned."

—Laura Elliot, author of *Guilty, Sleep Sister,*
and *The Betrayal*

"Tightly paced and impossible to put down, *Not Her Daughter* is a cleverly written story that challenges what it means to be a mother—or not to be one. A thought-provoking and poignant debut."

—Clarissa Goenawan, author of *Rainbirds*

"*Not Her Daughter* is an interesting and emotional debut about women stuck in lives they never wanted and the desperate decisions they'll make to get out. Certain to keep readers turning pages and guessing as to who the real villain is."

—Cate Holahan, *USA Today* bestselling author of
The Widower's Wife and *Lies She Told*

Also by Rea Frey

Not Her Daughter

Because You're Mine

Rea Frey

St. Martin's Paperbacks

This is a work of fiction. All of the characters, organizations, and events portrayed in this novel are either products of the author's imagination or are used fictitiously.

Published in the United States by St. Martin's Paperbacks, an imprint of St. Martin's Publishing Group.

BECAUSE YOU'RE MINE

Copyright © 2019 by Rea Frey.
Excerpt from *Until I Find You* copyright © 2020 by Rea Frey.

All rights reserved.

For information, address St. Martin's Publishing Group, 120 Broadway, New York, NY 10271.

www.stmartins.com

ISBN: 978-1-250-62104-7

Our books may be purchased in bulk for promotional, educational, or business use. Please contact your local bookseller or the Macmillan Corporate and Premium Sales Department at 1-800-221-7945, ext. 5442, or by email at MacmillanSpecialMarkets@macmillan.com.

Printed in the United States of America

St. Martin's Griffin edition / August 2019
St. Martin's Paperbacks edition / June 2020

10 9 8 7 6 5 4 3 2 1

For my agent, Rachel Beck, and my editor, Alex Sehulster.
You are my dream team.

a note to readers

Ten days after my fifteenth birthday, I let a boy ride the bus home with me—after my mother explicitly told me not to. It was a boy I liked. A boy who was two years older than me. A boy I was *interested* in. A boy I considered a boyfriend.

I thought I was ready for a physical relationship. (I wasn't.) I thought, when he came home with me, we were going to experience something special. (We didn't.) When he disappeared to the bathroom, and I was alone in my bedroom, something told me to run. Get out of my own house. *Go.*

But I stayed. When he entered the doorway, naked, with a removed look on his face, I knew what happened next was not going to be good.

In that bedroom, on that day, with this boy, I said no. I screamed no. I cried. I was held down. I bled. I went numb. He had a one-track mind, and I closed myself off, too afraid to do anything about it.

After that day? I continued to see him, even though I questioned myself: How could I *ever* spend even one second with someone who did such an unspeakable thing?

Because I wanted to pretend it never happened. I wanted to turn my saying no into some version of *I brought this on myself.* I felt, in some sick way, like he owned a part of me. I wanted—no, needed—to make it okay, to make him okay, so I wasn't a victim.

I continued to see him at school, outside of school, at parties, until I just wanted to get away from it all. At the time, I was confused. I felt guilty. I accused him. I hated him. I needed him. This awful thing had happened to me, but I felt tied to him because he'd taken something from me I could never get back.

Finally, I confronted him. (More specifically, I punched him. That was when I found boxing.) I switched schools. I found my own forms of therapy. I started kickboxing, then boxing, then dabbled in a bit of jiujitsu. I learned how to protect myself, how to protect my body, my mind, and my heart.

More than anything, during those tenuous times, I found writing. Those horrible moments in a childhood bedroom led me to cutting, an eating disorder, angsty teen rebellion—but finally brought me to (and kept me on) the page.

Though this is something I have never spoken about publicly, I want to assure people that sexual assault can be confusing. There are two sides to every story, and it's not always a stranger violating you, or taking you by surprise. It can be someone you know, someone you trust, even someone you love. Someone who can take something from you that they are not allowed to take.

This novel features characters dealing with serious subject matter, such as sexual assault, alcoholism, and suicide. If you've ever dealt with any of these issues, it's important to confide in someone: a friend, a parent, a teacher, a trusted colleague—any of these people can help you find support.

If you don't want to talk to someone you know, there

are many services that provide free, confidential help to anyone struggling with sexual abuse or suicidal thoughts.

Here are a few well-known providers:

THE NATIONAL SUICIDE PREVENTION LIFELINE

The lifeline provides free and confidential support for people in distress, twenty-four hours a day, seven days a week. The toll-free number is 1-800-273-8255. The website is suicidepreventionlifeline.org.

THE NATIONAL SEXUAL ABUSE HOTLINE

This hotline provides support, information, advice, and referrals by trained support specialists. It is free and confidential and is available twenty-four hours a day, seven days a week. The toll-free number is 1-800-656-HOPE. The website is rainn.org.

Remember: you are not alone.

prologue

She is going to die.

She doesn't know it yet. She knows she should be sleeping. She knows she shouldn't have come out here in the middle of the night. She knows she should have skipped the wine.

But the girls gave her such a hard time about not making the hike this morning. They'd come off the trail, sweat stained and endorphin soaked, ready for coffee, green juices, and egg whites. While they were enjoying nature, she was sleeping, which was the entire point of this weekend.

Now, a branch pops under her boot. Pine and dirt create a sensory cocktail as the mountain air bites her lungs. The moon is a guiding half bulb that cranks her skin to the lightness of milk. She struggles to find her footing on the path that weaves in a zigzag. She checks her reception: two bars. Her fingers swipe for the phone's flashlight, but she thinks better of it and switches it off. She'll need the battery.

Her breath severs into short inhales and sharp exhales as she climbs. She is not a strong hiker, has never been. So why is she climbing a mountain?

She is climbing to get away from the secret just revealed,

moments before, the way it slugged through her body, word by word. She is climbing to get away from herself.

She trips over a tree root and steadies her footing. "Careful," she warns. It will be a miracle if she doesn't sprain an ankle or get mauled by a bear. The app on her phone shows the peak is half a mile up, the spike of the mountain a phantom through the swollen trees.

Her body spasms the higher she climbs. Her lungs flame. The wine coats her tongue in a sweet, black film. The alcohol's effects crush her senses. She surrenders to the discomfort of her limbs and shakes her head in an attempt to clear it.

The darkness consumes her as the moon disappears behind a wispy cloud. She exhales into the muted night and releases the pain. She decides to focus only on the hike, the clean air, the sizeable stars that pop like diamonds scattered across a black cloth. The wind shoves forcefully at her back and propels her onward. The betrayal stings, but she needs to forget about it now. She sucks a ragged breath.

"Just get to the top," she murmurs.

If she gets to the top, she will have accomplished something. If she gets to the top, she can forget about tonight. The trail makes a sharp left, but she mistakenly steps right. Her thighs quiver and she attempts to right herself. If she gets to the top, she will have done something no one thought—

Her right foot swipes altitude as if she is knocked to the side. One moment she is steady, and the next she is not. Vertigo consumes her. Her heart stutters and threatens to stop while gravity scrapes her body toward the earth in a relentless wrench. She hears the sound of her bones crack against branches, then the sound of her voice—a startled whisper instead of a terrified scream.

She anticipates the pain, the silent reel of her life making its final playback in the few seconds she has left. The reckless, ill-timed decision to take a midnight hike. The lies. The secrets. The truth, still burrowed inside, tangled and safe. Her. *Him.*

She battles for breath while she falls farther, faster, and harder. Her child's face blasts into her mind—motherless—as the ground hurtles into view. She can see it swimming toward her in a swath of green, jagged black rocks, and skinny trees. She keeps her eyes open.

Here, in death, is where she will finally be brave. She stops the questions; the panic; the wonder; the wild, unexpected truth; and feels a small punch of relief. It's all going to be over. Her life, her history, being a mother, everything.

Gone in an instant.

Her arms blade through the night. Her legs flutter through nothing. Now, it's just air. Stars blur the inky sky. Trees whiz fast-motion around her. The shrill, displaced leaves, awakened birds, mossy boulders, bear shit. The path shrinks. She plummets facedown. Is she ready?

She thinks only of her child as she smashes into the earth with impossible speed, her torso skewered between trunk and rock. There is a final, anguished breath and then nothing, as her scattered and torn body comes to its premature conclusion and sits, undisturbed, until daybreak.

Part 1

in the dark

We are all searching for someone whose demons play well with ours.
—Meghan Coates

1 week before the fall

thursday

1

grace

The car idles. Grace cuts the engine, cradles the parking brake, and pulls. Her secret swirls inside her. She presses a hand to her belly and takes a deep breath to kill the nerves.

After a hurried morning school drop-off for her son, Luca, Grace checks her hair in the rearview, hoping Lee can squeeze her in for a quick trim before work. She loves that her best friend owns a hair salon in her home, and that Grace can test the latest hair potions and coloring techniques when Lee needs a guinea pig. She knows it comes at a price: Lee's gifted son, Mason, her chronic singleness, her insistence on being housebound. Her entire world is shrink-wrapped.

Grace registers what she has to tell Lee and doesn't know where to start. She imagines the shock, the aftermath, and how it might affect their relationship. She shakes her head, knowing it must be done, and exits the car.

Lee's small ranch—a rental in the up-and-coming Donelson Hills neighborhood—begs for fresh paint, new windows, and an updated roof. The rusted railing outlines a weather-worn front porch, unruly shrubs, and a once gorgeous magnolia has recently been struck by lightning. Now, a singed black nub is the only reminder of shady mornings spent beneath its leaves.

On more than one occasion, Grace has offered to hire a mowing service or landscaping company, but Lee insists she's got it handled.

Grace lets herself in the side door. Lee's voice rumbles from the back in a succession of pleas. "Come on, buddy. You've *got* to work with me."

She tiptoes toward Mason's bedroom and stalls in the hallway as Lee struggles to get Mason's shirt over his head. No matter how wide Lee stretches the necks of his shirts, that moment his head disappears, he panics, punches, and claws against the thin womb of fabric as the claustrophobia—one of his main phobias—takes hold.

Mason and Luca are both seven, but Mason refuses to get dressed by himself. As a result, mother and son work in the same order: right sock, left sock, underwear, pants—never shorts, even on the hottest days—long-sleeved shirt, short-sleeved shirt over the top (soft cotton only), and a plain rubber band around his left wrist.

"Buddy, please work with me."

"I can't if you're *doing* it wrong." Mason's tone splinters his mother's resolve. Lee's ribs quake with every breath, but she starts the process over, layer by layer. She knocks a flock of hair from her forehead with the back of a knobby wrist. Grace taps gently on the wood, careful not to startle Mason.

"Hey, hi. I didn't hear you." Lee swivels toward the giant wall clock. "Is that the time?" Grace knows Lee is calculating the morning routine: Mason's breakfast, her breakfast, shower, waiting for Noah—Mason's homeschool teacher and occupational therapist—mixing color, and prepping the salon. Lee's cell rings and she abandons her task to grab the call from her office.

Mason rolls his eyes and turns his attention to Grace. "Please help me."

She kneels down. "I'm always here to help."

"Why can't she do it right? We've been doing it the same way since I was *five*."

Grace smiles. "I know. Come here."

He reaches his arms overhead as she removes the fabric. She drinks him in. His unruly mop of kinked hair. His impossible paleness, despite hours of sunshine. His slight build. The patches of red that sometimes crop against his cheeks like poppies. "What do we have here?" She inspects the shirt and pinches the tag. "The culprit."

Mason crosses his arms and taps a foot. "She's slipping in her old age," he says. "Clearly."

Grace chuckles and snags a pair of scissors from Lee's desk to snip the tag. "You know, your mom's got a lot on her plate. You should cut her some slack." She glances at Lee, who's still on the phone, her back turned to both of them.

"*You've* got a lot on your plate, but you always remember to remove Luca's tags."

"Luca doesn't mind tags."

He shrugs. "Well, if he did, you'd remember."

She winks. "Maybe." She helps him with both shirts and stands back to assess. "So handsome."

He bows.

Lee returns. "How'd you get him dressed?"

Mason straightens and eyes his mother warily. "Grace found a *tag*." He says the word as if it's grotesque.

"There was a tag?" She looks bewildered. "I could have sworn I cut all of them out."

"Hey, it's fine. It happens. Right, bud?" Grace gives him a stern look.

He sighs and bumps against Lee's bony hip as he walks to the dining room.

Lee presses the pads of her fingers into her eyes. "Sometimes I feel like he hates me."

Grace fondles her shoulder. "He doesn't hate you. It's called being a mother. It's their job to give us a hard time."

"Luca doesn't give you a hard time. Not like that."

She shrugs. "Luca and Mason are totally different."

Lee looks at the time again. "Shit, can you . . ."

Grace already knows the rest of that question. *Can you make him breakfast?* "Sure." Their shorthand developed quickly when Lee was in the throes of Mason's diagnosis. Grace's divorce from her ex, Chad, was old news by then, and she was available to help as much as possible with Mason. When Lee realized homeschool was going to be the best option for a child with sensory processing disorder, she quit her job at a well-known Nashville salon, Parlour & Juke, morphed her garage into a studio, and began taking clients at home.

"Noah's coming in an hour," Lee continues. "I can't afford to cancel any appointments today, but I'm just . . ." She rattles her head. Grace knows that Lee needs close to six clients to make enough money to pay Noah, and the bills. Though Noah works for a steep discount, Lee barely makes ends meet.

"Go get ready. I've got breakfast."

Lee snorts. "What? This isn't professional?" She motions to her sweatpants and wrinkled T-shirt.

Grace assesses Lee. She is rail thin, thinner than she's been in a while, with prominent elbows, hips, and kneecaps that protrude when she crosses her legs. Grace clocks her concave middle, her tiny breasts, and settles on her face. With bone structure to make a model cry, Lee could have made a fortune on the runway as a living fashion hanger if she'd wanted to. "You look beautiful. Even in pajamas. A little thin, if you ask me, but . . ."

Lee rolls her eyes. "Well, if I had time to eat." She gathers her hair into a ponytail and gnaws a rubber band from around her wrist with slightly crooked teeth. "You sure you don't mind making him breakfast? I'll be quick."

"She doesn't mind!" Mason shouts from the next room.

"See? He knows what's up," Grace says. "Gluten-free toast?"

"Yes, with—"

"SunButter, not almond butter. I remember. Cut into squares. Berries on the side. Not touching."

Lee sags. "What would I do without you?"

"Go. Shower. Be clean."

Grace longs to flush away Lee's overwhelming sense of responsibility. When they'd first met, Luca and Mason had been budding, exploratory babies. Lee had been looser, happier. Now, everything revolves around her mini daily dramas, and though Grace always listens, she knows their friendship has shifted in the last few months. Their conversations focus almost *entirely* on Lee: what she's dealing with, how her past issues keep cropping up, how her stress surmounts everyone else's, her sobriety, and how money is tight. Sometimes, Lee even makes cryptic comments about the night Mason was conceived, alluding to the answer to everyone's question—*who is Mason's father?*—but then, as if afraid of confiding too much, she shuts herself off like a faucet.

Grace doesn't want to add to her stress. She has something big to tell her, but she's not sure this morning is the right time. She joins Mason in the kitchen. "So what happened besides the tag?" She opens the fridge and removes the bread.

Mason taps out a rhythm on his pants. "She's trying to quit coffee *again*. And we all know how that goes."

"So we've found the heart of the matter, at last." She

pops the bread into the toaster and washes her hands. "I have an idea. What if I make a pot of coffee just to get her—and you—through the day? Would that be okay?"

"Is the pope Catholic? Yes. *Please,* yes."

She peers closely at him and cocks her head. "Are you absolutely, one hundred percent *positive* you're not a middle-aged man? I could have sworn seven-year-olds don't say things like that."

"I can't wait to be middle-aged."

Grace snorts. "Trust me. I'm over forty. It's not all it's cracked up to be."

"Lies."

Grace's heart swells at their banter. Though Mason suffers from sensory processing disorder and carries his own aversions and anxieties around people, noises, touch, and even food, she knows he's simply a divine being who is tangled in a complex world that doesn't often understand him. But Grace understands him. Ever since he came into her life, she has been there for him, feels connected to him in the same way she does to Luca. She would do anything for him, and Lee knows it.

Grace makes a pot of coffee and his breakfast. When it's ready, he receives his plate and bows again. Grace curtsies. He shuffles to the table that's pocked with dents and stains from years of use.

"All good?"

Mason nibbles an edge and arranges his fruit to spell y-e-s.

"Impressive you are," she says in her best Yoda voice. Mason's lips twitch into a smile. The shower cranks off with the groan of old pipes.

"How we doing?" Lee emerges a few minutes later in a pair of black jeans, motorcycle boots, and another (cleaner) V-neck T-shirt. She fingers her thick fringe of bangs into place and swipes under her bottom lip to remove a smear of red lipstick that's migrated out of place.

"We're all good here, right, Mason?"

Mason nods and chomps another crispy edge.

"Don't be mad," Grace says as she edges back into the kitchen. "But I made us coffee."

"Oh my God, I love you. Thank you." She greedily takes the cup Grace offers and inhales. "Why do I even try to quit? It's pointless."

"Totally pointless!" Mason offers.

Lee playfully rolls her eyes and leans against the counter. "Sometimes I think he has X-ray ears."

"Because I *do* have X-ray ears!"

Grace takes a sip. "Have I told you lately how much I love him?"

Lee absently circles a finger along the rim of her cup. "Did you see Carol's email?"

Grace rummages in the fridge for cream. "I did."

"Why does she keep sending them?" Lee extends her mug and Grace pours in a splash of half-and-half.

"I think it's just her way of contributing. You won't ever let her help."

"Because her type of help is *too* much," Lee jokes.

"We don't need extra helpers," Mason adds.

He's such a little gossip, Lee mouths. "Hey, bud." She peers around the corner. "Why don't you get ready for your session with Noah?"

Mason lifts his head and wipes crumbs from his mouth. "Because I'm having too much fun listening to your conversation."

"We're going to the studio." Lee slides the pocket door closed as they step down into the converted garage.

Grace laughs. "Sometimes I feel like you're hiding from your little brother."

Lee offers a tight-lipped smile. "He's just very nosy right now." She takes a sip. "What were we talking about? Carol?"

Carol bombards Lee's in-box with the newest alternative therapies for Mason's sensory issues. While some people provide a list of traits for children with SPD, Grace (and Lee) knows what does and doesn't work. He doesn't fit any singular checklist. While he struggles with hypersensitivity in some areas (tactile, movement, sounds, oral input), in others, he is hyposensitive (visual input, auditory-language processing, and certain social-emotional areas). Anything Carol sends is generalized and not specific to Mason. Lee has worked hard with Noah to devise a home-school curriculum that works—the Waldorf method. As a result, Noah teaches Mason three days a week and completes his at-home occupational therapy sessions two days a week to work on gross and fine motor skills.

"I do appreciate it," Lee says, "but the whole 'quick fix' thing just isn't applicable for him, you know?"

"I know. But it's not just you. She sends *me* emails all the time about the best way to handle being a divorced parent or being on a single-parent income. Or coparenting with a touring musician. Or starting my own business when she knows I'd love to do it but can't afford to take the risk." Grace shrugs. "That's Carol's way of helping."

"But it doesn't help."

"I think she just wants to ease your stress in some way. We all do."

Lee is accustomed to doing everything herself. She grew up just minutes from here, raised by a drunk who'd died years ago when Mason was just a baby. When Grace, Alice, and Carol had become friends, they could all tell she was unaccustomed to receiving help. She seemed private, reluctant to let them assist with Mason in any way. Now, she accepts help—even if she still feels she should be able to handle everything herself.

Grace thinks about Noah. She introduced him to Lee after Luca needed some occupational therapy for handwriting. With working overtime and some extra budgeting, Lee was finally able to hire Noah full-time six months ago. Though he's only been Mason's teacher and therapist for less than a year, he's drastically altered Lee's outlook on Mason—and men.

Lee chugs her coffee and tilts her head. "How's Luca?"

"He's okay. We had a bit of a rough morning of our own. I'm slammed with board meetings today. Which is going to be a bit of a nightmare, but you know." She shrugs.

"Sorry to keep you."

Grace ignores the prick of annoyance. Lee rarely asks about her work anymore. Maybe because it's boring or she can't relate, but it would be nice to have *her* interest, however small. "Can I ask you for a quick favor before I go?"

Lee laughs and pats the back of her styling chair. "Sit."

Grace takes her seat and spins in the plush leather. "Just the ends?"

"Yes, ma'am."

Lee gathers Grace's hair and pulls it behind her ears. "I don't know why you won't let me do a bob. Or straighten it. It would work wonders for your face."

Grace shakes her hair free. "I like my face. And it's just easier to keep it long."

"You're no fun."

Grace almost snorts. *She's* no fun? She takes a small sip of coffee and lets the frustration fade. Instead, she focuses on the space: the huge ornate mirror, rimmed in leafy gold; the soothing playlist crooning from tiny tacked speakers; the painted concrete floors. The lighting is a nice touch, as it smooths her crow's-feet and neck wrinkles that have suddenly sprouted with the passing of her forty-second birthday. Her skin is still porcelain, her cheekbones high, her mouth wide and sensual (or so she's been told). Where her features are strong and sturdy, Lee's are small and delicate. She angles forward to set her mug on Lee's vanity. A gray journal with an engraved *L* catches her eye.

"What's that? A new appointment book?"

"Hmm?" Lee removes her scissors from a sleeve and drags the blade across a cloth.

Grace motions to the book. "New appointment book? It's pretty."

"Oh, no." Lee combs through Grace's hair with damp fingers, spritzing only the ends. "It's a journal actually."

"Oh? I thought you stopped that a while back."

Lee shrugs. "I did. I got so busy, I stopped writing, but a few months ago, I picked it up again. Cheaper than therapy, right?" She smiles, but it doesn't quite reach her eyes. "I have to keep moving it though, because suddenly Mason has taken an interest in what I'm writing and keeps trying to steal it. No matter where I hide it, he finds it."

"Kids are good that way. Like miniature sleuths."

"Yeah, but there are some things your seven-year-old should never read."

Grace wants to ask *like what* but refrains. She would hate for Luca to read her private thoughts, her secrets . . . especially the one she needs to reveal. Besides, she knows Lee respects privacy above all else. She's relieved she's getting her feelings out in some real way, though, even if it isn't by confiding in her.

The trim goes fast. The scissors hack her ends. The excess hair scatters across her shoulders and spills onto the floor. She removes the smock once Lee finishes and kisses her on the cheek. "Thanks for the trim." She steps back into the kitchen, dumps the rest of the lukewarm coffee in the sink, washes her hands again, and waves at Mason. "Have a good day, okay?"

He barks at her, and she barks back. Lee's face twists into a mask of concern. "Lee, we're just playing. We're dogs, right?"

Mason bobs his head and smiles at her. Lee doesn't always get to witness their special conversations, the way he opens up with her. She sees moody Mason. Difficult Mason. Challenging Mason. She waves again, hesitating only for a moment, and then slips out the door. Her secret pricks her conscience. She has to tell her soon, no matter how stressed Lee is.

But today is not the day.

2

lee

Lee retreats to the bathroom to blow-dry her hair. She clicks the dryer on and off, listening to Mason's light conversation. She wishes he would talk to her like he talks to Grace.

When she's done, she rushes back to the kitchen, but Mason's chair is cocked and tossed. His stacked fruit leans in a quadratic equation. She rotates in the small room as panic clogs her throat. "Mase? Mason? Where are you, buddy?" She checks under the table, the closets, every corner of his room, and even the hamper, where he can sometimes still fit if he makes himself very small. She rummages through piles of clothes, opens and closes doors, then hurries to the kitchen window, where she can see him standing under a tree by the garden.

She tiptoes out the back door, careful not to surprise him, and announces herself about ten feet out. He jerks his head toward her. "Quiet, or you'll scare it away."

"Mason, we've talked about this. You can't go outside unless you ask."

"Shh." He stabs his index finger at something by his feet and she edges closer.

"What is it?"

"It's a bird. Judging by the color of the breast, I'd say

this is a rose-breasted grosbeak, though . . ." He tilts his head. "No, I'm positive. Grosbeak."

Lee inspects the small mound at his feet. "Is it hurt?"

Mason toes the bird, but it doesn't move. "Dead, by the looks of it."

"Well, don't touch it. Birds carry diseases."

Mason clicks his jaw. "I'm not going to *eat* the bird, Mother. I'm studying it."

"Let's finish breakfast." She rotates her watch on her wrist. "I have a client and Noah is coming."

Mason crouches even closer. "This bird is not rare," he mumbles, completely ignoring her request. He stands. "I want to study the Christmas Island frigatebird before he gets here."

What the fuck is a Christmas Island frigatebird? "Okay."

They begin to walk back toward the house.

"Did you know that Christmas Island frigatebirds have *nothing* to do with Christmas?"

"I didn't."

"Did you know that the Christmas Island frigatebird has nothing to do with Christmas and lives in the Indian Ocean?"

Lee shakes her head.

"Did you know that the Christmas Island frigatebird is the *rarest* seabird on Christmas Island?" His single-minded focus instantly washes away the curiosity for the bird in the garden as they step inside.

"Did you know that the Christmas Island frigatebird is the rarest seabird on Christmas Island, *Australia*?"

He ambles past her—on the balls of his feet, always in a shuffle—and resituates himself at the table. Carol has suggested the easiest thing to do would be to toss an iPad at Mason, to let him search, swipe, and play. But Mason isn't a stim-seeker. Stim-seekers like textured fabrics, music, flavorful foods, even vibrant colors, technology sometimes. Lee discerned quite quickly that Mason is stim-avoidant. He craves less, not more. He prefers organic cotton, noise-canceling headphones, and sunglasses for bright lights, and he does not enjoy physical touch. He possesses a heightened focus that some would call obsession.

She knows Mason hasn't been in her friends' lives on a daily basis as he has in hers—except for Grace—and she tries to remind herself of that. Their kids seek constant stimulation, wanting to go, see, and explore everything until their parents collapse at night, utterly exhausted from their unwavering energy. Though Mason is one of the most curious humans she's ever met, his intelligence so far surpasses that of an average seven-year-old that people—adults even—just can't keep up with the speed of his mind.

It draws a fine line between *them* and *her* during public outings, and while Lee accepts this divide, welcomes it even, Alice and Carol constantly try to urge her and Mason to "step outside" their tiny boxes.

Lee grabs the encyclopedias he loves, the only possession of her mother's that remains after all these years. The pages are yellowed and musty, the majority of the print gummed from snacks she used to devour while reading. She runs her fingers over the crispy pages, and they crackle beneath her touch.

She loves flipping through all the highlighted pages now, witnessing her own self-prescribed education. She used to make lessons for herself on those boring, sticky, endless summer days, or the heavy winter mornings back when it actually used to snow, and the white would drape across her house like a blanket.

Lee leaves him to find the bird section, hoping it contains what he is looking for. She scours the cabinets for more coffee—she and Grace used the last bag—but has to settle for herbal tea. As she waits for the kettle to boil, dreaming of Turkish coffee thick as pudding, the exhaustion settles into her bones, and it isn't even nine.

She studies Mason's profile, thinking, as parents often do, how quickly time has flown. Wasn't he just a baby? She remembers those early years—the complicated past she tried to outrun. The things she's done. The secrets she's kept. She craves wine then, so much that it almost makes her dizzy. *No.* She grips her mug of tea and descends into her studio, sweeping up Grace's hair and rearranging her styling products until the rap of knuckles alerts her to Noah's arrival.

She rushes to the back door, eager to see him, as always. She pulls open the door and her heart palpitates as she says hello. She has memorized every bit of him: his dark hair that sweeps off his forehead with the firm part dividing his hair like a scar; the swimmer's build with clothes impeccably tailored to accentuate his muscles; the smooth, olive skin; the natural musk he exudes that makes Lee want to devour him.

"Hey, you." His green eyes soften when he sees her.

She swallows as her body involuntarily heats with desire. A few nights ago, when he stayed late, they'd talked for hours. She thought he might kiss her good night, *finally,* but he didn't. She's been obsessing about that missed opportunity ever since. She rearranges her face to neutral and opens the door wider. "Hey, yourself. Right on time."

He flashes his watch, a vintage Rolex. "Actually, I'm three minutes early."

She moves aside so he can step through. "Tea?"

He glances at the kettle. "Off coffee again?"

She shrugs. "Ran out." He knows her constant up-and-down battle with caffeine. One week, she offers him the strongest brew, and the next, it's nothing but herbal blends that taste like flowers.

"I thought as much." He reaches into his bag and produces a thermos. "I came prepared. Just smell that." He wafts the canister under her nose, and she gently slaps it away.

"Not nice." She does a double take at the army-green thermos with the silver top. Where has she seen that thermos recently?

Noah brushes past her, their elbows touching, and an electric shock jolts her below the waist. He enters the dining room, says hello to Mason, and arranges all of his materials in a straight line. She watches his body descend into a chair, and she longs to massage his shoulders and kiss the back of his neck.

Get it together, Chambers. She clears her throat. "Are you guys okay here?"

Noah turns and flashes her a sexy smile. "All good. Thanks."

She pours herself another cup of tea, buries the sexual hunger that has bloomed in the last few weeks, and tugs the pocket door into place. She paces her studio floor in socked feet and spins in her styling chair as Grace did moments ago, cranking to a stop in front of the mirror.

It's ironic that she and Noah both grew up in Nashville, in opposite neighborhoods, but they never met. It wasn't until Grace introduced them that she learned he was an occupational therapist. She couldn't believe her luck, but at the time, she couldn't afford his services.

Once she'd opened her own salon and squirrelled away some cash, at Grace's suggestion, she asked Noah for a professional assessment of Mason. He was kind enough to work out a deal, and now, seeing how well Mason is doing, she wishes she'd found him years ago. Noah is so good with him, so different from Mason's biological father, that she could cry from relief. She shakes away the thought of his real father, just as she had the wine.

Not today.

Because Noah gives her a discount on services, she cuts his hair every two weeks for free. Secretly, she relishes that time, stretching the appointments as long as possible. She loves the moment his head tips back over the sink and her fingers move across his scalp. The way his Adam's apple bobs while he relaxes beneath her touch. It is the only time she feels sensual: when she rakes conditioned fingers across the slick flesh of his neck, up the base of his skull, and across to his temples and forehead. Sometimes, she even massages his shoulders, loving how the knots dissolve beneath her touch. He always says she should have been a masseuse, but she only gives him such special treatment. She only craves *his* wet hair against her hands.

Every time she has him in this chair, she thinks about leaning in to kiss him. The exact way she would do it. She imagines his response, how he would pull her to him . . .

She blinks away the daydream and faces herself in the mirror. Tired eyes—large and gray, fanned by a set of thick, inky lashes, easily her best feature—blink back. Alice recently told her about some new laser treatment to "brighten and tighten" tired eyes. Though she's never had work done (mainly because she can't afford it), she should start taking better care of herself, at least invest in a good eye cream. It wouldn't hurt to make a little effort.

She hears Noah in the dining room, and she sighs with

longing. There is the promise of more—she can almost taste it. All she has to do is tell him how she feels and see what he says. She's given it enough time to make sure Mason likes him and is comfortable. What does she have to lose?

She whirls away from the mirror and lets any sort of physical desire evaporate. There will be time for romance, but she has to stay focused. There's such a precarious balance to her life at the moment: Mason comes first, her sobriety second, then her business. She spins back toward the mirror. There's more to that balance. Of course there is. A knock at the door—her first client— snaps her out of her reverie.

She rises to answer it.

There's the deep, underlying truth.

She plasters on a smile as she pulls the door open.

The truth she keeps only for herself.

secret [see-krit]

<u>adjective</u>

**1. done, made, or conducted without the
knowledge of others**

**2. kept from the knowledge of any but the
initiated or privileged**

*Sometimes, I wonder if we ever really know the
people in our lives: their layers, their hidden
truths, their complexities, their lies.*

I wonder how many secrets each of us juggles.

Are we afraid of not being liked?
Are we afraid of being judged?
Are we afraid of consequences?

I know I am.

*I've always been good at keeping secrets—other
people's secrets, friends' secrets, family secrets,
strangers' secrets. But I'm even better at <u>creating</u>
secrets.*

*No one ever guesses them . . . even if I beg them
to try.*

3

lee

"So, I have to tell you what happened last night. You'll die. Seriously, you will just *die*." Alice reworks her scarf around her clavicle and yells at her daughter, who is suctioned around the Two Rivers playground fire pole. "Olivia, get off that pole. Now!"

Carol peels an orange for her daughter, Zoe. "Let's hope you're not telling her that ten years from now."

Lee sits next to Carol, Alice, and Grace on the park bench, her eyes glued to Mason, who constructs a kite by the swings. This is their post-school afternoon ritual, at least one day a week.

Alice uncrosses her legs, her jewel-tone skirt swishing across her ankles. "Right? Seriously. She's obsessed with poles right now. Anytime she sees one, she wraps herself around it and just hangs there. I asked her why she does it, and do you know what she said? She said, 'Because it feels good.'"

Grace laughs. "Isn't she a little young for that?"

Alice lifts her sunglasses to her forehead. "Are we ever too young for that?" She arches her eyebrows and lets the aviators slide back into place. "So. Last night. Fred and I finally had sex, because, it's been, I don't know, fucking forever, and we start and it's just . . . awkward. Like, I feel *awkward* underneath my own husband. I'm trying to get past that, but then I'm paying attention to the damn condom—"

"Gross! How can you guys still use condoms? In your thirties?" Carol asks.

"Because not all of our husbands jump at the chance to get a vasectomy."

"Point taken."

"So, I'm totally grossed out by the condom, and then . . . there was an incident."

"What kind of incident?" Grace asks.

Alice inhales. "Like a chest fart incident."

Carol laughs, strangling juice from one of the oranges. She licks her fingers. "Oh my God. That is seriously the best thing I've ever heard."

Lee rolls her eyes beneath her sunglasses and laughs good-naturedly. These ladies and their sex stories. Lee hasn't had sex since Mason was *born*. Since before actually. While Alice and Carol complain about their snoring husbands or their inability to spoon, Lee has slept alone, night after night, for as long as she can remember. The loneliness has become an actual living thing. Noah flashes through her mind again, but she buries the fantasy. She smiles at Grace. Thank God she's single too, or she'd be on an island all by herself.

"Like full-on chest-against-chest *farting*," Alice continues. "I was like, 'What's next? Clinking our teeth like we're sixteen?' I mean, what is that? Olivia, seriously, get off that pole right now and let the other kids slide down, or we are leaving! Do you hear me, young lady?"

"Did you guys finish?" Grace inquires. She side-eyes Luca, who is busy flying down the slide, belly first.

"We did," she says. She gathers her skirt in her fist and knots it below her knees. "I don't know how because we were both so embarrassed by ourselves. It's tragic when I think back to how we used to rip each other's clothes off every chance we got. Now, we're like clumsy, middle-aged virgins."

Carol nods and hands the squished orange to Zoe. "I've got one better than that. Charlie and I had sex for the first time in three months the other night. Three entire *months*. It lasted about twelve seconds. We suck."

"It's these kids." Alice's eyes drift to Zoe and Olivia, who chase Luca across the playground. Mason pieces focuses on the kite, seemingly immune to the activity around him. "I mean, do you remember the days of waking up on weekends and . . . I don't know, taking a few minutes to come into the day instead of being forced into it by these little voices that have to tell you every last detail of their dreams, or what they want for breakfast, or that they had an accident or whatever?"

Lee wants to scream no. Life before Mason was haunted, dark, and . . . no. She can't imagine. Mason is the hardest thing she's ever done, but he keeps her grounded. He keeps her alive. She could never go back.

"What about when they pounce on your bladder, like they have radar for the exact spot you have to pee?" Grace asks.

"I'm not kidding, I think Olivia actually punctured my bladder with her knee." Alice sighs. "I was just talking to Fred the other day about all of this. Do you know what I used to do? Every morning, I would smother him with kisses—"

"Vomit," Grace jokes.

"And go make pancakes and coffee. We'd have leisurely sex, lounge around, and decide what to do with our day. Usually, our biggest decision was where we were going to get takeout from and what video to rent. Back when Blockbuster was a real thing. I mean, we'd *decide* what to do with our day. Do you know how foreign that feels now?"

"Uh, yeah, I do. Obviously." Carol looks at Lee, finally registering that she's been silent. "You okay, Lee?"

Lee forces a smile and shakes her head. "Sorry. I'm a little out of it today. Didn't sleep well. Sounds awful though. The chest farting stuff."

They laugh, and Alice wipes away tears. "When did passion switch places with, I don't know, a roommate?"

"I have a theory," Carol interjects. "In my experience, parenting and romantic relationships don't really go together. I read this article that your spouse becomes like a relative or something. I think they call it familialization."

Grace nods. "Exactly. I've been saying that forever. Hence my divorce. No one wants to sleep with a relative."

As much as Lee reads about divorce rates or failed relationships, she'd still take one over having none. She's never had a successful relationship. She craves that as much as she craves happiness for Mason. Noah floods her thoughts again, and her entire body warms.

"We do live in the South, you know," Carol jokes. "So, the whole sleeping with a relative thing . . ." She glances at her phone, which vibrates in her hand. "Ugh. It's my mother."

"Answer it," Grace demands.

"Please answer it," Alice begs, tenting her fingers in mock prayer. "Cheryl is the highlight of my day."

"Speaker," Lee adds, suddenly interested. "For us?"

"Fine." Carol sighs, hits speaker, and feigns enthusiasm. "Hey, Mom. I'm just at the park with the girls, so I won't be able to talk long—"

"I think I have cancer."

Lee balks. Normally, Cheryl's outbursts, though bordering on hypochondria, make them all laugh. The time she almost got arrested for stealing a mannequin from Kmart because she wanted *that* particular garment, even though it wasn't for sale. The time she refused to stand up on a bus so a pregnant woman could sit down because she insisted the elderly were a forgotten group and that pregnant women all over the world carried baskets on their heads and babies on their backs, so standing on a bus was the least of the soon-to-be-mother's worries. The time she made her granddaughter almost cry because she insisted that watching a Disney princess movie meant that she would grow up relying on men. No matter the preposterousness of the situation, Cheryl keeps their lives entertaining.

Carol rolls her eyes at the group. "You do not have cancer."

"I *know* I have cancer."

"I repeat: you do not have cancer."

Grace mouths to Alice, *She totally doesn't have cancer.*

"Well, your *father* had cancer. And he died, Carol. He died. That could happen to me too, you know."

"Mom, I was there, remember? I know Dad died."

"Then you should know that I have cancer and that I'm going to die too. And leave all you girls without a mother. Oh my. This is"—her mother inhales sharply and lowers her voice to a whisper—"the real deal."

Cheryl launches into a tirade about her right breast, which has become sore and lumpy. This week it's her breast, last week her brain, the weeks before that her thyroid, her pancreas, her lymph nodes, and her colon, if Lee is remembering correctly. She is a true hypochondriac, and the girls fear that when the "real deal" actually comes for Cheryl, no one will believe her.

"Are you giving yourself breast exams regularly?" Carol snaps her fingers at Zoe and hisses at her to drop the branch she's chasing Luca with.

"Well, no. But when Arnie and I were fooling around, he grabbed my breast and he said—"

"Mom! Stop! You're on speaker."

Grace and Alice laugh and lean in to say hello to Cheryl. Lee knows that Cheryl dating someone besides Carol's father is hard enough; the fact that it's Arnie—Cheryl's mailman of all things—might push the envelope a bit too far.

"I've got to go. You do not have breast cancer. Okay?"

"But I went to this one website, and you would not believe what it said. Let me find it . . ." The rustle of papers explodes over the phone.

"Did you actually print out the article? I thought your printer wasn't work—listen. It doesn't matter. Just stop googling stuff. You do not have cancer. You are fine. Every time you go to the doctor, you are always fine. Better than fine. You're the healthiest senior I know."

"Har har, Carol. Very funny."

"I really have to go."

"Give that delicious granddaughter of mine a huge kiss from her Maw-Maw."

"I will, Mom. Love you." Carol tosses the phone back in the bag, and the women look at her with slight concern. "Ridiculous, right? She does not have cancer."

"I'm sure she's fine," Grace assures her. "She's always fine."

"I mean, what would I even do? When we created our

will, it states that Zoe will go to her if something ever happened to me and Charlie, but is that a mistake? What if she dies?"

Lee shudders. Unfortunately, she's been there, going through the horror of losing one parent and being left with another parent who could care less about the responsibility of raising a young child. It's her worst nightmare—leaving Mason without a parent.

"That's why I sometimes think friends with kids are the better choice for that type of thing," Alice says. "Our parents have all been-there-done-that with raising kids and don't have the energy anymore. We've seriously thought about changing ours."

Grace looks at Lee and offers a comforting smile. They've had this conversation on numerous occasions. Since they are both single mothers, Grace urged Lee to get her affairs in order.

A month ago, Grace had arranged a meeting with her lawyer and they'd drawn up legal papers for Lee to get notarized. When Lee was creating the draft, she'd watched Grace painstakingly comb through the documents to make sure they hadn't missed anything. Certainty had swirled in Lee's chest.

"Will you?"

"Will I what?" Grace had removed her reading glasses and turned her attention to Lee.

"Mason. If something happens to me, will you take Mason?" It was the hardest thing she'd ever had to ask. Grace had pressed a hand to her chest, shocked.

"Are you sure? That's a monumental decision."

She'd nodded. "He adores you. You two just click. I see it every time you're together."

Grace had crushed her in a hug and told her what an

honor it was. "I'd ask you to do the same, but I'm pretty sure Chad would fight you for Luca." She'd rolled her eyes and dabbed her tears with her sleeve. It had been such a huge decision, but she'd never been more certain that Grace was the right choice.

"Your mom will be fine," Lee says now. "She's not going anywhere."

"Because she wants to annoy me until I'm old and gray."

Lee shrugs. "You're still lucky to have her."

"Until she's your mother." Carol sighs and scrolls through a few new texts.

Lee would take any type of mother. The anniversary of her mother's death is tomorrow. Every year, it eclipses daily life—from parenting to work to making dinner—until it's all she can think about. It's the elephant in the room, the sole memory her mind snags on, the day she can't change, the day *everything* changed, the day she became . . . different.

It used to be alcohol that quelled the ache of remembrance. She'd drink wine until she passed out and wake the next day, groggy and swollen, realizing that horrible footprint in history was gone. Until the next year.

Since her sobriety, Grace is now her crutch. She literally can't imagine getting through the tough stuff without her. It's been years since she could rely on a best friend, and it's one of the things she is most thankful for, even when daily life wears her down: Grace.

"Zoe, let's go, baby!" Carol calls.

Lee hurtles back to the present moment—the friends; the playground; the packing of various snacks, bags, and water bottles; Mason; and the laundry list of to-dos for the rest of the day. She waves good-bye to the group, thinking once more of her mother and what she would give to have even one more day with her. A day like this. A day chatting on the phone. A day fighting. A day laughing about her with her friends.

She steps forward and calls to her son.

4

lee

Mason launches his kite and watches it sway, unwinding the string when necessary. She's always amazed at his ability to get so engrossed in a project that he doesn't share the need to run, play, jump, and explore. She brings him here to be with his friends, but every week she vows not to do it again, because he's always off on his own.

"You ready, bud?"

He nods and begins to wind the string and lower the kite to the earth. He scoops it up and deposits the fabric in the trunk. In the car, he buckles himself into his booster. They drive home in silence—Mason isn't in the mood for the radio today—and she lets the same handful of thoughts accost her. Who she is. What she's become.

"I'm hungry. I'm so hungry. I need food right now or I will faint." Mason's words pull her from the repetitive mental abuse.

"You will not faint."

"I am *so* hungry that I will faint in exactly forty-six seconds if I don't consume something *substantial*." He grips his stomach for effect.

She laughs. "Well, forty-six seconds is not a lot of time."

"You should have thought about that before I was about to faint."

"We'll be home in five minutes. You can wait until then."

He kicks the back of her seat in sets of threes—thunk, thunk, thunk—and she grits her teeth. "Mason, please stop kicking my seat. That doesn't feel good."

"*You* don't feel good."

"Well, that doesn't really make any sense."

"Yes, it does. It makes perfect sense." He settles down almost immediately, knowing that if he throws a tantrum, it will do nothing but agitate them both. She resists the urge to get to the bottom of what is wrong. He will tell her when he's ready. Her mind sorts through the possible reasons anyway: is it the playground? The other kids? He has promised her that he doesn't feel left out, but really . . . why wouldn't he?

She drives the rest of the way home on autopilot and replays Carol's conversation with her mother. She's so flippant with Cheryl, the two of them sharing an almost comical relationship. Lee wonders what she and her mother would be talking about if she were still alive right this very second. Would she offer some parental words of wisdom about how fast childhood goes and to pick her battles?

As she takes a sharp right into her neighborhood, she is brought back to the night her mother died. She fiddles with the radio knob, but then remembers Mason wants it off. She searches desperately for something else to take over her mind. She doesn't want to think about that night yet. She doesn't want to catalog the loss, as she does each year, bit by bit. Not until she can call Grace.

She comes to a stop sign, eases her foot off the gas, and waits.

"Mom, what are you doing? There aren't any other cars."

"Sorry." She presses the gas after almost a full minute of stillness, and they lurch forward toward their street.

She is restless to get Mason settled, to call Grace and get it over with, as she does every year, in a passionate rush. If she doesn't talk about it, she will forget her. If she forgets her, there is nobody left to remember.

The timeline of her mother's death unfolds in quick snapshots. Lee was a child and had been sick. All she'd wanted was 7UP and crackers. It was her father who was supposed to go to the store, not her mother. But he was drunk and watching the game. Her mother had shrugged into a coat, kissed her hot forehead, and said she'd be right back. That was the last time she'd seen her alive.

She cringes from the memory and tucks it away once they pull into the drive. Mason slams the car door and runs inside. When she's set up an afternoon project for him, she calls Grace. "Hi."

"Right on time."

Hadn't she said the same thing to Noah that very morning? "Can I . . . ?" The memories surface and repeat, a barrage of images she can't undo or erase until she talks about that day.

Grace chews something and swallows. "Of course. I'm here."

"Where should I begin?" Lee asks in a whisper, but she knows exactly where she will start. Tears disturb her cheeks, but she lets them fall.

"Wherever you want," Grace says. "I'm listening."

Lee launches into it, offering the shortened version she's gone over in her mind a thousand times. The grocery store that was only a few blocks away. Her mother, who promised to be back in less than ten minutes. The unexpected robbery that happened on the way out.

The fluorescent lights had highlighted her mother lying near the exit behind a roll of wavy caution tape—her head knifed apart like a coconut, all the innards of her magnificent brain scattered across the floor as if her body were a bag of trash mauled by a starving dog. There were three shot civilians, her mother the only fatality.

She'll never forget the mound of her mother's belly, budding with her unborn baby brother. The pretty yellow scarf, dotted with blood, blown from around her neck. The waistband of her skirt, twisted and mangled. The way it felt to stand there, witnessing her like that, like someone was physically carving out her heart. That was her *mother* on the floor. That was her brother in her mother's belly.

Two lives lost in a single night.

Lee gets lost in the recollection, but Grace stays silent, listening, as she always does, until Lee comes to the very end. Every time she shares this loss, she remembers something new: a smell, a sound, a different sadness that cuts into her like a blade.

There's no amount of talking that can undo the past, but she tries anyway. She tries to bring her mother back—if only for a moment, if only to say good-bye. She finishes. The silence hangs. Grace knows there is nothing she can say to make her feel better.

She ends the call.

5

lee

When Lee hangs up, she feels better. Every year, like clockwork, she has to purge the memory. She doesn't ever talk about the funeral, how her father looked like he was made of crumpled paper in his oversized suit. She doesn't recount the irritating fabric of her stiff black dress, the raw ring it left around her neck, or how she set fire to it after the service in the bottom of a trash can.

Lee hadn't really had a chance to mourn her mother or baby brother because she stepped into her mother's shoes seemingly overnight. She'd learned to adapt to her father's moods, to stay out of his way, to stay *gone*. She learned to cook, give herself baths, forge permission slips, and even pack her own lunch on days she didn't have enough change for the school lunch. It wasn't about childhood—it was about *survival*. Neighbors stopped by almost every day, bringing wrapped casseroles and laundry detergent, and inspecting the place as she assumed Social Services might.

She abandons the memories and shoots Grace a quick text. *Thank you for listening. I don't know what I'd do without you.*

She waits for the response: *I'm always here for you. Thank you for trusting me enough to confide. Love you. XOXO*

Lee opens her laptop and checks her in-box. She almost deletes the group email from Carol, wondering if it will be yet another way to improve her or Mason's life, but this one is for a potential girls' trip. Intrigued, Lee opens the email. The images sweep her away in possibility. A getaway in the North Carolina mountains, where they can hike, hole up in a bed-and-breakfast, and spend time kid-and-husband free.

Yes.

Lee clicks the link. A Cape-style home fills the page, replete with a bustling garden, a pristine white-bricked chimney jutting from the roof like an oversized Lego, and an aquamarine plaque on the white picket fence that reads ARBOR HOUSE.

She explores some of the trails; giant monuments ratcheting into the sky; beautiful, carved bluffs; dappled leaves; and men and women posed in pictures with pink cheeks and walking sticks. Lee closes the hiking window and traces her fingers over the photo of the home. How she longs for a real getaway with her friends. She scans the rates and balks at the nightly price. Despite the money, which she doesn't have, she has *never* left Mason—not for more than a few hours, tops—and there is no way she could leave for an entire weekend, much less *next* weekend.

Can she?

She closes the page, wistful at how easy the other girls will jump to say yes, regardless of price or logistics. When they'd first met, at a playground meet-up, she'd edged into their lives when Mason was still asymptomatic. They'd bonded over Lee's killer haircut and her absolute desperation for mom friends.

They'd taken her in, each of them shuffling into their proper roles: Alice the workhorse, Carol the organizer, and Grace the reliable friend. Though she appreciates

Alice and Carol, she and Grace recognize something in each other—maybe it's having boys, maybe it's being single, maybe it's having lost someone important in their lives (Lee's mother, brother, and father; Grace's sister), and that sad residue it leaves just beneath the surface—but she feels safest with Grace.

She thinks again about the trip. Grace splits custody with her ex-husband, Chad, but Lee is the only one without an extra set of full-time hands—besides Noah—and it roots her to the spot. No vacations, no impulsivity, and no sudden getaways.

She will have to let the girls down at Carol's barbecue on Sunday, and she steels herself against their insistence and inevitable justifications on why she can and should go. *He's seven years old! He has Noah! He has our husbands! He'll be fine! Live a little!*

Carol has even made the trip short—a quick two-night, three-day getaway. She rests against her pillow, imagining uninterrupted baths, sleeping in, reading by the fire, exploring a new city. These are things people do all the time, but not her.

The idea dissolves as she waits for Noah to arrive for his second shift. She has two more clients before dinner. Then she can relax, read her son a story, get fractured sleep, and begin again tomorrow.

lie
__LIE__
lie
__LIE__
lie
__LIE__

Big lie, little lie.
I lie.
You lie.
We all lie.
Do you know how many lies I've told in the last seven years?
Probably too many to count.

Lying comes as easily to me as breathing.
Everyone believes me.
I'm good.
I'm safe.
I'm trustworthy.
Most people like me.

Which is why no one suspects me of lying.
I have no reason to lie . . . I have no outward reason to stray from the truth, right?

Wrong. So wrong.
I lie to protect myself.
I lie to protect the people I love.
I lie because I'm biding my time.

I lie so you have no idea what's coming next.

FRIDAY

6

grace

Grace opens the email from Carol, and hope crackles through her body. A vacation with the girls is exactly what she needs. She has been so burdened lately—with work, with Chad and his ever-changing schedule with Luca, with Luca's recent bullying at school, with house repairs, and specifically with what she needs to tell Lee.

She can't think of anything better than shedding the daily grind and relinquishing control for a few days. It's what's been missing. It's what they all need. She rattles off something to her boss, estimating the new summer budget, and hangs up the phone, turning her attention back to the details of the trip. The bed-and-breakfast is in Black Mountain, just outside of Asheville. Carol reiterates there will be hiking, possible canoeing, bonfires, and a nearby Japanese spa.

She shoots off an overly friendly email to Chad, asking if he's available, as the trip is next Thursday. Lately, he has backed out of several parenting duties, and Luca, feeling blown off, has been taking it out on a boy at school. She double-checks the parenting calendar. It isn't his weekend, but he owes her. He owes Luca.

She adjusts the photo of Luca on her desk and smiles. She's disturbed by his recent behavior but finally got him to admit what it's really all about: his father. Though he is surrounded by empowered females, she knows Chad's semiabandonment gets to him.

Her ex's schedule as a touring musician is erratic. But like most little boys, in Luca's eyes, Chad has swiftly become the infallible caretaker. No matter how many times Luca is crushed by his father's absences, he still has hope that *this time* will be different.

She takes another call, already distracted by the promise of Black Mountain. She can't wait to get some fresh air, jump-start the season, and spend time with her friends. She wonders if Lee will even go . . . she can already guess what her objections will be. No matter what she says or how Grace reassures her, Lee will still put up a fight. This might be the perfect opportunity for Mason—to give him a little room, to let him breathe without her there every single minute of the day.

She waves good-bye to her coworkers as the day winds down. Chad is picking Luca up today, which means she has all night and the entire weekend to herself. While it kills her to see Luca go, as she always wonders what Chad's feeding him, if he's reminding her son to floss, if he's helping Luca read or do his homework, she relishes the alone time.

She steps onto Church Street and tips her face to the sky. It is unusually chilly for spring. She sets her thermos of coffee on the ground, buttons her jacket, and walks to the parking garage.

The trip would be a perfect time to tell Lee. She is a firm believer in practicing hypothetical situations and envisioning several possible outcomes *before* they happen so she's prepared when shit goes south. If Lee getting upset is a given, then she can figure out how to respond. She briefly practices telling her and clocks how suddenly her face will change. How her affection might tip to frost. All the accusations she'll fling. The objections. The blame.

She won't think about that now. Instead, she focuses on the solo weekend ahead. There will be time for the truth.

She just has to get Lee to Black Mountain.

7

lee

It has been a long day. Lee's feet ache. Her shoulders bunch in repetitive knots. She's not heard a peep from Noah or Mason, as they are hard at work. She rummages in the fridge, searching for ideas for dinner. So many nights, she wants to go out, but Mason doesn't enjoy the loud restaurant noises and inconsistency in routine.

She revels in the brief quiet as she creates mock meals in her head. Chicken and rice. Chicken and broccoli. Bison burgers and sweet potato fries. They seem to go through the same roster of meals every week. Tonight, she wants something different.

She peeks around the corner, and her heart flips. She is in constant awe of how Noah keeps her son so even-tempered, like they are cut from the same cloth. Lee seems to agitate him over the smallest things. "You boys hungry?"

Mason continues scribbling answers in his workbook and ignores the question.

Lee surveys the wilting contents of the fridge again. They've been on a Paleo kick for a while, but she can't afford all the organic meat. She hesitates, closes the fridge, and leans against the door frame to the dining room. "Would you like to stay for dinner?"

Noah glances up from checking Mason's work and locks eyes. Her heart skips an actual beat, and she reminds herself to breathe. She senses hesitation, but then he smiles.

"Sure." He looks at his watch. "I had a thing I was supposed to do, but I can skip it."

"Are you sure?" A surge of relief and a possessiveness she can't quite explain overtake her. She has no idea if he's dating or what he does when he's not with them, but she desperately wants to be a part of his outside life.

"In fact, why don't you let me pick up dinner?" Noah asks. He stacks his workbooks and crafts and slides them back into his satchel. "Nectar sound good? I can get him a burrito bowl and grab us some tacos?"

"Are you sure? That place is pricey." She rummages in her purse for some cash but finds only coins. "Here, take my card." She fishes her First Tennessee debit card from her wallet and hands it over.

Noah stands. "Lee, stop. I've got it. It's my treat."

She thinks about protesting but stuffs the card back into her purse. "If you're sure."

"I am. Hey, Mason. Do you want chicken on your burrito bowl?"

"Is it organic?" Mason's pencil hovers in the air.

Noah ponders the question. "I'm not sure."

"If it's not organic, it will be full of antibiotics and hormones, which can affect my mood, hormones, and overall growth. I need to know the answer to that question before I can answer *your* question."

Noah hides a smirk. "How about I ask them when I get there?"

"That'll do." He taps a rhythm on the table with his pencil.

Noah grabs his keys, puffs his chest, and gives his best Schwarzenegger impression. "I'll be back."

Mason eyes him. A smile cranks his mouth up to the right. "That was a *terrible* Arnold impression. You should really work on that."

A spike of pride warms Lee's heart at their friendly exchange. "How do you even know who that is?"

Noah looks sheepish. "Ah, we may or may not have watched *The Terminator.*"

Lee laughs. "For research, I'm sure."

"Totally for research." He waves and disappears out the door before she can even tell him what kind of tacos she wants. She doesn't care what he brings her as long as she doesn't have to cook. She collapses back against the counter and studies Mason.

"Would you like some water?"

"Yes, please." He continues tapping his pencil in the steady rhythm that helps him concentrate.

Her cell rings, and she reaches for it. She's changed her ringtone to Prelude and Fugue no. 1, Mason's favorite composition. Blocked call. Her heart pumps faster, as it always does, if an unknown number ever flashes on the screen. She declines the call and pours Mason a glass of water.

She gazes out the kitchen window and catches the last remnants of the sun as it descends below the horizon in a delicious swirl of pink. Spring has brought a gorgeous bounty of various breeds in her garden, and she and Mason have spent a good amount of time discussing each of them. Maybe she'll bring some snapdragons to Carol once they've bloomed, despite the fact that Carol's garden makes hers look like an amateur's paradise.

Lee has invited Noah to come along to the barbecue on Sunday. Though they've all spent time together—

briefly interacting at parks, playgrounds, and birthday parties, or passing through the house—she wants her friends to like him as much as she does. He's become vital to the makeup of her insular little family.

She hands the glass to Mason and analyzes the differences between her and her friends. She can never quite relax like they can, letting their kids play in Carol's massive backyard. She has to keep an eye on Mason, because he could riffle through all of their belongings, repeat a random fact that is much too old for their seven-year-old ears, or start digging a tunnel in the middle of her yard in search of moles . . . The options are endless, and she always guts herself with worry while her friends drink, laugh, and tell stories, so certain of their kids' behavior and boundaries that they can detach while their children play.

Lee realizes she's never had that parental freedom, except for the last six months. Noah has brought a peace to their lives that she hoards like a stacked poker hand. She can't be identical to her friends, but with Noah's help, she's starting to relax about things that once kept her up at night.

Noah rustles through the door half an hour later with stiff paper bags. Mason presses his stopwatch. "You took exactly thirty-one minutes and thirteen seconds."

"Is that all?" Noah winks at Lee as he sets the bags on the counter.

Lee notices—for what seems like the hundredth time—his sturdy chest and muscular arms. She wonders what it would be like to wake up with him wrapped around her like a blanket. "Can't you smell the salt?" Lee dumps the contents of the containers onto separate plates. Her mouth waters at the chips and guacamole she is dying to devour.

"You can't smell salt, Mother. That's impossible," Mason says.

"Oh, just eat your organic chicken," she jokes. "You know what I mean."

She grabs the forks and a couple of spoons and moves to the refrigerator. "I'm afraid I've only got water."

"Water's perfect," Noah says.

Lee finishes dishing Mason's bowl onto separate plates: chicken, rice, cheese, veggies, and corn, his food never allowed to come in contact. Mason watches the exchange of easy conversation between her and Noah as they eat, and it dawns on Lee that Mason has never seen her interact much with men. As if reading her thoughts, Mason speaks up.

"I like this."

"Like what?" Lee asks between bites.

"This. I like this. I like the three of us eating together."

Lee beams at Noah. "I do too. We should do this more often, right?"

"It feels like a family. Are we family?" Mason looks between them.

Noah ponders the question and wipes his mouth with a napkin. "Well, we're kind of like family, but we aren't related by blood."

"That's right," Lee adds. "Friends can sometimes be just like family."

"But you should only trust your family," Mason says. "Because family is good."

Noah places his napkin by his plate. "It's not that simple. People aren't only good or only bad."

"And you can trust people other than family," Lee explains.

"So people—all people—can be good *and* bad," Mason affirms.

Noah's eyes glaze at the loaded statement, and Lee

wonders what he's thinking about. "Yes," he says. "People are both. Whether they are your family or friends. People aren't any one thing."

"I don't have many friends," Mason says.

Lee's heart snags. "Sure you do."

"No, I don't. I don't like anyone. Except for Noah, Grace, and Luca."

"That's three friends right there," Noah says. "That's more than a lot of people." He lifts his hand. Mason, a boy who loathes physical touch, who rarely lets her hug him or physically comfort him, slaps hands with Noah and returns to his food.

"I don't understand how you do that," Lee says, lowering her fork to her plate. "You and Grace are the only people who can touch him."

"I'm sitting right here, you know."

Noah smiles. "That you are, bud." He turns his attention to Lee. "You know what? I find that when you stop worrying about the reaction and instead focus on the *interaction,* miraculous things can happen."

"Huh." She moves her food around. "I've never heard it put like that before. Focus on the interaction not the reaction. I love that."

"It's hardest for you because you're his mother. But Lee, I promise"—he places his hand on hers and her heart thumps—"he is thriving. He's doing great. Really. He's a brilliant child."

"I am. I *am* brilliant."

Noah rolls his eyes good-naturedly. "Note to self: don't call your students brilliant in front of them."

Mason studies their hands. "Are you going to get married and have another baby?"

Lee retracts her hand, though she wants to leave it under his.

"I said, are you going to get married and have another baby?"

"No, sweetheart." She smiles nervously at Noah. "We are not getting married. We're just friends." As she says it, that word feels like a betrayal. She doesn't want to be friends. Friends are *bullshit*.

"But are you going to get married and have another baby? Babies take forty weeks to be born, and you are getting old. Having babies past the age of thirty-five significantly ups the risks for abnormalities."

"What are you, a gynecologist?" Lee's skin warms. She excuses herself to get a glass of water.

Mason goes on about pregnancy, reciting facts he memorized from a human sexuality book. Noah offers his two cents every few minutes, sharing even more facts Mason isn't aware of. They are like dueling encyclopedias. She thinks of her life before Mason. She thinks of the pregnancy. She thinks of what happened when he was a baby . . .

She clears her throat and enters the dining room. She is no longer her past. She is no longer that person. She is no longer responsible for that life.

Maybe one of these days she will start to believe it.

8

lee

You done, bud?" Lee rearranges her face to neutral. "You can finish your project in your room before your shower. I'll set the timer."

Mason abandons his dishes on the table and escapes to his room, where he is building a model of Tokyo. She should insist he come back and take his dishes to the sink but relinquishes the demand. Instead, she winds the timer to sixty minutes and scoops his plates and containers from the table. Noah helps her scrape, rinse, and stack the plates in the dishwasher.

"Want to sit for a bit?"

"Um . . ." Noah looks at his watch again, and for the second time tonight, she wonders what other plans he has. "Sure. I can hang for a bit longer."

Lee suggests they move to the living room. They bring their ice waters. Not for the first time, she wishes she could offer him beer or wine. She appreciates he never makes a big deal of not drinking in front of her, though she's insisted that it's fine if he wants to stock a few beers in her fridge for days when he stays late.

"He's so excited about the project," she offers.

"I used to love building models too. Kept me busy."

He fluffs a pillow behind his back and sinks into the cushions.

"Good instincts." She leans forward to set her glass on a coaster. "It's insane how much he likes you."

Noah laughs. "Well, I'd hope so."

"Are all your other students as brilliant as Mason?" she teases.

"No." He spins his glass around. "He's my brightest star." He smiles. "But you already know that."

She tilts her head. "I do know that."

He takes a sip of water and sets his glass on the coffee table beside hers. "I really do feel like he's progressing. Some of the therapies we're implementing . . . both his fine and gross motor skills have developed tremendously."

Lee studies him as he talks. The exact way he sits, spine erect, crisp shirt, right ankle over left knee. She appreciates his attention to detail, the way his body language is always composed yet relaxed, the way he actually listens when people talk. He is an *appropriate* person, which is one of the things she likes most about him. She has never had appropriate. She craves appropriate, responsible, honorable.

"Well, whatever you're doing, it's working." She licks her cold lips. "I wish I could have the same effect."

"It's my job." He stretches his legs in front of him, crossing the opposite ankle over his other knee. A sliver of paisley sock catches her eye. "And you're his mother. Kids are always different with their mothers."

"True." Lee thinks about Carol's email. "So, Carol emailed me today."

"Oh? Did she finally figure out a cure?" He tents his fingers into double quotes around the word *cure*.

"Right? No. Actually, she and the girls are going to Black Mountain next Thursday and invited me to go too."

"Lee, that's great. You never take a vacation. You should go."

She fumbles with her fingers in her lap and retrieves her water to give her hands something to do. Her nails tinkle against the glass. "I'd love to, but I would have to leave Mason. I've never done that before."

"Well, I'd be here to help."

She flicks her eyes toward his. "I can't ask you to do that."

"Why not?"

She shrugs. She is nervous tonight. She reminds herself that she trusts Noah—that Grace trusts Noah, that Mason trusts Noah—and that, at her very core, she knows what she has always wanted: a man in Mason's life. In *her* life. How she wants to present the image of a happy family to the world, but mostly to herself. She wavers for a moment, the seconds eating the silence. Finally, she looks at him and gathers her nerve. "I have a confession to make."

"Oh?" He jiggles the few remaining ice cubes in his own glass and is clearly thrown by the change in topic.

Lee leans her head against the cushion, eyeing him. "I never know how honest I can be with you. Or what you're really thinking."

"Is that your confession?" he teases.

"No."

"You can always be honest with me. You know that." His eyes are sincere.

She fingers the tassel on a small throw pillow. "I just don't want to screw anything up between us."

He cocks his head. "How would you screw anything up?"

Lee's past rips across the fabric of her mind. All the missteps, the failures, the earth-shattering mistakes. She lifts her head. "I . . . like you. As lame as that sounds."

"I like you too."

How honest should she be? "Yeah, but I *like* you like you. Like a woman likes a man she's interested in. Romantically, I mean." She sounds ridiculous. Her heart prances around her chest, and she resists sneaking a glance at her T-shirt to see if the imprint of her pulse is punching through the fabric.

"Lee." Noah inches away slightly. "I'm flattered."

She follows the movements of his body, how it transforms from relaxed to stiff in an instant. "But you're physically pulling away." She jokes, but deep down, the rejection stings.

No one ever chooses you.

"I'm not. I'm just . . ." He waves toward Mason's room. "He's the priority. I would never want to do anything to get in the way of why I'm here." He searches her face, but she can't look at him.

Instead, she stares into her lap. Why is he here? He's here because Grace introduced them. He's here because he agreed to teach Mason. He's here because she wants a man in her house, in her life . . . and yes, even in her bed. Is that really so difficult to conceive? She finally drags her gaze to his face as she stands. Her body thrums with nerves, desire, and the initial rejection post-confession.

She thinks about scooping his frigid glass from his hands, refilling it, and changing the subject. Instead, she stands in front of him as if to pass, their knees touching, and abruptly leans over him. Noah inhales and looks toward Mason's room, then directly at her. She can barely think over the pounding of her heart or the fierce hue of his eyes, like twin domes of jade, but she moves closer, never breaking eye contact, and hovers inches from his lips. His hands stutter against her shoulders—caught between pulling her in and pushing her away—but she holds her position. She is never this bold, but she's so tired of waiting.

He swallows. His Adam's apple bobs, and she senses it: desire. She can smell the husky scent of his aftershave mixed with his natural scent. It consumes her. She slides her hands against the sides of his face. Moisturized skin slicks her palms. She moves even closer. He sighs, his eyes fluttering closed. He leans toward her, meeting her, but before their lips meet, Noah grips both of her arms and gently pushes her back. "We can't."

She stands, every part of her pulsing with need. "Why not?"

"We just can't." He thrusts a hand through his hair.

"But why not?" She sounds petulant and tries again. "Look. I know you don't want to mess up our working relationship, and I get it. I do. I respect how professional you are. It's one of the things I love—*like*—most about you." She reddens at the word *love*. "But I've thought a lot about this. It's *all* I've thought about, actually." She replays their easy conversation at dinner, how much Mason enjoyed the two of them talking, the three of them sitting there, like a family. It's her turn to have a family, isn't it? After all this time?

"Lee." He stands, rejecting her again, and something braces inside her. She works to keep her disappointment in check.

"Look, I'm sorry . . . I just can't." He palms the jaw she just touched, and she follows the path of his fingers, unable to look away.

"Are you seeing someone?" The thought of him with another woman boils her blood. She hasn't waited six months to make a move only to be rejected for someone else.

He doesn't say anything. Sadness flickers then retreats

as he studies her, and she knows there's something he's not telling her. Against her better judgment, she walks into her bedroom and locks the door. She wants to stay and talk, but she's afraid of what he might say.

The weight of his refusal presses hard. In her bathroom, she splashes icy water on her face. She looks in the mirror. A barrage of criticism attacks her: why she's always second, why she doesn't get to have what others have, why she has no right to be angry. She calms herself after a few moments as the truth reminds her, and she finally exits the bathroom to apologize.

9

lee

Noah is not on the couch. She walks to Mason's door and listens, but she doesn't hear Noah's voice. In the kitchen, she notices his keys are gone from the table by the back door. She steps into the night, the air crisp, and sees a pop of taillights escaping down the street.

She retreats inside. Regret and shame consume her. She takes deep breaths, but emotion soars. Before she can stop herself, she opens her mouth and screams. It has been so long since she's used her voice in any obvious way, that at first, it startles her. But then, as the sound rips through her chest and throat, she gains momentum, and screams louder. Mason bolts from his room, eyes wild. His aversion to noise is never lost on her, but tonight, she can't help it.

She screams until he cups his ears and disappears back into the safety of his room and the consumption of his project. She collapses onto the tile, wanting someone to comfort her, to love her, to want her too.

She remembers when it all started, of course, this horrific feeling of being unwanted. That sudden beginning that had been birthed in the span of a single night—her mother's murder. Then it was her father's emotional abandonment. Then it was navigating the mean kids in middle and high school, friendless, without a boyfriend, or a parent to rely on. It was staying up nights worrying about the bills. It was coming home in the afternoons to find her father sitting in the bathroom with a knife, threatening to kill himself from his consuming grief. (He never did; he never would.) Lee felt sorry for him, sorry for the both of them.

It was her father finally getting hurt on the job at the auto shop—which caused spinal arachnoiditis—that led to disability. When he had an excuse not to work and still received a paycheck every month, he blew it on pain pills and booze and felt his contribution to their lives was enough.

Lee thought about leaving him so many times. Leaving the house, leaving him in it, leaving Nashville, but the fear of showing up and finding him dead kept her rooted to the spot. She cleaned, she made dinners, and she worked her way through cosmetology school right after high school to hopefully give them both a better life. His checks weren't enough; there would always be supplementation. It was only when she met Shirley that her life completely cracked apart.

Lee sighs and peels herself off the floor. She doesn't want to think about her past. She wipes away her tears, blows her nose, and knocks on Mason's door, her apology already working itself out in her head. She shouldn't have yelled like that. As she waits for him to open the door, she replays Noah's rejection like a dull knife to the gut.

She knocks again. Maybe it's just her lot in life to be alone, to raise Mason without a father. Isn't that what she deserves? The gnarled truth burrows deeper until she wants to cry. She bites back more tears as Mason cracks the door and she steps over the threshold, apologizing for scaring him.

As she says the words *I'm so sorry, I didn't mean to,* she's saying it to him, of course she is, but really, she means it for someone else.

despair [dih-spair]

<u>noun</u>

1. loss of hope; hopelessness

2. someone or something that causes hopelessness

I know about despair. I practically created it.

The way it wraps around you.
The way it tightens.
The way it chokes and squeezes.

I've lived in despair for so many years—agonizing, torturous despair that cuts you off from a normal life.
What's another word for despair?
Anguish. Desperation. Despondency.
Check, check, check.

The only thing that makes my despair better is if someone else—someone who deserves it, someone who's asking for it—feels that same misery I feel.

If just for a moment.
If just for a lifetime.

How do you ensure someone's despair is greater than your own?
I think I've figured out the answer to that little riddle.

Now it's time to put my plan in motion.

10

noah

On the way home, Noah replays what happened. His heart pounds and his throat constricts. He unbuttons his collar and sucks in a breath. His fingers tighten and release on the wheel. Traffic thickens as he heads to his side of town. He checks the time on his phone. Is it too late to call?

Lee fills his head. Her lips. Her breath. That pleading look, followed by a wounded one. Anyone in their right mind would be crazy about her—would jump at the opportunity to date her—but he can't. For many reasons. All that conversation about good and bad with Mason at dinner has made him uncomfortable. His stomach coils. He possesses his own version of bad—everyone does—but he also has a secret. The more he spends time around Lee, the more he wants—no, *needs*—to tell her.

But if he does, it could jeopardize his progress with Mason. Mason is the one he really cares about. Mason is the one he wants to keep safe.

He exhales and loops onto the interstate. Friday night activity buzzes around him, but he has tunnel vision. *Mason. I must think about Mason.* No matter what happens, he does not want to fail this boy. He can't taint that with convoluted feelings for Lee.

He swallows and thinks of the dream he had the other night. In it, he'd packed a bag for Mason. They'd gotten in a car and driven away from Nashville. Mason hadn't even asked questions. He'd been happy just to go with him.

Noah knows what it means. Of course he does. He doesn't have to be a therapist to figure that one out. There's a direct line that connects *there* to *here*.

He grits his teeth and knocks away the despair. "Forget about it. You are not your past." He almost rolls his eyes at the corniness of his statement, but it's a mantra he clings to like a lifeline. He is not his past. So he can't make decisions based on those screwups for his present.

He cranks up the volume on the radio and listens to the latest bubblegum pop hit. Twenty minutes later, he is at his front door. He parks, but then thinks better of it and makes a call.

His heart rate slows when he hears *hello*. "Want to meet at the Patterson House for a drink?"

He waits for confirmation, ends the call, and makes the short drive to the makeshift speakeasy. He thinks of the dim lights, warm booths, and oversized cocktails. He just needs an escape—from Lee, from Mason, from his own secret, from the dueling thoughts in his head.

As he parks and walks to the nondescript building, he makes a decision to stay focused. Everything will happen as it should in due time.

He just has to be patient.

SATURDAY

11

grace

Grace opens the doors to Ugly Mugs. She inhales the fresh baked goods. Her mouth waters at the thought of her gigantic cinnamon donut and steamy chai latte. She orders and twirls her wooden number as she searches for a seat. All the tables are taken, but the bar along the bay windows is open. She claims two stools and removes the novel she's just started from her tote. Midmorning sunshine pours through the glass, and she leans into the warmth.

She can't concentrate on the novel, of course. She's thinking about Lee. She will gauge her mood first and then decide what to do. Her donut and latte come in record time. The pleasure erupts over her tongue with the first doughy bite. She washes it down with her drink.

"Sorry I'm late." Lee appears over her shoulder, sunglasses on, her nude lips downturned and tight.

Grace is mid-bite and covers her mouth. "Hey." She motions to her food. "I was starving. Sorry."

"Oh, please. Eat. I'm not even hungry." Lee pats her flat stomach and scoots closer on her bar stool.

Grace wonders if she should just get it over with. *Forget the trip. Do it now.*

"You wouldn't believe what happened to me last night." Grace devours another edge. "Oh? Is Mason okay?"

"It has nothing to do with Mason." Lee flushes. "Noah and I . . . last night. On the couch."

Grace swallows a large bite and shakes her head, certain she hasn't heard right. "What?"

Lee flicks her thin wrist into the air, her bangles sliding toward her elbow. "We didn't have sex or anything. I kissed him. Well, I *tried* to kiss him, but he rejected me."

Grace opens her mouth, unsure of what to say. She knows Lee has a crush on Noah, could sense it the moment she hired him. But she knows rejection runs deep for Lee, and being rejected can have more than one implication. "What happened exactly?"

Lee chews one of her nails, a terrible habit she's always trying to quit. "Well, I just screwed everything up. Professionally, I mean. I feel like a fool."

"No, hey. You're not a fool." Grace's heart begins to thud as she wraps a protective arm around Lee. "I'm sure he just doesn't want to muddle the lines between employee and employer, you know?"

She snorts. "That's exactly what he said."

"So I'm sure it's true. I mean, who wouldn't be interested in you? Look at you. I'm sure he's just trying to do the right thing."

"But why is that the right thing? He's always at the house. Mason adores him. Just last night, Mason asked if we were going to be a family."

"He did?"

"Yeah. It makes perfect sense. *We* make perfect sense." Lee turns to face her. "Do you think he's seeing someone? Is that what this is all about?"

Grace sits back and crosses her arms. "I've never heard you even imply that you were interested to this degree. I always thought you might have a crush, but . . ." Grace buries her own confession. Not now.

"Of course I'm interested. I was interested when you first introduced him. Who *wouldn't* be interested?"

"Then why didn't you tell me?"

She lifts one shoulder and drops it just as suddenly. "Why would I?"

Grace dabs her lips with the napkin and slides her plate across the bar. "Because I'm your best friend? Because it's a big deal? Because you need someone to talk to?"

"I know. But I feel protective over him. Like, the thought of him dating . . ." She shakes her head. "The thought makes me insanely jealous, and I never get jealous. How ridiculous is that?"

Grace doesn't know what to say. *Lee is jealous? Lee is crazy about Noah?* The complexities of their working relationship fly into focus. If Lee makes a move, she could ruin everything for Mason. "Listen. I'm sure being so good with Mason makes you more attracted to him. You've never had a guy around Mason. Noah's the first, right?"

Lee nods. "So?"

"So that probably has something to do with it."

"What do you mean?" Lee sweeps her hair over one shoulder.

"I mean . . . the first guy who's good with Mason will obviously tug on your heartstrings." She makes her voice as tender as possible. "That doesn't mean he's necessarily a match made in heaven for you though."

"Where were you last night?" Lee's eyes are blank behind her sunglasses.

Grace is thrown by the change of topic. "What do you mean? I was home."

"I called you after he left. I couldn't get you." Lee taps her knee nervously, and it reminds her of Mason.

"Well, I don't know then. Did you leave a message? Or text?"

Lee crosses her arms. "No."

"Sorry. My phone's been weird since I updated the operating system." She scoots closer. "You know I would have answered if I saw you called." *Because I always answer. Because your issues are more important than mine.* "I'm here now."

Lee exhales and uncrosses her arms. "I know. It's just . . . why can't it ever be easy? Girl likes boy. Boy likes girl back. Boy is good with girl's kid. Boy, girl, and kid become a family."

"Because life isn't some fairy tale, that's why." She should know. Grace rummages in her bag for ChapStick, desperate to change the subject. "Before I forget. Did you get Carol's email about the trip next week?"

"I did. I can't go."

"Why?"

"What do you mean why? Because I've never left Mason. And because I've probably ruined any chance at freedom by coming on to Noah."

"Hey, seriously. Stop." Grace squeezes her elbow. "You didn't ruin anything. Was Noah acting normal when he came over this morning?"

She shrugs. "Mostly."

"See? I'm sure he's fine." She rattles her elbow, as if she can shake some sense into her. "Flattered, even. You don't need to worry about anything. And you should really consider coming to Black Mountain. I'm sure Noah would be happy to help."

"I don't even know if he does that sort of thing." Lee scratches her bare, thin arm. "Stay with him overnight."

"You trust him though, right?"

"Obviously."

Grace knocks away a few crumbs from her lap. "Then I'm sure he'd be overjoyed to help. You deserve it. As long as I've known you, you haven't taken a single vacation."

"True." Lee spins one strand of glossy black hair around her finger. "I brought it up last night, but we didn't get to talk about the details."

Grace balances one elbow on the bar and leans her head into her hand. "Do you remember when we first met? I asked you about your killer haircut and we became fast friends?" Grace begged Lee to give her all of her magic hair potions, as her hair, no matter what she did, ended up frizzed and slightly curled from the relentless Nashville humidity. "It's just like that. I wanted to know something, so I asked. Don't overthink this. Just ask him. He can either say yes or no."

"I'm not like you."

"You don't have to *be* like me, but anxiety from any decision comes from thinking about the decision, and not the decision itself."

"Thanks, Yoda." A hint of a smile curls one side of her mouth.

Grace playfully pushes her. "Just think if I had never talked to you that day."

Lee relaxes and her shoulders drop. "I can't even imagine."

"See? So ask him."

She nods. "I will."

"Today. You'll ask him today."

"Yes, pushy. I'll ask him today." Lee types something into her phone. "I'm even making myself a note so I won't forget. Happy?" She drops her phone back into her bag. "I'm sorry if I ruined your morning." She faces the window, the smile wiped clean. "I just thought for once in my life, something might work out. That's all."

Grace's heart aches, but she stays silent.

"I need to ask Mason. About the trip. Make sure he's okay with it first."

"Good mama." Grace's hands rest on her satisfied belly. "Want to go for a walk?"

"Where? The greenway?"

Grace and Lee love the Shelby Bottoms Greenway. Whenever their schedules allow, they walk the trail, winding around the water with the occasional fisherman, past the baseballs fields and the playground with exhausted mothers pushing babies in swings, under the old train tracks, and onto the actual greenway itself with its thick paths of trees, bamboo, and cyclists huffing *on your left* as they get lost in conversation.

It's where Grace feels closest to Lee—away from responsibility and free to talk or walk in comfortable silence. Sometimes they don't even talk. They observe the rust of the train tracks, the rushing water, the nature museum, the natural playground with its piles of sand and homeschooled children, the path that first winds around the sprawling dog park and uncoils near the glittering lake. It's the only time they are both free.

Lee glances at her watch. "I told Noah I'd be back in an hour and a half. Do we have time?"

"Plenty. Do you want to get coffee first?"

"Nah. I'll get one after."

"I'm going to get one to go."

She pays for a regular coffee and hooks elbows with Lee as they step outside. They separate to their cars to make the quick drive to the greenway entrance. Grace lets the earlier tension fade as she parks in the half-empty lot.

Her secret hammers her conscience, and she grits her teeth. She fires off a few texts and feels better. She takes a breath, plasters on a smile, and joins Lee on the path by the trees. But underneath that smile, she knows what is coming. The truth will drive a wedge between them, one that—no matter how hard she tries—cannot be removed.

SUNDAY

12

lee

Sometimes, when she wakes, Lee forgets where she is, in what fragment of time, as if the contents of her life have been sliced and reshuffled like a deck of cards.

She will come stumbling into consciousness and reach for the bottle on the nightstand. When her fingers swab the lamp or her phone, she will think only: then.

That was *then*. How many mornings before this has she come into the day still drunk and wanting to take the edge off? Lee is built on edges. If it isn't wine, it's work, worrying, remembering, or trying not to remember. But today, when she stirs, it isn't Mason she thinks of first, or the wine she reaches for.

It's Noah.

Lee lies in bed and eyes the dated ceiling fan. Her gaze shifts to the water spot on the ceiling, newly patched but still showing a blown-out brown stain. Her eyes travel down to the bedroom windows, recently afflicted with wood rot.

She's tried her best to spruce up the house, but it's still an outdated ranch, and a rental. Though her friends don't live far—Carol only a few streets over in Lincoya Hills, Grace and Alice in Green Hills, a more affluent neighborhood with better schools—Lee is the only renter. But to her, this house, on this street, signifies her fresh start with Mason, and she's proud of it.

Lee slides a hand over the pillow on the other side of the bed. It's been empty for as long as Mason has been alive. She has a switch, and she simply turned it off. But with one mistaken moment of throwing herself at Noah, the switch has been flipped, and she doesn't want to turn it off again. She can almost feel what it would be like to have him here beside her.

She tiptoes to Mason's room and presses her ear against the cold wood. Still asleep. Mason is a troubled sleeper. For a few years, he sleepwalked. She'd jar awake at the sound of him jiggling a doorknob to go outside or insisting, confused, that it was time to start his lessons for the day. Later, it had turned into the occasional thrashing or swinging of a pillow, disjointed sentences muffled by sleep. There is no rhyme or reason to what constitutes a good night versus a bad night, but she recently started giving him melatonin, which seems to help.

She dresses and puts on the kettle for tea. As she drops a tea bag into an empty cup, her eyes drift to the backyard, the garden, and the trees that fill the perimeter with their tiny, pregnant flower buds and dancing branches. She's just planted anemones, poppies, and a row of ranunculus and can't wait to see the wonderful bounty for late spring.

She needs to get to a meeting today. The uncertainty of what Noah's rejection means makes her feel antsy, and she'll be damned if she's going to take it out on Mason or erupt into a tantrum again. Even though Sunday mornings are packed, she clears her schedule.

She can't stand over all those talking heads today, nodding and giving her opinions about her clients' inability to spend the summer completely abroad because little Billy has science camp, or how a bonus should be spent, or which Jet Ski to buy for Percy Priest Lake. She always listens and smiles, painting wiry, gray hairs, or neatly slicing split ends, when all she really wants is to fist a bottle of wine and drink until her teeth, lips, and tongue grow black. The relief with every drink—how it eases the knots of aggression, disappointment, and frustration like the hands of a masseuse after a marathon—has left her without a comparable release.

She asks Noah if he can come over a bit early today. He quickly texts back and asks if he can talk to her about something.

Lee's fingers hover over the keys as she rereads the text. She types out a curt response: *sure.* She wavers between worrying it's something to do with Mason and hoping it isn't a rehashing of the Almost Kiss.

Lee yawns and waits for the kettle to whistle. Twenty minutes later, Noah knocks softly at the back door. What would he say if he knew he was her first thought this morning?

"Hey," she says as she opens the door. She rearranges her face to some semblance of normal, but it's strained, tight.

Noah places his satchel by the mud bench, and something about it reminds her of husbands all over the world coming home after a long day's work to their wives. His hair is slightly wet, and she wonders if he's just taken a shower. He glances toward the hall. "Is he up yet?"

"Not yet."

"Is now an okay time to talk?"

"Sure." She fixes herself a cup of tea, offers him one, and sits at the dining room table. "I feel like I'm in trouble or something."

"No. It's nothing like that." Noah struggles to find the words.

"Is it about what happened on Friday?" She senses his hesitation and hurries to fill the gap. "Please tell me you're not quitting because of that."

"Lee." Noah rests a hand on hers. "I don't know how many times I have to tell you this, but I'm not going anywhere. I'm not quitting. Relax."

She smiles, lips tight over her teeth, and loves the heaviness of his hand on hers. "Okay, I'll be quiet. Speak."

He drags his hand across the table and back to his lap. "I'm not sure the best way to say this, so I'm just going to say it, and I want you to listen. Okay? Entirely. Until I'm done."

Lee's breath sticks in her lungs. She only nods.

"It's about this trip with your friends."

She exhales, relieved that it's not about the kiss, but also anxious about what he's going to say. She wants to go—everything in her wants to—but the reality of packing a bag, getting in a car, and driving away from her life and Mason seems impossible. No one but her knows what a monumental step that is. No one but her knows exactly what that means.

"I'm thinking about it."

He narrows his eyes. "No, you're not. I know you."

She laughs. "How do you know I'm not going to go?"

"Like I said, I know you. You're easy to read. Have you talked to Mason about it yet?"

"Not yet. But I will."

"Okay, fair enough." He spreads his hands on the table and tips back in the chair. "Still want to hear my prepared speech?"

He's prepared a speech? She extends one hand, not needing one more reason to find him adorable. "By all means."

He clears his throat. "Here goes: you need to go on this trip. Not just because it's a fun thing to do, or because you need a break. But because *Mason* needs this. Mason needs to know that his mother can be gone for forty-eight or seventy-two hours, and his world will not fall apart. Mason is capable, even at this young age, of coping with his limitations. His mind is exceptional. You know that, and I know that. But it's his emotional health that needs a real test. This is why he needs this. He will be fine. You will be fine. You will be a better mother once you take a few days to yourself." He scratches his head. "I mean, what? You've never even been away from him, unless it's for coffee or to run an errand, right? Most seven-year-olds leave their parents eight hours a day every day for school."

"I know." The guilt washes over her. She often worries he's not getting the socialization he needs by staying at home.

"He will have familiar faces around him. He'll be protected and safe. Okay?"

She nods, but inside, the nerves begin their frenetic dance. No one understands that if she goes, she'll be thinking about what could happen while she's gone. It would be nothing more than obsessing if he's okay, if he's missing her, if he's having a meltdown that Noah can't fix. She's come to realize that she relies on Mason more than he relies on her. Which probably means that she's taken on a new addiction.

Noah's strong, masculine face and earnest eyes await her response. She lingers on the lips she would love to kiss and drifts down to the hands she would like to hold.

This man wants to give her a break. Even if he doesn't reciprocate the same romantic feelings, he still wants to take care of Mason so she can go have fun. It's the nicest thing anyone has ever offered.

"Why are you here?" Mason rubs the sleep from his eyes and stands in his Star Wars pajamas, hair mussed and static-prone. He checks the time. "It's not even nine."

"I needed to talk to your mom about something. Let's get you some breakfast and then we can start."

"I'm going to get dressed first."

Lee stands to help.

Mason stops in the hall and calls over his shoulder. "I have decided that I am now old enough to get dressed by myself. Grace is the only one who does it *right,* and I don't have the luxury of living with Grace. So I'm going to do it from now on." He disappears to his room.

Lee laughs but smarts at his comment about living with Grace. *Does my son prefer everyone but me?* "That's new," Lee says. She takes another sip of tea.

"You're probably going to see that more and more. He's exerting his independence, which has been a key component of our lessons lately."

"That's great."

Noah covers her hand with his again. "Talk to Mason about the trip. You'll feel better once he gives you permission."

Her heart races, both from the contact and from the conversation she knows she needs to have. "I don't think it's his permission I need."

"I know. It's yours."

Noah looks into her eyes and she could swear there's something he's not saying, some hidden desire he feels compelled to hide. She waits for him to remove his hand, physically aching for that contact the moment he does.

She stands and dumps the rest of her lukewarm tea into the sink. What she doesn't say, what she can't say, is that she is starting to feel obsolete. Mason isn't responding to her in the same way. She's used to his preference for Grace, but she thought that was singular. Because he's known Grace forever. Because she's like family. But in the span of a few months, Mason also prefers Noah. Not her.

She turns at the sink. "Are you still cool to go to the barbecue later?"

"Of course." He stacks his workbooks along the dining room table. "Looking forward to it."

She nods and searches his face. "Do you need me?"

He shakes his head. "You're free to go, young lady."

She hesitates, wanting to clear the air about the other night, to make sure they are *really* okay, but she simply retreats to her room and sits on her bed. The tears—sudden and loaded—push to the surface. All of her feelings have been kept at bay for so long, and they are coming at her in a wild rush: possible (failed) romance, freedom, handing some of the responsibility of Mason to someone else. It is a lot, and sudden. She flicks away the tears and exhales.

She needs to call her sponsor.

13
lee

The meetings are held about a mile from her house, in an old church off of Fairway, across from an elementary school. She first discovered this AA chapter when she was walking the neighborhood and instantly recognized the group congregating in front of the church. Some were smoking. Others were pacing or talking. She'd walked right in, sweat-soaked and nervous, and has been attending regularly ever since. She's kept her sobriety in check since Mason was little, which is the only way her friends know her. As sober Lee. As responsible Lee. As cautious Lee.

They've never seen the real her. They've never seen her at home, navigating the land mine of her father's life and mourning a mother who is never coming back again. Trying to save a best friend who has no interest in being saved.

She pushes through the doors and walks to the back of the church. Sally always goes to such trouble to spruce up the place. Two sturdy tables draped with floral tablecloths hold local coffee and an assortment of snacks. Fabric-covered chairs that Sally spent a week refinishing complete the circle—not those awful folding ones like in her early meetings—and in the corner, two diffusers spit out Young Living essential oils that she sells on the side.

It is a lovely place to confess and it makes her feel safe. Lee lifts her hand in salute as she enters, a few of the regulars already huddled around the donuts supplied by Shipley's. She grabs a donut and coffee and takes a seat. A blast of powdered sugar coats her palms.

"Looks like you've been mauled by a sugar monster there."

Lee glances up to see Gary, lifetime alcoholic. A corset of blue veins branches the width of his nose, his eyes a slurry inside his skull. He is her worst-case scenario, and yet even he keeps showing up, after every lapse, after every stumble—and let's face it, there will always be a stumble, because the stumble is his real addiction.

She swallows. "Yeah, love the sugar," Lee says. The donut rests on her lap. Not for the first time, she questions why she still comes to these meetings when she's been sober for so many years. Yes, it gives her strength, but it's still painful to listen to other people's stories and struggles. Their setbacks. Their fears. When she listens, she shuttles back to that place *before* Mason, to a time in her life she wants to wipe clean, like a whiteboard. But she attends because she knows without these meetings, she might slip.

The meeting begins and she pitches in with the greetings: "Hello, Stacy; hello, Gary; hello, Tina; hello, Harper; hello, Elliot." Once it's her turn, she falters. Her mind sorts through all the information they already know, wondering what she can possibly talk about today. She's told them so much about her life already: her mother, the alcohol, the party, the blackout, her father, Shirley.

She clears her throat. "So, there's this guy I've mentioned, Noah. He's my son's occupational therapist." A rosy flush blooms across her cheeks. "He's incredible. And smart. And so compassionate. He's great with Mason." Her breath unspools and sends a puff of sugar into the air. "The thing is, I'm interested in him, but I don't think he's interested in me. In fact, I *know* he's not, because I tried to kiss him the other night, but he rejected me." She scratches her forehead. "The lines are too blurry, I think. Work and romance. It feels complicated."

They listen to her talk. About how long it's been since she's liked anyone. About how she's scared to let someone into her weird little world. They do not know her real secrets—of course they don't—but once she starts talking about Noah, she can't seem to stop.

"And then what, right? Like, what if he finally makes a move, and it doesn't work out? What about Mason? Nothing is worth upsetting the wonderful rhythm he's developed with Noah these last six months. But in spite of all of that, I still want to take the risk. To see if it could work out. Am I being totally selfish?" She waits for more answers she knows aren't allowed to come. No one can interrupt her. It's policy. The person has the floor until he or she is completely wringed of words.

She completes her thoughts, and the room is a collection of breath as Lee dabs her tears and waits for someone to say something. Anything.

Sally places a hand on her shoulder. "Thank you for sharing, Lee," and then they move onto Harper. It's over, just like that. Harper launches into the latest battle with her sister, who also has a problem with alcohol, and Lee zones out for a moment to collect herself. It feels good to talk about Noah like that. If only she could talk *to* him . . .

At the end of the meeting, her chair snags along the

well-worn carpet. She mingles with the others. Sally approaches and pulls her lean body into a hug.

"Lee, that was a big step."

She hugs her back. "Thank you, Sally."

"We'll see you next week?"

Lee nods. "You will." She excuses herself as Gary calls after her like a pet. She waves good-bye and pushes through the double doors. She stands in the parking lot, torn. She's confessed her feelings about Noah and wants to be anywhere but home with the boys. It seems like Noah will be able to see right through her. But where else can she go? Carol's? She checks the time and knows she needs to get back. The walk is short but steep with rolling hills.

On the walk, Shirley pops into her mind again. They used to go to meetings together. The women met when they were both twenty-five. Shirley had just moved to Nashville and wanted to pick up some extra cash as a hair model. The two had become fast friends. Shirley was bold where Lee was reserved; Lee was sensible where Shirley was reckless.

Shirley, sensing Lee's shyness, had taken her under her wing and treated her like a sister. She took her to parties. She joined her at the movies. She advised her while shopping. She slept over. She urged her to come on double dates with bad boys who had zero interest in getting to know Lee, but she went along anyway, because she adored Shirley and didn't want to look like a prude.

But as their relationship progressed, the dynamic shifted. Shirley began to look up to Lee. She envied her career, the way she provided for her family, and mostly, her ambition. Lee knew what she wanted to do with her life; Shirley didn't. While Lee coveted the ease Shirley shared with men—men at clubs, men at shows, men at bars, men on the street—Shirley craved Lee's stable life. They were the perfect yin and yang.

The drugs had already started, but Lee, as always, had been the last to realize. It began with Shirley sleeping over more and more and swiping Harold's pain pills. That, mixed with booze, placated Shirley for a while, until it just wasn't enough.

Lee felt responsible for her, like she did for her father. Shirley's entire family was back in Atlanta, and though Shirley didn't mind being alone and never spoke of them, Lee knew she had to miss them. Shirley tried to fill that familial void as she bounced her way through jobs and crashed on Lee and Harold's couch when she was in between gigs: bartender, waitress, hair model, art model, drug dealer, then finally, hair stylist. She swore that Lee was the only family she needed, but deep down, she always felt Shirley was running away from something.

But really, weren't they all?

Lee wanted to be there for her, but she was scared. When she'd found the first batch of needles in her bathroom wastebasket and glimpsed the track marks in the crooks of her arms, she knew Shirley was taking a wild leap into something that could get her killed. It wasn't until later—too late—that Lee realized it was more than the drugs.

Lee pockets her headphones as she reaches her driveway. Noah and Mason are in the middle of a lesson, and neither acknowledges her as she enters the room. There's so much she wants to say, but now is not the time. If Noah takes one look at her, he will be able to read her.

She steps into her studio, locks the door, and fists her hands from all the pent-up emotion: from talking about him, from wanting him, from thinking about what almost happened between them. She collapses in her chair and listens for the sound of his voice, wanting him to come knocking, but knowing if he does, she will not answer.

Once she's calm, she joins the boys.

~~buoyant~~
~~strong~~
R-E-S-I-L-I-E-N-T
People think you're special if you're resilient.

But aren't we all?

Don't we deal with our fair share of mishaps, tragedy, and setbacks, only to bounce back better than before?

I am built on resilience.
Only, I am not elastic.
I am not <u>recovered.</u>
You don't recover after you've been through what I have.

It's just not possible.

(No one has to know that.)

I'll just keep pretending to be supple and tough, snapping back again and again to take on more and more.
To change shapes.
To become the version of who I'm supposed to be.
The better version.
The best version.
The resilient version.

But no one knows just how hurt I really am.

14

lee

Later that afternoon, Lee helps Carol arrange the tea sandwiches, organic juice boxes, and trays of fruit for the kids. Mason is finishing a lesson with Noah, and because Carol's house is only minutes away, Lee has agreed to let Noah drive him.

Though it is the weekend, Mason and Noah still meet for a few hours on both Saturday and Sunday, to keep Mason's routine intact. Lee worries he should have at least a few days without lessons or sessions, but Noah insists it's beneficial for consistency and to ease anxiety. She checks her watch and sneaks a cucumber sandwich from the platter.

"I saw that," Carol jokes.

"Sue me." Lee swallows.

"Can you help with these?"

"Outside?" Lee takes another bite. She scoops the tray of sandwiches into her arms and follows Carol out the sliding glass door. Charlie works the grill, charring and flipping hot dogs and burgers, as fragrant smoke drifts into the clear blue sky. The smell of the sizzling meat reminds her of summers at various campgrounds: Land Between the Lakes, Pigeon Forge, Gatlinburg, Dale Hollow. She stops, platter in hand, as she recalls her mother, standing in flip-flops and a bathrobe, flipping meat on the community grill.

"You okay, Lee?"

"Hmm?" She releases the platter on the cloth-covered table. "Do we need anything else out here?"

Carol wipes her hands on her apron. "I think we're good."

Lee follows her back inside. Fred, Alice, and Olivia wave as they remove their shoes in the playroom. "We knocked, but nobody answered."

"Hey, Olive Tree. Zoe is already outside," Carol says, affectionately rubbing her head. "Want to go play?"

Olivia rockets out the door and into their sprawling acre with the giant wooden swing set perched along the fence line. Fred says hello and follows. A massive flower garden, accosted by countless butterflies, lines the entire right perimeter of the yard. Lee is envious of the land, the house, and the marriage.

Carol constantly disparages the house, regaling them all with tales of the family they bought it from. On the positive side, they left the swing set, and despite the downfalls of the house—the wall full of dried boogers from the previous owners' four children, the rattling toilets, the creaky floors—they've transformed it into something lovely and warm. In Lee's opinion, it's everything a family home should be.

"Hey, A. What's up?" Lee asks.

"Just dying to talk about this trip," Alice trills. "And counting down the minutes until I can get a drink. We brought this." She hands Carol a bottle of red, and the three ladies venture toward the kitchen.

Alice motions for Carol and Lee to step farther into the kitchen, out of earshot. "I'm freaking out."

"About?" Lee asks.

"What?" Carol queries at the same time, opening the drawer to find the wine opener. "About the trip?"

Lee glances at the wine. "It's a screw top." She can practically taste it on her lips—the burst of fruit and alcohol at the back of her throat—and takes a swig of her water instead.

Carol rolls her eyes as she examines the wine bottle. "Duh." She replaces the wine opener and reaches for two stemless glasses.

"Well, let's see. Where should I start?" Alice laughs. "Fred got fired."

"What?" Carol and Lee exclaim together.

"How did Fred get fired?"

Alice lifts her hands and drops them. "Performance is down. Disappointing numbers in his sector. New management. Blah, blah, blah. I own a nonprofit. What the hell are we going to do?"

"I'm so sorry," Lee says.

"Does he get severance?"

Alice nods. "A few months. And," she adds, lowering her voice to a whisper, "we had unprotected sex, and he . . . you know."

"Oh God," Carol says. "Did you get the morning-after pill?"

Something twists inside Lee. "Were you ovulating?"

"I wasn't. And I didn't. I hate that stuff. I mean, I don't think I was ovulating, so it's fine, right? It's got to be fine." She scratches her forehead. "What would we even do? I have the business, and Fred is now *unemployed*." She says the word as if talking about the current political landscape. "I'm halfway to seventy . . . the baby could have all sorts of medical problems. What if we had a sick child? Or a disabled child? How would that change Olivia's life? Our lives?"

Lee bristles at the word *disabled,* and Alice darts an apologetic look her way. "I didn't mean disabled like that. Mason's not disabled. Shit. I'm not explaining myself right. You know what I mean."

Lee places a reassuring hand on her arm and suppresses the annoyance just below the surface. "Relax. I know what you mean."

Alice takes a breath and the full glass of wine. "Thank you. Hopefully, I'm not poisoning a fetus." She raises her wine in an invisible toast and swallows. Lee is transfixed by the wash of liquid over her teeth and gums, the way she exhales—satisfied—when done. An entire world crashes back into focus: pregnancy, wine, uncertainty, dread. All of the insane risks.

"So, the trip. Who, what, when, where. Let's talk details." She slugs another gulp. "I just want a few days of breathing fresh air, eating good food, and endless conversation. And that spa. Can we go?"

"Yeah, it's in Asheville," Carol says, as the two sip their wine and chat about the details.

"Hello!" Grace calls as the side door bangs shut.

"In the kitchen!"

Lee perks up as Grace enters the galley with a chocolate pie covered in plastic wrap.

"I know, I know. Don't kill me. I wasn't supposed to bring anything, but you know I love to bake, so too bad." She hands Carol the pie and kisses them all on the cheek, as Luca runs outside to join the girls. "Whatcha drinking?"

"A blend. Want some?"

Grace glances at Lee's water bottle and lifts her own green thermos in the air. "Nah. I'm good. Still drinking coffee. Thanks." She looks down the hall and then moves to the sink to wash her hands. "Where's Mason?"

"I was wondering the same thing," Alice says.

Lee smiles. "He's with Noah. Finishing a lesson."

"Are they coming?" Grace dries her hands on the dish towel.

"Yeah. He's driving him over."

The women look at each other. "That's huge."

"That is beyond huge," Carol adds.

Lee leans against the counter. "Well, if you A-holes are going to bully me into going on this trip, I better start loosening the reins a bit, right?"

"Cheers to that," Carol says, clinking her wineglass against Lee's water bottle. "Are you really going to come?"

Lee shrugs. "Noah said it was fine. I just need to clear it with Mason."

"And we'll help," Carol offers. "Charlie would be happy to help. And Fred, I'm sure, right, A?"

Alice nods. "Totally. Maybe he can be a full-time manny."

Grace laughs. "What did I miss?"

Lee's stomach tightens as she hears Noah knock. What if they don't like him once they spend more one-on-one time with him? What if they don't see what she sees? She knows she has Grace's approval at least, since she and Noah are already friends. The women drift back to the playroom. She can't wait to see Mason, but she is just as excited to see Noah. Despite his polite refusal, she's not giving up.

She drowns the nerves and opens the door.

15

lee

Mason enters first. He assesses the floor littered with shoes, Zoe's play kitchen stacked with various wooden pots, pans, and cups in the corner, and the bookshelves bulging with too many chapter books.

"Ladies." He nods, folding his thin arms across his T-shirt. "Carol, this place is messy."

"Mason, that's not nice," Lee scolds.

Carol laughs. "Sorry, bud. Zoe isn't as neat as you are, I'm afraid."

"You should tell Zoe that it has been scientifically *proven* that if you are messy as a child you will be messy as an adult. You're training her to think this is *normal*." He motions to the mess. "Is this normal?"

Carol nods. "I'm afraid so. This is, in fact, normal."

The ladies smother their laughter as Mason dramatically steps over strewn toys to get to the patio door.

"Oh my God, I love him so much, I could cry," Grace says, wiping away tears.

Noah lifts his hand. "Messiness aside, it's nice to see you all again."

They say their hellos, and Lee approaches Noah. "How did it go?"

"Really well. Mason now knows everything there is to know about sperm whales. And Komodo dragons."

"Wonderful." She laughs. "I'm sure that will come in handy someday."

"Why don't we head outside?" Carol asks. "What can I get you to drink, Noah?"

"A beer would be great. Or whatever you have."

They step onto the deck, and Carol makes the proper introductions. Carol checks on Charlie and the food and yells to the kids that Mason is here.

She's been taught to announce him. Lee appreciates it, even if Mason doesn't engage. The girls keep playing, but Luca comes running and waves.

"Hey, Mason. Want to come play?"

Mason rocks to his toes and thrusts two fingers of each hand into the pockets of his navy pants. "Did you know that the largest lizard is the Komodo dragon? It grows up to ten feet long and weighs a hundred and seventy-six pounds."

"Oh." Luca looks to his mother for help. "Dragons are cool."

"They are total carnivores and eat deer, snakes, pigs, fish, and water buffalo. Adults are cannibals and even eat their own *species*."

Luca looks alarmed. "They eat other dragons?"

"Hey, Mase. Let's maybe cool it on the facts," Noah suggests.

"*Yes,*" Mason says emphatically. "In fact, nearly ten percent of their diet is made up of their *own* newly hatched Komodo dragons."

"They eat their own babies?" Luca whispers. "Sick."

"They *do* eat their own babies. They even—"

"Okay, okay. Time to play," Lee says.

Luca shrugs and bounces back to the swing set, where the girls take turns sliding before seeing who can climb the ladder the fastest. Mason edges into the backyard, as if dipping a toe into an icy pool. He slinks toward the swing set, stops, and makes a beeline for the garden instead. Lee opens her mouth to warn him not to step on any of the flowers, but Carol anticipates what she's going to say and drapes a hand on her arm.

"He's fine. He can't hurt anything. I showed him where he can and can't step. He's always great at following directions."

She had? When? Lee looks for Noah. He is speaking animatedly to Grace. Her best friend holds her thermos to her lips and lowers it. Noah leans in almost affectionately, and Grace laughs at something he says, her fingers near his forearm. A stab of jealousy disrupts the moment. Why is Grace allowed to touch him, but he rebuffed her so blatantly when she tried to get close? She knows it's not the same thing; she's essentially Noah's boss. And she *wants* her friends to get to know Noah. That's the entire reason she invited him. Plus, Noah and Grace have known each other for years. So why is she so bothered? Nothing has changed . . . except her own feelings. She brushes away the envy as Grace walks over, and the women fan in a semicircle on the deck. The men finally join them, beers in hand.

"So, let's finalize this trip, ladies!"

The guys groan, everyone except Noah, as the women launch into lavish detail about the massages they will have, the hikes they will take, and the utter kid-free relaxation.

"And you're leaving us poor, defenseless men to take care of these little monsters? The inhumanity!" Fred exclaims.

Carol turns to Noah with a timid smile. "And you're okay with staying?"

"Of course." He nudges Lee with his elbow. "We've already discussed it, right?"

Lee looks into his eyes. "We did."

"Yay, it's settled then," Alice exclaims. "We're all going. Our first girls' trip without kids. It's a miracle." She glances at her watch. "And it only took about a hundred years to get here."

Carol narrows her eyes at Alice. "The real miracle will be if you don't overpack. We are taking *one* car, which means one suitcase per person."

"What? I don't overpack, do I?" Alice asks. She flattens a hand against her chest.

"Oh, please. You are the definition of overpacking," Grace adds.

"So, I won't overpack." She makes an *X* over her heart. "Cross my heart."

"And hope to die?" Lee teases.

"Oh totally," she says. "Hope to die."

Fred jumps in to change the subject. A few minutes later, Lee glances to the sliding glass door. *When did Mason go inside?*

He stands, forehead flattened against the panes, arms and legs splayed like a starfish. She waves to him, and he stares back, not blinking, frozen, a complicated child lost in a set of thoughts she can't possibly comprehend.

Lee thinks about the trip, about leaving her little boy, and something catches in her chest. She truly wants to go, *needs* to give herself a break, but can't imagine being away from him for even one night. She studies her friends, their lightness almost infectious. She tips her head to the sky and takes a cleansing breath.

She glances at Noah, who is laughing at something Grace said. The trust she has for him . . . it is unparalleled. She should go. She deserves some fun.

He will take good care of her son.

16

lee

Lee goes through the routine. Rise. Dress. Schedule. Get Mason settled. As he exits the bathroom, Lee asks him to sit. She sorts through the various ways to approach this conversation. She can be calm mom, excited mom, or direct mom.

The steam from her coffee drifts and changes shape. A wispy snake. A giraffe. The beginning of a genie from its bottle. She shelves the obvious distraction and focuses on Mason as he sits across from her.

"Carol, Alice, and Grace have arranged a short trip to the mountains in North Carolina, and I want to go. That means I would be away from you for seventy-two hours. Two full nights and three days. How do you feel about that?" She will be direct mom.

Mason forces the pads of his fingers together, flexing his knuckles in rapid-fire succession until she knows his fingers will start to feel like glass. "Where will I be?"

She keeps her voice even and calm. "You will be here with Noah. It will be this Thursday and Friday, and we will come back Saturday. Noah will complete your sessions during the day, and then he will sleep here at night."

"Where will he sleep?"

"Probably my room." Best not to offer open-ended answers. She has to present a detailed plan. At the thought of Noah peeling back her sheets and sleeping where she sleeps, she wonders if she is really ready for that kind of intimacy. Or if *he* is. "Would you be okay with Noah staying here?" She waits for the words to process, for him to run through the minutiae of their days and replace her with Noah. Noah making him breakfast. Noah making sure he flosses before bed. Noah tucking him in. Noah in the room next door in case he has a nightmare. Even as she imagines it, she falters. How can she not be here if he needs her? Noah is an exceptional therapist, but he isn't *her*. She almost tells Mason to forget about it, that she doesn't really have to go.

"I like this plan." He pushes away from the table.

"Wait." She reaches toward a body already retreating. "Does that mean you're okay with me going? And you're okay with Noah staying here for two nights and three days?"

He blinks, his eyes bright and as piercingly blue as the day he was born. "Yes, Mother. That's exactly what that means." The click of his door signals the end of their conversation. He doesn't ask her for specifics or structure. She simply said the word *Noah* and he said okay. Why doesn't she feel better about that? A knock on the back door fragments her thoughts. She straightens her shirt and hair, fisting her hot mug in one palm while she tugs the door open with the other.

"How'd it go?" Noah doesn't even say hello, his nerves as fragile as hers.

"Perfect, actually." She is still digesting her son's acceptance of her request. "No apprehension, no questions."

He steps inside. "He might have more questions later, but as I said, I'm available." He leans toward her and for one glorious moment, she thinks he's going to kiss her. But instead, he tips forward to glance into her cup.

"Ah, the good stuff. Thank God."

She rolls her eyes. "I'm an addict. What can I say? I'm assuming you'd like a cup?"

"You assume right."

She pours him a fresh cup and they sit across from each other at the table. "Should we discuss the logistics?"

"Sure." He takes a tentative sip. "Mason and I have a very set schedule. The only thing that will be different is I will be sleeping here."

"Of course. I know. It's just . . ." She swallows the knot that slithers up her esophagus. "Strange, I guess. Strange that I have permission to go. Not *permission*. But you know what I mean."

"I do know what you mean. You need this. You'll have a great time."

She nods as her heart attempts to catch up to her mind. Another knock on the door startles them both. She looks at the clock, but it's not yet time for her first appointment.

"Anybody home?" Grace enters the kitchen and Lee whistles at the tailored suit and sexy bun.

"What have you done with Grace?"

"Wow, thanks." Grace's eyes drift to Noah and she lifts her hand in a friendly wave. "Hi, you."

He gives her an appreciative once-over. "Hey."

Grace looks between them. "Am I interrupting anything important or . . ."

Noah directs his attention back to Lee. "Nope. This one here is going on the trip. Just decided. Right, Lee?"

Grace claps her hands, and suddenly, Lee feels like they have been pushing her to go before she's ready. She doesn't want to feel pressure. But isn't this what she's been waiting for—spontaneity, fun with her friends, a break from routine, freedom—*and* her son granting it to her without an issue? That's the most important part. Mason is comfortable. Lee stands. "I have a client." She turns to Grace. "Did we plan something I forgot about?"

"No. I just wanted to see if you had time for a cup of coffee. Should have checked your schedule first."

Lee hesitates. "You're welcome to hang out for a bit, unless you have to rush off?"

Noah sorts through his OT bag. "Stay. Mason and I don't start for another twenty minutes. Want to join me for a cup of coffee?"

Grace's eyes flick to Lee's face for permission. "Sure, if that's okay with you, Lee?"

"Don't be silly. Of course."

Noah pours Grace a cup of coffee as Grace washes her hands. Lee refrains from rolling her eyes. She jokes that Grace's fingers must be devoid of fingerprints from her obsessive hand washing. She dries them and joins Noah at the table. Lee listens to their easy conversation and wishes, selfishly, that she made people as comfortable as Grace. "I'll call you later?"

"Sounds good." She laughs at something Noah says. Lee fights the jealousy rioting through her heart and reaches across the table for her coffee cup. He barely acknowledges her as he waits for Grace to finish her story.

While they talk, she imagines another scene: Noah grabbing Lee's wrist and gently easing her back. Leaning down, her freshly washed fan of hair sweeping across his cheek. His aftershave clinging to her nose as she kisses him. She imagines the words: "I'll miss you when you go." She imagines her fingers rippling along his skin until he shivers.

Instead, she steps into her studio, not wanting to leave her best friend and love interest alone. She knows Grace is older than Noah and isn't interested in him, but still.

Her mind moves in a chaotic flurry, her heart zooming around her chest. Like a snooping child, she presses her ear to the door and strains to hear their conversation. Grace laughs. Noah laughs. She steps back, somehow feeling betrayed. She knocks away the silly thoughts. Yes, Noah and Grace are friends, but that's not what bothers her. *She* and Noah don't laugh like that. They don't share a lighthearted relationship. But Lee doesn't really share a lighthearted relationship with anyone except Grace.

"Hello?" Her client, Tally, enters through the garage door.

Lee plasters on a fake smile and buries her thoughts. "Hey, come in."

Tally sits in the chair and Lee pumps her up to chest height. She runs her fingers through the thick, blond mane. A few strays catch in the webbing of her fingers and float beneath the chair. The black smock goes around Tally's throat, but all she can think about is Noah. Noah's throat. Wanting Noah. Wanting to take Grace's place in the other room.

All this time, she's been too afraid to admit what she really wants. She removes her scissors, ready to give a dry cut, and catches sight of herself in the mirror. Her cheeks flame. Her body is primed for retreat, or attack, or both.

Her hands get to work. She should know better than anyone that wanting something and *having* something are two different things. Her past is a prime example. Lee has worked hard for what she has, but a relationship with Noah is what she wants, no matter the effort.

She snips the dead ends from Tally's hair and begins to create soft layers to frame her face. She cranks the music as she works and loses herself in the moment.

All she needs is time to convince him why she's worth it.

jealousy [jel-uh-see]

<u>noun</u>

1. jealous resentment against a rival, a person enjoying success or advantage

2. mental uneasiness from suspicion or fear of rivalry, unfaithfulness, as in love

I have always been a jealous person.
When I was a child.
As a teen.
In my twenties.

And now.

Everyone thinks I'm so calm.
That I'm <u>appropriate</u> (I despise that word), but they have no idea how spiteful I can really be.

I have to be careful though . . . jealousy is truly a green-eyed monster that rears its ugly head when you least expect it.

And haven't you heard?

Jealousy kills.

TUESDAY

17

grace

I have to tell her. I can't go another day without telling her. I'm losing my mind."

Grace waits for some sort of reassurance on the other end of the phone. She mouths the directions from her open cookbook, while attempting to talk and have dinner prepared before Luca makes it home from soccer practice.

"What are you so worried about?"

She wipes her hands on a dish towel. "Nothing. Everything. Her never speaking to me again. I don't know."

"But you're her best friend."

She tosses the towel across the counter. "Exactly. That's *exactly* my point. I'm her best friend."

After a moment of hesitation: "Just tell her."

Grace stirs the meat and rice with a wooden spoon and adds some more soy sauce. "I know, but I think I want to wait until the trip. She'll be more relaxed. Happy, even."

"But you just said you have to tell her."

"I know. I'm going insane." She lets out a small laugh. She wants it to be done. No matter what, she must get this secret off her chest, regardless of what drama Lee tries to upstage her with. Chad's pickup truck appears in the drive and she waves through the kitchen window.

"Luca just pulled up. Gotta go."

"Okay. Breathe. It's all going to be okay."

"Thanks." She still doesn't feel reassured as she disconnects the call and hears the stampede of her son's cleats.

"Hey, bud!" She soaps her hands in the sink and dries them on the slightly damp dish towel.

He makes a beeline for the living room, but she stops him. "Shoes off! And go wash your hands, please. Dinner is almost ready."

Chad reverses out of the drive, not bothering to come in, but she prefers it that way. His taillights fade along Estes, and she almost texts him to slow down in a residential area. Instead, she gazes at the other houses as she drops chopped red peppers into the cast iron skillet. Though the houses in this neighborhood easily swoop into seven figures, she bought years ago post-divorce, when she offered a huge down payment and was able to tailor the house to her exact aesthetic. Alice lives down the street in a massive Victorian. They used to spend their weekends perusing estate sales for antiques, or meeting up on Saturdays to talk appliances. She misses those days, back when she was still creating her nest. Her life has changed in such a short period of time. She used to be such an open book and now she's keeping secrets from almost everyone.

"I'm starved," Luca says. His face is flushed, and his uniform is stained from grass and mud.

"Go put on some clean clothes."

He opens his closet and balls his clothes inside, the wheels of his dresser drawers sliding and slamming as he plucks out fresh pajamas.

She scoops the stir-fry onto his plate, then hers, and carries them to the back door.

"Want to eat outside?"

He struggles to get his T-shirt on. "Sure."

They settle on the patio. He regales her with soccer stories and tells her all about Chad. She listens patiently, never slandering his father, and sits back, ogling the stars. "Isn't this nice?" she asks. Unexpected contentment spreads—for her life now, for the upcoming trip, for her secret—and she smiles into the darkness, feeling like nothing can go wrong. She has worked so hard for this life in this exact moment in time. Nothing is going to screw it up.

Nothing is going to take away her happiness.

18

noah

He should say it. He doesn't like keeping things inside, doesn't like pretending one thing when he feels another. Why doesn't he just tell Lee? He knows she is nervous about the trip. He knows she's probably still embarrassed about what happened the other night. He also understands, more than anyone, what it's like to leave someone who needs you.

While he gives Mason his last lesson of the day, he finds himself thinking of his brother, Wyatt. He'd had a dream about him last night—more of a nightmare really.

He watches Mason write. The clock ticks. He shifts in his chair, and the hardwood floor groans beneath his weight. They are working on Mason's fine motor skills. Simple things like holding pencils, buttoning and unbuttoning shirts, and passing objects through the midline have improved drastically over the last few months. Mason stops, erases, restarts.

"It's okay. Let's try this phrase." He tries to stay present with Mason, but thoughts of Wyatt drag him back.

"I don't understand this," Mason says. "Tell me another way to do it."

Mason looks at him. He could swear Wyatt stares back. The curly hair. The pensive brows. The tapping. It's like a constant mirror that shuttles him back in time and gives him an emotional kick.

Though he's been working with Mason for six months, every day it's an adjustment. He has to regularly remind himself that Mason is not Wyatt. That they are different. He feels unnaturally close to him because of the parallels. He knows he's not alone—lots of therapists show preferences for students for all types of reasons.

They continue to work, and once the day dies down, Noah drives the short distance home during rush hour, eager for a beer and the game. The city is now overrun with transplants from New York and California. The streets have been scooped with potholes, the traffic giving LA a run for its money. There's the hope of the overpriced transit system. Tall skinnies popping up on plots of land once unoccupied. Bachelorette parties dominating downtown. Price tags swooping into the millions. His hometown has become a *destination*. Luckily, he bought his condo years ago before the whole city lost its mind and inflated its prices.

Despite the influx, he enjoys the urban boon of energy. He likes that he can walk to bartaco when he wants to feel like he's at the beach, to imogene + willie when he needs a pair of custom jeans, or to the farmer's market to load up on produce.

He misses his family, but he's invested in Nashville. He's spent his entire life here, building his career. He left his teaching position at a school to start his own private practice. He now has good friends and a group of students he looks forward to teaching.

But then there's Lee. He doesn't know how to handle what's happening between them. He can still see her lips, wet, pink, and searching for his. The way her body had ignited. The way she looks at him. The way he looks at her.

The interest . . . *No*. It's far too complicated to ever get romantically involved, not to mention highly unethical.

He shakes his head, parallel parks his car, and enters his home. It is cold and quiet. He should get a dog. Maybe two. Something to kill the silence. He unpacks his folders from his bag and rustles through paperwork as he does at the end of every night, sorting through various client files.

He takes a quick shower, shelves the files of the children he won't see until next week, grabs a beer, and flips on the TV. He looks at his phone, checks his texts, and smiles. He wants to go out tonight, but he should really get some sleep.

He types out a lengthy reply, takes a swig of beer, and sinks onto the cushions. His eyes grow heavy as all the various thoughts swirl—Wyatt, Mason, Lee—until he wakes, mouth dry, TV blaring, and drags himself upstairs to bed.

He still can't shake thoughts of Wyatt. The day of graduation, the day he left him. The day *they* left *him*. He brushes his teeth and climbs into bed, not wanting to remember. What good does it do? He closes his eyes and lets his mind wander. It's hours before he falls asleep.

THURSDAY

19

lee

Thursday comes.

Lee tosses her new novel into her carry-on, makes sure she has all her toiletries, and knocks three times on Mason's door. How will she say good-bye to him? How will he ever really understand why she's leaving?

"Mase, open up, please. I need to talk to you." She waits the obligatory thirty-three seconds, and then he yanks the door.

"Password, please?"

"Sassafras."

He performs a ceremonious bow, his spindly arm cradling his waist. "You may ent*ah*."

"Why thank you, kind sir." She and Mason went through a *Downton Abbey* phase, and he'd become obsessed with accents. She steps into his tidy room and soaks in the order: the books alphabetically arranged, the science projects lined up on pristine shelves, the globes of varying shapes, the calming posters of the solar system tacked to the walls. "I need you to sit. Can you do that for me?"

"Of course I can sit. I have legs that bend, *don't I*?" He crosses his legs on the edge of his bed, and the weathered mattress squeaks beneath his weight.

"I'm leaving for my trip now. I will be back in seventy-two hours. Noah is going to take great care of you. Are you still okay with me going?"

"Yes."

"Is there anything you want to talk about before I go?"

"Can you shut the door on your way out?"

She snorts. "I can. Can I tell you something?"

"I don't know. *Can* you?"

"I can. I love you."

He sighs and recrosses his legs. "I love you too."

She absorbs those three precious words Mason often withholds and wishes she could press *pause*.

"Are you ready to go now?"

She swallows. *No.* "Let's say good-bye."

He cocks forward and offers his forehead, their own version of a hug or kiss. She kneels by his bed and presses her head to his. The bones of his skull meet hers. He pulls away first. Before she stands, she quickly kisses his cheek.

"No thanks. No thanks. No thanks." He smears her kiss from his flesh and simultaneously stomps his feet.

"I'm sorry. I know you don't like kisses, but I'm just going to miss you so much." She chokes on the last words and retreats a few steps. Her fingers graze the top of his head. He swats her hand. "You be a good boy, okay, Mason? I will be back very soon."

"Seventy-two hours is not very soon. It's three *days*," Mason states.

She grapples with how to respond. "Well, in the scheme of your entire life, that's very short, remember? We talked about how in the scope of all time, three days is not long."

"But you've never been gone that long." He shrugs. "To me, it's long."

"You know what I think? I think you're going to have so much fun with Noah, it's going to go fast."

"Maybe. Okay, bye-bye." He shoos her out the door, and she shuts it like she promised. Her hand lingers on the knob while panic seizes her chest. Should she stay? Is he nervous about the amount of time she will be gone? She palms her roller bag and purse and meets Noah in the dining room.

"All set?" Noah asks.

He stands in her home, as if he already lives here. Possession trumps her fears of leaving, and she longs to cling to routine, to undo the promises she made to the girls and instead crawl back in bed and stay put. But she doesn't.

As if reading her mind, Noah approaches her with compassion. "Look, I know this is hard, but we're going to have a great time. I promise."

Lee looks at her feet so he doesn't register the anguish in her eyes. "I know you will."

Noah pulls her into a hug, and she inhales his intoxicating smell and the warmth of his skin.

"Take good care of my boy, okay?"

He nods and steps back, his eyes searching her face. "Lee, when you get back . . ."

Her heart shoots to her throat. She can actually taste it, the blood, which traverses like silver across her tongue. "Yes?"

"I want to talk about something."

"What do you mean? Mason?"

"No. Not Mason. Just something between us."

Us? There's an us? She nods, unsure of what to say. "Sure." She reaches up to give him another hug. His arms linger, and finally, they separate.

"You have nothing to worry about. I promise I'm going to take good care of him."

"I know." His words swirl inside her like helium. "Please keep me updated."

He wags his phone in the air. "Hourly. I'll have it on at all times."

They step onto the front porch and he waves as she rolls her bag to the car. She hesitates before starting the engine, her emotions all twisted and coiled.

She makes the short drive to Carol's. The girls are already hoisting their bags into the back of Carol's rented SUV, laughing about something. Lee smiles as she parks and pops her own trunk. She *does* deserve this. No matter how she got here, she's here. She belongs.

"We thought you might not show," Carol teases.

She locks her car, the alarm chirping. "Sorry. But you'll be happy to know I'm late for a possibly exciting reason."

"Oh?" Grace asks.

"Noah." Even saying his name makes her smile.

Grace lifts her eyebrows. "Did something happen?"

"I'll tell you on the way." Lee wiggles her own eyebrows and piles her belongings into the car. She sits in the back with Grace. Alice distributes mimosas in to-go cups—a virgin one for her, made with kombucha, even though she longs for champagne. She feels celebratory, almost sees no harm in taking a tiny sip. Though she wants to revel in a bit of normalcy with the girls, she raises her virgin glass in a toast as Carol backs out of her drive onto Windemere and winds her way to I-40E.

"Everyone got everything?" Carol asks.

They all scream yes, and off they go, merging onto the highway from Briley Parkway. As the girls laugh and Alice cranks the music, Lee has never felt happier—or more uncertain—about what lies ahead.

duplicity
duplicities
duplicitous
Sometimes I feel like two different people.

The one I present to the world and the one no one knows about.
It's not that I don't think people would like the real me . . . I just don't think they'd understand who I really am and how I've gotten here.

All the things I've done.
All the things I'm doing.

People really do just see what they want to see, don't they?
They never expect betrayal.
They never expect deceit.
They never expect you can hide who you really are because it's all part of the master plan.

But I'm ready. I feel it.

I'm feeling duplicitous.

Part 2

black mountain

I can handle the truth. It's the lies that kill me.
—Anonymous

20

grace

Lee talks about Noah almost the entire five-hour drive. Grace wants to interject—*he says he isn't interested, don't get your hopes up, don't spin this out of control*— but she lets Lee get it all off her chest. Still, it fuels Grace's anxiety. The way Lee takes Noah's words out of context. The way she revs from zero to sixty. But it's the first conversation in a while that hasn't been filled with worry or stress, and Grace knows it's good for her to be excited about something.

After they unload their bags and check into Arbor House, they step toward Lake Tomahawk. The crisp mountain air revives her skin. The women walk the short .55-mile loop, stepping over duck droppings and past yapping dogs and walkers. Grace takes it all in: the mountain peaks that slash the clouds in horizontal zigzags, the blue sky that rubs against the blossoming trees, the orange buoys that bob in placid water. She trots up to Carol and slings an arm around her shoulder. "This place is heaven."

"Isn't it? It's just dreamy here."

"Dreamy. Magical. Amazing. Any good word ever invented. Thanks for arranging this."

Carol adjusts her sunglasses. "My pleasure."

They walk in silence. Grace expects Carol to launch into the oodles of research she's collected about the city, all its various merits, its nut-free schools, its healthcare, its little city center, and the specific details about Arbor House, but her chatty friend says nothing.

"Everything okay?"

"What do you mean?"

"You're just abnormally quiet."

Carol shakes her head. "I'm fine."

She's not fine. Her brain works overtime. Marriage issues? Financial trouble? Zoe? Grace's tongue preps all the questions, but she knows not to push. "I hope it's nothing too serious?"

Carol smiles and shrugs—she isn't much of a shrugger; she is a definitive person, a nodder or a head shaker, someone who always says yes or no—and leans against her friend. "It's definitely serious. But it will be okay."

"I'm here if you need me."

"I know." She lifts her head. "What's up with you?"

"What do you mean?"

"Something's going on with you. I can tell."

Grace reddens. *Is it that obvious?* "I don't know what you mean."

"Okay. Fine. We'll both play the *nothing's-going-on* card. I'm cool with that."

"You know me too well." Should Grace tell her? Carol has an uncanny ability to get friends to confide, but then in a matter of minutes, the entire world knows. No. Lee should know first.

She glances behind them at Lee and Alice, laughing and walking. Grace is relieved that Lee stepped outside of her comfort zone, away from home, open to a new adventure.

The first night, they venture into town and stop for drinks and gourmet cheese at the local wine shop. Grace decides not to drink, in solidarity with Lee. Lee pulls her aside and insists she enjoy herself, but Grace assures her it's fine.

"Hello, cutest town in America! I love you!" Alice exclaims. Grace smiles and eats another cube of cheese, as Lee obsessively checks her phone.

She's been gone almost a whole day, and there's not been one issue with Mason. No matter what Noah says to reassure her in his texts, Grace knows that Lee is waiting for the life-changing message that Mason has accidentally burned down the house, choked on a grape, or somehow escaped and been run over by a speeding car.

They walk through the tiny town square, settling on a delicious seafood restaurant.

"Who's up for a hike in the morning?" Carol asks.

Everyone raises their hand, except Lee.

"Oh, come on." Alice takes a generous sip of wine. "It will be so refreshing. We never get to hike at home."

Lee smacks Grace on the shoulder. "We hike. Tell them."

Grace laughs and stabs a piece of lettuce with her fork. "Well, we *walk,* sure. But we don't hike. I haven't hiked in ages. Is it a tough climb?"

"Hiking *is* walking. You walk," Carol reminds Grace. "You two walk the greenway all the time!"

"And Marge says the view from the top is worth it,"

Alice urges. The inn owner had told them about the two-mile trail close to the house.

Grace nudges Lee. "I'm in if you are. Could be a nice way to start the day."

"Look," Lee says, swallowing a bite of her own salad, "part of my coming here is to do things I never get to do. And those things might sound boring to you guys, but sleeping in sounds like heaven."

"I get that," Grace rushes to add. "You really don't ever get to sleep in."

Alice and Carol look at each other. "Neither do we."

"Yeah, but you two have husbands. It's just different," Grace says.

"How about this," Lee offers. "Let me just see how I feel in the morning."

"Fair enough," Grace says. She lifts her glass and offers a toast. She wants her to take the hike. She can tell her on the way up. Or on the way down. Or over breakfast.

A few hours later, they walk the short distance back to Arbor House, giggling and shushing each other as they climb the porch stairs.

Grace washes her face, brushes her teeth, and crawls into bed as Lee gets ready. The light from the bathroom slits beneath the door. She can hear Alice and Carol, slightly drunk, whispering about something in the next room. She hopes Luca is doing well. She grabs her phone from the nightstand to make sure Chad hasn't texted, but she knows Luca is not awake.

Lee tiptoes into the room in her pajamas, her cosmetic bag tucked under one arm.

"You don't have to be quiet. I'm not asleep," Grace says. She clicks on the lamp beside the bed. "Actually, I should set out my hiking stuff. Just in case you sleep in."

"I'll do the same, though I doubt I'll go."

They both rummage through their clothes. Grace pulls out yoga pants, workout socks, a sports bra, tank top, and windbreaker. "Did you hear from Noah tonight?"

"I did."

Grace takes the opening. "Anything you want to share?"

Lee tosses a pillow at her. "No."

Grace tosses the pillow back and sits on the edge of her bed. "I'm serious. I want to know what's going on."

Lee grips the pillow to her stomach and rests against the headboard. "I don't know, other than what I told you on the way here. He said he wants to talk about *us* when I get back."

Grace waits for her to continue.

Lee sighs. "Grace, he's just so . . . loyal. And unwavering. He really looks at me when I'm talking. He never seems distracted. He's meticulous. He's direct. He's incredible with Mason. And those eyes . . . I could get lost in them."

"So just see what he says when you get back. And then go from there." Grace hesitates. "Just don't get ahead of yourself, okay?"

Lee stiffens. "Who said I'm getting ahead of myself?"

"I don't mean it *that* way. I'm just saying that you don't know what he's going to talk about, so don't get your hopes up."

"Why are you being so negative?"

Grace wavers. "I'm not. I'm totally not. I'm just listening to what you've said, and I don't want you to get hurt. That's all."

"You're not my mother."

Grace almost laughs. "Who said anything about being your *mother*? I just want you to protect your feelings."

Lee launches the pillow across the bed and sits up.

"Maybe I'm tired of protecting my feelings. Maybe I just want to throw caution to the wind and take a risk."

Grace lifts her hands in surrender. "Go for it then. You know best."

"That sounds like a real vote of confidence, Grace. Thanks."

"You know that's not what I mean."

"Then what *do* you mean? I thought you wanted me to be happy. I thought you liked Noah."

Grace scratches her forehead, suddenly exhausted. "I do like Noah. I want you to be happy. That's not what I'm saying at all."

"Then what are you saying?"

"Forget it." Grace climbs back into bed and flicks off her lamp. Her heart thuds in her ears. She doesn't want to be this worked up. She doesn't want to fight.

Lee peels back her own sheets and sighs as she crawls into bed. Grace considers apologizing but thinks better of it. She attempts to ignore the frustration, emotion, and nerves.

She rolls to her side and blinks into the darkness. She counts backward from one hundred, but no matter what she does, she's wide awake.

"Lee?" she whispers into the blackness. "Are you awake?"

She waits for a response, but none comes. She rolls onto her back. *Tomorrow then.* She closes her eyes, recites what she will say, and begs for sleep.

FRIDAY

21

lee

Sunshine filters through the shades. Lee glances at the alarm clock. The red numbers flash ten. She sits upright in a panic, thinking of Mason. Has she missed any critical texts? She fumbles with her phone and sees a few messages from Noah. She stabs them with her thumb to find photos of Mason eating breakfast and working on an engineering project. She smiles, relieved, and types back a succession of apologetic but enthusiastic replies. She sinks back into the covers and attempts to relax. She hasn't slept this late in years. She didn't even hear the three of them leave this morning.

She replays her argument with Grace. Why can't she just be happy for her? Grace is always supportive . . . but for once, she wishes she would stop acting older and wiser and just listen.

Her stomach grumbles. She heads downstairs and smells fresh coffee. A crew of familiar voices bounces around the kitchen. She rounds the bottom of the stairs to find the girls clustered around the table in their workout gear, digging into omelets and green juices.

"There she is!" Carol exclaims.

"Morning, sleepyhead."

"Did you get good rest?" Grace asks. Her tone is tentative.

Lee smiles. "Hey, sorry. I can't believe I slept so long. Are you guys back already?"

"We are. We were there by six-thirty. It was amazing," Alice says.

"*So* amazing," Carol says.

"Marge wasn't lying about the view," Alice adds.

Grace shrugs. "I didn't go either. I slept until eight, and they had already left. I went for a walk around the lake, though."

Lee helps herself to coffee and leans against the counter. "Where's Marge?"

"Went into town. But not before making us all of this."

"Fancy," Lee says.

"And the coffee too, which is divine," Carol says. "Almost as good as the Lounge's, A."

"Hey now," Alice teases. Alice owns the Germantown Lounge, a nonprofit artistic haven where patrons can paint, write, strum guitars, type, and drink coffee for free.

Lee takes a sip. The thick dark roast dissolves the fog in her brain. "So, what's on the agenda today?"

"We thought we'd go into Asheville and do some shopping," Carol says as she bites into her eggs. "Does that sound good?"

She doesn't have the extra cash to spend. The thought of aimlessly wandering from shop to shop as the girls try on clothes and collect toys for the kids sounds like the opposite of relaxing.

"You know, I think that claw-foot tub is calling my name."

Carol opens her mouth to protest, but Grace interjects.

"That sounds fabulous. You do what you want. It's your vacation too."

Lee appreciates the support and hopes the tension from last night is gone. She surveys the food again and chooses an egg white omelet and a piece of toast. After they eat, she helps scrape plates and load dishes. Alice and Carol head up to shower and change, but Grace lingers on the stairs.

"Are we okay?"

Lee nods. "Yeah. I'm sorry about last night. Truly. You were just being protective, which I appreciate." She cradles her mug against her chest.

Grace smiles. "Okay, good. I'm going upstairs to shower. Just come in if you need the bathroom."

"Thanks." Lee walks outside with her second cup of coffee. The morning air shocks her body awake. She sits on the steps. Lake Tomahawk glitters just a few feet away. People scatter around the water with their dogs. A few kids squeal from the small playground, spraying sand into the air. Would Mason like it here? If he weren't so married to routine, maybe. She tips her face to the clear, cloudless sky. She doesn't have to worry about that now. All she has to do is enjoy herself.

The door creaks behind her, and the girls, refreshed and dressed, bound outside. They step around her toward the gate.

"Sure you don't want to come, Lee?"

"Retail therapy can't be beat," Alice jokes, swinging her tote.

"A really good bath could give shopping a run for its money any day."

Grace leans down and kisses her cheek. "Enjoy."

Lee waves and watches them walk toward the SUV.

She stares into her coffee cup, drains the last few drops, and goes back upstairs to fill the claw-foot tub.

She finds complimentary bath salts and sprinkles some into the steamy water. She undresses, places her phone on the bathroom sink, and observes her body. She is still lean. Her stomach is flat. Her breasts are small and perky. She runs her fingers across her flesh, wanting to see what others see. She tilts her head and imagines Noah watching her like this, touching herself. Would he be aroused?

She slips into the scalding water inch by inch and surrenders to the heat. She closes her eyes. Noah's distinct face and strong hands fill the space behind her eyelids. One hand slips beneath the water. She touches herself and imagines his fingers—not hers. She finishes in minutes, breathless and sweating. What would he do if he knew she just used the idea of him to get off?

She dries her body, drains the tub, and gets ready. She checks her phone again. Noah, true to form, has sent regular, timed updates. She wonders again what he wants to talk about, if he is going to confess something to her.

She creeps downstairs. "Marge, are you here?" She assesses the charming cabin: the wood-paneled rooms, the hutch filled with fine china, the sectional positioned in front of a massive wood-burning fireplace.

Lee doesn't understand the appeal of loading your house with strangers. To charge them to stay on your property, to clean up after them, and hope they don't murder you while you sleep. She looks around the house, wondering what secrets are kept here. She glances at the ornate brick fireplace, remembering how she used to squirrel away her treasures behind a brick she'd sawed loose with a bread knife. She'd stuffed Troll dolls inside, small journals, her allowance, and later, money she earned as an adult. She double knots her tennis shoes and lowers her sunglasses as she steps outside onto the path.

Mason turns eight at the end of summer. She thinks about where she was eight years ago and cringes. All of the ways she's gotten here . . . no one would understand, not even Grace. She hits the pavement with her iPod and breathes deep. She spends so much time in her studio, with hair products and chemicals, or in the house, with Mason, that she never feels she can take a deep breath.

The sun warms her pale skin as she walks the loop three times. Her past whips around her like a storm, as it always does when she is alone with her thoughts. She is in a constant state of rehashing events that happened, almost happened, or should have happened. She thinks of the night she started drinking. She thinks of the party. She thinks of her father, of Shirley. She thinks of Mason as a baby, plump and happy, gurgling in his car seat. She thinks of what happened after.

On her last loop, she ducks inside to grab water. Marge is still out. She checks her phone again and sees a single text from Noah that says: *Nothing new to report. I hope you are having fun.*

Pleasure spasms through her body. She unlocks her phone and texts him back. *I am having a lot of fun. Thank you for making me come.*

She laughs as she sends it, knowing that the last sentence bears more than one meaning. She waits as the ellipsis blinks, and then his message comes through: *My pleasure. You are missed, but Mason is doing well.*

She's missed? By whom? She can still imagine the kiss that almost happened, his smooth face in her hands. She fantasizes about what he would feel like inside of her, all the ways that that would crack her life apart. She sends one more text just as Carol, Grace, and Alice parade inside.

"Finally!" she says. She slides the phone into her pocket and smiles at her friends who are laden with bags of trinkets for their kids.

They show off their gifts—Grace even bought Mason a wooden toy plane—and she makes the appropriate comments. But Noah consumes her thoughts. He misses her. Noah misses *her*. Suddenly, she can't wait to get back.

22

grace

Grace tells the girls at dinner.

She promised she'd tell Lee first, but she wants to gauge their reactions before she tells Lee. They will be her trial run. They can give her advice. She wanted to tell them while shopping, when they'd stopped at Hole for donuts and coffee, but the timing hadn't felt right. Now, when Lee excuses herself to FaceTime with Mason, she releases all of it in a quick rush. Carol and Alice look at each other, wine stems in hand, truly shocked.

"Wait, wait, wait." Carol waves her hands. "How did we not know?"

"Why didn't you tell us?" Alice asks, swirling her wine in a nervous frenzy.

"And *why* haven't you told Lee?" Carol's eyes widen.

Grace pinches a piece of fresh, warm bread and pops it into her mouth. "I wanted to. For months. Trust me. But I also wanted to see for myself first . . . to make sure it was real."

"Are you going to tell her tonight?" Carol asks.

"You have to," Alice says. "She needs to know."

Grace cringes but nods. "I am. I just wanted to tell you first so that you can make sure she doesn't murder me while I sleep."

"Oh, stop. She'll be fine," Carol insists.

"And we're happy for you." Alice pats her hand affectionately.

"Really? I'm not the worst friend ever?"

Carol rolls her eyes. "Oh, please. Hardly."

"However it ends up, thanks for making this trip a hell of a lot more interesting," Alice says as Lee returns to the table.

"Sorry. What did I miss?"

Grace almost chokes on her bread and raises her glass in a toast. "To real friends," she says.

"To real friends," they echo as they clink their crystal against hers.

Tonight, she will tell Lee, and then it will all be over. There will be no more secrets.

After dinner, the women pile into Carol's rental and drive the fifteen minutes back to Arbor House. Marge is waiting out front. They cluster together, somehow wondering if they are in trouble.

"Ladies, may I?" Marge ushers them to the back deck. A blazing fire pit, a tray of graham crackers, squares of expensive dark chocolate, homemade marshmallows, skewers, two bottles of wine, and freshly folded blankets are artfully arranged around each of the chaises.

"Marge, are you serious right now?" Alice exclaims. "This is amazing!"

"You ladies enjoy, and just let me know what else you need." Marge pulls the back door closed. They each grab a blanket and get cozy under the stars.

"Okay, this is pretty divine," Carol says.

"Beyond," Alice adds.

Grace claims the chair beside Lee and relishes the night sky.

"Thank you for convincing me to come," Lee finally says. "Really. I would have been so sad to miss this. I didn't know how much I needed to get away."

Carol leans forward and cups her hand around her ear. "What was that?"

Lee stretches her legs in front of her and takes another bite of her s'more. "I said, thank you. You were right. Don't be an ass about it."

"That would mean she'd have to be someone other than herself," Grace jokes.

"Wow." Carol tosses a piece of graham cracker at her. "Let's dump on the organizer. Fine."

"We love you," Lee says. "But you are a total control freak."

"It got us here, didn't it?" Carol nibbles sticky marshmallow from her finger.

"The s'mores are a nice touch, I have to admit," Grace says, trying to distract herself from what's to come, from what she has to say.

"I have an idea." Alice chews and swallows, making brief eye contact with Grace. "Let's all go around and tell each other something we don't know. Kind of like Truth or Dare. Without the dares."

The confession snags in Grace's stomach and flips. *Here we go.*

"How about no?" Lee scoffs.

"Oh, come on," Carol says. "It will be fun."

"Why don't you start?" Grace asks. She needs time to formulate how she will say it. Where she will even begin.

"How about Alice starts? Since it's her game."

Alice sits up straighter. "Fine." She clears her throat. "I think I've decided to turn my nonprofit into a for-profit business. With Fred as my manager."

"Whoa," Grace says, genuinely surprised. "A, that's an amazing idea."

"Do you think you and Fred will kill each other?" Carol asks.

Alice shrugs and twists the cap off the first bottle of red. "Probably. But I'm not going to 'Alice' the situation and freak out. I can handle this."

"Did you just use your name as a verb?" Carol laughs.

Alice tosses the cap at her. "You go."

Carol catches it and looks at Grace. "No, why don't *you* go?"

"Because I'm not ready yet," Grace says, an edge to her voice.

"I just thought the older and wiser one would want to go next." Carol shrugs.

"Ha-ha," Grace says. "Asshole."

"Stop calling me that!" She launches an entire cracker, and Grace lifts her blanket to shield herself from it. The cracker breaks apart and scatters crumbs along the deck.

"Guys, we can't make a mess," Lee whispers.

"She started it," Carol says around a mouthful of s'more. "But fine, I'll go."

Grace resituates herself under her blanket. Her heart is a jackhammer, and she takes long, slow breaths as she waits for Carol.

"Mine's not good, I'm afraid."

"What do you mean?" Lee asks. "Is it Zoe?"

"No, it's my mom."

"Did she call you an asshole too?" Grace jokes.

Carol smiles and swirls her wine. "I wish. Turns out

she has stage-four breast cancer. She just told me a few days ago."

Grace sits up. "My God, Carol. You mean when she called in the park last week . . ."

"Yep. Totally legitimate. I just assumed she was being her normal paranoid self. But you know how my mother is. I want to make sure she's *actually* stage four and not, you know, cancer-free, as she very well could be."

"Oh God, now I'm the asshole. I'm so sorry."

"You're fine." She dismisses Grace's apology with her hand. "It will be fine."

"But we all heard her on the phone that day," Alice says, "and it all seemed so trivial."

"Well." Carol shrugs. "It wasn't."

"Cheryl seems like she'll live forever," Lee murmurs.

"She does. But after Dad died . . ."

Grace sits forward and touches Carol's knee. "Please let us know how we can help. You know we're here for anything."

"I can't think of anyone better to have in her corner though," Alice says. "You're the most devoted daughter I know. Your love coupled with your affinity for research will have her cured in no time."

"Ha. I'm sure she'll still find some way to annoy the piss out of me until the end of time." Carol clears her throat and glances at Grace, but she shakes her head. *I'm still not ready.*

"So, since we're all revealing our deepest, darkest secrets . . . ?" Carol turns to Lee.

Lee shifts in her chair. "What?"

"Oh, come on. You know what everyone wants to know," Alice urges.

"I don't get to pick what I tell you?" Lee rearranges herself under the blanket.

"We're dying to know," Carol says.

"What, how I wake up looking like this?" Lee laughs.

Grace knows she needs to interject. It's her turn. This is about her, not Lee. She should have told Lee separately and not gotten Carol and Alice involved in the first place.

"Come on."

"Come on what?" Lee's voice hardens.

"Who is it?" Alice asks. "Who's Mason's dad?"

Despite what Grace has to tell her, she pauses. It's the one thing Lee has never revealed. With Alice's and Carol's confessions, maybe tonight is the night Lee will come clean.

Lee closes her eyes. She opens them after a long, uncomfortable moment and blinks into the fire. "No one."

"Are you, like, the Virgin Mary?" Alice jokes.

"Was it a sperm donor?" Carol offers.

"No one is judging you here. Believe me," Alice says. "We all have shitty sex stories."

Lee watches the fire, seemingly haunted. Grace leans forward. "Lee? Are you okay?"

She shakes her head. "I'm fine. It's just . . . not a good memory, you know?" She searches for something to say.

Grace clears her throat and looks around the group. "I'll go."

Lee looks relieved, but Grace dreads what's coming. How it will change their relationship. How Lee will look at her. The exact moment their friendship will shift. She calculates all the ways to begin. When it started. What it was like the first time. How it got from *there* to *here*.

"Will you hold that thought? I'm dying to pee." Lee's blanket pools at her feet as she disappears inside to the bathroom.

The girls lean forward once she's out of earshot. "Just tell her," Carol hisses. "Get it over with."

"I'm trying! I can't stop her from needing to pee."

Alice grabs Carol's forearm. "Maybe we should give them privacy. So Lee doesn't feel pressure to respond in a certain way."

Grace knows Carol wants to stay. She wouldn't miss a good bit of drama for anything, but she reluctantly nods. "Fine. Have at it." The women say good night and toss the empty bottle of wine into the recycling bin, the second one unopened by Carol's lounge chair. "Good luck."

They head inside. Grace takes a staggering breath as she waits for Lee to come back out.

It's finally time.

23

grace

A few minutes later, Lee appears on the deck and notices the empty chairs. "Where did they go?"

"Tired, I think. Here, come sit for a second." Grace pats the chair beside her.

Lee sits and then lies back. "Can we just lie here for a second and not talk? There's been so much talking."

"Sure." Grace reclines. The fire crackles. Reams of black smoke lift into the night. She needs to tell her, but she wants Lee to relax first. She closes her eyes and takes deep breaths, the exhaustion and nerves taking over. She startles when hands shake her awake.

"Grace, let's go up. You fell asleep."

Grace swipes a hand across the back of her mouth. "Did I?" Her voice is groggy. "Sorry. What time is it?"

"Midnight. Come on. We'll go get ready."

Grace clamps a hand on Lee's arm as she turns to go inside. "No, stay. I want to talk about something important."

Lee sits and gathers the blanket in her arms. "Okay."

Grace licks her dry lips. She swallows, her mouth robbed of moisture, and coughs. Her mind files her confession in the right order, and she gathers the courage to start. She exhales roughly, but before she can speak, Lee looks at her with tears in her eyes.

"What's the matter?" Grace asks.

"I know you have something to say, but can I go first? If I don't, I'm afraid I'll lose my nerve." Lee's feet tap nervously against the deck. "It's about what the girls asked."

Grace nods, but her secret inflates and threatens to pop if she doesn't get it off her chest right this minute. "Sure."

"I never saw his face."

Grace studies her, confused. "Whose face?"

"Mason's dad. I never saw his face."

"What do you mean?" A jolt of panic flutters through her abdomen.

"I mean that I was passed out, drunk, and when I woke up, he was, you know, inside me."

Grace absorbs what she's saying, the words clicking in her brain. "Lee, were you . . . ?" The word *rape* fades away. She can't say it out loud. She doesn't want to believe it.

Lee works her bottom lip with a trembling hand. "I was wasted at some dumb party. I went upstairs to the bathroom and then the next thing I know, there's a guy having sex with me."

It's like a punch to the chest as Lee says it. Grace steadies her voice, but it slices across the silence. "And he forced you?"

Lee cracks her knuckles. "All I remember is waking up, and he had his hand around my throat and squeezed until I couldn't breathe. And then he said . . ."

Needles of caution flood her entire body until she can't breathe.

"He said: 'I could kill you. Do you know that? Do you know what I could do if I squeezed?' I literally thought he was going to kill me, and then just as fast, he was done. I passed out. When I woke up, he was gone."

The confession is startling. Suddenly, Grace is at that party. She can see it, feel it. The words bring her to her knees. She moves to Lee's chair and slides a comforting arm around her shoulder. "Oh, Lee. That must have been . . . I don't even have words." She holds her there, rocking back and forth the way she does for Luca after a bad dream. "Why didn't you ever tell me any of this? Does anyone know?"

Lee shakes her head.

"Did you ever think about reporting it?"

"How could I?" Her hands rise and drop. "I had no idea who he was. We were in the dark. I mean, *complete* dark. I was beyond drunk. I've tried to remember if I met someone that night, if I was flirting with anyone, but I was so wasted. I just don't remember anything. Except what he said."

"And he never came back around?"

"No." Lee stares at her lap.

Grace stutters over her next question. "How soon did you know you were pregnant?"

Lee exhales. "Not until five months."

"What?" Grace looks at her, perplexed. "How is that possible?"

"I was in denial." Lee twists her hair at the nape of her neck. "I wasn't really showing yet. I just wanted to pretend it didn't happen, and by the time I knew, it was too late to do anything about it."

"My God." Grace shields her mouth with both hands. She imagines the heavy breathing. Her own face on the floor. Hands strangling her neck, the hard ramming of flesh against flesh. The realization of a rapist's baby in her belly. Her dinner rises in her throat and she bolts inside to the downstairs bathroom. Lee's confession ravages her heart. She vomits into the toilet, her gut a lining of ragged nerves. Her mouth drips with leftover dinner. She rises on unsteady legs, splashes cold water on her face, and washes her hands. She grasps for the door, wrenches it open, and finds Lee's tall, willowy frame against the backdrop of the moon's reflection.

"Are you okay?"

Grace's body begins to twitch and tremble as she moves toward her friend. She should be asking Lee the same thing. How can she reveal her secret after what Lee just confessed? Lee's arms find her in the blackness, and Grace lets herself be held. She can't find the right words. She pulls back and swipes mascara from under her eyes. "Sorry. Something I ate. Let's go back outside." Her fingers are clumsy as they work to adjust her top.

They descend the deck steps and crawl into the comfort of their blankets. Grace tilts her head toward the night sky. The stars pop and twinkle on their inky canvas. "I'm so sorry you went through all that, Lee. I can't even imagine how confusing it must have been to have a baby like that."

Lee nods. "It was. It is." Lee looks at her. "God, it feels so good to finally tell you that after all this time. I was so worried you would judge me."

"Why in the world would I judge you for that? Knowing you went through all of that *alone* breaks my heart. I wish I'd known sooner."

Lee rises and envelops Grace in another hug. "I love you so much," she finally whispers. "I couldn't get through even a day without you. Thank you for being the best friend I've ever had."

Tears threaten to spill, but Grace just squeezes her tighter. "Thank you for saying that. That means the world."

"Ugh. So much crying." Lee wipes away her tears and

curls back under her blanket. "Okay, wow. Talk about therapy."

Grace laughs. "Right?" She adjusts her own blanket. "That will be three hundred dollars, please."

"Pricey."

"Damn right."

Lee smiles. "Thank you for letting me get that off my chest. I know you have something you want to talk about too."

Oh shit. Grace considers waiting another day. Lee is in a good place. Lee trusts her. Lee feels closer to her. But it's now or never, and she knows it. "Okay. I don't know how to tell you this, so I'm just going to say it." Grace closes her eyes. The wind cools her cheeks, the night sounds a guide around her. The fire is almost dead, but tiny flames still lick the bottom of the pot.

"Just tell me," Lee says. "You're killing me."

"I'm pregnant."

Silence balloons around them. All of the ways Grace has been practicing to tell her amidst the array of emotions has come undone, those tenuous weeks of withholding finally leading to this very moment. She's said it. It's out. Step one.

"What?" Lee shakes her head and angles forward, staring at Grace in disbelief. "How far along?"

"Eight weeks. I obviously didn't want to tell anyone yet because of my age and all the risks . . . Luca doesn't even know."

"Wait, wait, wait." Lee waves her hands. "Back up. Who's the father? You're not even seeing anyone, are you? Oh my God, is it *Chad*?"

"That's the other thing I have to tell you." Grace takes a shuddering breath. "It's Noah's."

Shock contorts Lee's face. The open mouth. The frozen eyelids. The petite, flared nostrils. The veins in her neck that swell into ropes. Grace watches her rib cage expand and contract. Her fingers harden into tiny pale fists.

Finally, Lee stands and tosses her blanket to the ground. "*What?*" Her voice howls across the night, and Grace realizes how ugly things are about to get.

"*My* Noah? As in Noah Banks, my son's therapist? The man I'm romantically *interested* in, that Noah?"

Grace wants to remind her who introduced them. They were friends first. "Look. I know this is hard to understand." She can physically feel the dynamic transform; the defensiveness Lee clings to like a lifeline. "I didn't tell you at first because . . . well, honestly because I wanted to make sure it was real. Noah and I have been friends for a long time, so I wasn't sure it was even going anywhere." Grace registers the stricken look on Lee's face and rushes to continue. "And I didn't know you had a crush on him when we started seeing each other. I swear. By the time I did know, we were already pretty serious. I didn't want to hurt your feelings. I'm sorry."

"My *crush*? You have no idea what you're talking about, Grace. It's more than a crush. He's like family. You know how I feel about him!"

Noah has wanted to tell Lee about their relationship for months, but Grace thought the truth should come from her. The pregnancy escalated the sense of urgency, and now, here they are. "Lee, I'm so sorry. We never meant for it to happen. We really were just friends, and then we just kind of . . . fell for each other."

"How could you do this to me? And not tell me when you're with me almost every single day? How could *he* not tell me?" Though Lee is tiny, her voice stretches across the backyard, and Grace worries the entire neighborhood is on the verge of waking. "Oh my God. The thermos. You guys have the same coffee thermos, because you're *sharing* it."

Grace shakes her head. "What?"

"That fucking green thermos! Noah brought it the other day and I couldn't place where I'd seen it before. But it's *yours*. And the two of you in my kitchen, pretending to be friends." She turns her back and then pivots to face her. "God, you both must think I'm a total idiot. How *dare* you not tell me this?"

"Because we thought you'd react like this, that's why." Part of her is furious. Just once, she wants news not to revolve around Lee. For one moment to be entirely about Grace. For her best friend to be happy for her, understanding, compassionate even. This is big news. This is happy news. Why does she constantly have to be upstaged with tragic tales, anger, and so much darkness?

"How in the world do you expect me to react? I like him, Grace. And you knew that."

"I do know that *now*. Which is why I was trying to wait and find the right time."

Lee fastens her hands on her hips and eyes her stomach with murderous eyes. "Well, I hope you guys make a wonderful little family. Because you just destroyed mine."

"Oh, please stop with the dramatics." Grace stands, her entire body alert. "For once, this is about me, not you. Noah and I really care about each other. We *are* starting a family. That doesn't take anything away from yours."

"The hell it doesn't."

The two friends face off in the dark, and suddenly Grace is beyond drained. "I can't do this. Let's just talk about this in the morning. I'm going up."

She doesn't wait for Lee's protests and instead leaves

her behind on the deck. She's tired of her childish behavior. She heads upstairs and listens for Carol and Alice, but all is quiet and dark in their room. She scrubs her face, changes into pajamas, and climbs into bed, but her heart races. Tears threaten to spill, but she is not giving Lee the satisfaction. She tries to calm herself, knowing at her age, stress is even more damaging to a fetus. She takes deep breaths and sends a good-night text to Noah, giving him the brief outline. She waits for his kind response and reassurance that she did the right thing. He is on her side. He is here for her. She lies in the darkness for what seems like hours, until her breathing grows heavier and she starts to fade.

24

lee

Lee soaks up the silence. Grace's words ring in her ears. *Grace is pregnant with Noah's child. Grace and Noah are in a relationship.* The betrayal snaps around her brain. All this time, lying straight to her face. She removes her phone from her pocket. She considers calling Noah right now, in the middle of the night, and telling him exactly what she thinks.

How dare he?

Who does he think he is?

Who does *she* think she is?

She thrusts her phone into her sweatshirt. Time stills and she focuses on her breathing. She notices the wineglasses and blankets scattered around and starts to fold, collect, and arrange them so Marge won't have a mess to deal with in the morning.

She brushes away the graham cracker crumbs and gathers the plastic packaging. Her fingers grip the second bottle Grace left by her chair. She pauses, her breath trapped somewhere in her throat.

"Put it down," she insists, but instead holds it tighter. She unscrews the top. The tiny foil seal pops beneath her grip and she inhales the tannins, grapes, chocolate, and oak. Her fingers tremble. She places the bottle at her feet and backs away as though it's a poisonous spider.

She knows what it would mean to take a drink. After all the effort, work, and reasons she stopped drinking . . . it would all be for nothing. She turns, keeps her hands busy, calms her mind, and stacks the thick blankets on the corner of the steps. She balances the wineglasses in her hands, walks inside, and deposits them in the sink. She flicks on the tap and fills each glass with a little hot water so as not to leave a crimson stain.

She should go upstairs, slip into the twin bed beside Grace's, and carry on in the morning. Forgive her. Forgive him. She thinks of Noah and Grace, in a full-blown relationship behind her back. She thinks of the baby they made, those intimate moments they must have shared, the conversations, the family they will create, how Grace will pull Noah away from her, from Mason, from *them*.

In one swift motion, she is back outside, palming the bottle and emptying half of it into her mouth in less than thirty seconds. Despite being away from her son and the pain from Grace's confession, she feels immediately like herself again—as if the temporary Lee has been acting in place of this woman with glass in her mouth. With one drink, she morphs back into her true self, because this ugly, wretched need is still a piece of her. It's the part that's in control; it's the part she can trust to tell her who, at her core, she really is. She lifts the bottle again. In less than five minutes, it's drained.

She ambles back to her chair, the buzz immediate. She stuffs the bottle deep into the recycling bin on the deck next to the other one, hidden under a pile of newspaper. The wine coats her lips with its sweetness. She wants more, is desperate for it, is desperate for *him*.

She's so tired of acting. After so many years of silence, she told Grace about the man at the party, about that night. It has taken a long time to close that section of her life, and with one confession, she's brought that night, its ugliness, and everything that came after to light again.

She fishes her phone from her hoodie and thumbs through the texts. Should she just text him? She hovers over the keys but thinks better of it. She blinks a few times and watches the treetops swish in the night. She's drunk. Her mind is fine, sharper than it's been in months, but her body is not. She needs to sleep and call her sponsor in the morning.

The varying thoughts ping-pong until she sits up and rubs her eyes. It's late, but she doesn't want to go upstairs, doesn't want to see Grace. She studies the houses around her, the rustling trees, the beautiful night. She can just make out the start of the hiking trail from the backyard.

"A hop, skip, and a jump, and you're there!" Marge had said. "One of the treasures of this little place."

Before her mother was murdered, they would take hikes at Radnor Lake and make weekend trips to Pigeon Forge and Gatlinburg. After her mother died, she gorged on reruns and scalding TV dinners and rarely went outside unless it was to check the mail. Here, everywhere she turns, nature pushes in, offering itself to her.

But it's not nature she wants. She wants Noah. She wants revenge.

She wrenches her body from the chair, flips up the hood of her sweatshirt, and sways on the deck. What should she do?

She stalks through the backyard, her striped socks protecting her bare shins. Wispy grass sweeps her ankles and calves, and she tugs her socks higher. Maybe she'll prove the girls wrong and do the entire hike. She thinks of her friends, women she felt so close to and now feels immediately removed from. They lead such cushioned lives. They have no idea what she's been through or had to deal with. Except Grace . . . and *this* is how her best friend repays her for being so vulnerable and open?

She advances toward the trail. Is it crazy to hike this late? No crazier than her getting totally wasted after years of sobriety. No crazier than her best friend and the man she's interested in—*has* been interested in—going behind her back. No crazier than thinking she can trust anyone.

Never again.

A wooden stake in the ground signifies the start of the trail. She wonders if poisonous snakes lurk in the grass, or if a bear or coyote will bide its time and then devour her on the way up. She can always turn around. She'll be fine once her body starts moving.

She pushes one wobbly leg in front of the other toward the base of the trail. She owes it to herself to do this. She owes Mason. The exercise and fresh air will help the wine wear off and give her a clear head. She'll deal with Grace and Noah after. The confession. The reaction. The real truth no one knows or will *ever* know, as long as she has anything to do with it. For now, she's doing the damn hike.

She steps onto the path and begins to climb.

25

grace

Grace cannot sleep. As much as she wants Lee to be happy for her, she knew it would go just like this. But as angry and hurt as she is, can she really blame her?

She has replayed her and Noah's relationship over and over, as if on a calendar. They'd met years ago at a coffee shop. He'd been dating someone else at the time, and Grace wasn't romantically interested in anyone. Then they'd joined the same gym. Once she found out he was an occupational therapist, she'd taken Luca in for a few sessions. After years of casual run-ins, occasional drinks, and professional referrals for her friends' kids, he'd asked her on a real date. She didn't even know if she was interested until she *was*.

She should have told Lee the first time she and Noah went out, but she knew Lee might find it problematic for her best friend to be dating her son's therapist. Grace didn't yet know how strongly they'd both feel or how fast they'd fall. She didn't want to add to Lee's worries if their relationship fizzled out before it had even started.

Their first date, they'd met at Lockeland Table, a sweet little slice of hipster heaven in East Nashville.

She'd worn a form-fitting dress. As she walked through the door, searching for him in the dim light among laughing guests, she realized that she wanted more than friendship.

She spotted him at a high-top by the window. Streetlight poured in and illuminated his strong features. There was a new intimacy to meeting like this, on purpose, alone. For a startling moment, she wondered if she could go through with it. There was Lee. There were boundaries. There were lines friends didn't cross. But that early on, she had no idea Lee liked him romantically.

Grace felt like she deserved some fun too, something just for herself. She spent so much time worrying about Lee and Mason that she owed it to herself to go on a real date with someone she already trusted. As she sat across from Noah, tossed back drinks, and flirted, something awakened for the first time in a while: genuine interest.

He'd kissed her that night, before they separated toward their cars, lingering on the front walkway. The new boutique hotel across the street thrummed with tourists spilling onto the porch, listening to music and getting rowdy, and just as she was making a comment, he'd gripped the back of her waist and leaned in for a deep, intensely intimate kiss. His thumbs grazed her cheeks. Her entire body—which had been dormant since her divorce—sprang to life. She left in such a giddy stupor that she'd speed-dialed Lee before she even knew what was happening. She made up some lame excuse as to why she'd called and hung up before she told her where she'd been.

Looking back, she should have. They should have had it out *then,* so it wasn't a secret now, so she could have shared every step of their relationship instead of treating it like some sinister secret. It could have even shifted Lee's interest in Noah, made her realize he was unavailable. Grace had seen the crush forming but had done nothing to stop it.

She sits up. Despite Lee's anger, she can't leave her out there. Grace thinks about the confession from the party and a protective rage settles over her. Though Lee puts on a good front, she's still fragile. She tries to bury all that sadness, but it's there. Grace recognizes it.

She tiptoes downstairs and listens for signs of Lee in the house. On the back deck, the chairs are empty and the blankets refolded. She scans the backyard, then heads inside. She searches the downstairs couch and the empty guest room and even walks up to their room again and hunts for the bathroom light shining beneath the closed door.

No Lee.

She checks her phone for a missed text and decides to go back outside. She'll do a quick loop, see if she can find her so they can talk. One way or another, they are working this out.

betray
<u>*betraybetraybetraybetraybetraybetraybetraybe-*</u>
<u>*traybetraybetraybetraybetray*</u>

What does it mean to be betrayed?
Now I know.
I know what it means to be betrayed.
I know what it feels like to be betrayed.

I know how it moves inside of me, a rage unlike anything I have ever known.
I think we've all probably betrayed someone: a friend, a lover, even ourselves.
But this . . .

I don't know how to handle this.
What do I do?
How do I get past this?

This is the type of betrayal you just don't forget.

26

lee

Lee woke to the sound of her father's laugh. How long had it been since she'd heard him laugh? She checked the time, groaned, and sat up. Last night's photo shoot barreled through her mind. It had been some of her best work to date, and Kevin, one of the industry's top stylists, noticed. She'd worked so hard to build a stellar portfolio and it was finally paying off.

Lee climbed out of bed, stretched, and went to brush her teeth. She hadn't told Shirley about the photo shoot. It was childish, but she wanted this one thing for herself. As she scrubbed, she thought about how much had changed in the past two years. Her best friend had gone to rehab and stayed clean. Shirley had even made it into cosmetology school and then apprenticed with Lee.

Lee knew it wasn't a competition, but she was getting tired of all of this copycat behavior. Yes, it was important for her best friend to have goals, but she wanted her to have her own goals—not just snatch hers. Becoming a hair stylist wasn't just something you did because you'd run out of other options. It took dedication and skill. Like everything else, Lee assumed Shirley would grow bored and move onto something else.

Laughter drifted from the kitchen again, and Lee

paused in the hallway. She knew that laugh. She rounded the corner. Had she missed a call or text from Shirley?

Leaning against the countertop, Shirley was wearing her father's Titans T-shirt and eating a bowl of corn flakes. For the millionth time, Lee registered how similar they now looked.

Shirley joked it was like the couples who had been together for long stretches of time, or dogs and their owners. They started to look and act just like each other, but Lee wasn't convinced. In the past few months, Shirley had taken an unhealthy obsession in wanting to be as skinny as Lee. In wearing Lee's clothes. In having the same hair. In wanting the same profession. In fitting into Lee's family.

Harold stood next to her, already slurping his second beer. He exhaled smoke from a nubby joint and admired Shirley as she lifted onto her tiptoes in search of a mug. Her calves tightened and Lee swallowed the revulsion for her father's leering stare.

"Hey, Lee Bee." Shirley turned and smiled. "Coffee?"

"Sure." She glanced at the clock. "What are you doing here so early?"

"I'm always here."

"I know, but what are you doing here . . . like this?" She gestured to the T-shirt and bare legs.

Shirley secured two mugs and offered them in her direction. "Drinking coffee."

"Dad?"

Shirley shifted back down to flat feet and fastened her hands around her tiny waist, the mugs dangling from her thumbs. "Well, I guess now is as good a time as any." Shirley looked at Harold then back at Lee. "Don't freak out."

"Why would I freak out?" Lee could tell she was

about to freak out, but she waited for Shirley to explain what was going on.

"We're together."

Lee looked between them. *No, not possible.* "Who's together?"

Harold's glassy eyes focused on his daughter as he exhaled smoke into the air. "We are."

Shirley took a few steps toward Harold and wormed against his chest. Lee watched, horrified, as Shirley situated *her father's* arm around her shoulders. She inhaled sharply as her entire body began to shake.

Sensing her discomfort, Shirley extricated herself and poured Lee a cup of coffee. "Here. Let's talk about it." She offered her the drink, and Lee had to refrain from slapping it out of her hands.

When Lee didn't take it, Shirley retracted the cup. "I'm sorry I didn't tell you. I knew you'd be mad. Are you mad?"

Her eyes were dilated, and Lee searched for the pills or powders scattered on the counter like roaches. She grabbed the crooks of her arms and ran her fingers over the unblemished skin on the inside of each elbow. How quickly she believed Shirley would relapse.

Shirley yanked her arms back, obviously insulted. "I'm not on drugs, Lee. Jesus."

"Well what the hell am I supposed to think?" She tried to untangle the truth. First her looks, then her career, and now her father? She glanced at him, awaiting some sort of logical explanation.

This was her best friend. They couldn't be dating. She almost choked on the word, on how ludicrous it sounded. She tried to say it out loud, but it rolled around her mouth like sour candy. Lee batted through the chaotic thoughts. Shirley patiently waited for her to respond, to somehow tell her it was okay, but she couldn't. She looked from him to her.

"I don't get it." She shot an incredulous look at her dad. Memories lurched to the surface of her mind . . . how he used to take her fishing, show her how to tie sailor knots, change tires, shoot cans on sizzling tin roofs. He was a decent father before her mother died. It was like she'd somehow forgotten that it hadn't always been so awful, that he hadn't always been such a lousy drunk.

"What's the problem?"

"The problem is that you're dating someone *my age* who now looks just like me. Doesn't that seem twisted to you?"

Shirley self-consciously fingered her new bangs. Did she not see the situation for what it was? Lee knew about her roster of men, how she met them after work or between shifts, sometimes early in the morning or late at night. She kept them away from Lee, that romantic part of her life highly secretive, just like her real family, even though Lee was desperate to know whom she liked and where she'd come from. Though they'd met years ago, Shirley never talked about her past. She only focused on today and tomorrow. It was one of the things Lee loved most about her—but also one of the things that frustrated her.

Every time Lee thought she'd figured out the man of the day or could decipher who she spent hours each night talking to on the phone, Shirley had already moved on. But this didn't seem like a fleeting male in a lineup of endless, faceless conquests. This was different.

Lee fixed her eyes on her father. "So, what? You two are in love or something?"

He shrugged and popped another top. "Would that be so impossible?"

Lee nodded. "Yes, Dad. It would. It would be extremely impossible."

He swiped the rest of the six-pack from the counter, along with the crumpled pack of cigarettes he clenched between dirty fingernails. He'd worked on the car yesterday and the oil spots and grime remained. Had he touched Shirley with those hands? Lee worked her way up to his face, one she rarely studied anymore. He was still handsome in a rugged, worn sort of way. He'd been compared to Clint Eastwood his whole life. So many of his sins had constantly been forgiven because of his face, and she was just sick of it. This behavior would not be tolerated in *her* house.

He pinched a white stick and wedged it between chapped lips, unlit. "Shirl, let's go to the lake. Want to?" The cigarette trembled with every syllable. He sniffed, looked at Lee, and moved past her into the hall. "I'm sorry, Lee. But this is my life too."

His life too? "What's that supposed to mean?"

"It means I'm entitled to be happy." He shrugged and retreated toward the bedroom.

The lake was her mother's place. Harold had taken her mother there every Saturday for as long as she'd been alive. He'd never taken Shirley there before. Had he? She wanted to shake some sense into both of them. Shirley was twenty-seven years old. Her father was fifty-two. He couldn't have sex with someone the exact same age as his daughter.

Shirley gripped Lee's elbow, and it startled her. She'd almost forgotten Shirley was even in the room. Ragged nails chewed into the flesh of her biceps until she wrenched free of the desperate fist.

"I'm sorry." Shirley retreated a few steps. "I know you're angry."

"Angry? I don't even understand how this happened. *When* this happened." When had they ever had a stolen moment, a furtive glance, a second to morph from her best friend's father to the possibility of romance? A thousand warnings she'd probably missed between them fired through her brain: suggestive looks, lingering conversations, time spent together in her absence. Had their budding relationship become obvious to everyone but her?

"I know. But I've always liked your dad. He just gets me." She shrugged her slight shoulders as her father just had, her clavicles pointy and somehow still highly seductive through the thin cotton of her dad's T-shirt. Were these the details her father had noticed, even fantasized about? The thought turned her stomach.

Why couldn't Shirley see Harold for who he was? That he would hurt her. That he wasn't good enough for her. That Shirley, in some sick way, was replacing her mother. It was the ultimate betrayal.

"No, *I* get you," Lee finally said. "You're my best friend. We're the same age. We like the same things. That's my dad in there. He's . . ." *Old. Sad. Tired. Off-limits.*

"I know. And I've tried to put myself in your shoes. I really have. I've thought about how I'd feel if the situation were reversed. What I'd say."

"And what would you say?"

"Well, I guess I'd just want you both to be happy."

Lee rolled her eyes. "What a crock of shit."

"Look, I know you think he's a bad guy, but he's not, Lee. He's just heartbroken." Shirley reached for her again and then lowered her hand.

"What, and your vagina is going to make him all better?" Lee crossed her arms. "This is not happening. I won't *let* it happen."

Shirley straightened, her jaw set. "It's already happened."

"So stop then."

"I don't want to." Shirley crossed her arms to match Lee's.

"What are you, five? I'm telling you right now." Lee leaned closer and refrained from shaking Shirley like a rattle. "Either choose whatever this is with Harold or your friendship with me. I mean it." She'd never given Shirley an ultimatum, but she resisted the urge to apologize. She wasn't the one who should be sorry.

Shirley gazed at her bare feet. "Please don't make me do that." When she lifted her head, she had tears in her eyes, and Lee recoiled. Did Shirley truly care *that* much about her pathetic father?

"You need to talk to me about all of this. Right now."

Shirley wiped her eyes. "I'm not talking to you about it. Not when you're being so aggressive."

Lee laughed. "Aggressive? Are you kidding?"

"Besides"—Shirley stood up straighter but her eyes were wildly insecure—"it's really none of your business anyway."

Lee felt as though she'd been slapped. "You're unbelievable." She swiped her car keys, slammed the front door, and slid into the driver's seat of her car.

27

noah

Noah pulled up to the school at seven thirty. He was taking a half day today so he could fly to Philly. He adjusted his tie and checked his teeth for lodged kale from his morning smoothie. He'd worked for Music City Open School since obtaining his master's degree, and he was thinking of going solo, of becoming a full-time at-home occupational therapist, because he could organize his days and work on therapies outside the confines of such a rigid curriculum.

Noah waved to the slew of teachers in the hallway and slipped inside his gym. He checked his email before first period, and then his texts. His parents expected him for dinner tonight. It was his brother's twenty-third birthday tomorrow, and Noah had snagged a set of *Saturday Night Live* tickets to surprise him. Wyatt had never been to a live production, or New York, but *SNL* had been his favorite program since childhood.

It had been a while since he'd been back to Philly. He used to go most weekends, but life—and work—seemed to constantly get in the way.

He breezed through the morning and left just after lunch, arriving in Philly early evening, tired and in need of a beer. He parked the rental car in the building's garage and took the elevator up. He calculated how long it had been since his last visit. Christmas? He knocked on the door and waited for his mother to open it.

Time had not been kind to her. Her eyes were marred by a network of lines that tugged her entire face toward her feet. Her shoulders stooped under her shawl. Her bones had grown smaller, and her silver hair reached for him, as though she'd been accosted by static. Errant hairs had escaped from her signature bun, and she hurried to tuck them back in with bobby pins she clutched in her fist like flower stems. His father, tall but spreading, sidled up behind her and pulled Noah into a hug.

"He finally comes home."

"Good to see you, Dad."

"You too."

He could smell Hamburger Helper, the childhood staple Wyatt refused to let go of, even in his second decade of life. He moved to the kitchen. The casserole bubbled on the stove—cooked in the same pot his mother had used for thirty-plus years—and felt a small tug in his heart.

"How's Nashville?"

"Good. Busy."

His father offered him a beer. "Good, good."

Noah popped the top. "I've been thinking of branching off on my own, actually. Getting some private clients."

"Why?" His mother grabbed a wooden spoon and lifted the top of the casserole dish. "That school adores you."

"They do, but there's so much red tape there, Ma." He took a swig. "More money and freedom on my own."

"But what about benefits? A 401(k)?"

"You do what's best for you," his dad said. He lifted his spectacles, angled them up to the light, and wiped smooth, even circles with the lip of his shirt. "That sort of stuff tends to work itself out."

"Where's Wyatt?" Noah could hardly contain the anticipation to see his brother. He thought he'd be waiting for him at the door, but no. His parents had probably not alerted him to his arrival.

"Getting dressed." His father glanced at his watch. "For the last twenty-five minutes or so."

Noah took another swallow and stood. "I'll get him." He walked down the carpeted hall and knocked on the first door to the right. Stickers covered the wood, and his eyes pored over all of the band names and hilarious quotes his brother had pressed there over the years.

"Who is it?"

"Noah."

He heard a sharp yelp, and the door opened. No matter how long passed between visits, he still saw the kid in him. Wyatt's pale, freckled complexion and blond hair were a stark contrast to Noah's dark hair and olive skin, but they shared the same green eyes. Wyatt's face cracked in a smile as he elicited their secret handshake. No hugs. Never hugs.

"How are you?"

"Good. I am very good now. And how are you on this fine day?" He stared at the floor as he said it and shifted from foot to foot.

"I'm great. Excited to see you. Do you want to come eat?"

"What are we having?"

"Hamburger Helper."

"Then yes. Yes, yes, *yes*." Wyatt ambled to the front room, knocking into the edge of the piano with his hip. He'd always been clumsy, especially after he'd broken his right leg falling down a flight of stairs. His bones had never set right, and he often dragged his right leg behind him like a lame limb. Their parents were whispering in hushed tones, their backs to the stove. Noah cleared his throat.

His father turned first and smiled. "Wyatt, is it good to see your big brother?"

"The best," he said. He turned to Noah. "How long can you stay?"

Noah hesitated. "I can stay for a few days." He scratched his chin. "Because, if I recall correctly, someone has a birthday."

Wyatt smiled and jerked a thumb toward his chest. "That would be this guy."

They shuffled into their proper positions around the dinner table. His mother scooped the casserole onto his plate, and he thanked her. Noah chewed a mouthful of the greasy fare and joined the small talk about the weather, the latest politics, and a recent school shooting in New York.

Wyatt soaked up the conversation and asked his brother everything he could. Wyatt loved big, grandiose stories, so Noah dug deep and told him about things he didn't over Skype. Things he only touched upon in his letters. He shared how he'd gone to Haiti last summer—though Wyatt already knew this story, he still loved to hear it— and built houses in the unforgiving sun; how he worked to bring clean water to small African villages and what vaccinations he'd had to get before going. (Wyatt was fascinated with needles.) He shared how he spent his free time on the weekends with kids like Wyatt, who were on the spectrum, kids with Down syndrome, and cerebral palsy. He told him about all the races he'd run for cures during the last twelve months, collecting jerseys like medals. How he'd crushed an Ironman in Hawaii. How he'd climbed Mt. Kilimanjaro. How he went scuba diving in the Great Barrier Reef. How he'd taken up indoor rock climbing.

What he didn't tell him was *why* he did all these things. How it was all a distraction. How it filled time. How, if he couldn't live in the same city as his little brother, he'd keep himself busy with other rewarding outlets. He'd spent so many years building his career, and he couldn't leave— not now.

Noah had always wanted to be there for his brother, to care for him in the same way he cared for his students, but his parents had moved from Nashville right before Noah started college. He'd already accepted his scholarship to Vanderbilt, and then his father had purposely taken a job in Philadelphia. It was too late to get into any other college or even apply. He was stuck with an impossible choice: move with his family or pursue his education and ultimately, his career.

He'd never forgiven them for their abrupt decision. Even as he'd concocted ways for Wyatt to stay behind in Nashville, their age difference prevented it. Wyatt had been just a kid. And, as his parents had been so quick to remind him, Noah was Wyatt's brother, not his parent. It was *their* job to raise him—not his.

Wyatt asked endless questions at dinner until his parents went to bed. Noah soaked up his brother's energy. This was what he'd come for anyway. He didn't care to spend time with his parents.

He just wanted his brother all to himself.

28

noah

Noah slept fitfully on the pull-out sofa. He could hear the city sounds drifting into the cheap apartment windows: horns, car alarms, ambulances, bums. He'd always been shocked his parents had moved somewhere so loud, but his mother insisted Wyatt loved it. Even all these years later, Noah wasn't convinced.

He heard footsteps in the kitchen. Noah worked himself to sitting. His left shoulder throbbed from the odd angle on the couch. He ran a hand through his hair, pulled on a T-shirt, and padded to the kitchen.

"Morning, Ma."

"Sorry. Did I wake you?"

"It's fine. Couldn't sleep."

She shook some grounds into the coffeemaker. He filled the carafe for her and turned it on, and they both waited as the water started to heat and hiss into the pot. She seemed so frail, weathered in places she'd once been strong.

"What's on the agenda for the birthday boy?"

"Well." His mother opened the cabinet and pulled down two mugs. "We normally take him to the YMCA because he can swim there. He loves to swim now. Did I tell you that?" She rotated in a tired circle and Noah removed the mugs from her hands. "There's a wonderful instructor, Heather, who keeps an eye on him. I think he has a crush on her, if you ask me. But it's been great for his leg. And then we usually do the library, a movie, or come back here." She poured him a cup and pushed it across the island. "Too much isn't good for him, you know . . ."

He ignored the prick of frustration and drank his coffee. They treated Wyatt so gingerly, like an ornament. Wyatt thrived with order, physical activity, routine, and set social engagements. He consistently sent suggestions to his parents, made appointments for Wyatt that they canceled, and encouraged them to put him on the same curriculum as his students.

But Noah didn't live here. Therefore, he could no longer dictate his care. As he sipped, the irony was not lost on him that he took such precautions with his other students. He had their routines scheduled to the most personalized detail, but the person who mattered most to him lived in a cramped city, up here, in this tiny apartment, like a bird in a cage.

"You need to expand what he's doing, Ma. It's important for him to try new things. Otherwise, he'll become resistant to change."

Her fingers flexed around the shell of an egg, and he thought it might burst in her hand. "You know, Noah, we do the best we can. He's doing just fine."

He set down his mug. "Is he? Is he really?"

Wyatt shuffled out, hair on end, and lifted his hand in a wave.

"There's the birthday boy!" his mother trilled.

"Happy birthday, buddy. How does it feel to be forty?"

Wyatt stopped at the entrance of the kitchen and tugged on the hem of his T-shirt. "I am not forty. I am approximately twenty-three years old. You are eight years older than me, so you're thirty-one years old. Which *is* very old."

"Don't dig me an early grave just yet." Noah hopped off the bar stool and rummaged in his bag to find the tickets. "I have a surprise for you. Sit."

Wyatt pulled himself onto the bar stool. "A surprise! It's been so long since I've had a surprise." He shot a knowing look at their mother. "Gimme."

"Close your eyes and hold out your hands."

Wyatt did as he was told. He could sense the nerves of his mother on the other side of the island as she wiped her hands on a dish towel. Noah laid the tickets in his waiting palms and watched as Wyatt's eyes attempted to focus on the tiny print.

"Do you know what those are?"

"Tickets. They are tickets."

"Yes. But do you know what type of tickets?"

Wyatt squinted and screamed. "*Saturday Night Live* tickets?" His eyes flew to Noah and toward his mother, just missing their mark. "Are we really going to go see *Saturday Night Live*? In New York City?"

Noah smiled and his chest warmed. "Just me and you, buddy. A night on the town."

"For my birthday?" Wyatt clutched the tickets and vibrated with excitement.

"For your birthday."

"For my birthday that's tonight? For this birthday that is today?"

"That's right. That's why I'm here. I wanted to surprise you." Noah almost tossed his mother a smug smile but refrained. They never made him *this* happy. Why didn't they surprise him? Why did they keep the world away?

Wyatt bounced up and down on the stool like a five-year-old, scraping the bottom of the wooden legs across the linoleum. His mother cringed and opened her mouth to protest, but Noah stepped in. "You know what? Why don't you get dressed, and we'll go play some basketball. Have you been playing?"

Wyatt shot their mother another look, as though the concept of basketball—something he used to do daily for hand-eye coordination—was as foreign as the tickets in his hand.

"That's okay if it's been a while. Go get ready, and I'll take you out today. For your birthday. We'll play basketball and go get some lunch. Sound good? Is that okay, Ma?"

His mother turned back to the counter so he couldn't read her face. "Sure."

His brother hopped off the stool, tickets clutched in his fist, as he yelled about going to New York.

She turned, one hand on her hip. "That was way too generous, Noah."

Noah shrugged. "My brother only turns twenty-three once."

"Look—"

His father walked into the room, a newspaper under his arm. "What's the birthday boy so excited about?"

"The *SNL* tickets," his mother said, scooping eggs onto a plate. "Eat, or your eggs will get cold." She dropped the pan in the sink and flicked on the water, and a plume of steam sizzled into the air. She wiped her hands again and left the kitchen, his father smiling uncomfortably as he grabbed a fork to dig in.

29

noah

After a long day spent together, Noah felt right at home. He'd forgotten their hidden language; how navigating Wyatt's mind was like a wildly inventive puzzle he loved to solve. He was a little rusty, but not by much. They showered back at the condo, got dressed, and gathered in the living room for a small birthday celebration. They sang to Wyatt, and then he blew out his candles on a cake bought at their favorite local bakery. His mother cut a wedge of vanilla cake with bright blue frosting and handed him a small, square piece.

"Your lips look like a blueberry," Noah said.

"So do yours," Wyatt added.

"Do you have everything you need for tonight?" his mother asked, as she poked at the frosting with a plastic fork.

"Tickets, check. Wyatt, check. I think we're all good." Sensing her nerves, Noah added: "Tell them we'll behave, Wyatt."

"We will behave, Ma. We will behave," Wyatt repeated. He dumped his paper plate in the trash and turned to Noah. "Let's go. I don't want to be late. If we are late, we cannot go in. I have researched the schedule this afternoon. They are very strict."

"You got it, boss man." They waved good-bye, took the elevator down to the first floor, and climbed into Noah's rental car.

"You ready?"

"Born ready. Born ready," Wyatt said, moving back and forth against the passenger seat. Noah had already memorized the directions, so he wouldn't have to rely on an app. The constant verbal interruptions agitated Wyatt.

Noah pressed *play*. He'd made a CD for him before he'd left. It was a compilation of his favorite songs—one for every year of his life. Wyatt sang, rocked, and clapped off-beat, and Noah joined in when he recognized the lyrics.

The ninety minutes went fast, despite the insane city traffic. Noah felt the vibration from his parents' obsessive texts in his pocket and clenched his teeth. He turned the music down as they approached the center of the island. "Welcome to New York, brother."

Wyatt gasped at the city streets. The glittering lights, clustered bodies, and urban mayhem took hold as Noah drove through Times Square. The city had a pulse, and they were situated right in the heart. Wyatt stabbed the button of the passenger window and thrust his large head into the noisy night. Life exploded in every direction. He reached out as if to collect the energy.

"Pretty cool, huh?"

"It's majestic! Look!" Wyatt had extremely good hearing and perfect recall. He could recognize ambulances, sirens, car alarms, and any sort of traffic coming from a block away. But those were individual noises, always stories below, always containable. Was this too much?

Wyatt turned and gripped the door with both hands—and for one frightening moment, Noah wondered if he was going to try and jump out of the car. "Why have Ma and Pop never brought me here?"

Guilt knifed Noah's conscience. He could have given him such a fulfilled life. He could have made him feel alive every single day. "I don't know."

Drivers laid on horns as they inched by. Saturday evening traffic lurched in every direction while digital billboards talked, flashed, and rotated. Tourists gathered on sidewalks and in streets. Stimulation edged its way to the very center of Wyatt's brain, rewiring it. They were so close to the plaza, Noah could just park in a garage and they'd be there in minutes. But he wanted to give Wyatt more than this. It was his one night away from home. He turned right and headed away from Midtown.

"Where are we going? Why are we leaving?"

"We're just going to park away from all the traffic, so you can see more of Manhattan. Is that okay?"

"Are we going to be late?"

"We have plenty of time, Wyatt."

He nodded rapidly. "Yes, then yes, then yes. I want to see more."

Noah thought of all his various trips to the city when he was young. His parents had taken him a few times before they'd had Wyatt. He had vivid memories of Central Park, The Metropolitan Museum of Art, and eating pizza in Brooklyn. Once Wyatt came, fussy and uncontained, they'd closed themselves in their house like an underground bunker. No more trips. No more spontaneity. They'd reduced themselves to rigor, order, and sacrifice for the past two decades.

He found a parking spot close to the subway and killed the engine. "Would you like to walk or take the subway?"

"Subway. Subway all the way."

Noah nodded. Wyatt loved subways and tunnels. He'd often sketched black, scary holes filled with trains in therapy sessions. He remembered that. They found the nearest station and descended down the stairs. Noah paid for their tickets. They pushed through the turnstile and stood on the escalator as warm, dank air rustled around them.

Wyatt leaned forward and back on the platform.

"Hey, Wyatt, what's the difference between a teacher and a steam locomotive?"

"One's a person and one's not."

Noah laughed. "That's true, but a schoolteacher tells you to spit out your gum, while the locomotive says *choo, choo, choo*! Get it?"

"That is a terrible joke, a terrible joke," Wyatt said. His mop of blond hair shot into tangled waves above his scalp.

Noah laughed again while the lights of the train flashed down the tracks. They illuminated his younger brother, and just for a moment, turned him golden.

"Train!"

Noah smiled and clapped him lightly on the shoulder. "I told you it would be here." He glanced at his watch. "Right on time too."

The train thundered closer and blew stale air into the jammed underground lair, as people texted, fisted dog-eared paperbacks, and held loud, personal conversations over the rumble of the approaching car.

As the train neared, Wyatt tipped back on his heels again—in gummy tennis shoes he refused to throw away—and then as quickly as he'd ever moved, darted forward three short steps, extended his arms, and took flight off the platform.

Noah watched him lunge, too stunned to reach for him in time. A woman beside him screamed. The timing—

never Wyatt's strong suit—was perfect as his soft body, built on a lifetime of Cheetos and Cokes, intersected with a sickening thunk into the front side of the train. His brother disappeared with the screech of brakes. "Wyatt!" He called his name in a futile attempt to retrieve him, to rewind, to go back just a few seconds. Time cracked apart, froze, shattered. Noah tried to move, but he couldn't. He could physically still feel his brother standing right next to him, smiling and laughing. He couldn't be gone. He couldn't have jumped.

Chaos erupted around him. People murmured and gathered in tight clusters while the train squealed to a violent shudder on the tracks. Noah's skin warmed and turned hot. He collapsed to his knees. He had to be dreaming. He'd just told Wyatt a joke. He'd laughed. He'd been excited for New York and *SNL*. *No, no, no.* Had Wyatt made some kind of horrendous miscalculation? Had he gone momentarily insane? He couldn't have done this on purpose.

He glanced again at the train, his eyesight blurred by tears. He couldn't imagine what they would have to do to remove Wyatt's body from the train, like gum stuck to a shoe. Noah vomited from the image, the blue frosting and cake batter splashing back onto his own wet cheeks.

People huddled around the front of the train, snapping photos and calling for help. Finally, someone crouched down and touched his shoulder with acrylic nails. Her perfume wafted into his nostrils, and he gagged.

"Sir? Are you okay? Do you know that person?"

He sat back on his heels. "It's my brother," he croaked. "My brother just killed himself."

He said the words, but he didn't believe them. He'd spent his entire life devoted to helping his younger brother function in society—teaching him to read, to communicate, to handle loud noises and confrontation, to be nice to waiters, to play ball, to drive, to vote—and now he was dead.

In minutes, the police arrived, and he stood on rubbery legs. He replayed those last moments in an attempt to understand what must have been running through his brother's mind. In the car. At the condo. Eating cake. Earlier in the day. There'd not been a single sign of distress.

Officers flanked him on both sides and escorted him away like a criminal. He glanced to the front of the train and saw his brother, broken apart like an egg. *Oh, Wyatt.* He fell again, dry heaving.

How would he ever explain this to his family? He would be blamed. This would forever be his fault. The teacher. The mentor. Noah, who always knows best. He closed his eyes as pain assaulted every part of his body.

"Sir. Are you alright? Sir?"

He ignored the officers and glanced again at the front of the train. He vomited again from the sight, the loss, and the shock of losing the only person he'd ever really loved.

There was no life without Wyatt.

Not for him.

30

lee

The hot steering wheel singed the palms of her hands as she drove. She'd woken up so excited about the photo shoot last night, and now this. What was she supposed to do with *this*?

She screamed and banged the wheel. Her mind drifted to the first time Shirley and Harold must have kissed. His lingering looks. How they were probably in his bedroom right now. Her *mother's* bedroom. The betrayal stung. Shirley was always so secretive. About men. About her family. About her past life.

But this wasn't about being private—this was her father. Though Shirley had taken such a visceral interest in Lee's life, getting involved with her father seemed unstable, sick. It made her realize that she might not really know who Shirley was. Best friends didn't do things like this to each other.

She wound down Lebanon Pike toward Mt. Juliet and then back again, wondering where she could go. For the first time in her entire life, she wanted a drink. She'd stayed away from it like the plague. Her father was an addict. What if she was too? Alcohol had taken away so much: her mother and brother, her father, even Shirley for a period of time when she was addicted to drugs.

She roamed the neighborhood. Lee remembered going on long walks around the neighborhood with her mother; water fights on humid days; picnics beneath their ancient weeping willow; driving to Whitt's Barbecue and feasting on hot, juicy sandwiches. They were snapshots in her brain, a series of quick images from their brief years together.

She circled the lot of her father's favorite liquor store and parked. She was a regular, buying his beer every day like clockwork. The tinkle of bells above the door welcomed her. She waved to Dan behind the register and then stopped with an icy realization: she'd spent years bashing her father for his choices, but she was the one *enabling* him with every six-pack she brought home. With every month that passed where she let him slide on helping with the mortgage. With never insisting he move out of her house—the house she paid for.

She was as much to blame as he was.

She bypassed the beer and let her fingers trail across the random bottles. Over the years, she'd become an observer of other people's habits around alcohol. How they used it as a reward—even a crutch. She assessed the brown and clear liquids aged inside thick glass. If she were to drink, what would she choose?

Even the thought of drinking sent her into a tailspin of grief. Her mother's beautiful face flashed through her mind, and she almost turned and left. Instead, she trailed by the vodka and bourbon and balked at the absurd prices. She hated the smell of liquor. Beer reminded her of her father. Cocktails were too much work. Wine? She turned down the aisle with various grapes from expensive regions. Wine was healthy, wasn't it? She'd just read an article about wine being good for your heart. She plucked a blend from the bunch. Her fingers shook, and before she knew what she was doing, she walked to the register. Dan smirked and hopped off his stool to ring her up.

"The old man trying something new today?" He tucked a greasy strand of hair behind his ear.

Lee rocked forward on her elbows. "Not for the old man."

He lifted the bottle. "Thought you didn't drink."

She didn't drink. She *never* drank. Her whole adult life, people told her to loosen up, to live a little, to come out for a drink after work, but she refused—so much so that people stopped asking. No one understood. Alcohol hadn't ruined *their* whole lives, hadn't stolen their entire family. For most people, alcohol was social, celebratory, happy. She looked at Dan and somehow felt guilty. "I don't."

He rung her up without question and lowered the wine into a paper bag. He twisted the top and dropped her change and receipt into her waiting palm. A jolt of anxiety expanded through her chest. What was she doing? Alcohol wasn't the answer. She gripped the bottle in her arms as she stepped outside. The weight of it felt dangerous. She turned back toward the entrance. Did Dan accept refunds?

In the car, her fingers hesitated before she screwed off the top and sniffed. As the glass cooled her fingers, she thought again about Shirley and her father. What a mess her home life had become while her professional life was finally gaining traction. She took a small sip and was surprised by the taste.

She sucked the spare drops from her lips and opened up Facebook on her phone, typing in Shirley's name. She looked for any connection to her father, any signs or clues she'd missed. He had an account he rarely used, and she constantly asked why he was even on there. Was it to be a voyeur into Shirley's life? Did they send each other messages?

She reviewed her friend's wall and noticed that a mutual friend was asking about a party in a few days. Shirley had mentioned it in passing. She clicked on the details. She needed to talk to her. Shirley owed her a conversation, an explanation. Did Shirley miss her own father? Was she just lonely? Or maybe she'd finally run out of men. There had to be a logical explanation for what was happening. Yes, she felt betrayed, but Shirley was also her best friend.

The anger loosened as she took another sip. Was she allowed to sit in her car, drinking like this? She screwed the top back on and wedged the bottle underneath the seat.

She had an entire day to kill. She couldn't go back to the house. She locked the door and began to walk. She thought about Shirley. How sexual she was. How powerful. How unapologetic. How free. How she could get anyone she wanted, whenever she wanted. She never thought about consequences or what could go wrong. But she was such a contradiction. She said she *wanted* to be more like Lee. That Lee was going places. That she wanted to be more responsible. But she did nothing to show that she really wanted those things, or that Shirley would ever be anyone other than what she'd always been: reckless.

As the alcohol laced her system, something stirred. It was time for a change. It was time for her to create her own life. She'd become almost dependent on Shirley's attention. While it had inflated her ego at first, she now realized it was a subtle power move on Shirley's part. She wanted the career Lee had. She wanted the house Lee lived in. She wanted to look just like Lee. She wanted her father. Had Lee simply enabled Shirley to want *more* of her family, instead of paying attention to her own life? Maybe that was her purpose in life—to be an enabler.

She shook her head and headed back to the car. Lee needed to reclaim who she was—independent of both of them. Her mother would have wanted more for her—to be bold and brave, to find love, to find herself.

She unlocked the car, pulled out her phone, and re-checked the details of the party. Maybe she'd show up at the party in some hot outfit and let confidence lead the way. It would be the perfect place to be noticed. Being noticed came *before* being loved.

She'd show Shirley. She'd show her father. She'd show herself.

She started the car and drove to Percy Priest Lake. She fished the bottle of wine from beneath the seat and walked to the water's edge. She cleared her mind, sat on a rock, and began to drink.

31

noah

When he got back from Wyatt's funeral, dreary from the late flight, he showered, made a double shot espresso, and walked to the basketball court to drop in on a pickup game. Hadn't he just been on the court with Wyatt for his birthday? He could still see the way his brother had excitedly gripped the ball, clumsy in his dribbles, but whooping with joy at every attempted shot.

He replayed the fight he'd had with his parents before he flew back. They'd confessed Wyatt had been showing suicidal tendencies for months, but they'd never uttered a word. He felt betrayed they hadn't warned him. It was dangerous to take his brother on a city outing where anything could happen.

Noah had worked with his fair share of suicidal students over the years, but Wyatt hadn't displayed any of the signs. At least not with him. But he had with his parents, and that's what mattered. He could have saved his life if they'd warned him. He could have prevented it. Wyatt could still be here.

The court was littered with shirtless, sweaty regulars. He laced his shoes and waved at Phil, an acquaintance he sometimes grabbed a beer with.

"You in today, Banks?"

"Yep." He stretched his arms over his head and heard his back crack.

"Cool. Four on four."

Noah's body was stiff from the flight and lack of sleep, but he ignored all the twinges and immediately fouled Charles, a loudmouthed show-off who loved to dunk.

"Take it easy."

"You take it easy." He was itching for a fight.

"What the fuck, Banks? Chill." Charles passed the ball back to Phil. "It's a game, dude."

Noah wanted to slam the ball in his face, but backed off and took a breath. "Just pass the ball."

Charles passed the ball, and Noah ducked around him to sink in a three-point shot.

"Ooh, look who came to play."

Phil passed the ball to Stewart, who passed it back to Noah.

"Something like that," Noah said, taking another shot and missing it. Every time he closed his eyes, he saw Wyatt with his arms spread like wings. How he'd wanted to be weightless. How it must have felt to be dragged across the train like something caught in a grater.

In one second, his beloved brother was there, and then he wasn't, and no matter what he did, how many games he played, how much he worked, how angry he was at his parents, or what punishment he doled out, it didn't change anything. Wyatt, his brother, his lifeline, his purpose, had taken his own life.

He kept seeing his mother's shattered face as he stormed out of their condo after the funeral. He knew his parents blamed him, and it felt like being stabbed in the fucking heart. He carried the burden of witnessing such violence—not them. He would never forget how beautiful his brother had looked on that platform, and then after, as he was carried away by the wind.

He needed to shut off his brain. He lost himself in the game, ending three points ahead of the other team. He squirted water into his mouth at the side of the court and wiped his face with a towel.

"Nice game, Banks," Phil said, clapping him on the back.

"You too."

"Why don't you come to my house tonight?" Phil asked as he removed his T-shirt and tugged on a clean one. "It's my birthday."

"Oh yeah? Happy birthday." Noah thought of Wyatt's birthday party and his blue lips as he licked frosting from a spoon.

"Lots of chicks, right, Phil?" Charles added as he stuffed his shoes into a bag.

"You seeing anyone, dude?" Phil asked.

Noah shook his head. "Nope."

"Come then. It'll be fun."

He hadn't told them what he'd just been through. The suicide. The guilt. His parents' blame like a whip. For one night, he needed to feel something other than this all-consuming, gut-wrenching anguish. The thought of getting blackout drunk was the only thing that sounded appealing. It beat sitting in his condo by himself.

"Sounds good, man. Thanks."

"Cool. I'll text you the details. Good game."

Noah slapped hands with the guys and watched them walk away. He collapsed on the bench. The exhaustion, the trauma, the flight, the drive, the funeral, and the game smashed into his body. He glanced at the time and wondered if it was too early to start drinking.

He'd go home, take a shower, and hit the pub. A few beers before the party couldn't hurt.

32

lee

Lee checked her makeup again in the mirror, fluffed her hair, and walked up the stone steps to the gorgeous bungalow. Shirley's client, Christy, was throwing a party for her boyfriend's birthday. Hopefully she'd slip right in as though she belonged. *Fake it until you* are *it,* Shirley always said.

Lee snorted as she entered the house and battled her thoughts. Shirley had literally taken that statement to a whole new level. She'd faked living Lee's life, when what she really needed to focus on was staying clean, standing on her own two feet, and getting away from her father. Why didn't she see that?

Bodies pressed into all corners of the house. Music blared, red Solo cups clenched in almost every fist. Lee hunted for any familiar faces but saw only strangers. She felt the customary urge to turn and run, but she squared her shoulders and went to get herself a drink. She'd never understood the draw of alcohol, but in the last twenty-four hours, it had taken the edge off. She felt more relaxed. She felt like she could do anything.

She shot Shirley a text and waited for her reply. What would Shirley do in this situation? Before Harold, she'd seek out the hottest guy in the room and have sex with him. Lee scoped out the men, spotting a few cute ones, but no one she'd want to take her clothes off for.

She got another drink. She'd already downed an entire bottle of wine earlier, alone in her room, while she listened to her dad and Shirley whisper through the thin walls. Probably talking about her, figuring out what to do. She couldn't think about them. The noises. The intimacy. The reality of what they were *doing* with each other. This entire train wreck had pushed her and Shirley's relationship into dangerous territory, and she wasn't sure they'd ever be able to recover. She poured herself a shot of something. She tossed it back, that lighter fluid sting warming her throat.

She checked her phone again. *Sorry. Not coming. Have fun.*

Lee resisted the urge to chuck her phone out the window. Instead, she fired off a text. *Get here NOW. You owe me. We have to talk.*

The ellipsis blinked at her, then disappeared. Lee gritted her teeth and wondered if she should just go home. It was too loud, and there were too many distractions for her to even think clearly. Instead, she walked to the middle of the living room, where a few girls danced by the couch, giggling and rosy-cheeked.

Lee began to tilt her hips left and right to the music. She locked eyes with some guy on the couch and let the alcohol numb her mind as her body sprang to life. She lifted her hands, ran them through her hair, and moved her body in ways she never had in public, soaking in the approving looks some of the men shot her way.

She danced until she was sweaty and drunk. She lurched back to the kitchen and realized she could barely keep her balance. She bumped into someone's back, turned, and apologized.

A hand on her shoulder forced her to turn, and she struggled to make her eyes focus.

"Lee?"

It was Shirley. She wore an amazing short black dress and jean jacket. How had she gotten here so fast? Shirley leaned in to smell her breath, and her intoxicating perfume made Lee's eyes water. "Are you *drunk*?"

Lee's eyes felt heavier than she wanted, and bile rose from all the dancing. "So?"

"So?" Shirley's mouth hung open. "Why in the world are you drunk? You don't drink."

"I do now." Lee suppressed the guilt. Shirley had been sober for two years and now *she* was the drunk friend.

"Why?"

"Why do you think?" she shouted. "You're sleeping with my father!"

Shirley looked pained and glanced around, embarrassed. "I know. I'm sorry. I don't know how it happened."

"Save it. You don't love him. You don't even care about my father. You could have any guy, and instead you choose him? Do you actually hate me that much or something?" She squinted at her. "Or is it daddy issues?"

Shirley gripped both elbows to keep her stationary. "Lee, you're my best friend. Don't be ridiculous."

She jerked free. "That man will eat you alive. He'll do the same thing he did to my mother."

Shirley stepped back. "That's not true."

Lee snorted. "Shirley, he's been utterly useless since my mother died. I've done everything to help him. All he does is drink and take up space." The moment she said it, she wished she could take it back. She didn't respect her father, but she still loved him.

"Look." Shirley gripped her forehead and dropped

her hand. "I don't know what you want me to do. What do you want me to do?"

"I want you to prove to me that my father is no different than any other guy."

Something fluttered across Shirley's face. "What does that mean?"

"It means I want you to sleep with someone else. Here. Tonight. At this party. Go find someone. Show me that what's happening between you and my father is nothing more than some sick joke."

Shirley rolled her eyes. "Let me take you home."

"*You* go home. I'm having fun." Lee headed for the bathroom. Throngs of people lined the hallway, so she climbed the stairs, careful to place one foot in front of the other. The wood of the staircase swirled, and the banister felt like a cool snake beneath her palm. She teetered on the top stair and gasped, afraid that she might tumble back and crash to her death in a pile of drunken bones. Not tonight.

Instead, she'd splash some water on her face, drink a few glasses of water, and head home. The talk with Shirley could wait. The noise of the party lessened on the landing. She stalled in the carpeted hallway, trying a few doors to try and locate a bathroom. Hall closet. Laundry. Office. There was a door at the back of the hallway to the left. She opened it and walked into a bedroom. It was dark, but there was light from a separate door—presumably the bathroom.

She thought of what awaited her tomorrow, a slew of clients and their stories of happy weekends or extraordinary adventures. She had no fun stories to tell, no crazy adventures. She couldn't even get properly drunk for the first time without messing it up. She twisted the knob and let herself into the bathroom. She splashed water on her face, wiped her hands, and took a few deep breaths. She flipped off the light as total blackness pushed in. Her reflexes slowed, and her world began to spin. The mixture of beverages rose and swirled. The back of her throat burned. She needed to get home.

She opened the door and jumped. The outline of someone hulked in the doorway. The person stepped forward, and before she knew what was happening, hands closed in on her as she was forced back into the bathroom.

Part 3

after the fall

I've learned that two people can look at the exact same thing and see something totally different.
— Anonymous

PRESENT

33

grace

Grace wakes to the strained rhythm of her own heart. The room is still dark, the blackout curtains drawn. Last night hurls into her consciousness. Lee's reaction. Her confession. The way she'd disappeared, angry and upset.

She doesn't know how she will explain herself this morning, or where she'll begin. She sighs into the bleak, dark room, realizing that probably isn't going to happen anytime soon; things are going to get even tenser before they get better. She needs to pee but can't see in the dark. She flicks on her bedside lamp and squints into the sudden bright light.

Lee's bed is empty.

It would be just like her to sleep on the couch, or even outside, just to prove her point. Despite her own confession, she thinks of what Lee told her about the man in the dark, the secret she's harbored all these years. She doesn't understand how a man could ever do that to someone else.

Grace rubs her hand over her belly. She takes a quick shower and heads downstairs. She checks the living room and kitchen. In the sink, the wineglasses sit, half-filled with soapy water. Outside, the skewers from the s'mores have been wiped clean and placed on top of the stack of folded blankets. The worry eases. Lee probably cleaned up and headed out for a walk this morning to clear her head.

She knows walking helps Lee sort through everything, just as it does for her. She fires off a text anyway. *Good morning. Can we have coffee?*

She inhales the clean, humidity-free air. She walks to the front, through the aquamarine gate, and to the edge of Lake Tomahawk.

Couples are already out, walking or jogging, and she wishes she had a cup of coffee and a book. She pans the path around the lake for Lee. A buzz vibrates her hip: Noah. She gives him an update and says she'll call him later. Lee's dark secret bubbles through the peace of the morning. Does Noah know about Mason's real father? Have they ever discussed it? It makes her sick to think of Mason being conceived out of something so depraved. How another human could take advantage of someone like that . . .

"What are you doing out here so early?" Alice, clad in expensive workout gear, jogs toward her.

"Me? What are you doing? Going for a run?" She approves of the expensive gear. "You look like an ad for Lululemon."

Alice strikes a pose. "Am I hired?"

Grace laughs. "Not when you pose like that."

"I'll work on it." Alice pauses by the bench and props up a leg to stretch her hamstring. "So, did you tell her?"

Grace sighs. "Did I ever."

Alice stops stretching. "Went that well, huh?"

Grace massages a temple. "She was outraged. Not that I'm surprised, but I shouldn't have told her like that." Grace thinks again about the confession Lee made and the selfish timing of her own. "I think I screwed everything up."

"She'll get over it," Alice says. "She has a crush. I'm sure it's hard to see through that. It's the first guy she's liked in a long time, right?"

Grace nods. "As long as I've known her."

"Right." She switches legs and folds over her quadriceps. "I'm sure she's just jealous, but you're her best friend. She'll be happy for you eventually."

"I hope so."

"I know so."

Grace glances at the house behind her. "Carol still asleep?"

Alice releases her leg and shoves her hands into her puffy vest. "Snoring like a trucker."

Grace laughs. "I'm so glad Chad never snored."

"Me too. Fred doesn't either. Does Noah?"

"What? Snore? No, thank God."

Alice sits and gently elbows her. "I'm super happy for you, by the way. Luca will be over the moon about having a brother or sister."

"You think so?"

"Of course. If I didn't think I'd lose my mind by adding another human to our household, I would have done it already."

Grace tries to think about holding a baby in her arms again after all these years. "Yeah, but there's something special about having just one too."

"True. Less expensive, at least." Alice slaps her thighs. "Should we go for a walk?"

Grace hesitates. "I really want to find Lee."

"Is she not sleeping?"

"She wasn't in the room when I got up."

Alice stands. "Maybe give her some space? It will do you some good to clear your head too."

They navigate the short path around the lake. Grace

searches the stray jogger or walker, hoping one of them will be Lee.

"So what did she do when you told her?"

"Well, let's see. She yelled. I listened. She told me I basically ruined her family. I finally went inside because I just didn't want to fight. But then I couldn't sleep, so I went and looked for her, but I couldn't find her."

"What do you mean?" Alice glances at her.

"She wasn't on the deck when I came back out." Grace recalls standing out there, searching into the black night.

"She probably just needed to process what you told her, don't you think?" Alice asks.

Grace shrugs. "That's what I was hoping, but what if she never came home?"

"Where else would she go? Clubbing?" She snorts.

A blast of sirens pierces their conversation. Two police cars whip down the curvy streets, to the base of the mountain Carol and Alice hiked yesterday. Grace can barely make out the trailhead through the thicket of trees.

"Jesus. I wonder what that's all about?" Alice murmurs.

"Hopefully no one got attacked by a bear," Grace says.

"Aren't bears still hibernating?"

"I have no idea. Carol would probably know." Grace checks her phone again and sends another text to Lee. An ambulance whines down the street, and the girls exchange concerned looks. "I don't like this," Grace says. "I have a bad feeling."

"About Lee?"

Grace can't tell her about their entire conversation, about the dark turn, the look in Lee's eyes as she revealed what happened at the party. "Can we just go look for her? Or wake Carol up? I just don't feel right. Lee *always* responds. I've texted her twice and nothing. And if anything happened to her, I don't know what . . ."

"Hey, slow down. It's fine. She probably just doesn't have her phone. Or maybe she's just not ready to talk yet."

They hustle back to Arbor House, just as Carol saunters out the front door in a fluffy white bathrobe and oversized slippers.

"Is Lee in there?"

Carol yawns and looks behind her. "Well good morning to you too."

"We can't find Lee."

Carol motions inside. "I literally just woke up." She cradles a cup of coffee and blows steam off the top. "What do you mean you can't find Lee?"

"She wasn't in the room this morning."

"So?"

"So, I don't think she ever came back last night." Her head fills with instant worst-case scenarios: a bear attack, being kidnapped, freezing to death.

"I'm sure she's fine."

Grace pushes past them and up to their room. Her heart births a staccato rhythm. She searches for Lee's phone. She dials her number, but it goes straight to voice mail. Her toiletries are untouched. Lee always makes it a point to go through the same bedtime routine: makeup remover, cleanser, moisturizer, teeth. It became a habit that started after she stopped drinking—when she used to fall asleep drunk and wake up to sour breath and raccoon eyes—and since she's become sober, Lee is obsessive about nighttime care.

Grace struggles to remember if there'd been a crack of light from the door last night, or a running faucet. Grace has always been a sound sleeper. Even if Lee had come in, she might not have heard her.

But where could she be?

"Come on. Where are you?" Grace sends another text, grabs her zip-up hoodie, and goes to find the girls.

34

grace

They scour the entire house to make sure Lee isn't somewhere they missed. Grace steps onto the back deck and looks for clues. She urges Carol and Alice to call Lee too, just in case Lee is only screening *her* calls.

She shakes out the blankets, searches under the chairs for Lee's phone, and then bumps into the blue recycling bin behind her. Maybe her phone fell in when she got up last night? She turns, crouches down, and rummages through it. The bottle of wine they had is there, and under a stack of newspapers is the other one. The truth slams into her as she stands, numb and unblinking. The bottle was unopened when she went inside. She's positive. "Carol?"

"Yeah?" She pokes her head out the back door.

Grace raises both bottles. "We only drank one of these last night, right?"

Carol squints. "The bin was empty except for the newspaper. I'm sure of it, because I didn't know if I could put glass in there. Why?"

Grace thinks of Lee out here, alone. She wouldn't have. Maybe she was tempted but just dumped it out. Grace notices the screw top back on the bottle. If it had been unopened, it wouldn't be empty. Grace gnaws the inside of her cheek.

"Do you really think she drank it?" Carol asks.

"Hey, you guys ready? Marge said she'll call if Lee shows up before we get back." Alice pulls on a light jacket and motions for them to follow. Grace lowers the bottles back into the recycling bin and joins Alice and Carol.

New worries fester along with Lee's absence. Did their fight cause a slip from sobriety, or was it the memory of her assault? They set out in the direction of the sirens, curious passersby popping their heads out of their homes or standing to gossip in the street about what's going on. The cool morning wind whips across their bodies.

"Windy," Alice mumbles, trying to keep the conversation light.

Carol joins in, but Grace's mind is elsewhere. Her skin drains of color with every step, and Alice, sensing her unease, latches onto her. "It's going to be fine. I promise. You'll see. This has nothing to do with Lee. It can't possibly."

She doesn't know what is possible or not possible. *Maybe Lee called an Uber to run an errand in the city center,* Carol suggests. *Maybe she's journaling in a park somewhere, or off on a walk on the opposite end of town,* Alice adds. *Maybe her phone is off.* Even as Grace calculates the different possibilities, none of them seems like a logical explanation for where she might be.

They all link arms as they round the corner to the start of the trail, a barrage of police cars, barking dogs, and one lone ambulance with its siren light shooting around in a silent circle. Grace searches for a dead body or crime scene tape. None. A small whoosh of air escapes her lungs.

Two officers sip coffee by their patrol cars. She turns to the girls. "Stay here, okay? I'll find out what's happening."

"Why don't you let us come with you?" Carol asks.

"No, it's fine. I just want to ask, then we can keep searching."

She crunches toward them, snapping twigs and leaves under overused tennis shoes. She stares between them, not knowing which one to address. "Excuse me, officers?"

The taller one looks down at her. "Ma'am?"

"May I ask what happened here?" Grace considers his answer: what she will do, how her body will respond, what words she'll say.

"We don't know all the details." He sniffs and looks at his partner. "Found a hiker at the bottom of the path."

"A hiker?" Icy fingers of dread began to peck her spine like a piano. *No, no, no.*

"It appears someone fell off the mountain."

"Man or woman?" Everything in Grace begs for the right answer. It feels as if her entire life depends on it.

"Woman."

Crushing grief pierces the flesh of her chest and rips. She sucks cold air, the woods around her starting to spin. Her hand finds its way to her belly and then up to her forehead, which is clammy and growing wet. "And this person is . . . ?" She waits for the reassurance that the woman—not Lee—is fine. That whoever fell is alive. That she is a *survivor.*

The officer clears his throat and the other one motions behind him. "Ma'am, we need to keep this area clear, so if you wouldn't mind . . ." He motions her along, like she is nothing more than a nosy neighbor clinging to small-town gossip.

Grace chooses her next words carefully. She focuses on her breath, on the officers' faces, on the truth. "I understand, but here's the thing. My friends and I are here on vacation, and we're worried because we can't find our friend. We're staying over at Arbor House, but she didn't come home last night. She's not there and she's not answering her phone, so we're just worried that she might have . . ." She can't finish the sentence. Might have hiked. Might have fallen. Might have died.

The officers straighten, as if she's said the right thing. "Can you describe her, please? Your friend?"

"She's about your height, kind of tall, jet black hair, thin . . . she was wearing a green hoodie. And black nail polish. She also had on striped knee-high socks."

The officers swivel their heads toward each other, their eyes confirming what she already knows. They look at the ground, the bottoms of their coffee cups, then somewhere toward the vicinity of her face, but never quite make eye contact.

Grace's legs start to shake, her heart knifed into a million bloody pieces. "Oh God, please. It can't be her." She grips the officer's arm until his flesh bulges between her fingers. Lee's outraged face from the night before sears her mind. How hurt she was. How devastated from the news. That tenuous exchange. Their last conversation.

The officer steps back. She releases his arm in apology. "She has a son. He's . . . he needs her. We need her. We're all mothers. We're just here on vacation. We've been here for less than two days. It can't be her. It can't." The rush of words crashes toward them.

"Ma'am, let's not jump to any conclusions. Can you come with us for a moment?" The other officer supports her elbow and ushers her a few feet away toward the trail.

Grace finds Carol's and Alice's expectant faces somewhere behind her. She tries to steady her features, to make them impassive, to emit total control with her eyes and lips, but she can't. Alice screams, and Carol's arms shoot around her as she collapses to the ground. This can't be happening. This *isn't* happening.

Grace chomps through the crispy leaves and bramble, praying for a miracle. She marches past hushed whispers, officials, and walkie-talkies spouting off commands. The air grows cooler as she nears the start of the path, snarled with overgrown trees. Just yesterday, she was giggling and joking with her friends, only thinking of vacation. Her baby. Luca. Noah. Her confession. Their growing family. Her best friend being mad at her.

Now, near a batch of trees, she spots a corpse under a dark rubber sheet. The outline of a petite body rises beneath it, all the swells and bumps that compose a human. She halts, steadies herself, and swallows the cottony dryness of dread. How many times has she seen this exact scenario on television? How many nights have she and Lee spent together, sprawled on her crumb-infested sofa, eating snacks, not even blinking as someone gets murdered or dies from some untimely accident? They've all been desensitized to scenes like this, and yet, this is real. This is *happening*.

The officers talk as Grace edges forward. She waits for someone to tell her to stop, or that she can't be here. She drops to her knees at the edge of the sheet. The earth soaks through her running pants.

An arm appears out of nowhere to peel back the sheet, inch by inch. Grace holds her breath. The face is marred and covered by dark hair and blood. At first, despite the horror, she exhales. This former person can't be Lee. The features are almost indistinguishable, the neck broken, the body's limbs crooked and limp. The coroner or whoever it is—detective? investigator?— pinches the saggy flesh of the corpse's cheeks and turns its face upward, and that's it: beneath all that death, there she is. The eyes, the locket that bears a picture of Mason, bunched in knotted chain around her neck, the black fingernails angled back, as if she'd been clawing for help, and the green hoodie, now blood-soaked, hiding fragments of her dear, dead friend.

She nods, mouth behind cold hands, the tears coming before she can talk, scream, or wail. She bobs her head once, twice. Her friends riot toward her, a stampede of fear, emotion, and disbelief exploding beneath the soles of their shoes.

Alice skids to a stop next to Grace, tossing out a primal scream. She collapses over Lee's chest and squeezes. Grace hears things pop and squish as the investigator pulls her off and tells her she cannot touch evidence. Lee isn't Lee. She is *evidence*. Carol stands at the edge behind them, unable to move, her face a ghost of surprise.

Grace replays the previous night's events. Only Grace knows about Lee's confession, but what about the rest? Had her disappointment about Noah caused her to drink, to hike, and ultimately fall? The sobering question slams into her before she can stop it: could she have jumped?

The contrasting thoughts clamp down, and she doesn't know what to say or how to abate the guilt. As Grace stands, her body stiffens, and a dreaded truth repeats itself over and over in her head: *You told her about the baby. You told her about Noah. You told her everything, and now Lee is dead.*

35

noah

Mason eats chicken straight off the bone. Noah studies his movements, the way his small teeth gnaw at the warm flesh. Since they discussed how chickens were killed, skinned, sprayed with chemicals, and processed in factories, Mason prefers they buy whole chickens, so they pass through fewer hands.

This is Mason's second rotisserie chicken in forty-eight hours, and Noah, never a fan of messes, has offered him a pair of latex gloves and a trough of paper towels, which he folds into a parallelogram. Mason dissects the bird with the precision of a surgeon, already having peeled back the oily top layer of skin. He pushes through twiggy bones, snapping a few like toothpicks, and then organizes the meat into neat little stacks: dark, light, pink, and purple, staring down into the bowl of the carcass, not disgusted but intrigued. He envies Mason's hyper focus.

Noah pours himself another cup of coffee and glances out the window. God, he misses Grace. He hates that she told Lee alone and that it did not go well. He knows their friendship will weather the storm, but he never should have let Lee think, even for a moment, that she had a romantic chance. He hadn't told Grace about what happened on the couch; how she took his face in her hands, how he was so reminded of . . .

His phone rings, and Noah rushes to pick it up, so as not to disturb Mason. He looks at the number, expecting it to be Lee or one of his clients.

"I was just thinking of you."

Ringing phones and voices converge in the background. Grace's voice crackles in and out over the line. He sticks one finger in his ear and ducks into Lee's studio. He attempts to string together the words into something he can comprehend.

"Wait. Slow down. What's happened?"

"It's Lee. *Lee*." Grace begins to cry.

"What are you saying?"

She starts spewing information between sobs: there was a fallen hiker. Or maybe a jumper? And Lee. Lee, Mason's mother. Lee, Grace's best friend. Lee, Noah's employer. Lee, the woman who likes him.

"She's dead, Noah. Lee is dead."

Her beautiful face flashes through his mind. "What?" It is an idiotic thing to say, but he can think of nothing else. His knees buckle, and he collapses in her styling chair. Grace says his name, but he can only focus on the word *dead*.

She tries to explain between sobs, but the dial tone thrums in his ear, and he realizes he's the one who ended the call. He looks in the mirror, his reflection pale and uncertain. *Dead, dead, dead*. His brother's death swoops back into focus—his last and largest loss.

"Please God. Not again." He drops his face into his hands. His entire body convulses. Sweet, hopeful Lee. He whips his head upright and catches sight of his own green eyes in the mirror. She'd been so hesitant to go . . .

had she had some sort of gut feeling that something bad would happen?

"Noah! You have to see this!"

Mason. How the fuck is he going to tell Mason?

He replays Grace's words again, and they rip right through him. He spins away from the mirror, but he can't escape. *Lee*. How many times has he sat here, drinking a cup of coffee, as Lee massaged his scalp with oils and held a razor to his neck? She'd washed, dried, cut, hummed, and moved around him, rotating the chair to face the slim horns of her hips. They'd decided on free haircuts in exchange for his reduced fee, and he looked forward to his time in this chair. He *liked* her. He knew the floral scent of her skin and adored the way her fingernails tickled his forehead when she was styling him. Had he been leading her on? Had he had feelings he didn't want to admit, even to himself?

He rotates back to the mirror. The glass is smudged, as if one of Lee's clients smeared their fingers across it to get a better look at their hair. Noah searches for an explanation as his phone tumbles to the rug. Grace told Lee about them. And now Lee is dead. The truth scrambles in his head until he can't make sense of it. Lee can't be dead. He just texted her. He pulls his phone out of his pocket and scrolls through until he gets to their text exchange. He reads them through his tears. The last text was right before Grace's confession.

Why hadn't he checked on her? Why hadn't he called to explain himself after Grace had told her the truth?

"Noah, *come here*!" Mason's chair scrapes against the floor in the next room. His heart slams around in his chest. Is he supposed to be the one to tell him? They hadn't gotten that far on the phone.

He wipes his eyes and clears his throat. "Coming, buddy!" He tries Grace back, but it goes straight to voice mail. He reenters the kitchen to pour himself a glass of water from the tap. His hands shake as he gulps it down. Emotion brims behind his stoicism, but he can't break. Not here. Not like this.

"Look at the rib bones compared to the leg bones. I have separated them into width and height."

Noah takes a step closer and observes the pile of bones. He closes his eyes and gathers himself. All he can think about is Lee. During months of working here, he's gotten intimate with her surroundings. He knows what Lee reads before bedtime, what magazines she subscribes to, what shampoo she buys in bulk. He knows what bills go unpaid, left in a stack on the kitchen counter, what type of dish soap she prefers. He's seen her razor, bits of stubble caught in the blade, her brand of tampons, her vitamins, and her vibrator, which Mason sometimes slips from her nightstand when she isn't looking and uses to massage the bottoms of his feet after a long day. (He and Mason had a long talk about that one.) In some ways, he knows Lee better than he knows Grace.

Mason mumbles something to himself and kicks his feet under the table. Noah studies the back of his head, his posture, and, as always, feels like he is shuttled back in time to his own childhood. To Wyatt.

Noah buries his own recollections and focuses on Mason. Though Mason has been comfortable in his mother's absence, it's only because he knows she's coming back. Losing a parent, especially for someone like Mason, could cause a truly irreparable regression.

He shoves aside his grief as the obvious next steps begin to arrange themselves in order of importance. He has to be deliberate about the way he handles this in front of

Mason. He can't let on that anything has changed until he and Grace figure out what's next.

He grips both sides of the sink and studies the garden. Lee loves her garden. *Loved.* God. A sob escapes his throat, and Mason turns in his chair.

"What was that?"

"Nothing, bud. Sorry. Frog in my throat." Sometimes, when Lee was done with a client, she would slip outside and sift through the dirt—just to be connected to the earth. She loved watching something grow from a tiny seed. She'd even gotten Mason interested in what lay beneath the surface: the cool, wet dirt, the roots, and the worms that slithered and broke apart if he pinched too hard.

"A frog is not in your throat." Mason snorts. "I don't know why people say that. We should find the origin of that saying."

"We should."

The phone rings. Grace. "I just need to take this." He retreats back to the studio. "Hey. I'm sorry I hung up. I tried you back, but it went to voice mail." He scans the room, gutted with the realization that Lee will never set foot in her beloved studio again. "I'm in shock."

"We are too."

He can hear the pain in her voice and wishes he could hold her. He thinks about the stress to their unborn baby and her higher-risk pregnancy. He listens as she recounts what happened, starting with their arrival, the bonfire, the argument, the unplanned hike, the body, and the police station. He slides the pocket door closed.

"Noah, I have to ask, and I know this sounds ridiculous, but did she ever imply that she was depressed at all . . . or anything like that?"

He replays their texts and many conversations. Lee

always skews a bit toward the cynical or sometimes pessimistic, but Mason keeps her grounded. "No, of course not. Why? Do you think she was suicidal?" The idea of Lee jumping off of a mountain willingly seems preposterous. But he knows all too well that sometimes people jump when you least expect it. Even when you think they're happy. Even when they have so much to live for. Or lose.

"We don't know yet." The rustle of phones and voices escalates in the background. "But I don't think so. I'm sure it was just a horrible accident." Her voice breaks and drops to a whisper. "Is this entirely my fault?"

"Grace, hey. Stop. Listen to me. Your telling her about us has nothing to do with what happened."

"But she was drunk, I think. I think she drank wine."

"What?" He knows Lee clings to her sobriety like a badge of honor. She wouldn't undo that for some petty jealousy, would she? "Look. Don't get ahead of yourself. The toxicology report will probably tell you all of that. Just breathe, stay calm, and tell me what you'd like me to do. Do you want me to come there?"

"No, no. I don't want Mason to know yet. Just keep everything normal, and please don't tell him anything."

"Of course not. I wasn't planning on it." He jots down notes as Grace rattles off a to-do list, and then goes back to Mason. Noah rearranges his mask of normalcy and helps clear away the tiny chicken bones and what remains of the carcass.

"Would you like to go outside and work in the garden?"

Mason nods and removes his latex gloves. Noah opens his hand and Mason deposits them there.

"Go wash your hands, and I will meet you outside."

Mason obeys and Noah disposes of the gloves, paper towels, and bones. He sprays disinfectant onto the table and scrubs away the remnants, bringing order to the mess. Mason needs order. He needs to know everything is going to be okay.

Mason explodes out of the bathroom and into the backyard. He bounds across the expanse of grass and plunges his now clean fingers into the waiting dirt up to his wrists. Noah is surprised he doesn't want another pair of gloves.

Noah looks around the house, clocking just how much there is to take care of. This house is a rental. They will have to sort through all of Lee's belongings, her will, Mason's guardianship. He's certain these are things her friends haven't even registered yet. All of the logistics of death. He will help take care of everything and allow them to grieve. Because he knows what happens when you don't.

He washes his hands, grabs another pair of food-grade gloves, and shoves them in his back pocket. Then he opens the door and joins Mason in the garden, maintaining the mirage that this boy's life, for at least one more day, is not about to fall apart.

36

grace

The girls sit at the station. They've answered every question they can about last night. Grace doesn't mention her hunch about the drinking or about what Lee has confessed. She's too consumed with their argument, for the horrible timing of telling her fragile friend such a huge secret and then leaving her alone to fester.

Grace can't stop seeing Lee's bloody corpse, how one body could be so dismantled. She drops her face into her palms, her eyes rubbed raw from tears. The officers continue to assure them that the way Lee came down the mountain is indicative of a slip. Her hands and wrists were covered in cuts, as if she'd been trying to grasp at anything to stop her fall. Grace can't help but wonder if she'd been aware of her flesh being scraped across the rocks. If she'd been scared. If she'd died angry.

Tears splash onto her lap, and Alice smooths circles across her back. Poor Mason. Poor Noah at home with Mason. She would never be able to keep incoming news like this from a child; it would be written all over her face.

She glances around the unit, all of them unsure of what to do next. Alice and Carol appear as bewildered as she is. Steam drifts from an ivory mug, her fingers wrapped around it. When had she been offered coffee?

Alice clears her throat. "What did Noah say?"

"Not much. He was in shock."

"He won't tell Mason though, right?" Carol asks.

Grace wipes her nose with her sleeve. "Of course not."

"Oh my God, Mason!"

Grace and Carol look at Alice. "Mason what?"

Alice's eyes toggle between them, wild and wet. "Who will Mason live with?"

Carol turns to Grace. "Did she have a will? Or a guardianship arrangement should something happen? Surely, she did," Carol continues. "She had to, right? She's a single parent with no extended family, and the father isn't in the picture."

Grace nods. "She does. I encouraged her to put something on paper since she's a single parent. Though I never thought . . ."

"So she has one?" Alice presses a palm to her chest. "Thank God. Oh, thank God."

"Yes." Grace's stomach clenches at the upheaval Mason is about to experience. She looks at the girls. "In the event of her death, Mason goes to me."

Carol and Alice exchange looks. "That's incredible," Carol says. "When did that happen?"

"About a month or so ago."

"A *month*?" Alice's eyes widen. "Talk about a premonition. What would have happened if she hadn't written that?"

Grace shrugs. "I have no idea."

"Well, thank God it's you," Alice says. "He adores you."

"And she doesn't have any other relatives?" Carol asks.

"No." Grace sits up and rotates the coffee cup in her hands. "Her entire family is gone. Her mother died when she was young. And then her father died right after Mason was born. She's never talked about any aunts, uncles, nieces, nephews, or cousins. I don't know if she even has any living relatives. She always said she didn't."

"Even if she did, we wouldn't let Mason to go to someone he doesn't know," Carol scoffs. "He needs special education, therapy, someone he trusts." She rests her hand on Grace's back. "I'm so glad it's you."

"What about Noah?" Alice asks. "Do you think he'll still be able to help?"

"Of course he will. Why wouldn't he?" Grace asks.

"I don't know. I'm all mixed up." Alice drops her head into her hands.

"What about a funeral? Would Lee have wanted one?" Carol asks.

Grace massages her temples. "I don't know. I mean, I don't think so. She wasn't religious." The truth is that Grace has no idea what Lee would have wanted in the unlikely event of her death, but she knows a church and graveside burial aren't it.

An officer appears, the shorter one from the scene. Handcuffs, flashlight, and a gun hang from both hips. "Ladies, thank you for your patience. This looks like a pretty open and shut case." He eyes each of them. "You can go back to where you're staying until we call you, but we do need you to start thinking about how you'd like to handle the body."

The body. What would they do with the body?

"So, we're free to go?" Alice asks.

"Yes, for now. Try to get some rest."

Carol rolls her eyes, and Grace knows she's thinking the same thing. Why do people always say that? She couldn't sleep if someone paid her a million dollars. She'd probably never sleep again.

They gather their belongings and walk back to Arbor House.

"I vote for cremation," Alice says. "That way, Mason can always have her close by."

"I second that," Carol says. "Especially if she didn't want a typical funeral."

"Is there anyone we need to call?" Grace asks. "Besides her clients, obviously? I know she keeps all of their information in her book at home. Noah can supply the numbers since he's there."

They all rummage through the people in Lee's lean, compact life as the breeze picks up. "Her sponsor?" Alice asks.

"Yes, her sponsor. And Mason's therapist. Her therapist." Grace ticks them off on her fingers. "I'll start a list."

"I just . . . I feel like this is all my fault. If I hadn't arranged this trip, then she wouldn't have fallen," Carol says.

"Hey, stop that." Alice loops an arm around her shoulder. "This is no one's fault. It's one of those freak accidents you hear about and now it's happened to us. But we will get through it." Carol leans into the hollow of her friend's shoulder. "We will. Okay?"

They stop in front of the bright gate, the day ironically clear and beautiful, not a cloud in the sky. If Grace hadn't left Lee alone outside, would she still be alive?

She brushes the what-ifs aside. She has a little boy to tend to, his mother's body to take care of, and arrangements to make. Becoming Mason's permanent guardian charges every nerve in Grace's body. She *adores* Mason. She is the closest to him out of the group, and she wants to prepare him for everything that's to come.

Doubt gnaws the lining of her stomach. What would Lee think about her taking Mason into her home when she'd probably died hating her? She can't think about that now; can't think of all the logistics, of their fight, of even telling Mason that Lee is dead.

They each separate to their rooms. Grace shuts the door, acknowledges Lee's roller bag, her made bed, and a novel, untouched, on the nightstand. She riffles through her bag. The journal with the engraved *L* is tucked inside a mesh pocket. She picks it up. Is there some clue in here, some indication of what she was thinking or feeling?

The emotions sweep over her like a tsunami and she gives in to them, so overwhelmed, she doesn't know what to do. She collapses in bed, all of the next steps crashing into her. She tucks the journal to her chest and flips it open.

She begins to read.

secret
lie
despair
resilience
jealousy
duplicity
betray

How many times can one person be disappointed?
Everyone thinks they know my motivations, my
fears, my purpose.

Do we ever really know the people in our lives?
Do we ever really share our deepest, darkest
truths?

No.

No one ever really knows someone else—all the
ways you can present a version of yourself to
the world that you want to be seen.
The rest stays hidden.
The rest stays yours.

No one will ever know the real me.
It's something I've decided.
It's something I will hoard just for myself.

I keep coming back to this one thing I heard over
and over again: the heart wants what it cannot
have.

But I will have it.
Because I deserve it.

I deserve what's rightfully mine.

37

noah

Noah waits for Grace on Lee's front steps. Mason is asleep. He still can't believe that he and Grace are meeting under these circumstances. They need a plan—a tell-Mason-his-mom-is-dead script. He can't fend off the questions much longer—where his mother is, why she's not back, why he hasn't talked to her.

Grace kills her headlights before pulling into the drive. Noah rushes down the steps to meet her. He wraps her in his arms and kisses the top of her head.

"I'm so sorry," he murmurs.

Slowly, he lowers to his knees and gently palms her belly. Grace holds him there, his hair in her fingers. His left ear presses against the dome of her stomach and listens for life, even though he knows it's too early. He releases her waist and stands. Ever since she found out she's pregnant, there's been no excitement—only cautious optimism. What would a loss like this do to her? To them? Finally, he eases her back toward the steps, which are cool and hard beneath his jeans.

"I just can't believe a few days ago, she was here, and now she's not, and . . . I just don't even know. God, I'm so tired. I feel so responsible." Grace drops her face in both palms.

"It's not your fault." He rubs her back.

She looks at him. "But if I hadn't left her out there."

"Don't do that." He slides his hand to the step behind her and sighs. "It won't help anything. Trust me." He knows the blame game all too well. He still plays it with Wyatt's suicide all these years later, no matter how many times he's been told it wasn't his fault.

"I still feel responsible." She wipes away smeared mascara.

"I know." It's all he can say because he *does* know. Nothing he tells her is going to change the way she feels.

"We have to tell Mason."

He nods. "We do."

"And then what?" Grace sighs. "I don't even know where to begin."

Noah pushes away the aftermath of his own brother's death, all of the logistics, the funeral, and what came after. "When a parent dies, it becomes about legal guardianship and not custody." He pauses, unsure how to frame his next statement. "Unless the biological father were to come forward."

Grace emits a short, harsh laugh. "He won't."

He looks at her, surprised. "Are you sure? Because if he knew what happened, he might step up and take responsibility."

"No." Grace shakes her head. "The father won't come forward."

Noah lets that information sink in. "How do you know?"

"Because she told me. She told me who the father is."

Noah bristles. He runs through every conversation he and Lee have ever shared, but she never alluded to who Mason's dad was. Despite the tragic situation, he's still curious. "Who is it?"

She sighs. "She doesn't know."

"Whoa." He thinks about the Lee he knows. He can't imagine her sleeping around with some guy and not knowing who got her pregnant.

"I don't want to talk about that right now." There is an edge to her voice. "I just want to talk about logical next steps. I need to know exactly what to do and in what order."

"Hey, it's fine." He rubs her back again. "I understand this is a lot."

"I've got the guardianship papers. I have a copy of her will."

"Wait, you've got guardianship papers?" he asks in surprise. "How?"

She glances at him, her face drawn. "Because she named me as Mason's legal guardian should something happen to her."

Noah registers this new information and feels immense relief that Mason will be with Grace. That *he* will be with both Grace and Mason. That, in essence, he will become Mason's guardian too. They haven't talked about being together forever, but with Grace's pregnancy and the hope of their future . . . it makes sense. "That will make it a lot easier. Because Lee signed papers, it should be a simple procedure. We'll set a court date. They will name you as his legal guardian, and everything should run smoothly. No pushback or anything." He clears his throat. "I know his sessions are expensive. His therapy, all of that. We can discuss alternatives if you like?"

"I don't care about money. I just want what's best for him. I don't want to disrupt his life or routine." Grace looks at him under the porch lights, her eyes glistening. "How are we going to do all this? We're having a baby.

I have a kid from another man. And now I'm about to take on the responsibility of another child who just lost his mother?"

"I know." He pulls her close and kisses her temple. "But I'll be with you every step of the way. You know that."

"Will you?" Grace searches his face. "I get it if you don't want to stick around for this, Noah. No one expects you to. It's a lot to ask. Plus, you have other families and responsibilities."

"What are you talking about? We're having a *baby* together. I'm in this." Noah works something out in his head. The future. The boys. The baby. Them. The thought of asking Grace to marry him flits across his mind, but he knows now is not the time. "Grace, you are my family. We're in this together."

Her entire body seems to relax. "You promise?"

"I promise."

"Because out of everyone, Mason loves you the most."

Something aims and fires in his gut. "I'm not sure about that. His bond with you is pretty incredible."

She exhales. "How's he been doing the past few days without her?"

"He's wondering why he hasn't spoken to her, and why it's been longer than she said."

"Ugh." Grace moans. "We should tell him as soon as possible." She fiddles with a stick she plucks from the steps and sweeps the branch back and forth in front of her. "We have no idea what we're really in for, do we?"

"Not really. But it will be okay."

"Poor Mason. My heart is just breaking for him."

"I know." He hesitates and decides to continue. "I know you have the papers, Grace, but I would suggest thinking really long and hard about this."

"About what?"

"The guardianship. Becoming a parent to Mason is going to change your life. You and Luca have a rapport, a routine, your ups and downs, and your little traditions. But all that will change."

Grace studies him. He can't tell what she's thinking, but he knows that having a baby will essentially do the same thing. A baby will change their lives. Having permanent custody of Mason will change their lives. Her best friend dying will change their lives. It already has.

She wipes a tear from her cheek. "It's not up for discussion."

He nods. "I wasn't saying it was up for discussion. I was just saying there are other options if you need them."

She whips her head toward him. "Like what? Giving him to a stranger? Don't be ridiculous."

"Hey, calm down. That's not what I meant." He's thrown by her clipped tone, but he knows she is hormonal, tired, and devastated. "All I'm saying is that it's normal to think things through."

"I have. I'm taking him." She stares straight ahead into the night, and he tucks a strand of hair behind her ear.

"That's an amazing, selfless thing. He's very lucky."

She moves closer to him on the steps. Lee sat like this, just days ago, scared to go on her trip. Scared of what might happen in her absence. And now her best friend is in her place, scared of what to do next.

Finally, her body softens and she glances at him. "I know she'd be happy to know you're here with him. With us."

"I wouldn't be anywhere else." Noah pieces together all the information they will have to tackle over the next few days: the logistics of the house, the funeral, telling Mason, the aftermath, making sure Grace stays healthy . . . It is a lot, but he's been here before. He survived Wyatt's death.

He knows he'll survive this too.

38

grace

Grace startles at the unfamiliar surroundings. She slides a palm across the fresh sheets, toward the open space that, hours before, housed Noah's body. She squints into the half-light. Not here. She stares at the ceiling—*Lee's* ceiling—and listens for Mason. After a few moments, she rises, her body still heavy with sleep, and finds Noah in the kitchen. Her arms circle his waist, and she breathes in the sharp smell of his skin, clean and masculine.

"Morning, beautiful. Did you sleep?"

"Some."

"I made you decaf. Are you hungry?"

"Sure." She knows they have to break the news this morning. From there, they will set a court date, do paper-work, pack, and help Mason move. God. She hasn't even thought of the process of moving, the emotional hell that will cause for him.

She helps with breakfast, heaping soft eggs cooked in butter onto three separate plates, and pours a fresh cup of decaf for herself. For one moment, she forgets that Lee is not here, and she grips the counter, almost spinning with realization.

They eat in silence, stabbing fork tines into their steamy eggs. She washes them down with her second cup of coffee and hears Mason's door open right at eight. She catches Noah's eye across the table, and they nod at each other.

Mason enters the dining room and rubs his eyes. For a moment, she sees the flicker of hope that she is his mother, but just as quickly it's abandoned when he realizes she's not Lee.

"Where's my mother? Why is my mother not here? Where is she?"

Grace attempts to smile. "Hey, buddy. Why don't you come have some breakfast? Noah and I need to talk to you about your mom."

Mason fingers a small hole in his pajama bottoms. He sniffs and crosses his arms. "Those eggs smell like fish. You can't cook them in the cast iron pan or else they taste like fish. Mom cooks fish in that pan."

Grace makes a mental note for future reference. "That's a great tip. I'll remember that." She moves the chair next to her and pats the wooden bottom. "Here. Sit. We need to talk."

Noah urges him to sit too, and finally, he does. He refolds his arms over his *Sesame Street* T-shirt and looks between them. "Okay, out with it. Where's my mother?"

Grace opens her mouth to explain, but she doesn't know how to convey the truth in a way that is not so gut-wrenching. She contemplates all the ways she can say it: *Your mother had an accident. Your mother went hiking. Your mother fell.* No matter how she frames it, the moment she says it will change his life forever.

"Mason, I'm going to tell you where your mother is." Noah clears his throat and glances at Grace, and she nods in approval. "While she was on her trip, your mother went on a hike late at night. She couldn't see very well and she fell."

"Is she in the hospital?" Mason's fingers begin to peck against the table.

Noah falters and Grace butts in. "No, Mason, she's not in the hospital. Your mom fell from the very top of the mountain. I'm so sorry to say that she died."

The blunt delivery slices through Grace—even though she knows Mason needs to hear a definitive statement to understand—but it's as if she is hearing it for the first time. Mason's breath quickens, his lungs punchy beneath his pajamas.

"I'm so sorry. It was a terrible accident."

Mason's face turns splotchy, first his right ear, then his temple, then the violent splash of color like a contagious rash across his neck. His eyes widen and brim with unshed tears. "My mother fell off a mountain?" Mason looks at her, the pain written all over his face. "And died?" His voice drops to a whisper when he says the word *died,* and not for the first time, Grace recognizes the vulnerable child beneath all that logic.

"Oh, sweet boy," she murmurs. She extends her hand to cover his but stops short at the edge of his nails.

"Grace . . . she's not really dead, is she? She's not dead." Tears wet his cheeks as he furiously shakes his head. "No, no, no. She's not dead. Not dead."

Noah leans closer. "We're so sorry, Mason."

Again, he looks between them, desperate to make sense. "Grace, please. You were *there*! You were with her! How did she fall? She promised she'd be back. She *promised*."

"I know. I know she did." Grace covers her mouth with her hand and tries to calm herself. She has to be strong for him, for them.

"But, but, but, but." He repeats the word, crying as he

says it, and Grace wraps a firm arm around his shoulder and holds him tight. "But she said she would be back. She promised. She *promised* she'd be back in seventy-two hours. She promised me!"

"I know. I know she did." Grace holds him tighter. "And if she hadn't gotten into an accident, she would have kept her promise. You know that."

He rolls into her chest and cries. She holds him, her own tears slipping across her cheeks and jaw. Noah watches them, the anguish apparent. She squeezes Mason tighter and waits for him to pull away.

Finally, he extricates himself and hiccups. "Is this my fault?"

"Why on earth would you ask that?" Grace says. She smooths his matted hair away from his forehead.

"Because I said something about living with you before she left." His eyes float between them, bewildered. "I made a *comment* about wanting to live with you. But I didn't mean it. I didn't want her to die."

"Oh, Mason, of course not. This is not your fault. It was an accident." Noah's words are gentle, but the meaning is firm.

"He's right. This is not your fault. Do you hear me? Mason, look at me. This is *not* your fault. It's not anyone's fault." Grace ignores the stab of guilt: the argument, the drinking, the unplanned hike, the fall.

He assesses the dining room, the living room behind him, the kitchen off to the right. "But where will I live? I live here with my mother."

"I know you do," Grace says. "And we will need to talk about that."

Noah interjects. "You will live with Grace and Luca."

Grace shoots him a stern look. Now isn't the time to

bring up details. She wants to let him sit with the truth and whatever that brings: pain, grief, loss, the love he has for his mother. He needs to process.

"So what I asked for is coming true then." He hiccups. "I *made* this happen!" He pushes back from the table and runs to his room.

Grace covers her face with her hands. "God." She knows the pain he is going through, how he must want to take the truth and destroy it.

"Let's give him a minute."

Grace lifts her head and glares at Noah. "Was that really necessary?"

He blinks at her. "Was *what* necessary?"

"Talking about where he would live at the very moment he's trying to process? That seemed so heartless."

Noah's jaw clenches, and it's the first time she's seen anything other than the easygoing side of him. "I understand how it seems, Grace, but he needs all the information. He needs to understand that his mother isn't coming back, but he also needs to realize that he will no longer live with her. He needs to know that at once, so he can work through both the grief and the actual logistics of the situation."

Grace doesn't agree. Something thuds in Mason's room, and she turns toward the hall. "Should we get him?"

"Trust me," Noah says, scooping up their plates. "He needs to work through the full emotions first. If we try to talk to him right this second, we won't get anywhere."

The mother in her aches to give him comfort. It's not about *getting* somewhere, it's about being there for him. Even if she can't hold him against her chest, she can still let him know that she's here. No child should have to process something like this alone. She stalks down the hall, against Noah's suggestion, and knocks on the door.

When he doesn't answer, she twists, expecting to find it locked, but the knob gives in her hand. She's careful to stand on the threshold. She knows he does not like people invading his personal space. "Mason?"

He rocks beside his bed, curled in a ball.

She crouches down and gently lays a palm on his back. "Hey, buddy. You did not do this. I need you to really hear that. Above anything else. You did not make this happen."

"But I *did* want to live with you!" He pops his head up, his curls frizzed. "I used to write it down: that I wished I could come live with you and Luca. That I wished you were my mother. And now it's true. I made this happen."

Grace knows there's no use arguing. If Mason believes it, then it's true. She eases into a cross-legged position beside him. "You know, years ago, my sister died. I know it's not the same thing as losing your mom, but it was very, very hard. I was extremely close to her, and when she died, I didn't know what I would do. I kind of felt like that was my fault." Grace almost seizes as she says it, the memory shuttling back into focus. How she couldn't believe it. How denial became her best friend. She doesn't ever talk about her sister's death; not with Noah, not with Lee, not with anyone.

Mason sniffs and stops rocking. "Why?"

Grace hesitates as a thousand memories float to the surface. The two of them creating obstacle courses out of pillows and furniture, fighting over boys, sneaking out of their windows, long nights of pillow talk, and then the painful separation of their lives as adults. "We grew apart," she finally says. "She moved away, so I didn't really see her as much. Sometimes, when family lives in different places, you aren't as close. When she died, I felt guilty I wasn't with her. That I hadn't been paying close enough attention to her life."

"What was she like?"

What a loaded question. "She was interesting. Hard-headed. Beautiful. Impressionable. Smart." Her heart catches, and she feels like she can't breathe. "I think you would have liked her."

Mason swipes his nose. "That's a weird thing to say."

"Is it?" She knocks away the memories of her sister and tries to stay present. "The point I'm trying to make is that it's never easy to lose someone, but it is not your fault. It's never your fault. Even if it feels like it." *Do I really believe that?*

Mason leans against her shoulder. Though Mason does not like physical affection, he is initiating this contact—needs it even—and she welcomes it. He has never minded her touching him, helping him, occasionally brushing a shoulder or his head.

"What am I going to do now?"

It is such a weighted question, and she wants to assuage all of his fears. But she knows only time will do that—not anything that she says in this moment.

"I'm going to be here to help you figure that out, okay?"

He nods. "Can I be alone?"

"Of course." Grace stands. "Noah and I are in the kitchen if you want to talk or need anything. We're here." She closes his door and returns to the kitchen. Noah has poured them both fresh cups of coffee.

Something buzzes from the living room office, and they turn. The fax machine. Grace constantly teased Lee about having a fax machine, but it was combined with her printer and scanner, and she couldn't afford to replace it with a newer model.

"Who would be sending a fax?" Noah asks.

Grace remembers she gave the station Lee's number for the toxicology report. "The police," she says. She is shocked there hasn't been more of an investigation, but really, what is there to investigate?

She can hardly think about that night, imagining Lee falling to the bottom. Her body intact and then not. Her heart beating and then the moment it stopped. She clenches her fists in an effort to erase the images that bombard her and impatiently waits. This will give them proof. Two sheets come through. The machine quiets. She plucks both papers from the bed and reads the results.

39

grace

Instead of the toxicology report, it's the bill for the cremation and urn. She exhales and scans the receipt. "Not the report." She folds both papers and shoves them into her back pocket. She is desperate for the report—desperate to know the truth. The autopsy will answer the question of whether Lee had been sober or drunk when she fell.

Mason's door opens. He shuffles into the room. Tiny red scratches streak both arms.

"Are you okay?" Grace knows it is a dumb question to ask, and Mason calls her on it.

"My mother is dead. I am not okay. I will never be okay *again*."

"Let's sit for a second," Noah suggests. He leads them all to the table. Mason glares at the floor, his cheeks sucking in and out with every breath.

"I know how hard this is," Grace offers. "And we want you to take some time to sit with this and ask any questions you need to. But we do have to talk about the next steps, okay?"

"Like what?" He kicks the chair across from him and it topples to the floor. "Sorry," he says.

Grace gestures to Noah to leave it. "Mason, your mom

didn't own this house unfortunately, so that means that you will, in fact, have to move. But you will live with me and Luca, and you will have your own room."

"When?" he asks.

"Probably soon," Noah says. "But we have a little time."

"I don't want to move."

Grace can see the wheels turning—all the ways his daily life will change. Getting used to new sounds, a new room, a new routine.

"I am *never* leaving my room, and you can't make me." Mason balls his fingers into fists and opens and closes them on the table. He finally flattens his palms and digs his fingernails into the wood and bears down until his face darkens.

"Mason, stop that. Do not hold your breath." Noah's voice is calm, but Grace recognizes the hint of fear at the edges. She watches Mason's face morph from red to purple and motions to Noah to do something.

"Look, Mason. Listen to me for a second. What do you think about me staying here with you until Grace gets everything ready at her house, and then we will move you and your things into your new room? Does that sound good? Hey buddy, does that sound good? Can you breathe for me, please?"

Just when Grace thinks he's going to pass out, he releases his breath in a loud whoosh and all the color starts to drain. He nods his head over and over. "Yes, I want to stay here. I want to *stay* in my room."

Grace balks at the suggestion. She knows Noah just said it to get him to breathe, but still. "Well, you can't stay here long, Mason. Just until we get your room ready, okay?"

"No, I want to stay here. I want to stay in my room. Noah just said I could stay in my room."

"No, that's not what I said," Noah interjects. "You can stay here *temporarily* until your room is ready at Grace's house, okay? Your mom does not own this house. We cannot live here after this month. They will rent it to someone else."

Mason keeps his arms crossed, eyes glued to the table. She doesn't blame him. She knows how unfair this is.

"Alright," Noah says, "I think we should give you some time to process everything. Then we can talk about your room, okay?"

Grace notes the time. Chad is dropping Luca off soon. She's dying to see him. It's been days. The possessive tug keeps her rooted to the spot, but isn't that why Noah is here? To help?

"I should go. I need to grab Luca." She walks around the table to Mason and deposits a quick kiss on his head. "I'll be back soon." He pulls away.

She is usually so good about keeping their personal space intact—he touches her only if he initiates—but she just kissed Mason like she kisses Luca. She will have to make a mental note of the differences—to bury her own natural impulses and find an appropriate response for Mason in times of peril.

Noah meets her at the back door. "So, listen. I have an idea. It might be crazy."

She grabs her purse and keys. "What?"

He rubs her arms as if trying to generate heat. "Don't freak out, okay?"

"Why would I freak out?" Grace prepares herself to not react.

"What if I sell my place and move in here? Take over the lease? That way, he can still come over and we can do sessions where he's comfortable."

Grace lowers her keys. "What? You'd give up your place to live . . . here? That's crazy."

He shrugs and gives her an easy smile. "Maybe. But I think it could really benefit him, especially in the short term."

"How so?" Tension stiffens her fingers around the keys. "He'd never want to come to my house if he has his house as an option. You know that. That seems confusing, even to me."

"I know, but . . ." He looks behind him. Mason sits still, staring at the table. "I was thinking we could split responsibility so it's not so much for you in the beginning. I don't know. We could figure it out."

"Split responsibility?" Her heart stutters in her chest. She tries to grasp his words, loses them. She looks into his eyes, searching. "You mean like split *custody*?"

"Hey, calm down." He reaches out to touch her arm, but she sidesteps. "It's just a suggestion."

She deflates. He's only thinking of Mason. She needs to figure out what would be best for him, not what would be best for her conscience. "I'm sorry. I'm just overloaded." Grace fidgets with her keys. "Let's just talk about it later, okay? Luca and I will come over in a few hours. I can bring food, or . . ."

"Sure. That sounds good. I'll text you."

She memorizes Mason's tiny, heaving shoulders, his unruly hair, his bewildered eyes. She doesn't want to leave and thinks about canceling on Luca, but she knows she needs to see her son and explain all the myriad ways *his* life is about to change too. But Mason . . . his entire existence has been burgled. Life just isn't the same after familial loss. She should know.

Before she leaves, she reaches into her bag and extracts

the wooden airplane. She places it on the table. "Your mother bought you this."

The lie slips from her lips, but she needs Mason to experience some comfort—even if it's as trivial as a toy airplane.

He greedily pulls it toward his chest. Satisfied, Grace leaves.

As she treads down the stone steps, Noah's offer brims to the surface. Though she appreciates the sentiment, Lee left Mason in *her* care, not anyone else's. She has to do what's right, not what's easy.

If Mason can't be with his mother, then she will make sure he is happy and loved by her. She revs the car. Snapshots plague her mind. The mountain. The loss. The body. The recollection of the party. Mason's world cracked apart by a single phrase.

She worries about Luca, her house, the move, the explanation. Only time will tell how this will all work out. She cranks the music, lowers the windows, and presses harder on the gas pedal to get home to her son.

synonyms for <u>GUILT</u>:
culpable
disgrace
remorse
shame
sin
crime
infamy
iniquity
offense
wickedness
wrong

BLAH
BLAH
BLAH
I used to think <u>guilt</u> was such a stupid emotion.
You either do things with conviction or you don't do them at all.
Why would anyone ever waste time feeling <u>guilty</u>?

Now I know.

I know what <u>guilt</u> does to you.
I know all the ways it can change a life—or a moment.
I know the way it festers and keeps you bound.

There's power in <u>guilt</u>.
There's advantage.

I know how to make other people feel <u>guilty</u>.
I know what <u>guilt</u> can do to a person.

What <u>guilt</u> can do for me.

40

grace

Grace is responsible for the body. She only gets to see Luca for one day before she is back on the road, headed to Black Mountain. The girls insist one of them should join her, but Grace wants to do this alone. She needs the head space.

She tells Mason where she is going—she's decided that no matter what he asks about his mother, she will tell the truth—and he hesitates before she goes, the fear of her not returning registering in his eyes.

On the way, she thinks about Noah's offer. Yes, he's a strong male figure in Mason's life. He understands him. He can provide a wonderful education and give him necessary coping tools they don't possess. He's just trying to help. Grace knows all of this, but something in her gut says no to him moving into Lee's house. Mason needs a permanent mother, not a part-time one.

Grace thinks of the process of cremation and hopes Lee would approve of the simple, silver urn. Grace combs through the details of her many conversations with Lee, shaking loose the inner lining of their friendship to reveal somewhere meaningful to scatter a few ashes. She loved all the parks: Shelby Park, Radnor, and Percy Warner. There are also the knotted, aged trees in

Centennial Park. Her garden. That spot on the Harpeth where they'd gone kayaking with the boys.

She has hours to ponder as she drives, sorting through lists of possible locations, until she arrives in Black Mountain. She's already contacted Lee's clients, her therapist, and Mason's therapist, thanks to her address book. She'd traced her fingers over each of the numbers, all of the people in Lee's life contained within a few creased pages.

She is picking up the urn at the police station. She could have had it shipped, but she couldn't imagine Lee wedged in the back of a UPS truck like an Amazon package. No. She wonders why the urn isn't at the mortuary, but theirs is a small community, and she supposes they are improvising. She has to pick up the rest of Lee's personal effects, so they instruct her to come directly to the station.

Grace isn't good with death. Though her sister was the hardest loss of her life, most of her other relatives are alive and well. She has little experience being comforted, because she is always the one providing it. Every time she realizes this is happening *to* her—and specifically to Mason—brings with it a fresh new wave of grief.

She parks in front of the nondescript building and opens the police station door to find Jerry, the officer who had been their point person for the case. He sits at his desk and rubs a hand over his bald spot.

"Jerry?" Grace knocks on the door.

He pushes back from his desk when he sees her, a look of sympathy on his face. "Hey. Come in. Thanks for coming . . ."

"Grace. I'm Grace." She eyes his office. "I just didn't want it—her—to be shipped."

"I understand." He fumbles with the keys on his hip

and unlocks a large filing cabinet behind him. His arms disappear then reappear with a plastic bag containing a few recovered items: a ring, Lee's necklace, her striped socks, dirt-stained and freshly folded, and four silver bobby pins. She opens the necklace and runs her fingers over the photo of Mason. He clears his throat and she looks up to find the urn in his hands. The silver catches the light as he cradles the vase.

She takes it with caution, as though it's a bomb that might detonate. Lee is *in* here. Lee was a human—a talking, feeling human with arms, legs, and a heart. And now she is ash in an urn in her hands.

"Strange, isn't it?"

She blinks. Does he mean it's strange that he's stored an urn in his filing cabinet or that the process of cremation itself is strange? She only nods and tucks the plastic bag of belongings under her free arm.

"Life is a very precarious thing."

His words blow through her as she clenches the icy vase to her chest. "That it is," she responds.

She signs a few papers, thanks the officer, and walks back the way she came. Four and a half hours in the car, five minutes in the station, and she's free to head back to Nashville and all that awaits. As the sun blasts into a clear sky, she inhales the clean air, air they had been raving about only a week ago.

She starts toward the lake, the urn wedged under her arm like a football. She sits at the edge of the glittering water. How can a place so calm bring so much turmoil? She tosses a couple of pebbles into the water and situates the urn closer to her side. God forbid it tip over and drift along the walkway.

The court date looms. She and her lawyer have already

met to go over any last lingering questions or logistics over the guardianship arrangement. She imagines standing in front of a judge, offering herself as a fill-in parent. Grace takes some deep breaths and closes her eyes. She tries to conjure what their new lives will look like, how swiftly it's all about to change.

She finally stands, grips the urn in her hands, and walks back to the car. She opens the door and sorts through all of the various contents from her and Luca's lives: untied shoes, water bottles, crayons, toy cars, crumpled pictures, food wrappers. She spots a baggie with a few spare Cheerios and empties them onto the pavement. Carefully, she removes the top of the urn and sprinkles some ashes into the bag. She lifts the vase into the padded box she brought, wedges it in the floorboard, and locks the car. She trots over to the trail, alone with her thoughts. With the baggie. With Lee.

A few people are out enjoying the weather. She stops at the base of the trail and reads the sign: WELCOME TO BLACK MOUNTAIN TRAIL. YOU ARE HERE. She studies the red asterisk and the dotted line signifying the trail to the top. Lee had been right here. Had she read this sign? Had she had second thoughts about hiking?

Instead of taking off up the mountain, she veers off the path and over to where they found her. She will never forget the tenuous steps she took to identify her friend, disassembled, beneath that rubber sheet. The images are seared into her brain no matter how many times she tries to scrub them away. She keeps her eye out for any fallen trinkets: another ring, a bracelet, or Lee's phone. They have yet to recover her cell. She figures it got swept away in the thicket of trees on the way down. She fingers the baggie in her pocket and edges back to the trail. She checks the time. She unspools her earbuds, opens Spotify on her phone, and decides to climb.

On the way up, thoughts consume her. The wind whips her hair around her face as Son Lux blasts its melancholy chorus. At the peak, she checks for people on the trail, says a little prayer, and casts the remnants of the baggie into the wind, a bit of blowback causing her to step aside. She will sprinkle a little more at home in a spot they all agree to. She says a few words and then begins her descent. Nature pulses around her, unthreatening yet powerful in what it can do. She absorbs it all, this backdrop of death, this sanctuary for those who find spirituality in nature. She will never think of hiking the same way again.

Back at the car, she climbs into the hot seat, now warmed from the afternoon sun, and plugs in the directions home. The car revs, and she takes the beautiful, winding roads back to the highway. She dreamed of coming here in the fall with Luca, to see all the leaves change. They would go camping, maybe. Or check out the amazing nature park.

The idea settles like sour milk. In the span of one night, so much has been ruined, taken away, and removed like a lame limb. She glances at the urn beside her, safely packaged in its box. Lee's life has met its tragic conclusion, and here Grace is, left to handle the aftermath. She urged Lee to have a will in case something like this happened, but things like this *never* happened. It is the stuff of movies, those rare worst-case scenarios reserved for other people.

Yet here they are.

She tells herself to stay focused. She can't break down. She can't give in. She can't wonder if things could have been different.

But the what-ifs strangle her: what if she hadn't told

her about Noah and the baby? What if she hadn't left her with the wine? What if she hadn't fallen?

She queues up a podcast to take her mind off of the questions. The miles roll by as she tunes in to the words of Brooke Castillo, but inside, only one question remains:

What if she had found Lee before she climbed?

41

grace

Grace meets Noah for drinks when she gets back. Every conversation has been in someone's house, where the reminders of death and sadness drape over them. They need to get *out,* have a good meal, and loosen up. Grace has even thrown on a flirty red dress and high heels for the occasion.

Once in the dark bar, she rehearses her speech. Mason will come to live with her full-time. It's Grace's responsibility to care for Mason's well-being, not Noah's. She downs her seltzer and lime, crushing an olive between her teeth as it slides in salty chunks down her throat. The boys are with Carol, a new arrangement that will soon become typical. She will need her friends' help; she has to trust them just like Lee trusted her.

A few minutes later, Noah breezes in. Despite the tenuous situation, upon his arrival, she drinks in his flawless appearance. The hair that's neatly trimmed, the face that's smooth and freshly shaven, the clothes that are ironed, the nails that are buffed, cuticles clipped.

"Hi, gorgeous." He kisses her neck, and a shiver cascades from her shoulders to her hips.

"Hey, you." She pushes her glass to the bartender and orders another seltzer and a gin and tonic for him.

"How are you holding up?"

Though they talked on the way back, she didn't go into detail.

"I've been better." She greedily eyes his gin and tonic. "The urn is beautiful."

"That's good at least." His eyes are warm as they press into hers, gauging her emotional health.

"She would have liked it." Grace crunches into a cube of ice. "So, I've thought about what you offered—about staying in the house—but I want Mason to come live with us now. I think it makes sense in terms of the most successful transition."

Noah nods. "I think that's perfectly reasonable."

She cocks her head. "You do?"

He smiles. "I do."

"Okay, good. I was also thinking once I get through court, maybe we could discuss a new schedule for him? I know he's been doing the Waldorf homeschool method, but I was thinking about entering him in the Waldorf school close to my house."

"Really?" His eyebrows lift. "That place is pricey."

She shrugs. "I have the money."

He exhales. "That's a big decision though. Normally, kids with SPD don't do well in a school setting until they're closer to ten or eleven. But," he's quick to add, "the Waldorf school isn't a traditional school. And he's already used to the curriculum." He tosses back his drink and orders another. The bartender slides the squat glass across the mahogany bar. "I can assess, talk to the school, and set up a tour for all of us if you like?"

"Thanks."

He raises his glass to hers in a toast.

"We'll start packing up Lee's stuff, and I'll let the landlord know we're breaking the lease. Just know that

I am one hundred percent here for the both of you. And you." He presses a warm palm to her belly.

Relief slithers through her. She's been so on guard, like she has to protect something that isn't quite hers. The knots in her shoulders loosen. "It's all going to work out." She says it as much for him as for herself.

"It is." Noah canvasses the room, landing on a few older couples swaying to Sinatra. "Want to dance?" He hops off his stool and offers his hand.

Grace hasn't slow-danced in ages. Her fingers fit neatly into his. He spins her onto the open floor, her red dress twirling into a small bowl of fabric. Her limbs soften. The future blends with her worries and then evaporates: the baby, the living arrangements, Mason, Luca, her and Noah's future, coparenting with Chad, everything.

For this moment, she wants to be nothing more than a woman with her boyfriend on a dance floor. Noah eases her to his chest. They move, tender and slow, song after song, preparing themselves for their new reality, but clinging to this simple moment—just the two of them—for as long as they possibly can.

42

noah

He holds Grace. Her body fits so perfectly against his. His mind is a flurry of activity: his grief for Lee, the possibility of not teaching Mason anymore, his absolute excitement over the baby, his protectiveness over Grace. While he wants to plan his and Grace's future, everything has stalled. She doesn't seem excited about the baby. She doesn't even want to talk about it, and while he understands, he worries for her health. The questions keep him up at night: what if she doesn't feel connected to this child? What if she sabotages her own happiness because of how Lee died?

He wants to remind Grace that they must move forward; they can't ignore all the wonderful things that are about to happen. He knows she takes loss as personally as he does; when you lose a sibling, it's like losing a best friend. And now she *has* lost her best friend, and he can't relate to that exact experience. All he can do is continue to be here for her, Mason, and Luca.

He holds her tighter, and her heart thumps against his. His body responds to the sensuality of her red dress. The relaxed fabric, her body hot and inviting beneath it. They haven't made love since Lee died, and their previously adventurous sex life has waned since he found out she was pregnant.

He recalls the first time they slept together. As Grace shed her clothes, gone was the relatively composed woman he'd come to know. In her place was a woman who demanded to be tied up, spanked, choked, and talked dirty to. She constantly urged him to push the boundaries. He was wildly attracted to that part of her and relieved he could be so free. He hadn't really been that way since . . .

"What are you thinking about in there?" Grace blinks up at him, her eyes heavily hooded and cheeks flushed. Her bottom lip is wet from where she must have just licked it. She has no idea how sexy she is or how much he loves her, though he hasn't said it yet. He isn't sure he's ever really been in love with a woman before Grace.

Yes, she is a few years older. Yes, she has a child and a clown for an ex-husband. Yes, she is now the guardian of her best friend's child. But the way she has handled everything is not lost on him. It's what he wants from a partner. It's what he wants for the rest of his life: *her.*

"I'm thinking about how nice this is." He leans down to meet her lips with his, and his stomach knots and releases. "How good you feel." He adores everything about this woman. The intensity of it scares him. He wants to marry her, knew it almost immediately, but he doesn't dare bring it to her attention. Not yet. He has to tread lightly, let the grief fade, and then he will ask.

"What else are you thinking?" She nuzzles his neck with her lips.

"I'm thinking that I wouldn't want to be anywhere else."

"Really?" She pulls back, her long, white neck exposed. He resists the urge to trace every curve of her delicate throat with his tongue.

"Really." He gazes into her beautiful eyes, mesmerized as always by her pronounced cheekbones, her full, wide mouth, her ivory skin. The curls, wild and free, that seem to float around her shoulders. Her body underneath the clothes—a real woman's body full of scars, marks, and curves. He loves that she doesn't diet, isn't self-conscious or obsessed about looking a certain way. She's comfortable in her skin, and that's one of the things he loves most about her. She is sure of who she is.

He waits for her response, hoping he hasn't revealed too much. Though he can be himself, he's always afraid he's going to come on too strong or chase her away. He knows how fiercely independent she is, and that she doesn't need a man to feel complete.

"I feel the same way about you." She kisses him again and loops her arms around his neck. Her fingers tickle his scalp until his entire body ignites.

"Let's go home," he whispers. He doesn't know which home they will go to, but he wants to make love to her now.

She pulls back and her eyes flash with desire. "Your place or mine?"

"Wherever you'll have me." His mouth finds hers again. He loses himself in the middle of the bar. He gathers the fabric of her dress in his fist. The music fades. The rush of blood fills his entire body until all he can think about is getting Grace alone.

43

grace

The door squeaks on its hinges. Grace waves hello. It's so odd that Noah is answering Lee's door, that they are packing up her friend's belongings to haul off, donate, or sell. She motions behind her. "Yard looks great."

The front has been freshly mowed. The weeds have been pulled, the hedges trimmed, and the walkway swept and tidied. Lee's lease is null and void at the end of the month, but they still have to spruce it up to re-rent.

Grace steps inside. The last week blurs from memory. Only a few days ago, she stood in front of the judge in her best suit, guardianship papers in hand. Her whole support system waited in the wings for the good news. It had been a frighteningly easy process. The judge had rushed through the docket, barely making eye contact over his spectacles, before cracking his gavel for the next case. Grace had glanced at her lawyer to make sure she understood what had just happened, and Kim had simply nodded and shuffled papers back into a file.

"And that's that. He's all yours."

Grace had rushed out of the sterile room into the hall to find Mason obsessively bouncing a ball against the wall, while Alice, Carol, and Noah met her with expectant faces. Afterward, they'd gathered at Shelby Bottoms with muffins and coffee under Lee's favorite tree to scatter a few ashes. She'd given the urn to Mason, and it was the first time she thought he might actually be able to get closure.

Now, Grace steps into Lee's kitchen and closes the door. It still smells like her: hair products and stale coffee. She and Noah have already packed as much as they can, the furniture sold, donated, or dumped. Tonight is for stacking boxes and dismantling her studio, which hasn't yet been touched. "How are you feeling, gorgeous?" He kisses her and pulls her close. "I missed you today."

"Me too." Their wild night from the bar comes back into focus. The uninhibited sex. Her requests. The physical pleasure. Those moments have been too few and far between since the pregnancy and Lee's death.

"Want something to drink?" He releases her and opens a cabinet.

"Sure, water's fine."

He pours her a glass. "How's Mason?"

"Asleep. Alice came over to watch him."

"Good. Hope he sleeps tonight."

"You and me both." Mason's night terrors have challenged her previously uninterrupted sleep. Lee used to talk about them, but she never understood their severity or prevalence. She's been researching different remedies. She assumes, like with everything else he's dealing with, that it will just take time. She takes the chilled glass, and the icy water shocks her lips. He slices a lemon on the cutting board and squeezes in a few drops.

"Fancy," she jokes.

"I think we've made good progress, don't you?" They walk from room to room. Most of Lee's belongings have been stripped, tossed, or boxed.

"Shall we tackle the studio?"

"Yep." Noah stops in the kitchen and refills her glass. "I was thinking once we get that cleared out, we can just stack all of the boxes in there, since it still has the garage door."

"Sure." Grace imagines loading all the boxes into a van and taking them somewhere. Never coming back to this house. Never driving down this street. The finality of it consumes her.

In the studio, they clear the boxes to one side of the room. As she pushes cardboard across cement, memories hurl themselves to the surface of her brain. "I can't believe we're doing this."

Noah lowers a stack and wipes his hands on his jeans. "I know. I can't either."

"She really liked you, you know." Grace hasn't said the words; hasn't talked much about Lee since she died, hasn't wanted to admit that she is really gone and Grace is here in her place, in her house, about to mother her child.

He straightens. "I really liked her too." He groans as he heaves another stack along the far wall. "Just not in the way she expected."

She appreciates his honesty. "True. It's so strange that you both grew up here and never met each other before I introduced you." *It's strange that you never made a move* is what she really means. "Did you ever know any of her friends or anything?"

"Not that I know of." He shrugs. "We didn't run in the same circles."

Grace tries to imagine Lee and Noah going for coffee or hanging out, but can't. She busies herself with packing products into their own boxes and labels them to donate to local salons. She tapes the top of one and carries it to the wall.

They pack in silence over the next hour, and Grace wishes she'd left the speakers hooked up. She finally swipes her phone, opens Spotify, and cranks the volume to capacity. "Well, that's far from impressive," she jokes.

"Here." Noah plucks a plastic cup from Lee's desk and deposits the phone into it. The sound amplifies through the room. "Instant speaker."

"Thanks." She looks around. "Want to take a break for a second?" She sits cross-legged on the rug. "You know, I bought this rug with Lee. I joked that it was like having a giant sheep at work." She runs her fingers through the threads. "She didn't want a rug because of all the hair she had to sweep, but I insisted vacuuming would be less work. And the cement would get so cold on her bare feet in the winter. She always preferred being barefoot." She chokes on her words and shakes her head. "Sorry."

Noah sits beside her. "It really doesn't seem real, I know. I don't think it ever does." He glances at her. "When you lose someone, I mean."

She wipes away her tears. "You mean Wyatt?"

"Yeah."

"It's crazy to me we both lost siblings. That's rare."

Noah hesitates. "How come you never talk about her?"

Noah has asked a few questions about her sister, but Grace always deflects. "Same reason you don't probably. Too painful."

"Makes sense." He glances at her. "Were you close?"

She shrugs and plunges her fingers back into the rug. "At one time, yeah. But you know how it is when everyone in your family is so consumed with their own lives. You miss things."

Noah exhales and nods. "You certainly do."

"Do you think you ended up working with autistic

kids specifically because of Wyatt?" She releases the rug and folds her hands into her lap.

"Probably. But I've always been good with kids. Kids like Wyatt and Mason. I have a knack for it, I guess."

"I can see that. You always seem in control."

"Oh, I am." He laughs.

She cranes her head toward the painted ceiling. "It was all so simple when I first met Lee. Mason was just a baby, and she was still working at the salon. She was happy. Everything was going so well for her. I didn't know she was a recovering alcoholic at that point—she was always so good at keeping things to herself—but, I don't know." She sighs. "We had a good time together. She was easy to be around. She fit into our group." She pauses. "Now, every morning I wake up, I think, 'Did that really happen?' The thought of never telling her something that happened, or laughing with her, or getting coffee and going for a walk . . . I mean, you should have seen her at the bottom of that mountain, Noah." She shakes her head at the memory. "And Mason."

Noah dangles his scotch glass between the fingers of his right hand and loops his left around her shoulders. "Mason will be fine. He's doing well."

Grace massages the back of her own neck. "He is, isn't he?"

Her cell blasts through the studio, cutting into the current song, and startles them both. She grabs the phone from the cup. "It's Alice." She forces herself to stay calm. Knowing Alice, she probably just wants to know where she keeps the good wine. She swipes to answer and instantly hears Mason screaming in the background.

"Alice? What's going on?"

"I'm so sorry," Alice hisses. "He woke up. He's so upset. I didn't know what to do. I . . ."

"I'll be right there. Okay? Stay calm." Grace disconnects the call. "He woke up."

"Should I come with you?"

Grace stands and gathers her things. "You don't mind?"

"Of course not. I'll drive."

Grace decides not to worry about her car as they pile into his and speed through the neighborhood. She shouldn't have left Mason with Alice. She should be there for him, even if she does have to get things done at Lee's. Twenty minutes later, Noah kills the engine in her driveway and shoves the gear into park.

She shuts the passenger door. The leaves blow gently against the trees, even though the air's too warm for this time of night. She can't even make out the stars from the thick smudge of clouds overhead. Mason's voice rocks her walls, even from outside. She checks her watch. Has he been screaming this entire time? Noah enters before her. She takes a deep breath, prepares herself, and steps inside.

44

grace

Her living room has been completely dismantled. Throw pillows, cushions, toys, blocks, and books have been ripped and tossed across the open space. Alice grips her elbow and steers Grace toward the door, her fingers like ice.

"I'm so sorry. I didn't know what to do. I've tried everything I can think of to calm him down. But I've mostly just been ducking to avoid getting hit."

"And Luca . . . ?"

"I checked on him. He woke up and was pretty freaked out, but I think he fell back asleep. You're lucky he sleeps like the dead."

Noah kneels in front of Mason, his small face twisted and red.

"You okay?" Alice places a hand on Grace's back.

"What do you mean?"

"You just look pale. Are you feeling alright?" Alice's eyes trail to her stomach.

"Just tired." She walks Alice to her car and thanks her for staying. "Sorry about this. I'll call you tomorrow."

She heads back inside, but Noah has already disappeared into Mason's room. She starts to clean and sort through the mess, stacking books, organizing the G.I.

Joes, rock collections, math cubes, and various toys, fluffing pillows, and replacing the books in their appropriate bins. What caused him to get so upset—a nightmare?

She moves to the row of banker's boxes stacked against the bookcase. He'd gotten into these as well, flinging the contents with abandon. Grace moved all Lee's documents to her house to sort through, but abandoned the project when she realized her quiet single mom moments were gone. She didn't have time for side projects, organization, baths, yoga, or binge-watching Netflix. The time she has on her own is now spent taking care of logistics: Mason's therapy sessions, the extra payments, school entry forms, extracurriculars for both boys, the last lingering court documents. Her life has become a series of appointments, paperwork, and new, expected compromises.

She dumps some of the files back into the box and primes her ears for Luca, but his door remains shut. He's always slept like a rock, not even stirring when tornado sirens blast through the neighborhood on stormy nights. She tiptoes to the end of the hall to check on him. The sheets tangle around his legs, his arms flung above his head in victory. She watches him sleep for a moment, adjusts his comforter, and presses her cool palm to his forehead, hunting for fever. He's had a bit of a cold and not much of an appetite the past few days. His skin warms her hand but isn't hot. On her way back to the living room, she listens for Mason, but all is quiet.

Grace surveys the hall, the bathroom, and kitchen, satisfied that the episode hasn't extended into any other part of the house. She resumes replacing Lee's personal items back into boxes. There are so many documents to compose a life. Most have to do with Lee's business: tax returns, write-offs, receipts, bills. She must take care of dissolving Lee's LLC too. She sweeps through the thick manila folders and slices her middle finger against last year's tax return.

"Shit." She sucks the blood from the thin cut and replaces the lid.

"Hey." Noah squints into the living room lights.

Grace turns, her finger still in her mouth. "Is he okay?"

He eyes her finger. "Are you okay?"

"Paper cut." She drops her hand and glances down the hall. "He asleep?"

"Yeah." He collapses on the couch.

"Thank you for that." She wedges in beside him. "Did he say what he was so upset about?"

Noah scratches his neck. "He said he was looking for something."

"Looking for something?" Grace inspects her finger for more blood.

"Of his mom's. Probably something personal he could keep."

Grace drops her finger. "Of course he probably wants something of hers. I can't believe I didn't think of that." Tomorrow, she will sort through and ask him what he wanted.

"I think you've had other things on your mind." He rests his hands on his thighs and stands. "Look, I was thinking I'd keep packing back at the house if you're okay with that? Unless you want me to stay?"

"No, go. We've got to have everything out of that house in two days." She walks him to the door and suddenly stops. "Oh shit. My car is at the house."

"We'll get it tomorrow." He tugs her against his middle and kisses her passionately. His hands trail the lower part of her spine and wind around to her belly. She pulls away. "You feeling okay? With the baby and everything?"

She folds her hands across her stomach, a barrier. "Yeah, why?"

He smiles and steps back in to kiss her, his tongue grazing across her neck. "Just making sure."

Her skin erupts into goose bumps. She pulls him tighter, and he kisses her again. They break apart. They haven't said they love each other yet, even with his baby inside her, but she knows it's coming.

"Sleep well. Call me if you need anything."

"'Night." She closes the door, collapses against it, and then heads to bed.

45

noah

He makes it halfway back to Lee's when he realizes he doesn't have his phone. "Shit." He thinks about leaving it but won't have any way to contact Grace in the morning. He turns around, hating how naked he feels without it, how addicted to technology they've all become. The ultimate crutch.

When he pulls up, the house is dark. Has she already gone to bed? He flicks Grace's key around on his key ring and lets himself inside. He whispers her name, but her room is at the back of the house. She sleeps with a sound machine. He knows he won't startle her. It's Mason he's worried about.

He flips on the interior light and searches for his phone. It's not on the entry table or on the couch. He hopes it didn't fall out of his pocket when putting Mason to bed. He sweeps the living room and pauses near Grace's desk. It's a beautiful antique they'd found together at the Nashville Flea Market at The Fairgrounds Nashville. He'd haggled on the price and gotten the dealer down, loaded it up on a cheap Budget rental they'd secured for the day, and helped her situate it in front of the bay window. His fingers trace the wood until he spots a corner of his phone edging out from beneath a banker's box.

"Gotcha." He assumes Grace placed it here. He lifts the box off the edge and notices the word *personal* scribbled in Grace's handwriting across the top.

They have both handled so much paperwork lately. All of Lee's business accounts, Mason's guardianship, the court documents, and taxes. Noah has done his part to arrange, label, and file all of Mason's physical, medical, and therapy files to make it easier on Grace.

Though this is private, curiosity gets the best of him. He flips open the lid and peers into the box. A few photographs are scattered over some journals and a folder labeled HARRY. Who's Harry? He prepares to close the box but hesitates. He eyes the photograph on top. For reasons he can't articulate, his heart begins to race. He plucks it from the pile. His heart gives a physical kick against his chest. Two women stare back at him—one of them is Lee. Their arms are looped around each other playfully, and Lee is cocked forward, mouth open, laughing. The women are virtually the same height with similar haircuts, painfully thin limbs, pale skin, and large eyes.

"What are you doing?"

He drops the photo and rearranges his face to neutral. "Hey, sorry."

Grace stands in silk pajamas. The outline of her body peeks beneath the thin fabric. He lifts his phone. "Must have fallen out of my pocket."

Her eyes flick to the box. "Was it in the box?"

"No, under." He glances again at the photo. "Sorry, I was just curious." He picks up the photo. "There's been so much paperwork lately that it's nice to see an actual photo of her. This is a great shot."

"Which one?" Grace walks to the box as he hands her the photo. She emits a painful smile and traces Lee's outline with her fingertips. "It is. This is before I knew her." She sets it down and replaces the lid. "I don't really know what to do with this stuff. These are all so personal. It feels wrong to toss them, you know?" She flattens her palm against the top of the box. "And I thought Mason might like to have them someday."

"I'm sure he would." Noah cocks his head. "Who's that with her? Her sister?"

"Lee doesn't have any siblings. That's her best friend."

"I thought you were her best friend," he teases. He attempts to keep his voice calm, his actions nuanced.

"I am. I meant before we met." She shoves the box to the edge of the desk and he reaches to help her lower it. She rolls her eyes at him. "I'm fine."

He lifts his hands in surrender. "I know you are a strong, capable woman. But you're also pregnant."

"*Barely* pregnant."

"Still."

"I'll fight you." She playfully leans into him, and his arms close around her waist. His question about the photo bounces around his mind as he inhales her intoxicating scent. He closes his eyes and focuses on the woman in his arms, not the one in the photo.

"I'm thirsty."

The two break apart as Mason appears from the hall and edges to the kitchen without asking for help. They hear the ice dispenser, a thin stream of water, an exaggerated yawn, and then he pads back to his room.

Noah smiles. "I'm so glad he's comfortable here."

"We're getting there." Grace glances at the clock. "Come to bed. We can finish up at Lee's in the morning."

"You sure?" He casts a cautious look down the hall. "What about the boys?"

"What about the boys?" She grabs his hand and looks at him suggestively.

"Will that be confusing for them to have me here in the morning?"

"Don't be silly. They love having you here." She tugs him down the hall, and he obeys.

The boys know they are dating, and so far, they haven't had an issue with it, but he still worries about blurring boundaries and introducing too many changes at once. Grace hasn't told Luca about the baby yet, and he respects her decision. She wants to get far enough along in the pregnancy to make sure it's safe. He gets that. But every part of him wants to scream from the rooftops that he's going to be a father.

He undresses down to his briefs and slips into bed beside her. His body is suddenly exhausted, but his mind is frantic. He tries to forget about the box, the photograph, the puzzle that's scrawled across it. He needs to know, but the last thing he wants to do is to give himself away. Grace is dealing with so much—too much. She wouldn't understand. She would be confused, maybe even angry. But he knows they have to talk about it. He will not keep secrets from the mother of his child.

He tosses and turns for hours as Grace sleeps beside him. He sees the women in the photograph. How had he never known Lee had an almost identical best friend? He hasn't let himself think about Lee since the accident, because he's trying to be strong for Grace. But the sadness challenges him now, and the guilt. Noah *knew* Lee liked him. Instead of dissuading her or just telling her the moment he and Grace became involved, he dodged and deflected. He pretended. He ignored the obvious. He kept secrets.

But at what cost?

If they'd just been honest right up front, Lee and Grace wouldn't have gotten into that fight. She wouldn't have had a reason to drink. She wouldn't have taken that dreaded hike.

He rubs his eyes. He can't keep doing this to himself. He can't keep obsessing over the same handful of thoughts. Wyatt was enough. Wyatt was *more* than enough. Though years have passed and he has forgiven his family, the hurt still burrows around in his heart like a defect.

He can't do anything to bring Wyatt back, just like he can't bring Lee back. But if he'd had all the information, he could have prevented Wyatt's death. Could he have somehow saved Lee too? He replays their relationship as if on a reel, wondering if he once again missed obvious signs.

He exhales and blinks at the ceiling, waiting for early morning. He should just go back to Lee's and finish the job. It would be better than torturing himself here. He clings to his secret and thinks of what's in the box. He works his way back to the party. Of what came after.

Of what happened that night in the dark.

the truth will set you free
the truth will set you free
the truth will set you free
the truth will set you free
the truth will set you free
the truth will set you free
the truth will set you free
the truth will set you free
the truth will set you free
the truth will set you free
the truth will set you free
the truth will set you free
the truth will set you free
the truth will set you free
the truth will set you free
the truth will set you free
the truth will set you free
the truth will set you free
the truth will set you free
the truth will set you free
the truth will set you free
the truth will set you free
the truth will set you free
the truth will set you free
the truth will set you free
the truth will set you free
the truth will set you free
the truth will set you free
the truth will set you free
the truth will set you free
the truth will set you free

the truth will set you free
the truth will set you free
the truth will set you free
the truth will set you free
the truth will set you free
the truth will set you free
the truth will set you free
the truth will set you free
the truth will set you free
the truth will set you free
the truth will set you free

but the lies are what keep me safe.

46

grace

The next morning, Luca wakes her by shaking her shoulder.

"Mom, get up. Mason's door is locked, and he won't open it."

"What?" She was in a deep, dreamless sleep. She fumbles for her phone on the nightstand, but her fingers swat air. "What time is it?"

"I don't know, but Mason won't come out of his room. I'm hungry." He runs down the hall. She hears the sharp scrape of a stool toward the kitchen cabinets. The bang of a plastic bowl as it slips from his fingers. The clumsy way he opens and shuts the fridge and ransacks the silverware. She really needs to start keeping his bowls and cups in a lower cabinet. Grace's joints stiffen as she heaves herself out of bed, a dull ache nipping the base of her spine. She plucks her sweater from the dresser, walks to Mason's room, and jiggles the knob.

"Mase?"

She presses her ear to the door. Images flash through her mom brain: he's hurt himself. He's stopped breathing. He's climbed out the window and been missing since last night. "Mason?" She attempts to keep the fear out of her voice as she knocks harder against the wood.

"Open the door, please." Noah says if she is firm and uses action words, he'll be more likely to do what she says. She peers down the hall. Where is Noah?

After a few minutes, he unlocks the door. "You know what a locked door means, right?"

She doesn't warn him about his tone. Unlike Luca, Mason speaks factually, not always emotionally. "Luca and I were worried about you. We don't lock doors in this house."

"Fine. Can I go back to reading?"

"What are you reading?"

"My mom's journal."

"What?" She pushes into his room, pauses, and waits for permission. "May I see?"

He points to a gray journal on the bed, its pages fluttering under the high whine of the ceiling fan. She flips off the fan and runs her fingers over the cover. It's the same journal she saw in Lee's studio. The one she brought to Black Mountain. "Hey, bud. You know that journals are for private thoughts, right?"

Mason hovers by the door. "Yes, I am quite aware of that fact."

"And those thoughts are for grown-ups, not kids."

"I have an IQ of one-fifty-six. That's a *landslide* compared to most grown-ups."

Grace laughs. "That's true, but this is still meant to be private."

He sits beside her and points to a random page. "Have you read this? My mom had a lot of secrets."

She refrains from just taking the journal. She would never dream of doing something so sudden with Mason, something she wouldn't even think twice about if it were Luca. She is growing accustomed to the two sets of rules, but sometimes it's hard not to fall back on her parenting impulses. "Is this why you were upset last night? Were you looking for this?"

He shrugs. "I found it, didn't I?" He plucks the wooden airplane from his nightstand and holds it. "I just miss her."

"Of course you do," Grace says. She eyes the journal again. "Sorry for coming into your room unannounced. Would you like some breakfast?"

"Yes, please."

"May I have the journal?"

He rolls his eyes. "Grown-ups really are no fun."

"Thank you." She tucks it under her arm and then places it on her desk. She heads into the kitchen and sees Noah bent over her coffeemaker. "That's a lovely sight." Grace smiles and kisses him on the lips.

"Well, good morning to you too. Didn't want to wake you." Circles deepen the hollows beneath his eyes.

"No sleep?"

"Couldn't for some reason."

"Coffee should help." She slips on her sweater, washes her hands, and pulls down two mugs.

"I can't find the decaf though. Where do you keep it?"

"Oh, you know what? I'm out. But the doctor said I could still have one cup of regular coffee a day."

"Even with your age and everything?" Noah raises his eyebrows. "She said that's okay?"

She doesn't take offense at his question and instead laughs. "Yes, even in my old age. One cup of coffee is fine."

His face relaxes. "Thank God. Because I need it today. One strong cup coming up."

Once breakfast is ready, Luca plays with two Transformers on the table, mouthing silent explosions as the plastic toys butt into each other, while Mason reads a science book.

Grace sips her coffee, not yet ready to eat. Noah wolfs

his eggs. "Everything okay? You seem nervous or something."

"No." He wipes away egg with his napkin. "Just anxious to get everything wrapped up today."

"We'll get it done. Carol offered to watch the boys while we work, since she's right down the street. They can play outside."

Mason's head pops up. "Can I come with you? I don't want to go to Carol's."

"I thought you liked Carol's," Grace says.

"Zoe is too messy. Can we just stay while you work? We won't get in the way, right, Luca?"

Luca nods. "Right."

Grace thinks of Mason's room, robbed of all personal items. "You know your room is empty."

"I just want to say good-bye."

"Fair enough."

Mason nods and returns to reading. She waits for the caffeine to assuage her pounding head. After breakfast, they pile into Noah's car. She makes sure the boys fasten their seat belts. Her mind drifts as Noah engages Mason and Luca in a game of trivia.

Mason is the first to bolt inside after pulling into the gravel drive. His arms slice in straight, stiff lines by his hips. He dashes into his old room, shuts the door, and twists the lock. Luca charges into the backyard and climbs onto the fraying—but recently reinforced—tire swing. She watches her unruly boy thrust his middle through the rubber and gain higher and higher momentum.

Grace hesitates outside Mason's bedroom door and then finds Noah in the kitchen, rummaging through cabinets. She leans against the counter and crosses her arms. "Hey, can we get on the same page about something?"

"That we should come up with a way to inject caffeine

into our veins to get anything done?" He spins in the room. "Have you seen Lee's coffeemaker? I made sure not to pack it yet."

Grace retrieves it from the upper cabinet by the refrigerator and plugs it in. "Problem solved."

"My hero." Noah kisses her, and for a moment, she gets lost in the feel of his tongue in her mouth and his strong hand gripping the back of her neck. He pulls away first. "What do you want to get on the same page about?"

"So this morning, I asked Mason not to lock his bedroom door. He likes to lock it, which I get, but we have a no-locked-doors policy in our house."

Noah nods and fills the carafe from the tap. "Sure, I get it. I'll talk to him."

"Thank you." Grace has a thing about locked doors. Her sister used to lock herself in her room. Bad things happened behind locked doors. They made her paranoid.

"Now for the important question." Noah reaches across the counter and palms a bag of Vienna roast. "Are you allowed to have another cup?"

"I won't tell if you won't." Did Grace turn off her own coffeepot? Noah shakes the grounds into the filter and presses *start*. The kitchen fills with the scent of roasted beans. She's so forgetful lately: misplacing socks in the linen closet, toothpaste in the freezer, mail dropped and forgotten under the driver's seat of her car. He hands her Lee's hair school mug.

She traces her fingers over the porcelain of Lee's favorite mug. How many times has she stood in this very spot, exhausted from a bad parenting night while drowning her sorrows in countless cups of coffee? Grace suppresses the memory as she pours herself a cup, clears her throat, and turns toward the studio. "Would you mind keeping an eye on Luca? I'm going to pick up where we left off."

"Sure. I've just got a few more things in here and then I'll join you."

She steps into the garage, eyeing the rug they sat on last night. She moves to it first, deposits her coffee on the edge of Lee's desk, and winds the shaggy white rug into a tight coil. She drags it to the corner of the garage, hoists it up with some effort, and smacks away the dirt, hair, and lint that blow back onto her shoulders. Maybe the rug had been a terrible idea.

She sweeps up the debris from the cement, pulling the clogged bristles of the broom across split ends, pennies, rocks, and dead ladybugs, and then tugs the neck of her shirt over her nose as her eyes burn from the stench of lingering chemicals—bleach, ammonia, glosses, hair spray. She dumps the sagging dustpan into the open trash bag and looks around again. So much has been packed, moved, and taken apart. Perhaps she is prolonging all of this because she really isn't ready to move on. Despite going back to Black Mountain. Despite the quick cere- mony in the park. Despite watching Lee's pebbled ashes drift away, carried high by the wind.

A cluster of products tumbles from Lee's desk, and she stoops to throw them into a half-filled box. She'll do- nate them to a local salon so they won't go to waste. She takes another sip of her coffee, still scalding. That's why Lee loved this mug. Her coffee, no matter long how long it sat, stayed hot.

The pocket door rolls open. "Refill?" he offers.

"Now we're going from one cup to three?"

"Hey, it won't kill you, right? You said so yourself."

She nods and he crosses the bare cement to top her off, looks into her eyes, and kisses her. "I want to talk to you about something tonight, okay?"

Her skin barbs. "Okay."

"Nothing bad, I promise."

Grace immediately begins to decipher their recent conversations and tries to pinpoint what he could possibly have to say.

He smooths the wrinkle from between her brows. "That's your worry crease, you know. It's your tell."

She fingers it self-consciously. *I have a tell?*

"Don't worry. It's adorable." He flips the coffeepot lid and retreats back to the kitchen. "Open or closed?"

"Open, please."

She shuffles through all of the things Noah could have to tell her. She knows everything about him . . . doesn't she? What could he possibly want to discuss?

She takes another sip of coffee and wonders if it has anything to do with the baby. They haven't talked about living arrangements yet, but of course the natural progression will be to move in together. Maybe even get married.

There's a small part of her that would take satisfaction in rubbing her newfound happiness in Chad's face, after everything he's put her through.

But is she ready for all of that?

She continues packing and cleaning and stops every few minutes to sneak a peek at Luca and make sure Mason is fine. Noah works diligently in the other room, and she admires his movements, the width of his back, the muscles flexing beneath his T-shirt.

Desire hums through her body but she wills it away. She focuses on the task at hand and waits for what he will inevitably reveal tonight.

47

grace

It has been a long day of packing, and all Grace wants is a beer. Her feet hurt. The boxes are gone. The floors vacuumed. The windows washed. The artwork removed. *Lee* removed.

On the way home they grab takeout, play a quick game of Scrabble at Grace's, and then Luca and Mason disappear to work on a project.

Noah sweeps the small wooden tiles back into the box. She collapses on her couch, legs extended, and hears the swift pop of the metal top on Noah's favorite local IPA, Bearded Iris.

"I would literally give my right arm for that beer."

"Then how would you carry our baby?"

"I've got this one." She gestures with her left hand.

He kisses her and places her legs over his. "Should we check on them?"

She relaxes against the cushions. "Not unless they give us a reason to."

He takes a deep pull and emits a satisfied sigh. "Good point."

"What a day."

"But we got it done." He massages her calves with his free hand.

"You mean *you* got it done. I feel like I wasn't much help."

"Are you insane? You cleaned that house until it sparkled. All while pregnant, I might add."

She waves a hand. "I don't feel any different yet. Except more tired."

"Still. I know it wasn't easy doing all of that. You should have let me hire a crew."

"Nonsense. I wanted to do that for her, at least." She blinks at the ceiling. "You know, it's funny. When I was pregnant with Luca, I was obsessive about every stage. How big he was, what was happening to my body, if he was the size of a seed, an avocado, or a grapefruit. This time, I haven't even had a second to really think about it. There's been so much going on, I . . ." *I want to pretend it all never happened. I want Mason to be happy. I want Luca to be happy. I want all of this to be easy.*

"I know. Look." He scoots closer to her on the couch. "This has all been the opposite of what anyone expected, right?"

"Understatement of the year."

He places his beer on the coffee table. "But we're getting through it. We're going to get through it. You'll see."

Her head rests against the cushion, and the fabric scruffs her ear. "Maybe. And next week will be a bit easier with Mason at science camp."

Noah smiles. "That's right. I forgot that was so soon. God, he's going to love it."

"I've never seen him so excited about something." At Noah's suggestion, they'd taken Mason to an orientation for sensitive learners, and to her absolute delight, he's been counting down the days until camp begins.

"It will be good for him." Noah rubs her legs. "And you." He pauses.

Grace wonders if he's going to reveal what he wanted to talk about earlier. She closes her eyes. Though she wants to hear what he has to say—has been thinking about it most of the day—what she wants more is intimacy. His mouth on hers. To get lost in feeling, not thinking.

With all of the aftermath, there's been no real room for intimacy, and she craves it. Whether it's hormones, grief, sleeplessness, or just desire, she wants to feel something other than the residue of the to-dos in deconstructing and simultaneously rebuilding a life. She runs the tip of her finger underneath the lip of his T-shirt and grazes his belt.

"What are you doing?"

She caresses his skin. "Taxes."

He glances toward the hall. "But the boys . . ."

"The boys are fine."

As if on cue, Mason's door opens and Luca bounds into the kitchen. She retracts her hand. "What do you need, bud?"

"Snacks."

"Want help?"

"No."

Grace laughs. "Help him, please." The last time Luca fixed a snack on his own, he'd broken a glass.

"I'm on it," Noah says.

Grace rises to check on Mason. Legos litter the carpet and form a few shaky skyscrapers. His record player spews jazz—a recent discovery Noah made at the local thrift store. "We're building," he says.

"That's a pretty impressive city you've got there. May I sit?"

"Suit yourself." He stacks more Legos with expert precision, building another few inches in the air.

She assesses his room, which is almost a complete replica of his old one. "How are you liking your room?"

"You did it proud."

Grace smiles. "I'm glad."

Luca enters with a silver platter of cheese, crackers, grapes, hummus, and veggies and places it on the bed. He crams two crackers and a cube of cheese into his mouth. "Come on, Mom. We need privacy."

She rises, hands up in surrender, and backs out of the room. Noah meets her in the hall and kisses her deeply. With the boys safely lost in their world of building and eating, Grace succumbs to Noah's hands on her face, his lips against her skin, and her body bound to his. He leads her to her bedroom and shuts and locks the door. They hurry out of their clothes. Passion throttles through her. She can think of nothing else but the need for him to be inside her.

His tongue twines with hers with an intensity she thought they'd lost. Though they often have uninhibited sex, it has been sweeter and softer since she found out she was pregnant, but tonight, she just wants to be consumed. She climbs onto her bed on all fours, and he silently moves behind her, urging her legs apart with his knees.

"Is this what you want?"

She nods and blocks out the world. He runs his hands the length of her spine and hips. He braces himself behind her, moving around but not in.

"Please," she insists.

He continues teasing her until he finally, slowly, eases inside. Her thighs throb with need. Grace moves back to meet him. "Deeper."

His left hand grips her shoulder, then works around to her mouth. She sucks his fingers as he rocks in and out of her. She tosses her head back and slams into him. Their breath ignites the room. Before she can ask for more, his hand pauses at her throat and then closes. She arches back, inviting it—she loves it rough—and can hear his fast breathing; how close he is already. She needs this to last. He whispers something, but the blood whooshes through her ears as she tries to breathe. His fingers are too tight.

She reaches a hand to loosen his grip. His mouth moves behind her, his body close to explosion, but she can only make out some of what he says between heated breaths. "Do you like that? Do you like it when I squeeze?"

Dread sweeps the room, her brain, her neck. His fingers tighten until she struggles for breath. Those words . . . she *knows* those words. What they mean. She wants to pry her throat free, but she has to know. She has to keep going. She has to hear the truth. "Yes," she chokes.

He fucks her harder until her body convulses at his will. His body suctions onto hers, and, with her throat in one hand, he cups her ear with his lips, licking and suck-ing. "Do you like being choked? Do you like thinking about what I could do to you?" He thrusts harder until he comes, still grinding into her hips.

His words drum in her ears. Lee's story at Arbor House, on the deck, reels into focus. Those words. The choking. The man in the dark.

She gasps as he finally releases his hand and she col-lapses to her belly. The flesh of her ass bounces as she lies there, her brain spinning. She coughs and struggles for clean air before flipping over and palming the sheet over her naked body. Wherever he'd just been dissolves as he cocks back on his heels, sweaty and swollen, blink-ing at her.

"What just happened? Are you okay? Was that too tight?"

She fingers her throat. "Yeah, a little."

"Shit. Sorry. That was just ridiculously hot. We haven't really gotten adventurous . . . since the baby."

"I know. Speaking of." She slithers to her feet and refrains from sprinting to the bathroom. "I need to pee." The door is too far. She swipes her clothes from the floor, shakes them out, and uses them as a shield. She focuses on getting her feet to move, the bathroom door now just an arm's length away.

Before she can get there, the pads of Noah's strong, wide feet pulse behind her. "Grace? Hey. Look at me. Are you sure you're okay?" He eyes her belly. His body blocks the door.

"I'm fine. The baby's fine." Her hand moves to her stomach. "I literally just have to pee." She reaches up on tiptoe to kiss him and shuts the door. She twists the lock. She looks in the mirror. Fingerprints bloom around her throat. Noah's fingers. Had she really heard right?

She replays the conversation with Lee in Black Mountain. Lee would have known. He couldn't be—

Noah knocks on the door. "Grace?" His voice sounds worried as he raps knuckles against wood.

She takes a breath and splashes water on her face. She slips on her clothes, unlocks the door, and edges a foot into the bedroom. Noah pulls on his T-shirt, his jeans already buttoned and loose around his hips. His back hulks in front of the bed. He turns. "Hey, you."

She can't read his expression. He takes a few steps toward her, and she holds her breath.

"You promise you're okay?"

Grace nods and touches her throat again.

His eyes trail down to her fingers and she quickly drops them. "Holy shit. Did I hurt you?"

She exposes her neck, her pulse thumping against her

aggravated skin. He grazes his fingers across her neck. "Jesus, Grace." He tenderly kisses her throat with his lips. "Do you want some ice?"

"No, I'm fine, really." She searches for her bag. Had she even brought it inside? "What did you say to me just now?"

"When?"

"When we were having sex. What did you say?"

"I have no idea what I said. I was just, you know, in the moment." His eyes reveal nothing. "Are you sure you're okay?"

Worry pricks her skin, a million questions hammering to the knock of her heart. She all but demands he repeat what he just said, what she *knows* she heard. "I'm fine," she says instead. "I just couldn't breathe."

They stare at each other. His words are sincere, but his eyes . . . she can't read his eyes. She fumbles for something to say. "Did that feel good at least?"

"Are you kidding?" He kisses the top of her head. "That was the hottest thing ever. Pregnancy suits you."

She forces a smile and refrains from wiping away his kiss. "Want to watch a movie or something?" She needs him out of her house, *now,* but she has to think. She has to figure this out.

"Sure. Want me to grab the boys?"

She nods. He disappears down the hall. Rage, fear, and disbelief swoop into focus. She replays the words—those *exact* words—he said during sex. Not just to her, but to someone else. Someone she loved. Someone who's dead and can't verify the truth.

She and Noah have had sex so many times, so why *now*? Why in this moment did he reveal who he really is? Grace's heart stutters around her chest. She wishes she had a recording to play back, to prove his words to the world.

Even though she doesn't have proof, she still *knows*. She knows what she heard. She knows Noah isn't who he says he is.

She knows the truth.

Part 4

the lies we tell

"You are one decision away from a totally different life."
—Mark Batterson

48

grace

Grace is numb. All this time, right under her nose. *Noah*. The guy from the party is Noah. It doesn't seem possible. How he ended up here, in this house. How she couldn't have known. How *Lee* couldn't have known. Wasn't there a look, his voice, her intuition, or something that would have tipped her off?

Luckily, Noah decided to sleep at his condo last night, as she worked to piece information together. Now, wrapped in a blanket with a cup of coffee, she watches the sunrise, takes a shower, and finally preps the lunches and snacks for the boys while they sleep. Her mind works at warp speed. Does she confront Noah and risk things getting out of hand? Does she demand he explain himself and tell his side of the story?

She weighs her options. She knows, for the moment, she has to keep things status quo until she figures out how best to handle him. She thinks of the girls and knows at some point, she's going to have to tell them the truth about Lee.

Luckily, with Mason in science camp, she won't have to make excuses to keep him away from Noah this week. It will buy her time to figure out her next move. She calls in sick to work and wakes the boys, getting Luca ready for school and Mason ready for camp.

They pile into the car after a quick breakfast. Despite what happened last night, Grace marvels at Mason's ability to deal with his grief, to move into a new home, to have a new sibling, a different parent, and even try something unfamiliar, like camp, with such courage. He has been attending counseling two times a week (up from once a week for extra grief counseling). She listens when he wants to talk, which is rare, but she is also careful not to push him. She realizes that Mason not only demands space, but he needs it, and Lee never felt comfortable enough to give it to him.

Her heart aches as she replays the scene from last night. It wasn't about the choking—they'd been rough before—but he'd *said* those words. The words from the party. She shudders at how willingly they all trusted him . . . how willingly Lee trusted him.

Grace drops Luca off first and then drives Mason the twenty minutes to the science center. "Are you excited for today, Mason?"

"I feel like I've waited my whole adult life for this day."

Grace laughs. "All seven years of your adult life?"

He cocks a finger in the air. "Soon to be eight."

"Getting up there, aren't you?"

He shakes his head. "Practically ancient."

Grace smiles at him in the rearview mirror. "Do you know what you'll be studying today?"

"The teacher said we are going to talk about anatomy, biology, and then end with robots."

"That sounds cool." She waits for him to say more, but he doesn't. "Would the old man like some music?"

"Ninety-one-point-one, please."

She hits the preset button. The classical music takes over. Ten minutes later, she parks in the massive lot flanked by a bank of overgrown trees. She walks him inside and signs him in. He removes his backpack and lunch to place in a labeled cubby.

"I'll be back at four, okay?"

He doesn't say good-bye as he is ushered down the main hall by a waving teacher. She checks her phone. Work email notifications, a few texts from the girls, and a missed call from Noah. She knows she can't avoid him forever, but maybe she can buy herself more time. She dials his number and rearranges her voice to sound neutral.

"Hey, I was worried about you. Everything okay?"

She fights the urge to scream. "Of course. Why wouldn't it be?"

"I just didn't hear from you last night before bed."

They always text before bed, or talk on the phone, but she couldn't force herself to go anywhere near her phone last night. "Sorry. I took a bath and fell straight to sleep. Just got the boys dropped off."

"How'd he do?"

"Like a champ. Didn't even say good-bye."

He laughs. "That's my boy."

Grace bristles at the term and bites her bottom lip until she tastes the metallic sting of blood. Has she been missing every obvious sign? His preference for Mason above all of his other students, his subtle manipulations in suggesting he move in as a "temporary" fix, his need to be around her. A horrifying thought jolts through Grace. Is Noah with her only to get closer to Mason?

"Want to do lunch today?"

"Let me check my calendar. Hold on." She pushes *mute* and takes a few deep breaths as she climbs back into her car. She presses the button again and sighs. "I have a lunch meeting with Jan today. Rain check?"

"Sure. Hey, you know what I was thinking?" he asks.

That you're a horrible, evil monster? She forces her voice to sound neutral. "What?"

"What would you think about a one-night getaway? Just the two of us? Maybe an Airbnb somewhere, or a cabin on the lake. Just a day and night to slow down and relax. We could use it."

I'd rather die. "How would we do that with the boys?"

"Well Chad has Luca on Saturday, right? Maybe Carol or Alice could watch Mason for the night?" Noah's casual suggestion slices across the line.

She shoves the car into reverse and backs out of the parking space. "You really think he'd be okay with that after everything he's been through? And his first week of camp, to top it all off?" His flippant attitude toward leaving Mason grates on her last nerve. How entitled he is to think *he* knows best.

There's a slight pause on the other end of the phone. "I do, actually. He's responding extremely well to change."

Grace calculates what to say, how to keep her distance without lying. "I just don't want to overwhelm him."

"I know."

She can hear the rustling of papers in the background.

"I'm prepping our lesson plans for next week. Maybe I could plan a really involved project for him this Saturday so he'd be totally consumed?"

Consumed. The word vibrates through her body. "You want to go on Saturday? Like this Saturday?"

"Yeah, why not?"

She hesitates and wants to protest all the reasons *why the fuck not.* Instead, she laughs. "Sorry. I must sound like a real mom, worrying about all the details. I'll check my schedule and get back to you, okay?"

"Want me to bring dinner tonight?" Noah's voice is hopeful.

"You know, I'm pretty buried. I was going to try and catch up when I got home and just have a quiet night. Is that okay?" Grace's voice is light but her entire body is on defense.

"Not trying to blow me off, are you?" His tone smarts underneath the teasing.

"Oh, please. The opposite. You know I'd spend every minute with you if I could. I just got Stacy's accounts because she's on maternity leave, so it's just been a bit nuts lately."

"Maybe she can return the favor when you're on leave," he adds.

"Maybe." She lapses into silence. Her fingernails dig into her palm until she feels the sharp bite of pain.

"Okay, well, let me know if I can do anything to help."

"I will. Hey, I need to go. Shouldn't be driving and talking." Grace wants to pitch the phone across the seat.

"Good girl. Have a great day."

Good girl. Her skin crawls. "You too."

She ends the call, tosses the phone onto the passenger seat, and screams in disgust. She can't do this. She can't pretend. She wants him gone.

49

noah

Noah balances the pizza box as he exits his car. He knows Grace said she wanted a quiet night, but he's not buying it. Plus, he wants to ask about what he found in that banker's box. He doesn't like keeping anything from her. He checks the time and knows the boys will be asleep. He hopes Grace hasn't eaten too much. She can never refuse 312 Pizza.

He uses his key and tentatively whispers into the hall. "Grace?" He slips the pizza in the kitchen, walks down the hall, and hears the shower running. He doesn't want to startle her, so he tiptoes back to the living room and glances at her desk. The box is gone, but he does a double-take as he sees a familiar-looking journal. Where has he seen that before? Feeling like a snoop for the second time, he opens it and quickly learns that it's Lee's. He's just about to close it, when something catches his eye. Despite his better judgment, he reads as fast as he can, absorbing the words. His body begins to heat, as if exerting himself. His palms grow clammy, and he suddenly finds it hard to breathe. He reads a few sentences about Lee's past. He flips back a few pages to gain some context and gasps when he reads the next paragraph. Words jump out at him. *That night. Wasted. The man in the dark.* If this is true, then . . .

"What are you doing here?"

He reluctantly pulls his attention from the journal to find Grace in a bathrobe with a towel wrapped turban-style around her hair. He holds the journal in the air. "I was just reading."

She tightens her bathrobe, walks to him, and plucks the journal from his fingers. "That's not yours."

"Have you read this?"

Grace shrugs.

"Come on." Noah resists the urge to roll his eyes. *Of course* she's read it. Who would ever refrain from reading their dead best friend's journal when it's lying right here?

"Come on what? These were Lee's private thoughts." She looks so earnest, he almost believes her.

He drags a hand over his face and glances around her desk. "I need to ask you about something. Something I just read. And something I saw the other night."

The silence hangs. She waits for him to continue.

"In that box the other day, there was a photograph."

"Okay." Grace perches on the edge of the couch and crosses her arms.

Noah attempts to remain calm. "Lee was with someone who looked exactly like her."

"So?"

He assesses how to frame the question. "So, you said it was her best friend, right?"

"Shirley."

"Shirley." Her name sounds foreign on his tongue. "But they look . . ." *Identical.*

Grace uncrosses her arms. "I know. They were both

hairdressers. Or, from what I know, Shirley wanted to become a hairdresser. Why, do you know her?"

Noah's heart bangs against his shirt, and he struggles to breathe. "I recognize her."

Grace cocks her head and looks directly at him. "From?"

"A party."

"A party with Lee?"

Noah shakes his head. "Lee? No, I don't think she was there."

Grace snorts. "Oh, please. Like you can't remember."

He recoils. "What the hell is that supposed to mean?"

Grace pushes away from the couch and paces the room. She turns back and her eyes are different, detached. "The choking, Noah. The words you said. I know what happened at that party. I know *every* fucking thing you did to her."

His blood runs cold. Grace knows about the party? "What do you mean you know about the party?"

"I know what you did. The choking, telling her you could kill her. I know that you left her in a pile of her own vomit. *That's* what I know."

"I . . ." No, that's not how it happened. Vomit? There'd been no vomit. "Where did you even hear that?" He works through the information.

"Lee," she finally whispers. She lifts her eyes to his, and his heart hardens. "Lee told me about that night. She said that's how she got pregnant."

The statement hits as if crashing against glass. The words break apart, but he can't make sense of them. Her sentences tangle and whip around the circumference of his brain. He's not sure he heard right. "She said what?"

"The night she died," Grace says. "She told me she was raped. That Mason was a product of *rape*. From that party. And that she was blackout drunk. That she woke up while someone was still inside of her. That she was left there, like trash."

Noah shakes his head in disbelief. His nerves sizzle, almost electric. "That's not possible."

Grace shakes her head and waits. "What's not possible?"

He sits beside her on the couch and grips the back edge until his knuckles are taut and white. "Because I never met Lee until you introduced us."

She snorts again, and her fingers tremble. "Give me a break. I'm supposed to believe that? After you choke me and say the *exact* same thing? After you've been lying about who you are this entire time?"

"I wasn't trying to hurt you, Grace. And I haven't been lying."

"Of course you've been lying!" She removes the towel from her head and shakes out her wet curls. "And those words . . . it's what you said to Lee at the party. What you *did* to her at that party."

"Grace, look at me." Desperation takes hold, and he feels like he's on the verge of losing everything: her, Mason, Luca, his unborn child, the truth, this moment. It all hinges on what he says next.

Grace finally looks at him, and he takes her hands. "I swear on whatever you need me to swear on. It wasn't her." The words leave his mouth in a rush, and he steadies his voice, demands that his heart rate come back under control.

She stares, unblinking, so long that he wonders if she's gone into shock. "*Who* wasn't her?"

Time slows. He can hear the ticking of the clock. The ice dispenser making fresh cubes. The way Grace breathes, ragged and unsure, across from him. He is so confused, but not about that night.

Grace impatiently removes her hands. "Who, Noah? Who wasn't her?"

"The girl at the party," he finally says. He blinks slowly, frozen in a memory he's catalogued somewhere in the recesses of his mind. But that night comes hurtling back, and he gasps at the clarity of it. He remembers everything about that encounter, especially her. "The girl in the dark." He says the phrase dramatically, like something out of a movie. He straightens, looks at Grace, means it. "The girl in the dark wasn't Lee."

darkness [dahrk-nis]

<u>**noun**</u>

1. the state or quality of being dark

2. absence or deficiency of light

3. wickedness or evil

I'll never forget that night as long as I live.
The way it changed everything in my life.
One moment, you think your life is a mess, and the
next moment, it is a mess—literally, figuratively,
permanently.

I've tried so many times to remember before.
How everything—even in chaos—was so much
better than what came after.

I've never been the same after.
I will never be the same after.
I won't stop until I prove what really happened . . .

I'm getting closer.

50

lee

Shirley startled her in the bathroom doorway. "Jesus, what are you doing? Move." Lee tried to push past her, but Shirley curled her fingers around Lee's shoulders.

"I want to make sure you're okay."

The room tilted, and Lee clutched the door frame. "I'm great."

"Let's get you home."

"What home is that? My home? The one I share with my father? I heard you," she hissed.

"Heard what?"

"In my mother's room, you and . . . him."

Even through her drunken haze, she could tell Shirley was ashamed. "Oh God. I didn't even think of it like that, as her bedroom. I'm so sorry. I would never . . ."

"Save it. Just leave me alone." She sidestepped around her and rushed down the stairs. She plucked a new red Solo cup from the pile and got herself some water.

She watched Shirley pause dramatically on the landing. Several men turned to admire her. Lee rolled her eyes and drank glass after glass of water in an attempt to sober up. She expected Shirley to storm out, but she didn't. Instead, her sober friend walked to the kitchen, plucked a cup from the teetering stack, and poured herself a drink. Lee, even in her drunken haze, moved to stop her.

"What are you doing?" She flattened her palm over the cup.

"The same thing you are." Shirley wrenched Lee's hand away and stared at the liquid in the cup.

Lee wavered. She couldn't let her do this. She couldn't let her throw away two years of hard work just to prove a point.

"You'll regret that."

Shirley looked at her. "So will you." She tossed back the drink and made a face. "If you're going to be stupid enough to drink after a lifetime of sobriety, then I am too."

Lee bit her lip and moved to the edge of the kitchen. She didn't want to play this game. Shirley was an adult. She could make her own damn decisions. (Except for dating her dad.) Shirley joined the drunken throng and returned to the kitchen to do shots. Lee ached to stop her. Shirley was punishing herself with alcohol. It was a tired game Shirley used to play, but not since she'd gotten sober.

Lee checked the time. She needed to call them both a cab. She'd worry about her car tomorrow. Lee cased Shirley for an hour, calculating how many drinks she consumed and how much more outspoken she became with each one. When Lee's guilt threatened to overtake her anger, she decided enough was enough.

Before she could grab her, Shirley walked back upstairs. Against her better instincts, Lee followed. At the top of the stairs, Shirley waited outside the bathroom. She heard the crank of water from whoever was inside. The flip of the light switch to darkness. Lee opened her mouth to say something, but then the door opened, and before the person could step out, Shirley disappeared inside and shut the door firmly behind her.

Lee rushed to the door. She twisted the knob, but it didn't move in her palm. She thought about banging on it, but instead listened through the wood. She could hear Shirley's voice and a guy's. Lee rolled her eyes. So she was going to sleep with a stranger after all. The drinking wasn't punishment enough.

She strained to listen, wavering between wanting to leave and needing to stay. Even amidst her anger, she felt responsible for Shirley. She'd just ruined her own sobriety and Shirley's too.

She raised her fist to knock, but something seized her, and she lowered it. When she closed her eyes, she saw Shirley and her father. She heard them in her mother's room. She felt the betrayal slice across her like a blade.

The conflict made her hesitate. Wasn't this *exactly* what she'd wanted Shirley to do? Lee's thoughts were fuzzy, but the hydration was starting to clear her head. This was just Shirley's typical way to prove to Lee that she would sacrifice herself. That they were like sisters. That Lee came first in her life, not Harold.

The knob felt hot in her hand. Her other palm flattened against the door. She needed to startle them both, to interrupt the moment, to get her out of there. She brought her hand back, but before it landed, she stopped: how could her very best friend consistently treat sex like it was nothing?

She pressed her ear to the door one last time and heard a slew of angry, muffled words: *I could kill you, do you know how easy it would be to kill you?*

Lee recoiled. *Kill her?* Who would say such ugly words? Fear throttled through her chest. She needed to get help. She stumbled toward the open door, ran to the landing, and quickly descended the stairs. The room swayed. She panned the crowd for Christy or a familiar face. Should she call the police? She extracted her phone, punched in 911, and hesitated before pressing *send*.

Her hand shook as she climbed the stairs again. She was going to kick the door down. She was going to save her friend. She approached the door, took a deep breath, and banged on it. She didn't wait for a response and tried the knob. It gave in her hand.

She spun around the room? Had the guy left? She flipped on the light.

"Oh my God." Shirley lay facedown, her head twisted, a pool of vomit by her cheek. Alcohol poisoning?

"Shirley. Shirley, can you hear me? Oh God, please wake up." She shook Shirley's shoulder and leaned down to make sure she was breathing. The room spun as she inhaled the vomit. Her own stomach bucked at the sight and smell. Before she could contain it, she lunged toward the toilet, hand splayed over her mouth, and emptied the contents of the wine and all the drinks after, swiping a hand across her sticky lips and collapsing next to the toilet bowl.

Shirley's panties stretched tight around her ankles like pink handcuffs. Who just said those words and *left* someone? Had he been drunk too? Suddenly, she hated alcohol; hated the myriad excuses it presented and how it blurred the lines. She looked at her friend. Though *this* wasn't blurry. She'd heard what he said. She was seeing the evidence.

Lee cleaned herself up and then yanked Shirley's underwear back to their proper place. Something oozed between her friend's legs. She could smell the semen.

"Oh, Jesus."

She washed her hands, rummaged in the medicine

cabinet for mouthwash, swished, and spat. There were no paper towels, so she grabbed the hand towel that was draped on the rod, wet it, pumped foamy hand soap into the fabric, and then scrubbed the thick, wet mess from the floor.

She shook the chunky towel into the toilet and flushed repeatedly, watching partially digested bits of her friend's food swirl away. She felt dizzy and unsteady, but she had to erase this scene. Make it look like it had never happened. If there was evidence, she'd be reminded whose fault this really was: *hers*.

It was her fault Shirley was even here, that she was left like this. This had gone from a dare to a nightmare. No matter how angry she was at her, or if Shirley had initiated this crazy, wild exchange, she hadn't wanted this to happen. She spritzed a plentiful amount of air freshener into the air, wrung out the hand towel in the bathtub, and draped it over the shower rod.

Now, for Shirley. She knew it was almost impossible to wake someone so drunk; she'd tried with her father. Lee needed to get her out of the bathroom. She scooped her up and dragged her limp body into the carpeted bedroom.

Music and voices thumped downstairs. She shut the bedroom door, locked it, and with effort, hoisted her slight friend onto the guest bed. It smelled like Febreze and stale cigarettes. She rolled Shirley to one side so she wouldn't choke on her own vomit. She'd twisted her dad's head too many nights, covering him with thin blankets and plying him with water and bread to soak up the booze.

She curled in behind Shirley, spooning her like a lover. She closed her eyes, the room tilting and twirling, and was relieved when sleep came heavy and fast. Her breath splintered, so much so that she woke a few times gasping for breath.

Every time she came to, she checked the skin of Shirley's neck with her index and middle finger, hunting for life, and then fell back into fractured sleep. She knew the hosts would find them eventually, that they would bang on the locked door, but she couldn't think of that now.

Her friend had just been sexually assaulted. This was bigger than her dating her father. This was bigger than her lapsing from sobriety. This was about more than the man who'd just left her in that bathroom.

This had happened *because* of her.

This was all Lee's fault.

51

grace

Grace replays Noah's statement in her head. "What do you mean it wasn't Lee?" She wants to call his bluff, wants to challenge him, but knows it will do her no good. They are at a crossroads of sorts, and neither of them knows what to do next. No matter who was in that bathroom, he left her there, spread-eagled, like an animal. There is no getting around *that*.

"It was her friend," he finally says. "That woman in the photo."

"What?" The truth spins into the room. "How do you know Shirley?"

Noah paces and pulls at his hair. "I don't. She approached me in the bathroom at that party. We . . . had sex." He reddens. "We were in the dark. I flipped on the light before I left. I remembered her face. I . . ."

Grace is incredulous. "Didn't you know that was Lee's friend? Didn't she ever bring her up?"

He shakes his head. "Even if she had, I didn't know her name. When I first met Lee, I admit I did a double-take. I thought it was her. But I quickly realized it wasn't the same girl."

"How?"

He shrugs. "I just knew it wasn't her."

Grace does not know what to say and balks at his casual gesture. She flicks through the secrets like cards in a Rolodex. The girl in the dark wasn't Lee. The girl in the dark was Shirley. Lee lied. About the party. About the man in the dark. About the nature of her pregnancy.

"Lee wouldn't just make up some horror story. She had to have a reason."

"Why would anyone use that as a false story? And to say that they were raped?" He lowers his voice on the last word and makes eye contact with her. "Which never happened, by the way."

Grace grimaces. "How am I supposed to know that? How could I possibly know the truth?"

"Because I'm *telling* you what happened. Because I'm a good guy. Because I'm the father of your unborn child. Because that's the truth."

Grace takes a few steps back like he'd slapped her. "How do you know that woman in the dark wasn't really Lee?"

He crosses the room to Grace's desk.

She continues. "Think about it. You were drunk. They look exactly alike. Don't you think you could have been confused? That the story Lee told *is* the real story?"

Noah hands her the journal. "No, I don't." He opens it and stabs a page. "Read this."

Grace takes the journal and scans the entry. Lee's loopy cursive jumps out at her.

After what happened with that guy at the party, everything changed. Shirley got depressed. It's like the feisty version of my best friend was replaced with a stranger.

She flips through a few more pages and then closes the book.

"See? I'm telling the truth."

Grace shrugs one shoulder, a loose gesture for what she's really feeling. "Okay, so it's true. I still don't understand why she'd tell me that *she* was the one who was sexually assaulted."

"Please don't use those words. I did not sexually assault anyone."

"Regardless of what you call it." She runs her thumb over the *L*. "You still had sex with a drunk woman and left her there."

"Grace, that was eight years ago. But it was completely consensual, I swear." He looks away from her and something dark flashes across his face. "I'd just lost my brother. I was out of my mind with grief. It was a horrible decision to leave her in that bathroom, sure—I'll admit that. But that's the only mistake I made that night. I did not force myself on her. I did not do anything that she didn't *demand* I do. And I certainly didn't leave her in a pile of her own vomit. She must have gotten sick after I left."

Grace doesn't want to go into all the ways men get away with things; all the ways stories are twisted to best serve them. She knows Noah has shown her nothing but kindness, but she can't get beyond what happened in that bathroom. Or what Lee said. What she needs to concentrate on now is what happens. How she handles him. How they move on. Or don't.

As if reading her mind, he speaks first. "What now?"

"I'm not sure. I want to believe you, Noah. But . . ."

"Look, I know Lee was your best friend. I get it. I do. But she blatantly lied to you about this, and I have no idea why. She's not the woman I slept with. I swear on whatever you need me to swear on. I never even saw that woman again."

Grace tosses the journal onto the couch by Noah's bag and folds her hands over her stomach. His eyes travel to the baby. She adjusts her robe and tries to formulate an appropriate response, but struggles for something to say. Instead, she flings her frustration into the room in a sweep of agitated breath and tightly crossed arms. She is so tired. She can't absorb any more information or talk about things she doesn't understand.

He takes the cue. "I know this is a lot. I'm sorry we have to deal with any of this, but what happened in the past doesn't really matter. We're a family. That's what matters now." He searches her face.

When she remains silent, he stands and grabs his keys and bag. "I'll give you some time. There's pizza in the kitchen." He steps toward the door and pauses. "Can I see you after work tomorrow?"

She rubs an invisible stain from the floor with her sock. "Maybe."

He nods, grazes her cheek with his familiar fingers, and tucks a curly strand of hair behind her ear. "I love you, Grace. Beyond everything. You have to know that."

Goose bumps stud her skin. He has not said those words out loud until this very moment, and she is angry that he's robbed her of that experience. She will forever link those three words to *this*. She only nods, shuts and locks the door, and spins around in her living room.

Now all she can do is wait.

52

noah

Noah climbs into his car and ransacks his bag for the stolen diary. He feels bad about taking it, but he has to read more. He has to understand where he fits into this story. Why Lee lied. Who Shirley is.

Ever since he saw that photo of Shirley, he can't shake the feeling that there's more to the story. More to *her* story. More to what happened at that party and after. More that Lee never told anyone about (because why would she?).

This tenuous and strange situation aside, he realizes that making sure things are fine with Grace is not only critical for them, but for the boys. Once he proposes to Grace, he will become Mason and Luca's stepfather. And a biological father to the baby. That sort of responsibility would scare most men, but he's been waiting his whole life for this. He's always wanted to be a father, and to have a special boy in his life who reminds him of Wyatt—who will now become a permanent fixture—it all seems right, on purpose.

The boys know he and Grace are dating—it wasn't some big announcement, but rather a quiet conversation that the boys had simply shrugged and said "cool" to. They will have a bigger discussion once Grace tells them both about the baby.

The wheels turn. Mason has gone through such dramatic changes lately. How will he feel about Noah stepping in as his stepfather? He knows he has to propose first. He doesn't want to get too ahead of himself. Grace needs time to sort through her emotions, but it's where they're headed.

As he pulls into his neighborhood, his thoughts drift back to Lee. He calculates all the different reasons why she would lie. He cringes at what she told Grace. He's never been one of those guys who takes advantage. But hadn't he just choked Grace during sex?

But Grace is wild in bed. She begs him to do the unthinkable, almost taunting him with her persistence. It's one of the things that is the most surprising about her. How calm she seems in day-to-day life. How she comes undone behind closed doors. Despite that dichotomy, he'd still somehow crossed the line. He'd said those stupid fucking words before he realized they'd even come out of his mouth. Why had he done that?

He parks his car.

He still doesn't know what Lee would gain from lying. Sweet Lee. She wasn't a liar . . . was she? He knew her better than that.

He gets out of his car and locks it, tracing the timeline of his and Grace's romance. He'd been interested right from the start, but she'd just wanted to be friends. He'd waited so patiently until he'd finally asked her out for drinks and she'd said yes. He never knew what changed, but once she was in, she was all in.

When she'd introduced him to Lee, his heart had almost blown right out of his chest. He thought it was the girl from the party, but then realized it wasn't. Still, he was uneasy for months after they met, and he'd asked Grace all sorts of questions to assuage his fears.

His stomach tightens again at the thought of hurting

Grace. The way she'd looked at him in absolute disgust. He'd assumed, despite all the trauma of recent weeks, that they were on steady ground. Now everything is fragile and uncertain, and he knows he has to concentrate on getting her to trust him again.

He steps inside his condo, settles in with the journal, and suppresses the guilt at reading something that doesn't belong to him. He knows, as he reads, that it's time he makes the ultimate commitment to Grace. To become the father that Mason and Luca need. To be the man he's always wanted to be.

He closes the journal. This isn't right. It's not his to read.

Lee must have had her own reasons for lying, but he can't worry about that now. He has to focus on his present and future with Grace, his unborn child, Luca, and Mason. He casts one last look at the journal, tucks it back into his bag, and then heads upstairs to bed.

53

noah

Noah got to the party late. He didn't know many people, except Phil and some of his basketball buddies. He found the birthday boy, handed him a bottle of booze, and poured himself a drink.

His parents had called him obsessively since he'd left Philadelphia. They wanted to know if he was okay. They wanted to know what they could do for him. The anger wrapped itself around him like a cord. If only he'd known what Wyatt had been feeling, thinking, or planning. He could have saved him. He *knew* it.

He blasted through shitty cocktails and moved onto shots with a set of guys as the music thumped and the bungalow filled with flowing bodies and women in flirty dresses and heavy-handed perfume. He was hungry for a warm body—he needed a release. He took his final shot. The tequila opened his sinuses and made his eyes tear. He blinked. Every time he closed them, he saw Wyatt, and then the pieces of him, scattered like leaves in the wind.

"Hey, didn't I see you at the Five Spot last week?"

Noah turned, and a pretty blond cocked her head, a strand of beads clinking against her breasts. "You were there, right? I remember you."

"How do you remember me if I was just turned around?"

"Because I was standing behind you thinking, 'That man has one fine-ass back.'"

In spite of his mood and maybe because of how drunk he was, he smiled. Did his breath smell like a distillery? "I wasn't in town last week."

"Are you sure?"

"I'm sure . . ."

"Patty. I'm sure, Patty." She offered her hand, delicate and manicured, and he kissed it, which made her blush. "A gentleman too? Now we *totally* have to hook up." She sipped beer from her red plastic cup—the raised eyebrow, the bait—and he pushed closer to her.

"And what's your definition of hooking up?"

"What's yours?"

He shrugged and was pierced by a pair of sharp elbows. He winced as they jabbed against his spine. "Will you excuse me for just a sec?" Pam? Peg? Patsy? Shit, he'd already forgotten her name. He moved past her and weaved through the throng of chatty, drunken bodies to look for a bathroom. The line spilled into the hallway, so he headed upstairs, hoping he wasn't going to find some couple hooking up in Phil's bed. He was too old for this shit. He felt like he was back in college. He should be married with a wife and kid by now.

He tried a few doors, found a bathroom attached to a guest bedroom, and relieved himself. He washed his hands and stared at his reflection in the mirror. Why was he even here? What was he doing with his life? He was thirty-one years old. At a house party. Alone. He wiped his hands on his jeans and flipped off the light. He opened the door to see the outline of a woman waiting to get in.

"Oh, sorry. I didn't know anyone was waiting." He fumbled for the light, but she pushed him back into the bathroom against the rim of the sink. The porcelain groaned under the weight of his back. The girl from downstairs?

"Do you want to leave?" The click of the door's lock pricked the darkness.

No, someone else. What was up with the women at this party? He could smell the alcohol on her breath, the angles of her body grinding into his.

"Hey," she said.

"Hey."

They were at a standoff in the dark, balanced between something happening and not happening. A sizzle of desire seared the base of his skull. She pushed in closer. "What's your name?" he whispered.

"What's yours?" Her tongue found his earlobe and licked.

For a moment, he forgot where he was, forgot why he was here, forgot about Wyatt. "Noah. Banks. Noah Banks." Why had he just told her his last name?

"Well, Noah Banks. It's your lucky day."

She moved in again. Her lips found his cheek in the dark and self-corrected until their tongues bumped. She sucked his lips and moaned. He closed his eyes, even though he could have kept them open, and focused on nothing but her. Their kisses deepened, and an urgency wound itself around them like a brittle web. This wasn't about her wanting him—she clearly wanted something or someone else—but he understood. He wanted to escape Wyatt, to escape his parents, to escape life.

He pressed her against the wall, his hands suddenly all over her body. She had small, high breasts and tiny nipples. He sucked on one and traveled down her trim waist to her hips. He bit the bone, and she laughed.

"I want you to fuck me."

Noah hesitated as he fumbled with the button of her

jeans. He could hear the desperation in her voice. Was she drunk? "Hey." He stood back up. One of his knees popped. "Maybe we should slow down a little." He kissed her again, but her small wrists flexed against his sturdy chest.

"No. Do it." She nibbled his ear, and he could smell tequila on her tongue. "Do anything."

"Anything?" He felt arousal mix with hesitation. The arsenal of his relatively tame sex life shook out like a bag of tricks.

"Anything," she whispered again. She ripped his shirt over his head. Her nails scraped across his belt buckle as she fell to her knees. She peeled his boxers down and took him into her mouth. Her hair tickled his thighs.

Please don't have whiskey dick. Please don't have whiskey dick. The mantra repeated like a prayer while the sounds of her sucking filled the blackness, and he came to full attention. Two minutes in, and he was already close, but he didn't want to be *that* guy, so he pulled her up off her knees.

"Do you want to go somewhere? Like to a bed or something?"

"Here's fine." She pushed his boxers all the way down and began to undress. She told him, in order, what she wanted him to do. He listened to her demands and almost asked why. *Why* did she want to be choked? *Why* did she want to be dominated?

He tuned out the logical part of his brain—the part that reminded him he was too old for one-night stands, the part that knew they were both drunk, the part that was now dead inside because of Wyatt—and shoved her facedown on the floor. He felt in the darkness for her panties and pulled them to the side, rubbing a thumb over her asshole as he began entering her with force. Just like that.

"Harder."

The slap of their flesh was the only sound in the bathroom until he felt his hamstrings cramp.

"Put your fingers in my mouth."

The need in her voice was palpable. He groped in the darkness for her face and swiped her cheek, which was wet. Was she *crying*? She grabbed one of his hands and sucked his index and middle finger.

"Stick your fingers inside me and shove them in my mouth again."

Her voice had softened, but the boldness made him almost come. He was a witness to this woman splitting open, spilling a need that he too felt. He missed Wyatt. He missed having a purpose. He missed himself. He did as he was told by this stranger, feeling her contract on his hand, the moans in her throat unleashing across the mildewed rug. He shoved them back into her mouth, and she sucked herself off of them. He needed this woman. And he knew, by her body, by her forcefulness, that she needed him too.

"Choke me."

He slid one hand around her throat but didn't close his fingers.

"Choke me. Tell me you could kill me."

"What?" He moved back. "Hey, no. I can't say that. I'm not—"

"Just say it!"

Her voice revealed something he recognized: pain, fresh and raw, that needed to be erased by being overtaken. Maybe she'd lost someone too, maybe she wanted to run away from her life, or maybe she just wanted to be punished. Just a few days ago, he'd wanted to die, and now here he was with a woman's throat in his hands.

"I need you to say it!" she screamed again. Her voice pierced the silence, but it shook with desperate intent.

Part of him wanted to let go and wrap her in a hug, but the stronger part of him just wanted to do what he was told. To feel something other than what he felt. He closed his eyes and felt the words leave his lips. *I could kill you. Do you know how easy it would be to kill you?*

To his surprise, his body reacted as he said the words. He thrust harder and harder, something wild cracking open inside him—desire, need, power—just from taking control of this moment, of his body, of *her*. His fingers tightened.

He felt her climax again. She moaned, her entire body writhing in pleasure. He continued moving in and out of her, his hand around her slender throat. He compressed harder.

"Do you like when I squeeze? Do you like thinking about what I could do to you? Yes, oh yeah. Oh God."

His own orgasm curled itself around his hips and then released harder than he could ever remember. In it was his grief, his anger, the betrayal he felt, this life that he was supposed to live without his brother. He tightened his hand even more, then finally loosened his grip and shook the contraction from his fingers.

He collapsed on top of her, his triceps twitching. A drop of sweat landed on her back. He wiped it away with his free hand. For one agonizing moment, he saw his brother's face. He blinked it away, but the blackness engulfed him. He couldn't breathe. He tried to calm his mind, to catch air, but the room felt too thick. He climbed off of her, sucking for breath, and finally found his voice in the small, dank space.

"I've never done anything like that before."

The girl had grown quiet and still.

"Hello?" He kneeled beside her, accidentally ramming into her ribs with his shin. "Oh sorry." He gripped her slick shoulder and shook her gently from behind. For a sickening moment, he wondered if he'd killed her.

He inched closer to her face, praying that she was alive, that she was okay. He hovered above her nose and mouth. She was snoring. He felt for her cheek in the darkness. Her head was twisted and warm on the tile. Had she passed out? He assessed the situation. He couldn't just leave her here.

Could he?

He should turn on the lights, wake her up, and put her in the shower to rinse her off. Maybe even take her home if she could remember where she lived. He tapped her cheek. "Hello? Can you hear me?" Her snores saturated the silence as he sat beside her.

He finally stood on shaky legs, peed, cleaned himself up the best he could, and fumbled around the sink to wash his hands again. He scrubbed her from his fingers, dragging the bar of soap under his nails. He didn't want to turn on the light. He didn't want to see her. The aggression, the impulsiveness. He wanted it to stay hidden, black, unseen.

As he dried his hands on his jeans, the reality of what he'd just done slid into focus. Why hadn't he used a condom? What was he thinking? He got down on his knees again, careful not to trip over her. "Hey. Please wake up." He didn't know if she was here with anyone, or if she'd taken something besides alcohol. He rattled her shoulders, this time harder, but she didn't move. Should he call 911?

He calculated his options. He knew how it would look, a girl passed out, his semen leaking out of her. He moved to the wall, fumbled for the light, and flipped it on. He squinted from the sudden brightness and stared down into the hollow shell of the woman he'd just fucked. He memorized her haircut, the high cheekbones, and the mole above her lip. Seeing her there, unconscious, sent a wave of repulsion through him, when, moments before, he'd had the strongest orgasm of his life. His heart cut out of rhythm against his ribs.

The girl's snores vibrated the tile. He flipped off the light and bolted down the stairs. The party rocked around him, but he edged past the sweaty bodies back into the night, deciding right then and there that he had to do something about the state of his life.

His brother had died. It couldn't be the event that ruined him and took him down a dark, dangerous path. People died. That's what they did. He knew this, and yet he felt responsible. He'd been only inches from Wyatt, and if he'd just reached out . . .

His entire life he'd lived by other agendas: Wyatt's, his mother's, his father's. Any emotion Wyatt had ever had, he expressed. And Noah, the therapist, Noah, the older brother, Noah, the mediator, had repressed his own feelings—all his feelings—until he was a seething ball of emotion.

Where was his release?

The chaos of the party faded as he walked closer to the end of the block, the cool wind drying the sweat on his face. He felt bad about leaving that girl up there, alone, to wake up with her panties around her ankles. What kind of a guy did that? What kind of a guy said those things to a girl during sex?

He was ashamed to admit that it had been exciting; it had awakened something in him to talk to a woman like that, to wind his fingers around a stranger's neck and do whatever he wanted. He felt powerful and in control. He wanted to hold onto that feeling.

He took a right and continued the few short blocks

to his house. But the words he'd said and what he'd done . . . he couldn't hold on to the feeling *that* way.

No. He had to erase what had just happened. He had to bury it.

No one could ever know about tonight.

PRESENT

54

noah

He arrives at Grace's early and slides the journal back into its proper place. Grace enters the living room, waves at him distractedly, and hustles Luca into the car for his soccer game. He knows she needs time to process their conversation from last night, but her icy demeanor is literally killing him. Their relationship has fissured, but he will do whatever it takes to make it right.

While Mason is eating breakfast, Noah formulates how to talk to him about this next phase of life. "Hey, Mase. I want to ask you something."

"Ask away, Professor."

Noah chuckles at the nickname. "So you know how much Grace means to me. That we are in a relationship and love each other very much."

"Yuck. Gag. Vomit. Yes."

Noah nods. "I know that stuff is gross at this age. But I want to talk to you a little bit about what that means."

"It means you're probably getting married." Mason shovels another bite of cereal into his mouth.

Noah nods. "Well, that's true." *At least I hope that's true.* "And do you know what that would mean for you?"

Mason taps out a rhythm on the table. "You want me to be best man?"

Noah's heart swells. "I'd love nothing more, buddy. But what I mean is since Grace is technically your guardian"—he says the word with some trepidation, not wanting to remind him of his recent loss—"I would then become your stepfather. If we were to get married."

"Why do they call it a stepfather? Are you a *stair*? Are you made of concrete? That would be a negative."

Noah smiles. "That's a good question. But I want to talk about how you'd *feel* about that. Me being kind of like a dad."

Mason cocks his head to the side and taps his spoon against his bowl. "I've never had a dad."

"I know."

Mason studies him. "I think you would be an acceptable father figure. You're adequate. And you don't annoy me, so that's a positive start."

"That is a good start." Inside, Noah's heart fills to almost bursting. Suddenly, a whole life together flashes before his eyes. Him and his boys. The baby. Grace. "So you'd be okay if I were to become part of your family?"

Mason bristles at the word *family,* a word designated only for his mother.

"I *had* a family."

The past tense guts Noah, but he only nods. "I know, and your mother will always be your family. No one will ever take her place. But now Grace is your family too, and Luca. I'm like part of your family. Family doesn't always have to be related by blood, remember? We talked about that."

"I know." Mason sighs and dips his spoon back into the bowl.

Part of Noah feels like everything he experienced with Wyatt brought him here, to have a do-over and take care of a child who needs him. Mason is his second chance.

As Wyatt's face flashes into his mind, he kills the memory in its tracks. He has to move on from that loss, and maybe this is how to do it.

"Okay, enough of that. Lesson time?"

Mason nods and puts away his dishes, and the two begin. They start OT with some bear crawls, crab walks, and exercise ball work. By the time they move onto putty work, Grace and Luca are already pulling into the drive.

"How was it?" he asks.

"We won!" Luca exclaims. He rushes off to grab a snack, and Noah turns to Grace.

"They're really on a winning streak, huh?"

"They sure are." She smiles at him warily and looks at Mason. "How's it going here?"

Mason squeezes the putty and passes it back and forth to each hand. "Noah is going to become my stepfather. We are going to be a family."

Noah reddens at the admission and glances at Grace, who looks stricken. "Oh?" She places one hand on her hip and assesses Noah. "Is that right?"

He stands and pulls Grace into the kitchen. "Sorry. We had a conversation about family."

Grace's eyes flash. "And *you're* going to be his family?"

"Hey, don't be like that." He reaches for her, but she steps out of the way. "I do want us all to be a family. Of course I do. Don't you?"

Grace's jaw tightens then releases. "Look. This is just going to take some time. It's not going to be easy for me." Her arms encircle her own waist. "I still need to sort through some things, okay?" She finally looks at him, hesitating just long enough to make him uncomfortable. "But yes. I do want that stability for the boys. I want them to have a family."

He kisses her forehead, relieved but cautious. "Just please don't shut me out, okay? That's all I ask."

Her eyes blink warily beneath the fan of lashes. "Okay."

"I'm going to finish up with Mason." He tunes out his worries as the two complete their therapy, says good-bye to both boys, and gets in his car. Something solidifies on the drive home. He makes a detour to the antique jewelry shop he's passed a million times in Hillsboro Village and finds a parking spot on the street.

He walks inside and hunts for the cases of rings. He knows Grace needs time to sort through her feelings. He doesn't want to rush her, but he knows what he has to do.

He summons an employee. The woman removes one ring after another. He holds each diamond up to the light, watching the jewels explode and dance.

After three rings, he finds it. He knows her ring size—six. (He'd found her old engagement ring and sized it.) He knows the cut of diamond she prefers—round. (She's talked extensively about Chad's cluelessness for diamonds.) The band—platinum. (She dislikes gold.) He pays for the ring, pockets the small velvet box, ignores the prick of worry, and begins to plan his proposal.

55

grace

A week later, Noah calls and asks if he can come over. They haven't talked much. She's been busying herself with work and the boys. He says he has something important to discuss.

"Why can't you just tell me over the phone?" she demands. She cradles the receiver against her ear as she shuffles through DVDs in the living room.

"I want to do it in person."

Luca begs to watch Harry Potter in the background, and Mason says he will watch too. She has to be selective about what movies she chooses. Luca has already mourned the loss of the silly, loud, over-the-top movies they used to watch together. Now, they have Mason's requests to consider, and they come with a slew of prerequisites: no egregious violence, no slapstick comedy, no romance, no superheroes.

Grace tells Noah to hold on while she loads the DVD and walks to the mailbox once the boys are situated on the couch. She gathers her mail and waves to Nancy, her neighbor, who is wrangling her Lab, Bailey, for an afternoon walk. "Then that's fine, I guess." She's trying to be nicer to him, but it feels like a betrayal. There's been so much deceit, so many lies, so many convoluted versions of the truth.

She looks up at the trees whose leaves stutter and tilt. A breeze tickles her neck and shoulders. Months from now, the leaves will detach from their stems, gathering in colorful clumps at the edge of everyone's yards. Once fall is in full effect—her favorite season—she will let the boys rake for allowance and then separate the piles into color values. Mason will get a kick out of that. She flips through the mail and tosses a few catalogues and credit card offers into the recycling bin at the side of the house. "I'm assuming you're on your way?"

"Yes."

She sorts through a few pieces of Lee's mail that have been forwarded. Should she just trash them? Save them? She lifts her head as a FedEx truck screeches by, and Nancy yells at him to slow down.

"It's a neighborhood. There are kids here. Am I right?" Nancy shakes her head, yanks Bailey to the edge of her driveway, and lifts her hand as they set off in the opposite direction. Grace waves back and returns her attention to the phone call.

"Pulling up now," Noah says.

On cue, he revs into the driveway, comes to an abrupt stop, and hops out of the car. His hand is wrapped around something small. *What is that?* Grace's heart begins to pound.

"Hi." He looks as nervous as she feels.

"Hi," she says back. They haven't seen each other all week, and the shock of him, standing in her driveway, takes her off guard.

"What's in your hand?" she asks.

He looks down and hesitates.

"Noah? What is it?"

He finally looks up. "I had this whole idea planned. I was going to take you out somewhere romantic, or maybe get the boys to help. But I couldn't wait. I couldn't wait another second."

The words register, but don't click. "For what?"

Suddenly, Noah is down on one knee with a blue velvet box. "Grace Vanessa Childress, love of my life. I never knew what that word meant before I met you. I never knew what family or sacrifice was. I have never been more certain of where I want my life to go or who I want to spend it with. Would you do me the honor of becoming my wife?"

Grace presses a hand to her chest and tries to concentrate on the words as the beautiful diamond winks at her beneath the sun. The timeline of their relationship unfurls. It hasn't been long enough yet, has it? She looks at him, uncertain. "Are you doing this just because of the baby?"

He falters, still on one knee. "Of course not. I love you, Grace. Will you marry me?"

Visions of Chad's proposal float back to her mind. How in love she felt. How romantic his proposal was. How she thought everything would work out. No, she's not ready for that again. She's no longer an impressionable twentysomething. She's almost forty-three years old. Life is not a fairy tale.

She pulls him up off his knee and stares into his hopeful face. "Noah, this is so thoughtful, and I appreciate it, but no." She shakes her head. "I'm not ready for marriage. Not yet." Maybe not ever.

His face crumples, and he closes the box. He clenches it in his palm and shakes his head. "Oh." He pockets the ring and finally looks at her. Tears brim, and he embarrassingly presses both palms to soak up the impending tears. He paces away a few steps, turns, paces back. "Is this about Shirley? Do you still not believe me?"

"I'm still working through it."

He sighs, and she sense his frustration. "Regardless of what happened in the past, we've got our own family to worry about, right? Can we please just find a way to move forward? We don't have to get married. I'm fine with that."

The desperation clings to every syllable, but she ignores it. She already told him she needs time. Why is he pushing? She's got so many other things to think about than his wounded ego. "I don't know. I really don't." She turns and leaves the door open for him to follow. Luca says something in the living room. Mason responds, and both boys laugh. Despite the situation, the confusion, the trauma, and the shock, Grace smiles at their easy banter.

No one will ever know the entire truth. She knows that now. About the party. About what Lee said versus what Noah said. But Mason is the important one in all of this. He's safe. He's thriving. He is adjusting to a life without his mother *and* without a father. He's let go of his old house—after a torturous process—and is forming friendships slowly but authentically.

She washes her hands and then dumps popcorn into two mixing bowls and sprinkles them with sea salt and Parmesan. Noah stands at the edge of her kitchen and waits. She hands the boys their snacks, and they mumble their thanks. She kisses Luca on the head and wrinkles her nose at the slightly sour smell of his unwashed hair. Definitely a shower tonight.

"Can I get you boys anything else?"

"I would like some water with three ice cubes, please, madam," Mason says.

"Right away, sir." She bows in his direction. She loves

their playful exchanges. In the kitchen, she presses his favorite glass against the ice dispenser and waits for three cubes to tumble out. She brings Mason his water and then reenters the kitchen. She opens the refrigerator, pulls out a bottle of white wine, and deliberately pours herself a glass.

"What are you doing?" Noah's tone is sharp as she takes a sip.

"I'm having a drink." She lifts the glass in an invisible toast. "Women in Europe drink while they're pregnant. One glass of wine isn't going to hurt."

Before he can protest, she joins the boys and settles into the armchair. The chilled wine slips down her throat.

She thinks of Lee, as she does at least a few times a day. Her friend has literally taken her secrets to the grave. She can't torture herself with one more puzzle she can't solve. She has to focus on what is here, on moving forward, on her role as a parent.

She watches the boys, coexisting on her couch. Luca has become more compassionate, and Mason has become more social. It is all working out in its weird little way, despite what has happened. Despite losing Lee. Despite the secrets. They are all doing the best they can, given the hand they've been dealt and the partial truths she clings to.

After a few minutes, the side door opens and shuts. His engine revs as he backs swiftly out of her drive. At first, she's offended. He doesn't even want to say good-bye to the boys? But then she realizes she doesn't want him here, that this is better. He needs time to come to terms with where they are. And so does she.

She does not miss him when he goes.

56

noah

Noah paces his apartment. He's gone through his roster of friends, but he doesn't feel like talking to anyone. He needs a drink. He needs a punching bag. He's on the verge of detonating.

Noah changes into running clothes and laces his shoes. He steps outside, turns left down Twelfth Avenue South, and jogs toward the park. Grace turned him down.

She doesn't want to marry me.

He grinds his teeth and picks up his pace as his quads burn and his lungs ignite. Grace hadn't even cared that he left. She hadn't said good-bye. She was cold, and he isn't sure how to snap her out of it.

He needs to give her space, but they have a family to think about. She's even gone to a doctor's appointment without him, and the betrayal is like a punch to the face. Regardless of what is going on with her apprehension, Grace is still carrying *his* child. He has as much a right to be there as she does.

He knows he can't push Grace, that she will back away even more if he tries too hard. But the need is heavy. He wants to fix this. He wants to fix them.

He turns toward Sevier Park and decides to do some

hill sprints. The humidity is high, and sweat pours off of him like it's the middle of summer.

He doesn't know how everything got so fucked up, but he's going to figure it out. He's one of the good ones, not a man who takes advantage of women. He loves Grace. He loves Luca and Mason and their life together.

That's worth fighting for.

He cranks his phone to a different song and makes sure his wireless earbuds are in place. He stretches at the bottom of the hill and then races to the top, his arms scissoring, his body contracted with effort. He makes it to the top and jogs back down. He flies up the hill again and again in an attempt to clear his mind. With every sprint, he goes faster and harder. His lungs wheeze, but he keeps going. Who cares if his heart stops? Who would even miss him?

He finally stops on his tenth sprint and attempts to suck in clean air. He paces back and forth with his hands tented on top of his head. His entire body shudders until everything begins to normalize and come into focus.

He needs to get it together and stop feeling sorry for himself. He has a family to think about now. *His* family.

He walks back to his condo. He pushes that glass of wine from his mind. She just did that to bother him. He thinks about her resistance, how she's still so hung up on that party and this version of he-said she-said that he's suddenly a part of. He wishes he had a way to prove what happened that night. That he didn't hurt Shirley. That *she'd* come on to *him*.

He has no proof. He just has to trust that their bond is strong enough to get through this. They love each other. They love the boys.

Eventually, Grace will come to her senses.

57

lee

Lee stood in the dirty bathroom stall with the box in her hand. She'd swiped the test without paying for it.

"Hurry up," Shirley demanded.

It had been five months since the party, but everything was different. Shirley had all but abandoned her career. She never went out. She was moody. It was like her wild, vivacious friend had been replaced with a shut-in. Was Lee entirely to blame?

She'd bullied her at the party. She'd let her sleep with a stranger and hadn't done anything to stop it. Since then, Lee had asked countless times if Shirley remembered anything about the guy, about those awful words he said, but she swore she didn't.

Lee wasn't convinced. Every time she came home from work, Shirley was whispering on the phone to someone in a heated debate and then would end the call in tears. She refused to tell Lee who she was talking to. She didn't tell her anything anymore. She'd never known how two friends could go from being so close to so distant, but she was trying to fix what was broken between them.

Lee held the pregnancy test in her hand and flipped the box around to study the back. She unwrapped the loud plastic and wadded it into a ball. Shirley ditched the directions and removed the cap before slipping the plastic between her legs.

"Not my first rodeo," she muttered.

Lee had never taken a pregnancy test. She'd barely had enough sex to even know *how* to take a pregnancy test. She watched Shirley hover over the seat, wondering how many women, girls even, had done just this very thing, shocked and unraveled by something as small as a plus or negative sign.

Shirley replaced the cap and wiped her fingers on her jeans. She left the stall and washed her hands.

"You look. I can't."

Lee plucked the test from the corner of the sink.

"Don't shake it, or it won't work right."

"I'm not shaking it. I'm holding it." She watched the test obsessively, wondering what would happen if Shirley was pregnant with her *father's* baby. She couldn't calculate all the ways that would change their lives, all the ways it would tie Shirley to their family forever. She'd known Shirley long enough to know that she didn't do well with crises or surprises.

In the past five months, the initial shock of Shirley dating Harold had worn off. What she thought was a brief fling had turned into an actual *relationship,* and she knew that it would reach its natural conclusion in its own time. The more she fought against it, the more Shirley would want to stay. So she acted like she didn't care and just waited until it would all fall apart on its own.

Finally, after counting to one hundred and eighty, Lee looked at the test again, and there it was. The word *positive* was digitized in the small, gray window, a word that meant the opposite of what it should.

She showed the test to Shirley.

"Shit." She closed her eyes, took a settling breath, and leaned against the sink. "I can't believe this."

"Did you suspect anything?"

Shirley shrugged. "Kind of. But I just didn't want to believe it."

"Is it . . . ?" *My father's baby.* That's what she wanted to know. If she was about to become a sister.

"Who else's would it be?" Shirley asked.

Lee looked at her, eyebrows cocked. "The guy from the party? He . . . you know. Inside you."

"No, no way." Shirley dropped the test into the trash can. "That was five months ago. I'd know if I was five months pregnant, right?" She gauged herself in the mirror and placed her palms on her stomach.

"I have no idea. You know you hear about those women who don't know they're pregnant until they're giving birth, so . . ."

Shirley pushed her arm playfully. "Stop. I'm not one of *those* women."

Lee studied both of their reflections. "I know you're not. But since the party, you've pulled away so much that I don't know what to think."

Shirley's eyes locked with Lee's in the mirror. "I know. I'm sorry. I'm just so pissed that I drank at the party, that *you* started drinking because of me and Harold. It's all such a mess."

Lee hadn't thought about it like that. That night had not only been unpleasant for her best friend—it had caused a relapse and a horrible new habit for her too. What could she say? That it wasn't Shirley's fault? It was, to some degree. She never would have started drinking if she hadn't learned about her dating Harold. Maybe she was more like her dad than she wanted to admit. Maybe becoming an alcoholic was inevitable.

"Let's not worry about any of that. Should we take you to the doctor or something?"

Shirley dropped her hands from her stomach. "No."

"No?"

"No." She turned to Lee. "I can't have a baby. Look at me. I'm in no position to be anyone's mother."

"So what does that mean?"

"It means I'm not keeping it." She exited the bathroom before Lee could even collect herself.

This wasn't the Shirley she knew. The Shirley she knew wanted to be a wife and mother *someday*. She wanted some version of the American dream: husband, house, career, kids. So why did she keep sabotaging herself?

Lee whipped out her phone and searched for an abortion clinic or Planned Parenthood in the area and found one not far from Walgreens. She punched in the directions. Shirley wouldn't actually abort a baby . . . would she? She probably just wanted to know her options.

In the parking lot, Shirley waited to get into the car. Lee drove them the short distance to the clinic and grabbed a tissue from her purse to wax each tooth, hearing the squeak of Kleenex against her enamel.

"What are you doing?"

"My teeth are purple. From wine." While Shirley had been sober since the party, Lee had been drinking nonstop. Because Shirley kept her distance, Lee had been staying in with her new friend, Cabernet Sauvignon.

"Lee, Jesus." She rolled her eyes lightheartedly. "We're not getting our pictures taken."

They used to always be a *we*, no matter what. Did she still feel that way? As they walked to the entrance, angry picketers gathered outside, holding signs with pro-life slogans. Lee stopped, but Shirley grabbed her elbow.

"Come on."

Lee ducked around the protestors and stepped inside. Shirley signed in at the desk, while Lee scanned the room. Women of various ages fanned out in gray chairs, filling out forms, chewing fingernails, or staring at their phones.

While Shirley completed all of her personal information, Lee sorted through the money in her purse—she was down to her last few hundred dollars, because she'd just paid the mortgage. Would Shirley even be able to pay for this? She extracted her credit card and checked the expiration date. She had no idea of its limit, if it was even active. She paid so little attention to the details of her everyday life these days. Only her job, which she loved, the recent drinking, which she didn't, and the guilt for what had happened to Shirley at the party. What if this was that horrible guy's baby?

A nurse in pink elephant scrubs called Shirley's name off a clipboard, and Lee followed. She nervously stood by her friend as she stepped on a scale and answered questions in her short, impatient clip. Lee tried to exchange pleasantries as the nurse uncapped a fat, silver needle and gripped Shirley's arm. The woman hesitated, observing the old track marks—still visible due to unfortunate abscesses that formed during her last bout—and glanced in her direction. Lee shook her head as if to say, *she's clean for now,* and looked away as the nurse pushed the needle into the wispy veins at the crook of Shirley's elbow. The glass vials filled with deep, dark blood. Lee felt woozy as the nurse pressed a cotton ball to the small prick in Shirley's arm and secured it with a tab of tape. Lee hated needles, had always despised watching Shirley get high. Next, she was handed a plastic cup and shown to the bathroom. Lee waited in the examination room.

Shirley rolled her eyes as she returned shortly after. "How many steps are there to confirm you're pregnant?" She slid onto the examination table and kicked her legs nervously on the crinkly paper. Lee wondered, briefly, if this was the same paper they used to cover toilet seats.

After an eternity, Dr. Connors stepped inside the room, a crisply dressed man with a bushy mustache and kind eyes. Lee watched his mustache twitch as the words confirmed it: Shirley was pregnant.

Shirley let her head fall back and sighed. "What now?"

"I'd like to get an ultrasound, just to see how far along you are."

They were ushered into another room. Shirley was told to undress and lay on more crinkly paper. Lee watched as Shirley shed her clothes. Her stomach was a little rounder than normal, but not much. Shirley hopped onto the table and waited for the technician. Lee wished she knew what to say, how exactly to comfort her in this situation. There should be a doting boyfriend standing in her place, someone to hold her hand, to begin a future together. Not her deadbeat dad, drinking himself to death across town. Not the stranger from the party. Not her.

Lee stood in the corner as the technician inserted a wand between Shirley's legs, clicked an obscene number of buttons, and measured the very real-looking blob in the gray sac. Except it wasn't a blob. There was a *baby* in there. A fully formed baby. With a head, arms, and legs.

"Oh my God," Lee whispered.

The technician drew lines from different points around the baby, tapping her fingers on the keys. "As you can see, you're pretty far along."

"How far along?" Shirley sat up, the long, lubricated handle slipping out as she watched the butterfly wings of her child's heartbeat flap on the screen.

"According to your measurements, I'd say—" she clicked a few more buttons and drew more digital lines across the screen—"approximately twenty-one weeks."

"Twenty-one *weeks*?" they both exclaimed.

"Well, you're not really showing yet." The woman gripped the handle, urging Shirley to lie back. She shifted the wand, as though stuffing in a premature limb, and continued with the measurements as the truth sank in. Shirley had been pregnant for twenty-one weeks and hadn't suspected *anything*? A flutter? A kick? Nausea? Lee thought of all the recent napping, the skipped meals, the constant late phone calls and persistent privacy. Had she known deep down that she was pregnant?

"Does it . . . does it look okay?" Lee asked.

"Just a moment," the technician murmured, leaning in to check something. Lee licked her dry lips and felt her heart racing around her chest.

"The baby looks to be about on target. Placenta is intact. No abnormalities that I can see here, but I'll have the doctor take another look."

"And is it too late to . . . ?" Lee asked.

"Terminate?" The woman pulled the handle free, set it on the paper-lined tray, and removed her latex gloves. "Yes, I'm sorry. It's too late to terminate."

Shirley moaned and covered her face with her hands.

"What's the latest you can terminate?" Lee asked.

"Technically, nineteen weeks and six days."

Shirley sat up again. "Nineteen weeks and six days?

But I'm barely past that. You just said I'm twenty-one weeks."

"Yes, ma'am, but that is the absolute latest, and many doctors will not abort that far into pregnancy. In your case, you are past any viable point to terminate. I'm sorry."

A cold sweat drenched Lee's entire body. Shirley didn't want a baby. She wasn't in the right mental state to bring a child into this world . . . was she? "Is there any way we could speak to the doctor again?" Lee asked.

The technician stood and urged Shirley to get dressed. "I'll send Dr. Connors back in when you're ready."

Shirley was eerily calm as she hopped off the table. She grabbed a few stiff paper towels and wiped the goo from between her legs. "Well, this isn't good."

"There's got to be something we can do," Lee said. "We'll figure it out." She didn't want to bring up the timing. If she was five months pregnant and the party was five months ago . . . She wanted to tell Dr. Connors with the mustache and kind eyes about the possible father of this baby, about *her* father, about the strange circumstances. The past drugs. The drinking. She wanted to tell him about all the men Shirley had been with before her father, and that despite it all, she'd never ended up pregnant.

"Do you . . ."

"Do I what?" Shirley shrugged on her clothes and turned.

"Do you want to get a paternity test? To be sure?"

She shrugged. "I guess we should, huh?"

Lee nodded. "I think so. Just so we know what's what." She couldn't even question what would happen if the baby was from the guy at the party. What that would mean. How Shirley would handle a child created from *that*.

A few minutes later, the doctor knocked. Despite the recent tension, Lee gripped Shirley's hand. She was here for her, regardless of what the doctor said.

Lee clasped her hand, and Shirley squeezed back.

"Come in," Shirley finally said.

PRESENT

58

noah

Grace is coming around. Finally. The uncertainty about their future seems to be waning. He's moving past the crushing disappointment of her refusal. But he's not giving up.

Once they are in a better place, and Grace is well into her second or third trimester, he will try again. Maybe he will get the boys to help set the stage for another proposal. One way or another, he is spending his life with this woman, with these boys. He thinks about the baby and smiles. They've decided not to find out the sex. Though he loves Mason and Luca, he is praying for a little girl. He has always wanted a daughter.

He's going to Grace's next doctor's appointment—his first, her third—and cannot wait to see the image on the screen. To hear the heartbeat. To see the shape of the baby. It will all start to feel real.

Despite all of the challenges they've had to endure, he is thankful. It's what has made them stronger. It's what will make them indestructible.

He pulls up to Grace's a little early and stalls in the driveway. He doesn't want to disrupt her morning routine, but he thought it would be nice to make her a pot of decaf and some breakfast. He grabs the grocery bag full of fresh whole bean coffee and bagels and finds her key on his ring.

He's finally started therapy—something he's always resisted—to move past the trauma of Wyatt's suicide. Wyatt was his own person, who made his own decisions. Losing him was the biggest tragedy of Noah's life, but it was not his fault. He knows that now.

He has his own life and his own well-being to worry about. He's talked about the party, going over it in such detail, his therapist is now as familiar with that night as he is.

He still can't work out the mystery of Lee and Shirley, and how all of that fits together, but he can't worry about things out of his control. He has to stay in his lane. Grace has custody of Mason, and that's what matters. He can't imagine Mason having a more wonderful mother than her.

He unlocks the door and finds her busy slathering toast for both boys in the kitchen.

"Hi." Her eyes are bright, and she wears that pregnant glow everyone talks about, even though she isn't showing yet.

He lifts the bag. "I was going to make you coffee and breakfast, but I see you beat me to it."

She waves her knife in the air. "Busy day, but that's a sweet thought. Thank you." She spreads some butter on the toast. "Are you still okay to pick up Luca from school?"

"Of course."

She checks her watch and licks the knife. "I might need you to feed them too. I have a meeting that might run a bit long."

"I've got it handled." He sets the bag on the counter and shoves his hands in his jeans to keep from hugging her.

"Great." She lowers the knife, washes her hands, and takes a few steps toward him. She hesitates and then finally speaks. "I just want you to know I'm really trying. With us, I mean. That's the best I can do for now, okay? I just need a bit more time."

He nods as utter relief floods his adrenals. She's skirted around saying as much but hasn't directly told him anything concrete. That she wants him as much as he wants her. He resists the urge to pull her against his chest. "That's more than enough." He kisses her cheek. His lips linger. The smell of her hair is intoxicating. His entire body springs to life, but he maintains his space. He will not push her. He will let her come to him.

"I'll see you later then?" She moves back and smiles up at him. A smile he wants to look at for the rest of his life.

"We'll be here," he says.

She nods and calls to Luca, then disappears down the hall to go about her day. He finds Mason reading a book.

"Hey, buddy."

"Hey, yourself. Guess what I'm reading?" Mason cranes the textbook toward Noah.

He gets lost in Mason's curiosity and scribbles something else in the lesson plan for today. Grace and Luca wave as they leave, and when she goes, his heart goes with her.

She belongs to him—he feels it.

He cannot wait to see her tonight.

mine [mahyn]

pronoun

1. something that belongs to me

what's mine is mine.
and it's about damn time I get it.

what's mine is mine
what's mine is mine
what's mine is mine
what's mine is mine
what's mine is mine
what's mine is mine
what's mine is mine
what's mine is mine

MINE
MINE
MINE

59

lee

Lee walked into the hospital after Shirley had texted three times. She'd gone into unexpected labor while out running errands and had driven herself to the hospital. Lee canceled her last few appointments to make it to the hospital in time. No one was in the waiting room with balloons and stuffed animals. No other friends. No family.

At check-in, she fished her ID from her wallet and handed it over. Lee received her visitor's badge and stuck it to her chest. She shifted the overnight bag she'd brought as she walked down the sterile hall, smiling nervously at random nurses. When was the last time they'd had a sleepover, just the two of them? She never thought they would be thrown together for a reason like this.

She couldn't wait to hold the baby. She couldn't wait to see that bond between Shirley and her child. She was relieved how quickly Shirley had softened to the idea of motherhood after the paternity test confirmed the baby was her father's.

In the room, Shirley was panting, her hair slicked against her skin. "Thank God you're here." She collapsed back against the pillow.

Lee moved to the edge of the hospital bed, taking in the IV taped to the back of her friend's hand. Monitors beeped. She wanted to ask how she felt, but that seemed like a rhetorical question. Instead, she smoothed a hand over her hair, and Shirley, still a vulnerable girl in there somewhere, closed her eyes and leaned into her palm. "I think I packed everything you need. I can run home if I forgot anything."

"Thank you." She shifted and winced. "I can't do this much longer. I need to get the baby out."

"You're doing great. Let me just . . ." She turned to find a doctor, to appease her best friend, even though she had no such ability to make anything happen faster than Shirley's body would allow. She found a nurse.

"Are you Shirley's sister?"

Lee nodded. She basically was. "Is she . . . close?"

"Last check, she was at nine centimeters. We're issuing another check right now, and then, if she's at ten, she should be able to start pushing."

Lee nodded. Would Shirley want her in the room? She'd never seen a woman's body opening itself to life. She needed a drink. She still couldn't reconcile this new person—the one who *needed a drink to get through something*—with the old her, who avoided booze like the plague. Despite going to a few AA meetings, she couldn't stop drinking wine. She waited in the corner while they checked Shirley's cervix, and then the nurse turned to her.

"Ma'am? It's time for her to push. Are you going to stay?"

Lee blinked and glanced at Shirley, who was hoisting herself up onto her elbows in the hospital bed.

Lee walked closer to the bed and took Shirley's hand. "Yes, I'm going to stay."

The nurses helped Shirley scoot to the end of the bed and spread her knees as wide as they would go.

Every time Shirley had a contraction, she pushed. Her face turned purple with every bit of effort. She pushed and pushed, until a head with dark brown hair emerged between her warm, slick thighs, and Lee watched, fascinated at all of the tricks and miracles a human body could produce.

The rest of the body slipped out after, and the doctor held the baby upside down and sucked fluids from its open mouth with a bulb syringe.

"It's a boy," he said, then snipped the cord and handed the baby off like a sack of flour. The nurse took the baby to a table and rubbed, wrapped, and wiped. The baby opened his mouth and began to wail. Lee felt life bleed into the room. With his cry, everything popped with color.

Tears bloomed on her cheeks at the absolute miracle of it all. She turned to Shirley, who was squirming uncomfortably as she delivered the placenta, which came out like a giant jellyfish, coated in blood. "You did it," Lee said.

Shirley smiled and collapsed back against her pillow. "Holy shit, that hurt."

The nurse brought the baby over to Shirley and deposited him into her arms. Shirley grabbed one of his little fingers. "I can't believe we were ever this small."

Lee nestled in beside her and smoothed a hand over his head. "He's perfect."

Shirley let go of his finger. "This doesn't feel like I thought it would."

She trailed a finger across the soft flesh of his cheek. "What do you mean?"

"I don't know. He's just . . ." Shirley looked at her and she saw worry flash across her eyes. "It's like he's a stranger or something."

The confession cracked across her heart. "Well, I'm sure that's perfectly normal. You literally just gave birth." Lee studied his red face and perfectly pink lips. "But it's incredible, isn't it? Moments ago, he wasn't here, and now . . ." Now he was here, in her arms.

The doctor stitched her up, while Shirley stared from the baby to the wall back to the baby. Shirley lifted him toward her. "Do you want to hold him?"

"Sure." Lee scooped him into her arms and memorized all the soft parts of this brand-new person. She couldn't believe she finally had a brother. "Hello, there," she cooed. "I'm your sister. Yes, I am." She lifted her head. "Did you decide on a name?"

"Your dad likes Harry. So that's what it'll be, I guess."

Her father hated hospitals and had vowed never to set foot in another one after her mother died. And true to his word, he'd never been back. Not for a checkup. Not for an emergency. Not for her. Not for his son, here in her arms. Not for anyone.

"Hello, Harry. I'm your big sister, Lee." The baby gurgled and gripped her finger tighter. "You're so strong. Yes, you are."

Lee laughed and looked at Shirley, whose eyes were closed. She was devastated that the magic of parenthood hadn't taken hold, like all of those books said it would; that when the baby was born, she'd know just what to do. But there was still time.

The only thing she could think about right now was her brother in her arms. She'd *have* to quit drinking. Or at least be responsible about it: only a single glass at a time, only after the baby was asleep in case he needed her. She couldn't have them all pass out with Harry crying in the other room.

Lee sat with him for two hours while Shirley slept.

She wondered if Shirley should try to feed him, but she didn't want to disturb her. She snuggled his delicious body closer to hers, wishing she could feed him herself, bathe him, take him home, and protect him forever. Fear gutted the peace.

Lee and Shirley had tried everything to get the house ready: converting the office into a nursery, vacuuming, cleaning, getting diapers, formula, and onesies with her tip money. Her dad had done nothing to prepare. But the baby was here now.

Whether they were ready or not, life was about to be different.

60
lee

Lee slept at the hospital for two nights, watching Harry around the clock until it was time to take him home. Shirley seemed content with letting Lee take the lead. While Shirley and Harry slept, Lee reread an email. Parlour & Juke wanted to hire her. She'd asked her boss to write her a recommendation letter a few months back, before the baby, and he had. She'd have her own chair. They would pay her a *salary*. Apparently, the girls she'd styled at the last hair show had made an impression on their boss. He was recruiting, and he'd asked specifically if she was interested. She'd built a great book, and now someone wanted her skills. Her talent.

Lee thought of starting over, of getting her own little house in another part of town. No real memories. No ties. No mistakes.

Nothing had ever sounded better.

"What are you smiling at?"

Lee closed the email and set her phone down. "Just an email."

"About?" Shirley groaned as she pulled herself to sitting.

Lee couldn't contain the excitement. "Parlour & Juke just offered me a chair."

Envy flashed through Shirley's eyes and was instantly replaced. "Lee, that's fantastic. That's what you've been wanting."

"It is. I just can't believe they offered it." Lee let her mind wander to how utterly amazing it would feel to walk into work every morning, knowing she had made it to the salon of her choice.

"I want to get back into it," Shirley said. She peered in on Harry in the bassinet beside her. "Would you help me with my portfolio?"

Lee was flattered. She'd been waiting for Shirley to take an interest in hair again. But building a portfolio was a lot of work. She'd recommend someone. "I actually know a few people who'd be perfect to train with. I'll text you their info."

"Thanks."

Harry's future started to solidify in her mind: his mother getting her act together. Harold getting sober. They'd both have someone to live for.

When it was time to check out, Lee gathered all of Harry's onesies, bottles, diapers, and wipes and figured out how to buckle him into the car, his impossibly tiny limbs folded into the fabric and straps of the bucket seat.

Shirley twisted around from the passenger seat. "Is he too small for the seat, do you think?"

Lee assessed. "I don't think so. The staff checked that everything was secure." She fussed over the baby's straps and climbed into the driver's seat.

"Okay, do we have everything?"

"I hope so."

She pulled out of the hospital lot and looped onto the highway. "Have you thought any more about nursing?"

Shirley nodded. "I want to. The lactation consultant showed me what to do."

"All the books say it really helps with their immunity. Not to mention bonding."

Shirley fiddled with the radio. "I'll try."

Lee tried not to worry that Shirley hadn't held Harry much or even looked at him too long. She knew every mother was different and she might be feeling over-whelmed. "How do you feel?"

Shirley ran her fingers through her greasy hair. "Like I've been through a meat grinder."

Lee grimaced. "Lovely. But I didn't mean physically. I just meant about . . . Harry."

Shirley turned around and looked at her child. "He looks like a little old man, doesn't he?"

"I think he's perfect."

A smile warmed Shirley's face. "He is pretty cute."

"You're going to be a great mom, Shirley. I know it."

Tears filled Shirley's eyes and she knocked them away. Lee reached out and held Shirley's hand.

"God, I'm a mess. Look at me." Shirley flipped down the passenger visor and dragged her fingers under her eyes and across her cheeks.

"You're beautiful," Lee said. "And it's just the hor-mones. It will get better."

Shirley leaned back against the passenger seat and closed her eyes. "I hope so."

Lee exited the highway and turned left onto Fesslers Lane. "Listen, I was thinking you and Harold could have a night out together if you felt up for it. I'll watch the baby."

"Really? Am I allowed to do that?"

Lee hesitated. "I mean, I think so. The doctors said you should rest, but I don't think having dinner would be out of the question."

"I'll see what Harold wants to do."

Lee nodded. She wished her father would get out of the house, but he'd probably want to stay in. She just wanted Harry to have a calm first night.

A few minutes later, she pulled into their driveway. The lawn was nothing but weeds. Shirley turned to her.

"Can I talk to him first?" She bolted into the house without receiving an answer, leaving the baby in the car, as well as all their bags. Lee rolled her eyes and unbuckled Harry.

"Well, that wasn't very nice, was it? Leaving you here like that on your very first day." She knew Shirley was anxious to see Harold. The fact that he had missed the birth of his son wasn't lost on either of them. Harry's whole life with her father began to flash before her eyes, and she bit back tears. All the ways he would disappoint him. All the ways Shirley would be there to defend a man who didn't deserve defending, just like her mother had. Lee detached the car seat and inhaled the clean scent of new life.

She gazed at Harry's sleeping face. Thoughts of her unborn baby brother made her almost capsize with grief. Here she was, so many years later, with her second chance at becoming a sister. But she was just one person. She couldn't be with Harry all the time. She had to work. She had to leave him every single day. She knew her father had already raised a child, but she still wasn't sure if he was capable of loving a baby. Not in this phase of life.

She looped the car seat handle over her arm and carefully walked up the front stoop. She opened the door and smelled cigarette smoke. Beer cans littered the kitchen counter in front of the patch of tile that had been ruined in a grease fire her father had accidentally set last year. Dirty dishes were piled in the sink. Mail was strewn across the floor.

"Dad, really?" She waved through the haze of smoke, kicked the mail out of the way, and stalked to the living room. Her father was on the couch. Shirley sat in his lap, the two of them already glued to some stupid show. He was drinking a beer. Lee searched the coffee table for drugs, so conditioned to look for signs. She knew Shirley had promised to stay clean, and she wanted to believe her. But deep down, she feared she'd be high again the first chance she got.

"Dad."

Her father ignored her and took another sip of his beer.

"Dad! Hello?" She snatched the remote off the coffee table and hit *mute*. "Would you like to meet your son?"

"Where's my boy?" he slurred. "Where's Harry?"

Lee stepped back. She didn't want to hand him the baby when he was drunk. He could drop him or make him cry.

She set the car seat at her feet and unbuckled him. He was sleeping, despite the noise, the smoke, and the unstable environment. She scooped his pliable body out of the seat and cradled his neck.

"See? This is Harry, your son." She extended the baby for him to take a look, protective as she pulled him back again.

Her father opened his arms. He stank. He was wearing the same clothes he had three days ago, when they'd left to go to the hospital. Though Lee had insisted he no longer smoke in the house, he had, and would. A baby wouldn't change that. She craned her arms so her father could see, but he closed and opened his fists.

"Give him to me, Lee. Jesus."

Shirley nodded. "It's okay."

Lee bit the inside of her cheek as she handed off the

baby. Harold bounced the infant, his head popping back on its soft, unformed vertebrae. He shook the newborn like a rattle until Harry was choking on his own cries. "Stop that crying, you." He looked at Shirley. "Ugly little things, aren't they?"

"Like aliens," she said, as she lit a cigarette and blew smoke into the air.

"What is wrong with the two of you?" Lee, unusually bold, inserted herself between them and moved the baby back into her arms. She snatched the cigarette from Shirley's mouth with her free hand and waved the smoke away. "You cannot *smoke* around a baby. What are you even doing?" She squashed the cigarette in the ashtray and glared at her father. "And you have to support his head, Dad. You can't hold him like that."

"Chill out, Lee. We're his parents, not you," Shirley scoffed.

"Exactly my point," Lee snapped. "I'm the one doing everything so far, and you just had him. You *literally* just left him in the car."

Shirley reddened and opened her mouth. "I'm sorry. I'm just tired. I'm not thinking straight. It's my hormones."

"Give her a break, Lee. Jesus."

Lee resisted the urge to tell her dad to stay out of it. "Look, I know this is a lot, but you two can't drink and smoke around Harry. Can we please just make a deal about that?"

Shirley nodded and elbowed Harold.

"Fine, fine," he said. "We'll be good."

Lee looked at Shirley. "Are you going to feed him?"

Shirley studied the baby, her eyes glassy and raw. "Can you give him formula right now? It's in the bag, I think. They gave me some free ones."

"I thought . . ."

"I know. I am going to try to nurse. I promise. I just need to rest for a bit."

Lee sighed and walked to the kitchen with the baby tucked safely in her arms. She wanted to remind her that if Harry got used to formula, he probably wouldn't want her milk. As she mixed the formula and warmed the bottle, spitting out a few drops on her inner wrist to test the temperature, she wondered how this was ever going to work.

It already felt like babysitting, except she had a *real* baby to think about now. Harry's lips parted as he took the bottle. He began to suck and soften, his cheeks pink from exertion. She stroked the top of his head with its silken hair, a few strands sticking up at the crown.

Shirley and Harold laughed about something in the next room. What happened to this child would largely be up to her. Despite all her best hopes for Shirley to get her act together, that meant that Harold had to as well. She could help Shirley with her career, but that was it. She had her own life to think about. She wasn't ready for the full-time responsibility of someone else's child.

She finished feeding Harry and took him to the nursery. Pale blue walls welcomed him, as well as a modest crib. She'd had fun decorating with an owl decal and matching curtains. She lowered him inside and cranked the mobile above his head. She watched him fall asleep, then tiptoed out of the room and shut the door.

61
lee

Okay, it's finally done!" Shirley entered Frothy Monkey and practically floated to where Lee sat at a corner table.

Harry was strapped to her chest, out cold. Lee smiled to see such a sweet sight. He was only two months old, but Shirley had swiftly warmed to motherhood after her initial uncertainty. While she'd dropped most of the pregnancy weight, she had curves again. Her hair was growing back to its natural blond, and she looked like herself.

"I'm dying to see it." Lee offered the chair next to her. "And this cutie." She stroked the top of Harry's sleeping head and slid over a decaf coffee. "For the nursing mother."

"Why thank you." Shirley took a long sip and grimaced. "God, I miss real coffee."

"It's only a matter of time. Now, give it to me." Lee opened and closed her hands while Shirley reached into her bag to retrieve her stylist portfolio.

Though she took several weeks off after the baby, Shirley had been hard at work building her book. For the last month, she'd done nothing else. There was a training spot open at Parlour & Juke, and though Lee had only been there for two months, she wanted to put in a good word for her.

Shirley proudly set the portfolio on the table. Her cheeks were flushed, her skin glowing, and Lee marveled at how well motherhood suited her. How much it had changed her. Even if her father was still the same.

Lee clapped her hands excitedly and prepared to open it.

"Before you get into it"—Shirley laid her hand on Lee's forearm—"I just want you to feel like you can be one hundred percent honest with me. I can handle constructive criticism. Ooh. Oh boy."

"What?" Lee looked at her.

Shirley lifted the baby as well as she could in his carrier and sniffed. "How can a baby poop while he sleeps? That's a talent in and of itself." She rolled her eyes. "Perfect timing. I won't have to sit here biting my nails. I'm going to change him. Have fun." She grabbed the diaper bag and headed for the bathroom.

Lee laughed and opened the portfolio, thick with photos of all types of cuts. Shirley had decided early on that she would be a haircut specialist and not get into color, which Lee thought was brilliant. She scanned the first page. She'd started with the long cuts, which had been Lee's suggestion.

A knot formed in her stomach as she peered closer and dissected each haircut. Sections were heavy where they should have been light. Layers at the wrong angle or overly hacked into the hair. Wrong scissors. Slightly uneven tips. Blunt, wide cuts that made the hair shaft expand, not shrink. Razor cuts on the wrong hair types. "No, no, no." Lee quickly flipped to the next page, hoping it would get better. It didn't. Medium-length hair that did nothing for face shapes. Short cuts that were completely uneven and outdated. Lee turned page after page and waited to see the right cut, a glimmer of *something* that showed promise. They'd trained together, for God's sake. She'd taught Shirley various tricks and tips, but the last couple of months, she'd been training with someone else. And Lee had given her the recommendation! How could she have been so off base?

Shirley had picked up so many bad habits, Lee didn't even know where to begin. She started to panic. She couldn't tell her how bad this was. She closed the book and sipped her coffee. God, did Shirley think this was *good*?

A few minutes later, she emerged from the bathroom. "Shoo-wee can this kid fill a diaper. Holy God in heaven. I'm afraid for when he starts solids."

Lee laughed. "You and me both." She'd taken on her fair share of changing diapers in the last eight weeks. Harry loved to eat.

Shirley glanced at the book. "So?" She stomped her feet like a little kid. "You're killing me. Tell me everything."

Lee smiled and fanned her hands across the top of the book. "First of all, I just want to tell you how absolutely impressed I am that you did this in such a short amount of time. This is a huge portfolio and a really big deal."

Shirley beamed and ran her hand in soothing circles across Harry's back. "Thank you. I worked hard on it."

Lee opened the book. "That being said though, I *do* want to ask you about a few of your stylistic choices, just so I can understand how you approached each cut."

"Okay." Shirley's hopeful tone shifted, and Lee could hear a bit of defensiveness edging in.

"For instance, tell me about the layering for the long cuts, if it was wet or dry, how you sectioned the hair. All that."

Shirley launched into the details, and Lee listened.

Wrong. It was all wrong. She moved on to the medium and short cuts, withholding judgment until they'd gone through the entire book. With every answer, she realized how little Shirley actually knew about how to approach a head of hair. She wasn't ready to go anywhere near someone's head, let alone be hired by Supercuts.

"Is there anything you think I could work on? I want to get this right before I show P&J."

Lee hesitated and then rested her hand on top of the book. "You can't show this to Parlour & Juke. Not like this." Lee's direct statement hung in the air, and she watched as Shirley's face visibly fell.

"Okay." She adjusted Harry's pacifier. "Why not?"

Lee exhaled. "I just think you need to refine a bit."

"But how? Lee, come on. Out with it." She bobbed Harry up and down.

Lee knew she wanted constructive criticism, but she wasn't sure how to say it without being cruel. "Shirl, if I'm being honest, there's something fundamentally wrong with every single one of these haircuts."

Shirley stared quizzically at the book. "What do you mean?"

Lee opened it to a random page. "From how you just explained your process, to the approach, and especially the end result." She motioned to one of the photos. "They're just completely off the mark."

"Well . . ." Tears welled in Shirley's eyes, but she blinked rapidly to prevent them from falling. "Isn't that just your opinion?"

Lee covered Shirley's hand with her own. "I've been doing this a long time. I know what salons look for. I know how they will assess your work. That being said, this is nothing we can't fix." She squeezed her hand. "I'm happy to help you rebuild the book, but whoever you've been training with the last few months has given you some bad advice. We need to start over with the basics."

"I don't have time to start with the basics." There was a desperate edge to her voice. "I need this job. I need this job like yesterday." Shirley's face reddened. "I am counting on you putting in a good word for me. I want to get my own place. You know that. I need the money. This is important to me, Lee."

Lee nodded. She was being put in an impossible position. She wanted Shirley to have a good job and her own place. "Of course I know that. But I'm telling you, you need more time. No one will hire you with this book."

Shirley stared silently at the table. Lee saw a few tears splash against the wood.

"Shirley, hey. Please don't get discouraged. My first book was a disaster too. But it can be fixed. We can fix it, okay?"

"My book is *not* a disaster," Shirley snapped. She snatched the book and shoved it into the diaper bag. "This is just your opinion. *One* opinion. You're not the deciding factor here."

Lee sat back. "I'm just trying to help. You just said you could take constructive criticism."

"By telling me I have no talent and that my book is a *disaster*?" Shirley stood and her fingers shook as she shouldered her bag. "Yeah, thanks for the fucking encouragement. I'll never ask for your help again." She turned and stormed out of the coffee shop. Lee didn't want her to be angry, but all she'd done was tell the truth. Shirley needed to put in the real work, and it took longer than two months. She couldn't have a job handed to her just because she knew someone who worked at the same salon.

Lee palmed her coffee and keys and checked the time.

She had to get to work. She knew they'd talk it out later, but she felt bad she'd hurt her feelings. She entered the parking lot. Shirley was strapping Harry into the backseat. As she approached, she could hear her sniffles before she snapped him into place and shut the door.

"What?" Shirley wiped her face and smeared mascara across her cheek.

"I wasn't trying to hurt your feelings. Hey, come here." She tugged Shirley closer. "Look at me. You *are* talented."

Shirley scoffed.

"You are. Let's just approach this like a challenge, okay? We'll do it together."

"I don't *want* to do it together! For once, I wanted to prove to you I didn't need your help."

Lee shook her head. "What's that supposed to mean?"

"You're right. You've been right all along. I've been so busy trying to be like you—dressing like you, losing weight like you, dating your father, living in your house, becoming a hairdresser . . ." She lifted her arms and dropped them. "I thought if I could prove that I was as good as you in some way, then I'd be worthy."

"Worthy of what?" Lee was genuinely confused. Lee's life, from the inside, was a mess. She was constantly trying to fix things, trying to escape a past she couldn't escape. She'd become an alcoholic and still couldn't kick the cravings. She had no romantic prospects. She was basically a babysitter for her father. Her job was her only saving grace.

"I don't know. I just . . ."

"Listen, this is *your* life, Shirley. You don't need to be anything like me. You're a mother now. You have your entire life to do whatever you want to do. Is hair really what you want to do?"

She nodded. "It is. I love it."

"So go after it. No matter what."

"But how am I supposed to do that if I have no talent?"

"You do have talent. And I'm sorry if I seemed harsh in there. Look, if anyone can do this, you can. Look at you. Look how far you've come. You're sober. You've become a phenomenal mother to Harry. You are getting your life together, and I couldn't be prouder of you."

Shirley collapsed against her chest. Harry yawned from the backseat. Lee's heart swelled for her tiny brother in his bucket seat and her best friend in her arms. She wanted to help make this right. She wanted to help her succeed.

Shirley finally pulled away and wiped her eyes. "I'm sorry. I'm such a hormonal mess."

"You're fine. It's going to work out," Lee said. "I promise."

Shirley smiled through her tears, but doubt lurked just behind those pretty irises. "How do you know?"

"I just know." A sinking feeling crept over her skin. Lee swallowed her apprehension and forced a smile. "It's all going to be great."

PRESENT

62

grace

Alice and Carol swirl their wine in Grace's living room. After a few uncomfortable moments of silence, Alice leans in and places a hand on Grace's knee. "Why didn't you tell us any of this?"

She shrugs. "I wanted to. I should have. But I didn't think it was my place to tell." She'd finally shared a condensed version of what Lee had told her the night she died. About the man in the dark. What she'd gone through. How many secrets she'd kept. She left out the part about Shirley and Noah for now; that what Lee told her about her own sexual assault might not have actually happened. And how Noah may or may not fit into the puzzle. It was too complicated to get into.

The back door opens and shuts, and suddenly, her house is filled with male voices, both large and small.

Mason enters first and steps into the living room, slapping a tiny hand to his chest. "Good lord in heaven, people. You're like a bunch of ghosts in here. Open a window! Turn on a light! Let's bring some life into the room." He claps his hands, thrusts open the curtains, and flips on the overhead light. "That's better."

Grace laughs. "How much sugar have you had, young man?"

"A *lot*," Mason confirms. "Don't judge. I'm going to read a book to negate the effects."

Luca bounds in after and darts straight to his room without even saying hello. She hears Noah setting down grocery bags in the kitchen. He took the boys to Whole Foods to grab groceries and lunch—and she's guessing ice cream or cookies too.

"Is it me, or is Mason becoming more humorous by the day?" Carol asks.

"And he doesn't even know it," Grace adds. She takes a sip of tea.

Carol leans forward and motions to Noah in the kitchen. *Are you two okay?* she mouths.

"Why?" Grace asks. Her skin prickles.

Alice chimes in. "Because we haven't seen him lately."

Grace sighs, closes her eyes, and adjusts her sweater. "He proposed."

"What?" Carol and Alice both exclaim. Their faces crack into goofy grins, but she holds up a hand to interrupt.

"Don't get too excited. I said no."

"You said *what* now?" Carols shrieks. "Why?"

"Because I don't want to get married."

"Oh, come on. You can't base marriage on your experience with Chad. That's not giving Noah a fair shot."

Grace's eyes flicker and she clears her throat. "It's complicated."

The women look at each other. "Life is complicated. Taxes are complicated. Marrying Noah? Not complicated."

"I don't know." Grace drops her voice to a whisper and she leans toward the women, her palms working around the hot porcelain of her mug. "Doesn't he seem—I don't know—abnormally close to Mason?"

"What do you mean?" Alice asks.

Grace shrugs. "He just seems to have taken an unnatural interest in him. Something just feels off about it all."

Carol and Alice share concerned looks. "Like, do you mean inappropriate or . . . ?"

A ding interrupts their conversation. Grace sighs and extracts her phone. "Never mind. Forget I brought it up. I'm sure I'm just reading too much into it." Her blood runs cold as she sees the new email. "Oh, shit." She sits up straight. "Guys."

"What?" Carol sets her wine down.

"What is it?" Alice asks.

"Noah!" She glances toward the kitchen and then turns back to the email. "Noah, come here!"

The women anxiously wait as Noah enters the living room and says hello to her friends. With shaking fingers, Grace looks at the group. "It's the autopsy and toxicology reports."

"What does it say?" Carol asks.

"Finally," Alice adds.

Grace blasts through the medical jargon, which explains death from internal injuries. That much they know. She scrolls to the toxicology report. She recalls the empty second bottle of wine. Did she or didn't she?

She scans the page and lands on the number she fears the most: Lee's blood alcohol level was 0.16 at the time of her death.

"You're kidding," she whispers.

"What?" Noah leans over her shoulder. "Oh."

"Yep. She was drunk all right." She passes the phone to Carol and Alice. That level means Lee basically downed the entire bottle. Because she went back inside the house, Lee slipped from sobriety. Because she'd slipped, she'd had an entire bottle of wine. Because she was drunk, she'd gone for a hike in the middle of the night and died.

"She was completely wasted. My God. This is all my fault." She drops her face into her hands.

Alice and Carol murmur to each other as they reread the email.

"Hey, stop. It's not your fault." Noah slips an arm around her shoulders but it doesn't help.

Grace thinks about how devastated Lee must have felt to turn back to alcohol; the news of Noah and the baby had made her *that* upset. The women finally put down the phone and stare at Grace with sympathy.

"At least we know now, right? There's no more mystery. She was drunk." Alice fiddles with her wine stem.

"Which explains why she fell," Carol adds. "At least she didn't jump."

"We still don't know that." Grace sits back in the recliner. "I mean, yes. You're right. She probably did slip." She shrugs. "But what if she didn't?"

Carol gnaws her bottom lip. "Grace, is there anything else about that night? Anything we should know?" She looks from Grace to Noah.

Grace swallows. "Like what?"

"I mean anything else that happened. Something Lee said. Any kind of warning or anything?"

"A warning? Like that she was going to do something stupid? No. Absolutely not." Her face reddens as she works out what her friend is implying. "If I thought she was going to go jump off of a mountain, I wouldn't have left her on the deck. We were in the middle of an argument. That's all. I went back outside to look for her. I couldn't find her."

"Why didn't you wake us up? We could have helped."

Grace balls her hands into fists and stands. "Look. I

have gone over this a million times in my head. I feel awful enough as it is. You two telling me what I should have done doesn't help anything. She's dead. She got drunk because of what I told her. I have to live with that, not you. Excuse me. I'm going to go lie down." She storms off to her bedroom as a splitting headache pierces her between the eyes. Even her best friends don't get it. She has to live with what happened that night—not them.

She hears Noah talking to them and then he knocks lightly on her door. "Grace?"

She sighs and rolls onto her back. "Come in."

"Hey." He sits on the edge of her bed and places a hand on her knee. "They're not blaming you, you know. They're just still trying to make sense of everything."

She sits up. "I know. But I feel terrible. I feel so guilty, Noah."

"Hey, stop. That won't help anything. Come here."

She folds into his arms—the first time since he proposed. She breathes in his familiar scent, sighs, and finally pulls away. "Do you mind if I rest for a bit? This baby is giving me a run for its money in the fatigue department."

"Of course." He kisses her forehead and pauses at the door. "It's all going to be okay. You'll see."

He leaves the room, but for some reason, his words don't bring her comfort. Instead, they bring with them a sense of impending dread.

63

lee

Over the past month, everything had gone downhill. Since that day in the parking lot, Shirley had become a different human being. It was like their conversation had never happened. She stopped eating again. She stopped nursing. She didn't even take an interest in Harry. She'd given up on becoming a stylist and stayed holed up in Harold's room.

Lee had taken on the child care almost exclusively, even with her busy work schedule. She kept waiting for Shirley to come to her senses and stop feeling sorry for herself, but a switch had been flipped. Gone were the days of Shirley fussing over Harry, singing him to sleep, giving him baths, and giggling at his sweet coos. It was heartbreaking. She didn't know what Shirley was trying to prove, but she was desperate to snap her out of it. She knew part of it was punishment for bashing her portfolio, but Harry was the one who was suffering, not Lee.

Lee hired a babysitter to keep him placated on days that Shirley was wasted. She'd started drinking again, and an occasional drink had grown into blackout binges with her father. Lee was irate at her friend's childish behavior. She still heard Shirley talking on the phone late at night or early in the mornings, and she often wanted to snatch the receiver out of her hand and scream at whoever was on the other end of the phone to help her. It killed her that Shirley wasn't confiding in her, but she couldn't save her all by herself.

She'd thought about finding Shirley's family so many times and demanding they handle the situation. Yes, Harry was her brother, but Shirley was his *mother*. Someone had to talk some sense into her, and nothing Lee did made a difference.

Today, she had a four-hour training, and the babysitter couldn't watch Harry. Sensing her hesitancy, Shirley had rolled her eyes at Lee.

"We're his parents. We can handle it."

She'd been completely sober when she said it, but Lee had still hesitated. "You haven't exactly been the best role model lately."

Shirley averted her eyes. "Just going through a rough patch. I'll snap out of it."

"Will you? You promised me that day that you were going to try with the job and for Harry. You were so excited. You were—"

"Lee, stop! Enough. I know. I *know* what I said. I don't want to talk about it, okay? Just go to your stupid training." She'd lost any amount of weight she'd kept since having the baby, now all sharp angles and ruddy skin.

"Have it your way." Lee turned and slammed the door on her way out.

Now, every minute that passed, she wondered if Harry was okay. She'd fed him two bottles of formula before she left, changed his diaper, and put him down for a nap. She reminded herself that Shirley loved her baby and that she *could* give him everything he needed. She already had. If only she would try again. As much as Lee cared about him, it could never replace the love Shirley felt for her son.

After training, Lee raced out of the salon and called Shirley. No answer. She tried the landline, as her father refused to get a cell phone. Nothing. The panic hammered against her skull. She sped through town, hitting every red light, as if the universe was trying to keep her away. As the minutes ticked by, the questions began their assault: what if something happened? What if he'd choked or fallen out of his crib? Suddenly, the realization of what she'd done—leaving a three-month-old with irresponsible adults—shifted from conceptual to a horrific reality.

At the house, she unbuckled her seat belt and sprinted to the front door. She fumbled with the keys, dropped them, and finally found the right one to jam into the lock. She could hear Harry crying, even from outside.

"Oh God." The smell of smoke hit her nostrils first. Harry's cries intensified as she went through the kitchen and circled around to the living room. She searched for candles or cigarettes. Where was the cause of the smoke?

Harry was situated in his car seat, cartoons blasting. She lunged for the baby, unbuckled him, and folded him against her chest. His onesie was soaked with urine and yellow shit, his round face streaked from hours of strained tears. She shushed him against her. "Oh, Harry. Oh sweet pea. I'm so sorry. I'm so sorry. Never again, I promise. Never again."

She searched for the remote, clicked it off, and listened for other sounds in the house. The low hum of the television in her father's room was the only indication that there was other life here. She got Harry cleaned up and warmed a bottle. She cradled him as he sucked greedily at the food, his eyes alert and then growing heavy as he fell asleep in her arms. She kissed his forehead and then lowered him into his bassinet and tiptoed across the hall, pressing her ear to the door. She wanted to kick it in, to finally let both of them have it. She didn't expect much from her father, but Shirley was breaking her fucking heart.

She tried the knob and it turned in her hands. The room was dark and rank. The source of the smoke was immediate. There were two lit cigarettes in her father's ashtray and a blazing candle with an inch-long flame. She blinked through the haze and saw her father on his back, legs and arms splayed. Snores strangled his airway as the fan, on high, whirred with the annoying click of the rusty chain.

She moved around the bed to Shirley. A pillow rested over her face. Shirley hated her father's snoring and had all but threatened separate bedrooms if he didn't do something about it. Shirley had taken to sleeping with earplugs, or, in rare cases, with a pillow over her face when socking him in the shoulder didn't work.

The bedside table was littered with ashes, rubber tubes, and a small plate of something that had been boiled and was now burnt. Lee searched for the needle and found it beside Shirley's left hip.

"Goddammit, Shirley." Shirley had promised not to turn back to drugs. She'd *promised* to stay clean for Harry. What had been the catalyst to push her over the edge—and today of all days? Lee wondered if she'd secretly been doing drugs for the last month. She scanned the room as if she'd find the answer. There, on the floor, was Shirley's hair portfolio.

Lee knelt by the book and flipped through it. Every single photograph had been destroyed. Photographs that had taken time and money, now unrecognizable. Lee closed the book. She'd criticized Shirley's work. *This* was why she was so angry. Because she'd hurt her feelings. She looked again at the small plate of drugs. So she'd turned back to something that made her feel good.

She cast the disappointment aside, along with the book. Lee grabbed a small towel from the floor, pinched the used needle, and deposited it onto the nightstand. Enough was enough. She had to get her help. Get *them* help. Shirley could still have a good life. She just needed to get her away from her father and prove that she could be a good mother to her son. She'd help her get a good job. Shirley could be her damn assistant if she had to. But she had to get her out of this house.

Lee knew she hated to be woken up, but she'd had it. This was *it*. Harry could have died in there, alone and crying, and then she'd have to live with that for the rest of her life.

She gathered every bit of restraint she possessed and lifted the pillow. "Oh my God!" Lee jumped back as if something grotesque and monstrous had been hiding there. Shirley's eyes were bloodshot and cocked up and to the left, her face a sickening shade of gray. Remnants of foam dusted the tops of her lips, which were ajar, as if she'd been surprised by something. "No!" She screamed so loud, she was sure her father would awaken, but he remained motionless too. She clutched her best friend, her waxy flesh cool in her arms, and prayed for a miracle. She screamed into her shoulder until she thought she would throw up.

She could not lose her best friend. Not after how hard she'd tried to save her. Not after all they'd been through. Not after she had a real chance to get her life together. Shirley's story could not end like this.

Lee finally pressed two shaky fingers against the side of her neck. No pulse thumped beneath the surface. No

twitches or automation of a body continuing to run after
years of trying to destroy it.

"Come on. Come on, please God. Please be alive.
Please." As Lee's fingers hunted for life, pressing so
hard that she wondered if she was going to puncture the
skin, she was reminded of that night at the party, when
she'd kept Shirley in a tight spoon, consistently waking
to check for her pulse. She rooted deeper and deeper,
knowing but not accepting.

Nothing.

She inspected her arms. There were three sets of fresh
tracks, tiny pinpricks of purple flesh that looked like
nothing more than a spider bite. How could something
so small destroy her? The sad truth swirled through
her chest, and Lee collapsed once more on top of her
friend. It was like her mother's death all over again. The
dread. The horrific scene. That moment from wondering
to knowing. The indescribable grief. Was she responsible for this death too? She'd *seen* Shirley going downhill these last four weeks. She'd tried to help her but
had selfishly given up. She was the reason Shirley had
slipped in the first place. Harry wasn't enough to keep
her clean.

She dropped Shirley's arm. Her entire body trembled.
She felt sick. How would she tell her father? He couldn't
take another loss. Not like this. She turned her attention
to him. His snores had stopped. She searched for the rise
and fall of his chest. Was he dead too? She climbed over
to his side of the bed and ransacked the nightstand: the
same ashtray he'd had since she was a child, the baggie
filled with white crystals that looked like sachets of sugar.
His own needle, doll-sized and unused, tipped by the
crumpled package of cigarettes. A prescription bottle lay
cocked and empty. She palmed it and cleared the cigarette

smoke with her hands. Sleeping pills. How many had he taken?

She needed to wake him, to make him finally understand all the ways he'd let her down, let her mother down, let Shirley down, let Harry down, and that this time, he'd gone too far. This time, there was a baby. This time—like last time—someone was dead. Anger slithered inside of her. Screw him. Screw him for everything.

Her whole life flashed before her. Her father before her mother's death, and her father after. All of the abandonment, the neglect, and laziness. And then Shirley. Shirley, who had been the only real friend she'd ever had. Shirley, who had disappeared into her father's sick web and couldn't find her way out again. She thought about Harry in the next room and what would happen to him, what was best.

The pillow rested at an angle above Shirley's head. She grabbed it and stared down at her father.

It would be so easy.

Her fingers shook, but she gripped the pillow tighter. With a full breath, she began to lower the pillow over her father's face.

PRESENT

64

grace

Grace stares out the window. The children run laps around each other in a game of tag. Mason stands in the middle with a paper hat he made earlier that morning from a menu. He holds his wooden airplane, which all of the other kids want turns with, but he refuses. Every time their tiny bodies lunge for it, he holds it high, wagging it like a bone. Mason wields commands as the children sprint and scream around him, and Grace knows, in that moment, with all of his quirks, losses, and complex thoughts, Mason will find his way.

So much has happened. Just six weeks ago, Lee was here. Now, she's not. She is still processing, still working out the next steps with Noah. He's worried about the baby, especially when she kept him from coming to her last doctor's appointment.

"Whatcha thinking?" Alice slides an arm around her shoulders.

"I'm thinking I'm utterly exhausted."

"I know what you mean," Alice says.

She doesn't know. She can't possibly. The fatigue is in her bones. She wakes up tired, she goes to bed tired. She doesn't want to eat. She lies awake at night, heart racing, unable to believe all that has transpired in less than two months. Though Mason has his regular therapy sessions, she realizes she might need therapy too.

"Mason looks like he's having fun."

Grace smiles. "He is." Cheryl and Carol bicker outside, the sliding glass of the patio door unable to block the audible sounds of their heated conversation. Cheryl is doing well with her treatment. Charlie and Fred are busy drinking beer, laughing, and watching the kids play. Alice is lost in a balloon of new business ideas and one-track thoughts as she chats beside her. It is good to be around so much normalcy, but she doesn't belong. She has never needed her friends more, but there is a new distance between them. They can't understand all that she's been through.

Summer is approaching, and Grace craves routine. Mason will start at the Waldorf school in August. It will be his first school experience, but after interviewing and initial assessments with the staff, she's confident he's going to thrive.

Alice transitions outside to the deck and Grace follows, the intense sun signifying the start of summer.

"How are you?" Carol asks.

"Fine." She is so sick of everyone asking her that. She isn't fine.

"Oh, before I forget. Here." Carol reaches over to the slatted side table and plucks Lee's journal from the wood. "Thank you for letting me read this. I know it was private, but . . . it helped me understand her so much more."

"No problem." Grace slips the book into her sweater, holding it tightly against her chest.

"Her childhood and the stuff about her dad . . . man. What a tragic life he had."

"Who, Harold?" Cheryl asks as she hands Grace an iced tea. Grace glares at Carol's inability to keep anything from her mother.

"Harold is a stupid name. It sounds like *hairy,* which makes one think of fur." Mason pounds up the steps. He has removed his hat, his cheeks flaming, and sets his plane by the edge of the deck.

Alice laughs. "It does sound like *hairy.*"

"Do you even know what the name Harold means?" Mason probes.

"I don't. Do you?"

"Yes, of *course* I do, or I wouldn't have brought it up. Harold comes from the Latin Herald, meaning a king. A man to lead a nation. A man with a perfectly round head. A man who has many thoughts but says very few words. That's a Harold. I need to go to the bathroom."

He pushes past Grace and the women, yanks open the sliding glass door, and lets himself in. No one follows him anymore. They let Mason breathe, explore, wander, and make mistakes, and because of it, he is thriving.

Alice looks at Grace. "How could he possibly know what that name means?"

She smiles. "Noah did a lesson on names last week. He's become pretty obsessed."

"Where is Noah?"

"With some of his other students." This is a lie. She didn't tell him about the get-together, didn't want him to come. She hasn't yet confided in her friends about Noah and Shirley. Not until she figures out how the two of them will end up.

"I wonder if Lee ever told Mason about her dad? I'm sure she had to talk about her parents at some point, right?" Alice asks.

"If he read her journal, he knows he wasn't really there for Lee," Carol says.

"Can a seven-year-old really understand all that though?" Alice takes a dainty sip of iced tea.

"Probably not." Grace closes her eyes. What's not in that journal is the truth. "Does anyone else need like a yearlong vacation?"

"Yes," the women chime in.

More like a lifetime, Grace thinks. And she means it. She leans her head against her own chair as they listen to the rustle of leaves and the kids chattering at the edge of the yard. The women talk among themselves; Fred and Charlie are still lost in their own conversation. She remembers when Noah was here the day of the barbecue, and Lee was so excited by the prospect of their budding romance, the trip, her life, everything.

Grace swallows the sorrow and takes a sip of tea. The sweet, cold brew coats her throat but settles in a wash of sugar and nerves. She closes her eyes and clutches the journal closer to her chest. The chorus of voices soothes her as Mason comes back outside, dashes past all of them, and charges straight to the backyard to play with the other kids.

65

lee

The baby stirred in Lee's room. It was just an adjustment cry, probably him transitioning between dreams, but it was enough to bring her back to the present. She paused with the pillow mere inches from her father's face and then lowered it to the nightstand with an uneven exhale. She couldn't do this. She wasn't a murderer.

She climbed off the bed. Something was tumbling out of her father's right pocket. She moved closer and peered at the roll of money with the red hair tie around it. She grabbed the cash and walked back to her room. She rummaged in her closet for her motorcycle boots and tipped them over. First one, then the other. Nothing. She thought she was so clever, stashing her money here.

She tossed the boots to the back of the closet. Her father had stolen from her. He'd stolen the money she'd worked so tirelessly for, to pay for the baby, his formula, his diapers, the mortgage, the food, everything.

Her entire body ignited with rage. Why had she allowed this type of abuse for so long? What did that say about her? Instead of standing up to him and changing her life, she'd started to drink. So she could numb herself to all the pain he'd caused all these years. So she could pretend he hadn't taken away the only real friend she'd ever had.

She checked on Harry and walked to the living room. Despite all of her efforts, this place was a disaster. It would never be anything else. Her whole life had taken place here, and she'd held on to it, because her mother had been part of it. But there hadn't been a trace of her mother in a long time.

She was a fool.

She marched back to her father's room, where her best friend lay, nothing but a corpse now. She should just let her father wake up on his own and see the woman he loved like that—reduced to decomposing flesh. The second woman he'd loved and lost.

Agony festered. Frustration. Worry. Anger. Disappointment. Hate. All of the things she'd had to teach herself, do for herself, do for the both of them.

Suddenly a *whoosh* lit the air, and she screamed. The pillow she'd dropped on the nightstand had ignited from the candle, and angry red flames seized the fabric and licked the curtains. She moved back and yelled to her father, but he didn't move. She needed to get him out of here before the whole house burned down. Could she even drag him? The flames caught and spread. She watched the fire, knowing she didn't have a lot of time. She made a quick decision, then retreated from the room. The baby. She had to get Harry.

She scooped him from the bassinet and curled his warm body close to her chest. He knew her smell. He trusted her. The realization dawned on her: Harry was *hers* now. Not Shirley's. Not her father's.

Hers.

She ran out the back door, tucked him into his infant seat, and started the car. She tilted the vents to blast the heat, as it was exceptionally cold for November. She made sure he was buckled and ducked back inside. The driveway wrapped to the rear of the house. No one could see her. No neighbors were out. The house wasn't obviously burning, no black reams of smoke edging out of the fireplace just yet. Shirley had removed the batteries from the smoke alarm months ago when it kept beeping. It constantly went off from their smoking. There would be no audible warning that the house was being seized by such wicked flames.

She scurried to her desk to grab Harry's birth certificate. She pocketed Shirley's ID, both social security cards, and the guardianship papers that were in the filing cabinet.

She tossed Harry's formula, clothes, and anything she could get her hands on into her suitcase. The hallway was pregnant with smoke, and she kicked open the hot door to look at her father's bed. It was engulfed in flames; his body was nothing but a wave of heat. The stench seeped into the hall. She looked at Shirley's side of the bed and choked on a sob. She escaped the house, gasping and sputtering, jumped in the car, and reversed out of the drive as fast as she could.

She was done with this house, this life. All these years spent in agony. And in minutes, it was all going to be destroyed. She pulled over a block away, unbuckled her belt, and twisted around in the back to stroke Harry's soft head, the downy fur sprouting in a semicircle around the top. Smoke clung to her skin, and she rolled down her window to suck in fresh air.

"You're safe," she whispered. "We're safe, Harry." She turned around again to study him, his round face, his shocking blue eyes, his pink lips. The thought of calling this baby by her father's name, of being reminded of this life and *them* every single day—no. Harry had her last name luckily—Chambers. She could pass for his mom. She *would* be his mom. Shirley had made her Harry's legal guardian when he was born, in the event that something ever happened to her. She had the papers to prove it.

Lee knocked away a sob and gripped the wheel. Had Shirley known, somewhere deep down, that this would happen?

She thought briefly of Shirley's family. Though she knew nothing about them, she wondered if they could possibly gain parental rights to Harry even though she had the guardianship papers. Would they fight her for custody once they learned of Shirley's death? The thought of losing him was terrifying. But she had been in his life from day one. There was no way a court would argue with that.

She readjusted his buckles, kissed his forehead, and put on the lullaby CD she'd bought on sale at Target. She circled the block again and paused to look at her small, brick house—the flames still hadn't started to curl from the windows, but in moments, the fire would win. Glass would crack and explode. Inky smoke would launch into the sky, and the overpowering flames would cause the entire structure to crumble and turn to ash.

She passed the house for the last time—the house of her childhood, the house of her nightmares—and then let it fade into the distance as she drove. She ignored the fear of the fire possibly spreading to other houses. It was a risk she had to take. She adjusted the rearview mirror to check on Harry. Names shuffled through her head: Grant, Stewart, Phil, Matt, James, Patrick, Colt.

She turned right to loop onto the highway, buying into the details of her backstory with all its layers, complications, and skewed facts. Where did she go now?

She'd have to get a new house. She needed to start a new life.

"What about Asher?" she asked. No, not right. "Louie?" No. "Mason?" she asked. Of course. Mason was his middle name. Harry cooed from the back and revealed a gummy half smile. She nodded in affirmation. "Mason. Mason is perfect." His birth certificate said Harry Mason Chambers. Mason would simply become his legal name.

She nodded again, the new name clicking into place. She thought of Shirley—his real mother, her best friend— and tears spilled onto her cheeks. Her crisped body. Those lifeless eyes. The waxen skin. All of that lost potential. What an incredible mother she could have been.

Lee would have to concoct her own story about how she became a single mother . . . unless she just wanted to tell everyone the truth. *No, she'd never tell anyone the truth.*

The night of the party flashed through her mind. That black hole of remembrance would serve as the perfect backdrop to how she got pregnant, if she wanted to play the single mother card. It would ensure she'd never have to talk about it, that her backstory was as painful as that night, that she'd had to fight hard for Mason, and that she didn't want to remember. It would feed into the lie so she could close down that area of her past and not think about what she'd done to get him. And it would keep her bonded to Shirley, keep the reason she was doing this fresh in her mind. It was her fault Shirley had gone to that party. It was her fault Shirley had ever met Harold. It was her fault she'd relapsed. So it didn't matter if the origin of where Mason came from was a lie. It was her lie, but Shirley's truth.

She was doing this for the both of them.

She shook her head, pressed harder on the gas pedal, and focused on getting away from the house. She adjusted the vent so it blew back onto Mason's soft cheeks. The streets were drenched by late-season rain, which would soon turn to snow.

The baby squeezed his plump fists together and stuffed one meaty palm into his mouth. "It's a new beginning, Mason," she said to him. "You'll see." Her heart slashed against her ribs. Though she ached for Shirley, the rest was a release: from her father, from the walls of that damn house, from the anguished, tangled memories of a happy childhood ripped away by murder and drink.

Even the thought of giving up alcohol made her pause. But she didn't have a choice. She wouldn't be like Shirley. She wouldn't disappoint Mason. She had to be here for him. She made a mental note to find the nearest AA chapter. She'd go on Monday. She'd go every single day if she had to. No more wine. No more drinking.

They bumped over a pothole and Mason laughed. "Is that funny?" she asked. She bounced in her seat, and he laughed again.

She reveled in the sweet, raspy sound of his laugh and kept driving, the town fading to blurred dots of trees and clusters of houses in the crooked rearview mirror. A few homes were already decorated for Thanksgiving, with inflatable turkeys, cornucopias, and oversized pumpkins on doorsteps. The thought of cooking a holiday meal in her own kitchen with Mason strapped to her chest excited her. She would soon forget about her father, the smell of death, and all the sins. And sweet Shirley. His mother. Her best friend. She cleared her throat and swatted away tears.

An hour later, racing on I-24E, she decided to drive

to Chattanooga. She'd check them into a hotel and stay there until she got the call about the house. She'd prepare herself for how to take the news, how to fake it. There would be insurance money. She'd have enough to start over.

With miles eaten beneath the soft rubber of her ancient tires, she looked back at Shirley's sweet little boy, asleep in his seat. A swell of love, real and thriving, pulsed behind her lids. The real question—could she be his mother—clung like static to her skin. The uncertainty broke apart and dispersed across the earth. She had Mason now. That was all that mattered. She *had* to pull this off. She didn't have a choice.

She'd done what she had to do.

~~sacrifice~~
~~penance~~
~~atonement~~
~~devotion~~
<u>loyalty</u>
I am a loyal person. I have sacrificed almost everything for a child who is not technically mine, but I love him anyway.
I love him as though he is my own.
I need him.
I want him.
He is mine.
(I have the papers to prove it.)

I owed it to Shirley.
I owed it to myself.

She would be happy knowing he's with me.
He's happy.
He's loved.
He's safe.

He belongs to <u>me</u>.

PRESENT

66

grace

Grace walks through the door. She drops her bag and sees the boys playing a game with Noah in the dining room. Mason hoards his tray of tile letters, arranging and rearranging with an obsessive discipline, while Luca rests his chin in his hand, bored. Noah sits across from them, nursing a beer, and winds the timer.

"Look who's home," Noah says.

She smiles and offers a small wave. They have been talking and working through the baggage, and Noah is regaining her trust. He takes what he can get, always on his very best behavior.

Grace shrugs out of her blazer and hangs it on the coatrack by the door. She loves this coatrack; she installed it with Luca. It is a giant slab of wood with skinny arms that fold down like levers. She chooses one at random, hangs her jacket, then removes her shoes. She massages the knots from her instep with her thumb and places her keys in the dish by the door.

She absorbs the idyllic scene with her three boys playing Scrabble. The harmony that exists between them, despite all the adjustments. The tragedies. The changes, both big and small. The months collect on themselves like dust. She tags them by event: moving to Nashville, befriending

Noah, the girls, Lee, the trip, the mountain, the aftermath, now. There's just been so much.

And so much left to do.

She will have to fake losing her pregnancy soon, make Noah experience that loss in the most excruciating way possible. She'll do it right before her next "doctor's" appointment. She flashes another smile—one that she's perfected by now—and motions to the bathroom.

"I'm just going to go wash my hands." Grace eases into the guest bath, flicks on the water, and studies herself in the mirror as she pumps organic foam into her damp palms.

No one will ever understand the patience it took to pull off something like this. The *painstaking* planning, the years of organizing, plotting, lying, and pretending. The absolute masterful performance she's given, in spite of everything.

She soaps and wrings her hands, pumps again. It is an obsessive tendency, this hand washing. Sometimes she worries she's turning Luca into a germaphobe, but better safe than sick.

As she scrubs, she thinks back to the catalyst. That dreaded phone call. She was acclimating to pumping milk at work and balancing her newly single life as a divorced mom. The phone had registered a Nashville number, and she'd just assumed it was her sister.

It wasn't.

She'd dropped her iPhone. She'd made arrangements. Once the grief had lessened, she demanded to know exactly what happened, and she couldn't do that long-distance.

She knew Shirley had been having troubles. Their weekly calls had all but disappeared once Shirley had Harry. Shirley made her promise not to tell their parents she was pregnant or about what had happened at the party.

Though Grace had tried repeatedly to encourage Shirley to get out of that house with that disgusting old man and her horrible best friend, *Lee*, she'd never listened. Shirley was stubborn and wanted to do things her own way. She insisted she was fine, that her life was turning around, and that she wanted to live on her own terms. Lee had literally ruined Shirley's life, and now she would never get to do anything except rot in a grave.

It was because of *her* that Shirley was in that house. Because of *her* that she'd gotten so drunk and been used and left by Noah at that party. Because of *her* that she'd gotten pregnant with that drunk's child. Because of *her* that she'd given up on her dreams. Because of *her* that Shirley had relapsed, overdosed, *died*.

Once Grace moved to Nashville, she immediately wanted to take Lee to court. But Lee had guardianship papers. She legally *owned* Mason, not her.

So she set a new plan in motion. She found Noah. *The* Noah. He'd been stupid enough to tell her sister his name at the party. Though Shirley never saw his face, they'd both done obsessive Google searches for Noah Banks. There were twelve. Without seeing his face, Shirley felt she couldn't identify him. She just wanted to move on. She just wanted to forget.

But Grace didn't want to forget.

After she found the right Noah, she befriended Lee. It was easy to get all her targets under one roof. People were so clueless at the power of suggestion.

It took years to build a meaningful friendship with Lee. To earn her trust, to suggest guardianship. She'd endured *seven years* to get back what belonged to her sister.

Grace thinks back to the night Lee died. She hadn't entirely decided to do it on the trip, but then Lee had told the story about the man at the party. That was *Shirley's* story—not Lee's. Everything happened quickly after that.

The unopened bottle of wine Grace left out on purpose. The confession of her "pregnancy" and relationship with Noah. Going upstairs to bed to let Lee brood alone.

When Lee stalked off to the woods, Grace followed. She'd trailed her all the way to the top, Lee much too drunk to check behind her. After Lee stumbled, Grace capitalized on the moment, bumped her shoulder, and watched her topple over the edge.

Left, right, gone. Bye-bye, Lee.

Grace finishes rinsing her hands. She cranks off the tap and then dries them on a freshly laundered towel. She flips off the bathroom light and walks back to the front to retrieve her phone. Noah rises to collect his belongings and says good-bye to the boys. He approaches Grace and touches her arm.

"I'll see you tomorrow, okay?" His eyes are kind, pleading.

She nods and waits for him to leave. The door clicks, and she exhales. Phase one is complete. Lee is gone. The papers are hers. Mason is hers. Now, it's Noah's turn. It's time for him to lose his unborn baby. It's time for him to lose Mason, the boy he really loves. It's time for him to lose her.

She's already planted the seed in all of the mommy forums about the handsome occupational therapist who is baseless and untrustworthy. She doesn't have physical proof of what he did to her sister—she knows that—but gossip will ruin him. In her mind, he doesn't deserve to be around children. She almost relishes the anticipation, what it will physically feel like to destroy the man who treated her sister like an animal in the dark.

She enters the dining room, grazes the cap of Mason's shoulder, and caresses the crown of Luca's head. Her spirits swell as she plots the next steps.

She crouches between them. Her knees pop as she lifts slightly and resettles. They both stop what they're doing to cast a fleeting look her way. She grins, makes eye contact with each of them, and then carefully leans in to whisper:

"Mama's home."

acknowledgments

What a whirlwind. As I write this, my first book has not yet launched. I don't know all of the things I'm in store for, or what the state of my world (or *the* world) will be when this book lands in your waiting palms.

I do know, however, that I couldn't have gotten here without the help of my team: both my professional and personal team. My village and tribe. In no particular order, I want to thank:

The entire St. Martin's Press family. The audio department. My publicists, both internal and external. My agent and editor, to whom this book is dedicated. Nikki Terpilowski at Holloway. The SimplyBe. team. The readers who picked up *Not Her Daughter*. My writing group, but specifically Cheryl Rieger and Cassidy Trom, who spent countless hours with me, over wine, in both of your beautiful homes in Nashville and New York, helping me figure out this damn book. (The second-book curse is real, y'all.) To the writers I've met along the way. To the writers who have provided blurbs. To the last-minute readers who sped-read the final version of this book and gave me invaluable feedback. To the members of Authors 18—you are all a revelation. To my family, who keeps me grounded and supports me in ways I can't even articulate. To my husband, who is my biggest supporter, the most creative man I know, and pretty damn dreamy. To my daughter, who is my greatest teacher and my deepest love. To Helena, who gave me the inspiration for Grace. To Lynette Hish, for educating me about sociopaths. To my village of women. To coffee, for keeping me sane. To Argent Pictures, whom I didn't get to thank in my first book.

And last—but never least—to the readers.

Thank you all for supporting this dream.

Read on for an excerpt from

UNTIL I FIND YOU

by Rea Frey

Available August 2020 in trade paperback

from St. Martin's Griffin

1

Someone's coming.

I push the stroller. My feet expertly navigate the familiar path toward the park without my cane. Footsteps advance behind me. The swish of fabric between hurried thighs. The clop of a shoe on pavement. Measured, but gaining with every step. Blood whooshes through my ears, a distraction.

One more block until the park's entrance. My world blots behind my sunglasses, smeared and dreamy. A few errant hairs whip across my face. My toe catches a crack, and my ankle painfully twists.

No time to stop.

My thighs burn. A few more steps. Finally, I make a sharp left into the park's entrance. Jackson's anklet jingles from the blistering pace.

"Hang on, sweet boy. Almost there. Almost." The relentless August sun sizzles in the sky, and I adjust my ballcap with a trembling hand. Uncertain, I stop and wait for either the rush of footsteps to pass, or to approach and attack. Instead, nothing.

I lick my dry lips and half-turn, one hand still securely fastened on my son's stroller. "Hello?" The wind stalls. The hairs bristle on the back of my neck. My world goes unnaturally still, until I choke on my own warped breath.

I waver on the sidewalk and then lunge toward the entrance to Wilder. The stroller is my guide as I half-walk, half-jog, knowing precisely how many steps I must take to reach the other side of the gate.

Twenty.

My heart thumps, a manic metronome. Jackson cries out and kicks his foot. The bells again.

Ten.

The footsteps echo in my ears. The stroller rams an obstacle in the way and flattens it. I swerve and cry out in surprise.

Five.

I reach the gate, hurtle through to a din of voices. Somewhere in the distance, a lawn mower stutters, then chugs to life.

Safe.

I slide toward the ground and drop my head between my knees. My ears prick for the stranger behind me, but all is lost. A plane roars overhead, probably heading for Chicago. Birds aggressively chirp as the sun continues to crisp my already pink shoulders. A car horn honks on the parallel street. Someone blows a whistle. My body shudders from the surge of adrenaline. I sit until I regain my composure and then push to shaky legs.

I check Jackson, dragging my hands over the length of his body—his strong little fingers, his plump thighs, and perpetually kicking feet—and blot my face with his spit-up blanket. Just when I think I'm safe, a hand encircles my wrist.

"Miss?"

I jerk back and suck a surprised breath.

The hand drops. "I'm sorry," a woman's voice says. "I

didn't mean to scare you. You dropped this." Something jingles and lands in my upturned palm: Jackson's anklet.

I smooth my fingers over the bells. "Thanks." I bend over the stroller, grip his smooth ankle, and reattach them. I tickle the bottom of his foot, and he murmurs.

"Are the bells so you can hear him?" the woman asks. "Are you . . . ?"

"Blind? Yes." I straighten. "I am."

"That's cool. I've never seen that before."

I assume she means the bells. I almost make a joke—*neither have I!*—but instead, I smile. "It's a little early for him to wear them. They're more for when he becomes mobile, but I want him to get used to them."

"That's smart."

I'm not sure if she's waiting for me to say something else. "Thanks again," I offer.

"No problem. Have a good day."

She leaves. My hands clench around the stroller's handle. Was she the one behind me? I stall at the gate and wonder if I should just go back home. I remind myself where I am—in one of the safest suburbs outside of Chicago—not in some sketchy place. I'm not being followed.

It's fine.

To prove it, I remove my cane, unfold it, and brace it on the path. I maneuver Jackson's stroller behind and sweep my cane in front, searching for more obstacles or unsuspecting feet.

I weave toward Cottage Hill and pass the Wedding Garden, the Elmhurst Mansion, and the art museum. Finally, I wind around the arboretum. I leave the Conservatory for last, pulling Jackson through colorful flower breeds, active butterflies, and rows of green. My heart still betrays my calm exterior, but whoever was there is gone.

I whisk my t-shirt from my body. Jackson babbles and then lets out a sharp cry. I adjust the brim of his stroller so his eyes aren't directly hit by the sun. I lower my baseball cap and head toward the playground. The rubber flooring shifts beneath my cane.

The park is packed with last-minute late summer activity. I do a lap around the playground and then angle my cane toward a bench to check for occupants. Once I confirm it's empty, I settle and park the stroller beside me. I keep my ears alert for Jess or Beth. I think about calling Crystal to join us, but then remember she has an interior design job today.

I place my hand on Jackson's leg, the small jingle of his anklet a comfort. Suddenly, I am overcome with hunger. I rummage in the diaper bag for a banana, peel it, and reach again for Jackson, who is playing with his pacifier. He furiously sucks, then knocks it out of his mouth. He giggles every time I hand it back to him.

I replay what just happened. If someone had attacked me, I wouldn't have been able to defend myself or identify the perpetrator. A shiver courses the length of my spine. Though Jackson is technically easy—healthy, no colic, a decent sleeper—this stage of life is not. Chris died one year ago, and though it's been twelve months since the accident, sometimes it feels like it's been twelve minutes.

Suddenly, Jackson's life flashes before me. Not the happy baby playing in his stroller, but the other parts. The first time he gets really sick. The first time he has to go to the emergency room, and I'm all alone. The first time I don't know what to do when something is wrong. The first time he runs away from me in public and isn't wearing bells to alert me to his location.

Will I be able to keep him safe, to protect him?

I will the dark cloud away, but uneasiness pierces my skin like a warning. I fan my shirt, swallow, close my eyes behind my sunglasses, and adjust my ball cap.

The world shrinks. I try to swallow, but my throat constricts. I claw air.

I can't breathe. I'm drowning. My heart is going to explode. I'm going to die.

I lurch off the bench and walk a few paces, churning my arms toward my chest to produce air. I gasp, tell myself to breathe, tell myself to do something.

When I think I'm going to faint, I exhale completely, then sip in a shallow breath. I veer toward a tree, fingers grasping, and reach its chalky bark. *In, out. In, out. Breathe, Rebecca. Breathe.*

I shudder and gasp, the murmurs of the other mothers apparent while I remember how to breathe. After a few toxic moments, I count my steps back to the bench.

I just left my baby alone.

Jackson's right foot twitches and jingles from the stroller, blissfully unaware that his mother just had a panic attack. I calm myself, but my heart continues to knock around my chest like a pinball. I open a bottle of water and lift it to my lips with trembling hands. I exhale and massage my chest. The footsteps. The panic attack. These recurring fears . . .

"Hey, lady. Fancy meeting you here." Jess leans down and delivers a kiss to my cheek. Her scent—sweet, like honey crisp apples—does little to dissuade my terrified mood.

"Hi. Sit, sit." I rearrange my voice to neutral and move the diaper bag to make room.

Jess positions her stroller beside mine. Beth sits next to her, her three-month-old baby Trevor always in a ring sling or strapped to her chest.

"How's the morning?" Beth asks.

I tell them both about the footsteps and the lady who returned the bells but leave out the panic attack.

Beth leans closer. "Scary. Do you think it was her?"

"I'm not sure," I say. "Hopefully."

"You should have called," Jess says. "I'm always happy to walk here with you."

"That's not exactly on your way."

"Oh please. I could use the extra exercise."

I roll my eyes at her disparaging comment, because Beth and I both know she loves her curves.

"Anyway, it's sleep deprivation," Jess continues. "Makes you hallucinate. I remember when Baxter was Jackson's age and waking up every two hours, I literally thought I was going to lose my mind. I would put things in odd places. I was even convinced Rob was cheating."

I laugh. "Rob would never cheat on you."

"Exactly my point." She turns to me. "Have you thought about hiring a nanny?"

"Yeah," Beth adds. "Especially with everything you've been through."

My stomach clenches at those words: *everything you've been through*. After Chris died, I'd moved in with my mother so she could essentially become Jackson's nanny. And then, just two months ago, she died too. Though her death wasn't a surprise due to her life-long heart condition, no one is ever prepared to lose a parent. "I can't afford it."

"Like I've said before, Rob and I are happy to pitch in—"

I lift my hand to stop her. "And I appreciate it. I really do. But I'm not ready to have someone in my space when I'm just getting used to it being empty. I need to get comfortable taking care of Jackson on my own."

"That makes sense," Beth assures me.

"It does." Jess pats my thigh. "But you're not a martyr, okay? Everyone needs help."

"I know." I adjust my sunglasses and rearrange my face to betray the real emotions I feel. "What's new with both of you?"

"Can I vent for a second?" Beth asks. She situates closer to us on the bench. Thanks to the visual Jess supplied, I know Beth is blond, petite, and impossibly fit— and is perpetually in a state of crisis. She's practicing attachment parenting, which, in her mind, keeps her glued to her son twenty-four hours a day. I've never even held him.

"Vent away," I say.

"Okay." She drops her voice. "Like I love this little guy, truly. But sometimes, when it's just the two of us in the house all day, I fantasize about just running away somewhere. Or going out to take a walk. I'd never do it, of course," she rushes to add. "But I just have this feeling like . . . I'm never going to be alone again."

"Nanny," Jess trills. "I'm telling you. Quit this attachment parenting crap and get yourself a nanny. And if they're hot, she can even occupy your husband so you don't have to."

I slap Jess's arm. "Don't say that. You'd be totally devastated if Rob ever did cheat."

"Would I, though? One less thing I'd have to do at night," she mumbles.

"That's not attachment parenting," I assure Beth. "That's how every new mom feels sometimes."

Beth bounces Trevor, her voice vibrating. "But am I a terrible human? Are you both sitting there judging me?"

"We don't have time to judge you," Jess jokes.

"You *never* complain, Rebecca," Beth says.

"Who, me?" I ask. "I complain."

I imagine Beth and Jess giving each other a look. "You don't," Jess says. "Ever. Which makes zero sense, considering . . ."

Considering your husband and mother died and you're raising a baby all by yourself.

I shrug. "I learned a long time ago that complaining doesn't change anything, so why bother?"

"Complaining is my hobby," Beth says. "And I realize I don't have anything to complain about. I mean, not really."

I roll my eyes. "Beth, you're allowed to feel however you want. Don't compare your life to mine. For your own good."

"But your baby is perfect," Beth whines. "If you ever want to trade, just let me know."

I laugh. "I'll let you know." I tune in and out as they gripe about their babies and husbands. I add in my two cents, wanting to tell them my deepest thoughts on the subject, but decide against it. Their voices come and go. My eyes flutter—closed, open, closed, open—and before I know it, I've accidentally fallen asleep.